[illegible]h Jeffrey was born in Wivenhoe, a small waterfront [illegible]n near Colchester, and has lived there all her life. She [illegible] writing short stories over thirty years ago, in between bringing up her three children and caring for an elderly parent. More than a hundred of her stories went on to be published or b[illegible]adcast; in 1976 she won a national short story competition [illegible] success led her onto write full-length novels for both adults and children.

Elizabeth Jeffrey titles published by Piatkus, in alphabetical order:

Cassie Jordan
Cast a Long Shadow
Dowlands' Mill
Far Above the Rubies
Fields of Bright Clover
Gin and Gingerbread
Ginny Appleyard
Hannah Fox
In Fields Where Daisies Grow
Mollie on the Shore
Strangers' Hall
The Buttercup Fields
The Weaver's Daughter
To Be a Fine Lady
Travellers' Inn

Elizabeth
JEFFREY
Strangers' Hall

piatkus

PIATKUS

First published in Great Britain in 1988 by Century Hutchinson Ltd
This paperback edition published in 2018 by Piatkus

1 3 5 7 9 10 8 6 4 2

A CIP catalogue record for this book
is available from the British Library.

ISBN 978-0-349-42145-2

Typeset in Sabon by M Rules
Printed and bound in Great Britain by
Clays Ltd, Elcograf S.p.A.

Papers used by Piatkus are from well-managed forests
and other responsible sources.

Piatkus
An imprint of
Little, Brown Book Group
Carmelite House
50 Victoria Embankment
London EC4Y 0DZ

An Hachette UK Company
www.hachette.co.uk

www.littlebrown.co.uk

I am indebted to L.F. Roker MA for the loan of his MA thesis 'Flemish and Dutch Communities in Colchester in the 16th and 17th Century'.

Among other books consulted were: *History of Colchester*, The Revd Philip Morant, 1748; *The Victoria History of Essex*; *East Anglia's Golden Fleece*, Nigel Heard; *Elizabethan Life*, F.G. Emmison; *Register of Baptisms in the Dutch Church in Colchester*, Moens; *The Revolt of the Netherlands 1555-1609*, Pieter Geyl.

To my husband, with love

Prologue

In the second half of the sixteenth century thousands of Protestant Dutch and Flemish refugees fled to England to escape the Spanish Inquisition, the religious persecution of the Low Countries by the Catholic Spanish Government. The cruel and tyrannical Duke of Alva had been sent with an army by Philip II of Spain to root out, torture and kill all those who refused to adhere to the Catholic faith. Many did refuse and died horrible deaths, but many managed to escape, some fleeing for their lives, forced to leave all their possessions behind.

A colony of these refugees came to settle in Colchester. Although mainly from Dutch-speaking Flanders, they were known as the 'Dutch Community' or the 'Congregation of Strangers' or even simply as 'Aliens'. For the most part they were hard-working, upright people, skilled artisans and deeply conscious of their Calvinist faith. They worshipped in their own church and had their own Bay Hall in the town. Due to their industrious nature they prospered and some became very rich. It was through the Dutch Congregation that Colchester became famous for its cloth-making industry.

But the Strangers were not popular with the indigenous population. Although the more well-to-do were conscious of the prosperity that the Dutch Community brought to the town, the poorer people were jealous and resentful. They felt, quite rightly, that the Dutch were robbing them of their livelihood and they resented the fact that even English cloth had to be taken to the Dutch Bay Hall to be checked and then sealed with the Colchester seal of quality. Another source of resentment was the fact that the Dutch were clannish, refusing to mix with the local population and clinging to their own language. It took well over a century for the Dutch Community finally to become absorbed into the local population.

That much is history . . .

Chapter One

I

Shivering in the first light of a bitterly cold morning in the second month of the year 1591 Jannekyn clutched her bundle of possessions and shrank back against the bales of raw wool piled on the quayside. At least here was a little shelter from the biting east wind and the rain that was rapidly turning to snow. She glanced round anxiously. Her uncle had promised that she would be met when she reached England but she could see no sign of anyone looking for her in the crowds that jostled among the ropes, the fishing nets, the oyster barrels, the waggonloads of sea coal and the bundles of raw wool that were being loaded and unloaded from the hoys tied up at the wooden jetty.

A pale, thin, bedraggled figure, wet and dirt-spattered from the voyage, she pulled her cloak closer, wishing it had been lined with some of the fleece against which she was sheltering instead of with perpetuana. Long-lasting and serviceable though the heavy, blanket-like cloth was, it did tend to let the wind through. But even as the thought struck her she was overwhelmed with guilt and homesickness, because the cloak had belonged to her mother.

Jannekyn rubbed her cheek against it, remembering how she

had protested when her mother gave it to her. 'But, Moeder, it is your good cloak. What will you wear if I take it?'

Her mother had kissed her. 'I have my shawl. I shall manage. I want you to have it, liefje. It will warm you as you cross the German Sea.' She had smiled at Jannekyn. 'You must look respectable when you meet Oom Jacob. He is a rich man, remember. And don't forget to give Tante Katherine my love and tell her I am well.' At the thought of her lifelong friend she had wiped away a tear. 'Even after all these years I still miss her.' She had kissed Jannekyn again. 'I shall miss you, too, liefje, but I'm thankful you have this opportunity to go to England. You will have a better life there.'

Jannekyn choked back the tears that threatened. The snow was beginning to fall faster now, drifting into the tracks made by the waggons as they rumbled about the quay, and powdering the heaps of merchandise stacked by the jetty. Soaked and dirty from a miserable passage on a crowded boat where the passengers took second place to the cargo of herrings, she was chilled to the bone, but nobody spared her a second glance as she waited. They were all intent on getting their business finished so that they could escape into the warmth of the ale-house nearby. A knot of fear in her stomach was beginning to twist itself into panic. Supposing her uncle didn't come ... supposing he had forgotten ...

'Jannekyn van der Hest? Are you Jannekyn van der Hest?' a man's voice asked, speaking in her native tongue.

She spun round, relief flooding through her. 'Oh, yes. Are you my ...?' Her voice trailed away. The man standing before her didn't at all have the appearance of a rich clothier.

'Me? Bless you, no. I'm not your uncle. But don't you fret, juffrouw, Jacob van der Hest'll be waiting for you at New Hythe.

He asked me to see you the rest of the way up river since the *Lady Jane* draws too much water to go any further than this. You came over on her from Antwerp, didn't you?' He nodded towards the large, square-rigged ketch that was disgorging her cargo of herrings on to the quay.

'Yes, that's right.' Jannekyn studied this man who seemed to know all about her. He was about forty-five, stocky, with a frizz of grey hair edging a shiny bald head, and a thick bushy beard. His leather breeches and jerkin had both seen better days and as he clamped a battered hat on his head she noticed with a shudder that all that were left of fingers and thumbs on both hands were ten uneven stumps.

'There's my boat.' He waved a maimed hand in the direction of a hoy called *Anne* tied to the jetty, just taking aboard the last bales of raw wool. 'Come on, m'dear, move yourself. If we can catch what's left of the tide I'll have you at your uncle's side in less than an hour.'

Jannekyn looked at him suspiciously, making no attempt to move.

He grinned, opening his whiskers to a red cavern lined with two rows of broken teeth. 'Don't trust me? Well, I can't blame you for that, I s'pose. But I'll tell you here and now you'll be safer with me than hanging about here all on your own. If you stay here for too long what you'll lose to cutpurses and pick-pockets will be the least of your losses. A comely little rose like you is just right for the plucking? He picked up her bundle and walked across to the jetty. 'Well, what're you waiting for?' Seeing her still hesitate he added, 'Dammit, girl, you don't need to worry about me. I've got a wife back home in Grub Street who takes all I've got to offer, I don't have to look for it. Anyway, you're Jacob van der Hest's niece and Jacob van der

Hest was good to me when I first came to Colchester. You've naught to fear From Henrick de Groot, child, nor from my crew. I'll vouch for them.'

Even while he was speaking a disreputable creature, reeking of spirits even at this early hour, came up to Jannekyn with a suggestion that was unmistakable in its meaning even though the words he used were not in the English vocabulary Minister Grenrice had taught her. Shrugging herself free of his clawing hands she hurried after Henrick de Groot.

The *Anne*'s cargo had its own distinctive odour but it was not nearly so bad as the stench of herrings that had accompanied her on the voyage over from the Netherlands. Even now she couldn't think of that journey, which she had spent for the most part retching over the side of the boat in time to its pitching and rolling, without her poor stomach beginning to heave again.

Henrick de Groot had settled her on a heap of sacks in the bow and once the boat was under way he came and sat beside her.

'Where are you from, then, juffrouw?' he asked, keeping a sharp eye on his crew as they piloted the boat skilfully between the mudbanks towards the ancient town of Colchester.

'A village not far from Ypres,' Jannekyn answered. 'I didn't want to leave but my father was anxious that I should come to England.'

Henrick nodded soberly. 'Aye, there'll be more bloodshed before this business with Spain is finished. Your father was wise to want to get you away.' He looked at what was left of his hands. 'It was Alva's men that did this to me, but that was twenty years and more ago, long enough before ever you were born. How old are you? Seventeen?'

'Eighteen.'

'Ah.' He nodded. 'Too young to remember what went on.'

'My father has told me a little about it,' Jannekyn said in a low voice. 'He remembers.'

'He was one who stayed, then. He didn't join the great escape to England.'

'No. He tried to but something went wrong and he was caught and flung into prison.' She shook her head. 'What he went through there broke his health, but he swears that he was one of the lucky ones. At least he got out with his life.'

Henrick de Groot nodded. 'He's right. I feel the same. I may have lost my fingers but that's nothing to what I've seen. I've watched men burned alive, turning on a spit like a slow-roasting pig.' He spat disgustedly into the murky water of the river, narrowly missing the bloated body of a dead cat floating by. 'Bah, and what was it all for? It'll all come to the same thing in the end. Papists, Calvinists, they'll all die and get shoved into a hole in the ground, so what's the point of fighting over it?'

Jannekyn looked up at him, surprised at the vehemence in his tone. 'You must have thought it worthwhile once, to have suffered as you did.' She pointed to his hands.

He shrugged. 'I was young then, and full of ideals.' He gazed at her for several minutes. 'You're young to have made the crossing alone,' he remarked, changing the subject.

'I came over with a family bound for Norwich,' she said. 'At least, I was supposed to be with them, but they all stayed below decks and I couldn't bear it down there.' She shuddered at the memory. 'It was bad enough on deck, but I think I'd have died down there.'

'Seasick, were you?'

She nodded.

'Feel better now?'

She nodded again. 'It helped a lot getting away from the smell of the herrings. I was just unlucky that a herring boat was the only one my father could arrange a passage on.'

Henrick de Groot drew a leather bottle from inside his jerkin and gave it to her. 'Here, this'll help to warm you. I can see you're wet through.'

She took a draught of the fiery liquid and choked. It tasted vile. But soon its warmth spread through her and she raised the bottle to her lips again.

'That's enough.' He snatched it away. 'I don't want to hand you over to your uncle the worse for drink – even if it is the best French brandy.' He tapped the side of his nose, a conspiratorial gesture that was lost on Jannekyn, ignorant as she was of the ways of the east coast smugglers.

He left her then and made his way nimbly aft, where, using his teeth and feet to assist his maimed hands, he hauled expertly on the sheets to get a better set to the sail.

Jannekyn surveyed the English countryside. With a powdering of snow over the low fields and woods sloping gently away from the river valley it looked grey and bleak, matching her mood. She looked back at the village they had just left; it was little more than a huddle of houses round the waterfront, the square tower of the church a landmark in their midst. Then, as the *Anne* rounded a bend in the river she saw the wide sprawl of roofs that was Colchester. This was the place her father had seen as his Canaan; a land, if not flowing with milk and honey, at least where those who worked might prosper. A land he had finally recognized he would never see.

So he had sent his only daughter instead.

Jannekyn stood up in the bow of the boat, anxious to get a better view of the place that would henceforth be her home. The town was built on a hill, with untidy rows of houses spilling crookedly down the sides, church spires and windmills set at random among them like sentinel giants. She felt no excitement at the sight of it, but rather a feeling of foreboding, a feeling that had persisted despite her father's repeated assurance of the welcome she would find in his brother's house. 'How could it be otherwise?' he had said. 'Your uncle is my brother and his wife was your mother's lifelong friend. Of course they will welcome you.'

As the *Anne* approached the quayside at New Hythe she smoothed her hair and straightened the creases out of her cloak, remembering her father's words and telling herself that it was only a combination of tiredness and seasickness that was making her feel so apprehensive. She took a deep breath and stepped on to Colchester soil determined to accept whatever challenges her new life had to offer with faith and courage.

She was soon to need both.

If she had thought the waterfront at Wyvenhoe busy the harbour at Colchester was a frenzy of activity. The quayside was crammed with goods coming in and goods going out; the wooden warehouses lining the quay were piled with bales of cloth waiting to be shipped abroad, each bearing the highly prized Colchester seal of quality. Raw wool was being loaded on to waggons, well-dressed merchants were haggling with ship-masters and each other over prices among the casks of wine, vats of oil, sacks of barley, the hops and malt for brewing, and the woad, madder, alum and fuller's earth for the cloth industry. It was all there, waiting to be loaded, waiting to be taken away – sacks being carried on strong shoulders on and off ships, vats and barrels being rolled. To Jannekyn it was all a bewildering jumble, with an all-pervading smell of tarred rope mingled with raw wool, fish and the stink of woad.

'Here we are, child, this is the end of your journey,' Henrick de Groot said, deftly throwing a mooring rope over a bollard on the quay. 'Follow me and I'll take you to your uncle. He's over there, by that warehouse, look.'

Jannekyn looked. There was a group of about six men, dressed all in black, with high-crowned copotain hats, talking together. Any one of them could have been the uncle she had never seen. With them, yet a little apart, stood a hawklike man, watching the commercial transactions with a shrewd and calculating eye that missed nothing.

As soon as he saw Henrick approaching this man broke away from the group and hurried over.

'Is this the girl?' he asked briefly.

'Aye, this is the little lady.' Henrick gave Jannekyn a comforting wink as he answered.

Jacob van der Hest looked her up and down, seeing a tall, too-thin, fair-haired girl returning his gaze apprehensively from wide, violet-blue eyes. 'So you are my brother's only child,' he said without enthusiasm. 'You look pale and sickly. I hope you are not going to be an encumbrance.'

'I'm a little tired, that's all.' She spoke falteringly. This was not at all the kind of welcome her father had led her to expect.

'She had a bad crossing, Jacob. Don't be too hard on her,' Henrick said cheerfully. 'She'll be a bonny wench when she's rested.'

'Hmph. Not too bonny, I hope. Girls that are too comely are a constant source of anxiety.' His voice was cynical. 'My carriage is over there. Wait in it for me.' He turned away and went back to his business, dismissing her from his presence and his thoughts.

Henrick grinned at her. 'This way, child. And take no notice of your uncle. He means well enough.'

She bit her lip, close to tears, and followed Henrick to the waiting carriage. He opened the door for her and settled her inside with her bundle. 'You'll be safe enough waiting here,' he said.

'Thank you, Mynheer, you've been very kind,' she said, with a break in her voice. After her first reluctance to go with him she was sorry to say goodbye to the rough and ready sailor. He represented kindness – the only kindness she had received since embarking on the *Lady Jane* and, did she but know it, the only kindness she was to receive for some time to come.

He waved her remark aside. 'Think nothing of it.' He turned to leave her, then came back. 'Grub Street is where I live, second house from the end. Ask anyone for Betkin, that's my wife; they'll know who you want. She's a good girl, she'll always make you welcome. If ever you're in any kind of trouble . . . ' He broke off and patted her arm with a grotesquely maimed hand. 'Anyway, good luck, my child.'

Jannekyn gave him a wintry smile and watched him go. As he passed her uncle, Jacob van der Hest stepped forward and spoke to him urgently, nodding now and then in her direction. Henrick listened, frowning, and once he glanced back at the carriage where she waked. Then he shrugged his shoulders and went on his way.

Jannekyn couldn't help wondering what they had spoken about, it had obviously been something concerning her. No doubt her uncle would tell her when he arrived. She settled down to wait for him.

II

It was a full hour before he came, shaking the snow from his black fur-lined cloak as he flung himself into the carriage, muttering about harbour dues and taxes, rogues and charlatans. He offered no word of explanation or apology at having kept her waiting for so long. In fact the carriage had rumbled nearly half a mile up the hill over bone-shaking cobbles before he put down the ledger he had been pretending to study and spoke to her.

'Your father is dying.' It was a statement rather than a question.

Jannekyn looked at him in surprise. His face showed no emotion at all. 'I fear you are right,' she answered.

'Of course I am right. Why else would he have written to me about you?' He picked at his teeth for a few moments. 'And your mother?'

'Reasonably well, thank you.'

'They had no wish to come with you to England?' Now he was watching her closely. 'Later, perhaps? When you are settled?'

'Oh, no. That's not possible. My father could never stand the journey. His lungs, you understand. His years of imprisonment broke his health. It's a miracle he still lives. Anyway, they have no money and little prospect of earning enough for the journey.' She bit her lip. 'I should not have been able to come if it had not been for your generosity, Oom Jacob.'

Her uncle eyed her coldly. 'Generosity? What do you mean, generosity?'

She flushed with embarrassment. 'You paid my passage. It was generous of you. And my father told me ... that is, I've very little money of my own ... ' She stopped, not knowing how to go on under the cold stare of this strange man who was her uncle, yet was so unlike her gentle, sickly father. She tried to remember what had been in the reply to her father's letter to his brother. '. . . I will pay her passage over to England and will give her food and lodging. Her skills will be much appreciated by my dear wife . . . ' Her father had been so happy when he read that out to her.

'There, child, I told you my brother would not refuse me,' he had said, relieved at being proved right, for neither Jannekyn nor her mother had wanted him to write and ask for any kind of charity from his wealthy younger brother. But he had been adamant. For why else would a Predikant, a Minister just returned from England, who chanced to pass through their village, let fall the news – again by chance –that Jacob van der Hest, who had years ago been given up for dead, was alive and well and living in the town of Colchester, a rich man? And why else would Nicholaes Bloemaert from along the road know a man who knew another man who'd heard of another Predikant who would soon be going to England and perhaps even passing through the town of Colchester and so could deliver a letter to Jacob, if it was not meant that Jannekyn should go to her uncle?

'Jacob will care for you. He'll see that you have the opportunity to marry well, liefje,' her father had said, determination giving him strength. 'You are nearly eighteen, Jannekyn. Your moeder and I worry about you each time you leave the house . . . the soldiers . . . the danger all the time . . . ' He had broken off with a fit of dreadful coughing. 'You are a clever girl . . . I shall tell your uncle . . . He will be glad to have you . . . '

And so he had written, and three months later, when even he had given up hope of a reply, Jacob had answered, briefly, but sending enough money for her passage over. Now she was in

England, but more to gratify the dying wish of her father than out of any real desire on her own part.

Her uncle regarded her without speaking for some time and she hugged her meagre bundle of possessions to her, trying to draw some comfort from its familiarity. She realized with misgiving that even in her mother's best cloak she looked filthy and shabby in the eyes of the man beside her.

At last he said, 'I see that I did not make myself clear when I wrote to your father.'

'What do you mean?' The knot of fear that had accompanied her across the sea began to ravel itself anew at his words. 'You paid my passage over, and you said you would give me food and lodging, didn't you?'

He inclined his head. 'I did. And it is true. My wife has given birth to a son within the last month. He is our third child and was somewhat unexpected; we had thought my wife past the age of childbearing. She ailed throughout and ails still. She will be glad of your help in return for your keep.'

Jannekyn relaxed and the knot of fear untied itself again. 'Of course, Oom Jacob, I shall be happy to help in anyway I can.' It would be a small price to pay for a comfortable home with a family.

He inclined his head again. 'Good. I'm glad you understand the position. I would not like you to be under any misapprehension as to my motive for bringing you here to England. Even your rather stupid, idealistic father would not have expected me to lay out money on an expensive sea passage without any prospect of gain. But as long as you understand that you are here as my servant . . . '

'Servant?' She sat up straight. That was not at all how she had seen herself.

'Of course. What else?' He turned a haughty gaze on her which reduced her to the level of an object that even scavenging dogs would disdain. 'Now, let me see your papers.' He held out his hand.

'Papers?' she said blankly,

'Yes. Papers. No Alien is allowed into Colchester without the written consent of the bailiffs.'

She bit her lip. 'I didn't know that.'

'Ha! I thought not.' He glared at her. 'It is well that you have come to me because I can speak for you and say that I am sheltering you under my roof. Only that way, if I make myself responsible for you, will you be safe. The English have lately decided that there are too many Strangers – that's what they call us – in the town, and have prohibited any more from coming in.'

'So what would happen if you didn't speak for me?'

'You would be turned out of the town to starve, or thrown into the castle dungeons until you could be sent back from whence you came.'

Jannekyn digested this. The thought of a journey back across the German Sea, even if her parents were at the other end, terrified her. But they wouldn't be there to meet her, she would have to find her way back to them as best she might. And with no money – and soldiers everywhere . . . She swallowed hard. How fortunate she was that Oom Jacob knew about these things. He would see that she was safe. And it would be better to be treated as a servant in his house than to be thrown out of the town.

'I shall be happy to do whatever you say, Oom Jacob,' she said, eagerly anxious to please.

'Good. Because I warn you, if you don't do my bidding I shall have no hesitation in reporting you to the authorities.' Jacob leaned forward threateningly. 'I brook no disobedience in my house. You are in my charge now and you will do exactly as I say or you know what will happen. Do I make myself quite plain?'

'Yes, Oom Jacob.'

She looked at her hands. They were soft and white. Her mother had kept her from the menial tasks, saying that no man would look twice at a girl with rough, work-worn hands. But no doubt a man as rich as her uncle would have several servants and she would only be required to help with the baby. She would enjoy that. Once more her spirits lifted.

The carriage rumbled on over the cobbles. Jannekyn felt a stab of pity for the beggars in their rags, waiting for alms outside the great gateway of the Abbey of St John, although she noticed that her uncle didn't so much as spare them a glance. On they went, through streets lined with huddles of houses, white-roofed with snow. A few people, their pattens clicking on the paving stones, hurried about their business, anxious to get out of the bitter weather. In the distance, the huge bulk of the castle that had been built by the Normans raised its four towers to the leaden skies and it was towards this that they went, the carriage finally coming to a halt outside a large house, clearly not long built, standing just inside the east gate of the town.

Jacob van der Hest alighted and left his niece to follow as best she might.

They entered the house through a massive oak door and Jannekyn found herself in a large flagged area from which an impressive staircase rose. There was a passage off to the right with three doors in it but her uncle pushed open the only door to the left. This opened into a great hall where the family ate and entertained. Jannekyn followed him, eyes wide with wonder. Until this moment she hadn't realized just how rich her uncle was.

'We have but lately moved into this house.' Her uncle tried to sound matter of fact but was unable to keep the note of pride from his voice. He waved his hand towards the great hearth, where a huge fire of sea coal burned. 'My wife finds her new chimneys a great boon in the burning of sea coal.'

'It's a beautiful house, Oom Jacob,' Jannekyn said warmly. 'I'm sure I shall be very happy here.'

Jacob spun round to face her. 'Happy? You've not been brought here at my expense to be *happy*, girl!' he said. 'You've been brought here to work!'

The vehemence in his tone was like a blow and she stepped back as if he'd struck her. 'I'm sorry, Oom Jacob.'

He stared her up and down for a moment. 'And I would prefer you to address me as Meester whilst you are here. And my wife as Mevrouw.'

She lifted her eyebrows in surprise.

'It is the custom here,' he told her briefly.

'Oh, I see – Meester.' It seemed rather strange to her but, she reminded herself, this was England, not Flanders. She must expect things to be different.

'And take your shoes off.'

'My shoes?' She looked down at her feet. She was wearing the only pair of shoes she possessed, of rather shabby leather, holed in several places, but over them a pair of stout wooden clogs, or pattens as they were known, which raised the feet to keep them dry. Obediently she slipped her feet out of the clogs.

'And the shoes,' Jacob said impatiently.

'But . . .'

'Do as you're told, girl.' He held his hand out for them. 'Juist. Good.' He nodded as she handed them over, and flung them into a corner. 'The kitchen is at the end of the passage.

Ask Garerdine to give you food, and water to clean yourself up with. Then come to the solar.' He indicated a door at the far end of the hall. 'And make haste,' he called over his shoulder as he strode towards it. 'I have work to do. I can't waste all day and my wife will be waiting.'

Jannekyn stood in the hall looking down at her feet after he had gone. They were spattered with dirt in spite of wearing clogs and her stockings had been darned until there was little of them left. This must be another strange English custom, removing shoes in the house, and it was one she didn't like at all. It made her feel little better than a beggar in the street. She sighed and headed across the hall, the stone flags striking chill as she went in search of the kitchen. She had much to learn in this strange, new country.

Jannekyn found the kitchen. Garerdine, an apple-cheeked woman of middle age and ample proportions, was busy kneading dough and was not pleased at the interruption.

'Help yourself to broth.' She pointed to the pot suspended over the fire, from which a delicious aroma was already making Jannekyn's mouth water. 'And you mun cut yourself bread. I do have no time to waste waiting on the likes of you.' The sharpness of her tongue belied her pleasant appearance and Jannekyn hastened to do as she had been bidden. 'There do be water in the pitcher in the corner,' Garerdine went on. 'Be sparing with it. It do be a tidy step to the stock well from here – but you'll surely find that out for yourself soon enough.'

Jannekyn said nothing. She was puzzled at Garerdine's attitude towards her master's niece. Even though her uncle had made it quite plain that she would have to work in his house she would have expected politeness at least from his servant. However, despite the fact that not one kind word had been offered to her since she arrived, once her belly was satisfied and she had washed her face and hands and smoothed her hair Jannekyn's natural optimism and cheerfulness returned. As she left the kitchen, followed by a disapproving sniff from Garerdine, she was not unhappy.

She paused in the hall to survey her surroundings more closely. There was a long polished table running almost the length of the hall, with benches to either side and a chair, clearly her uncle's seat, at one end. A livery table stood to one side and under the window was a carved oak chest. The walls were hung with painted cloths, each depicting a different bible story and between them hung lengths of cloth of every pattern and hue, samples, she was to discover, of her uncle's stock in trade. Jannekyn had never seen such a grand house. There was even glass in the lattice.'

She hurried across to the solar. The door was opened by a girl of about fifteen: plump, with a peaches and cream complexion in an incredibly plain face, for which the nightly agony of curl papers did nothing, except to frame it in an unruly yellow fuzz on which her cap refused to sit straight. She was dressed in a gown of dark blue frizado with a crisply starched ruff.

'She's tall, isn't she? And dreadfully thin,' the girl said.

'Now, Dionis, that's not very polite, even to a servant,' her mother said. 'I'm sure you'd be thin, too, if you'd lived in the gutter.'

'Gutter? I haven't . . . ' Jannekyn began, looking at her uncle to explain. Then she followed his gaze to her feet.

Jacob turned to his wife. 'Well, my dear, do you think she'll do?'

'I think so, Jacob.' Katherine van der Hest's voice was tired and flat. She had once been a beautiful woman, full of vitality, but this last pregnancy, which should never have happened to a woman of her age, had been fraught with difficulty and the birth had been such that she had been lucky to survive. Now her face was sallow and lined with pain and her once bright hair was streaked with grey under its snowy white coif. 'Come nearer, child.' She held out a pale hand and Jannekyn went over to the low couch where she lay propped with cushions and covered with a silken dornicle. 'She looks well bred and quite intelligent, Jacob. You were clever to find her. Had you been begging long, child?'

'I was *not* begging,' Jannekyn said between clenched teeth. She was seething with indignation at the ridiculous charade her uncle was playing. 'I came . . . '

'She came into Colchester without papers,' Jacob said smoothly. 'As you know, my dear, no member of our community is allowed into the town without the written consent of the bailiffs now.' He gave a little smirk. 'I think they're afraid we Dutch will outnumber the natives if they let any more in. But that's by the way. Anyway, I found this girl with no form of consent and I thought she looked honest and well enough bred to serve us, my dear.' He smiled ingratiatingly at his wife,

'Where did you find her, Jacob?'

'On the quayside at New Hythe. She hadn't long been in Colchester.'

Katherine gave Jannekyn a languid stare. 'It was foolish of you to come to Colchester with no papers, girl. You could have been incarcerated in the castle, or thrown out of the town, which might have been even worse. I've heard there are wolves in the woods beyond Lexden. You were lucky my husband saw you.' She closed her eyes, weary after what was for her a long speech.

Jannekyn looked from one to the other. She could hardly

believe her ears. This was not how she had expected to be received into her uncle's house. Yet what he had said was true. She had no papers. She hadn't been aware that she needed any. And he had first seen her on the quayside at New Hythe . . .

'Can you sew, girl?' he interrupted her thoughts.

'Yes.'

He raised his eyebrows at her, waiting.

'Yes, Meester.'

'Good. I'll find you some cloth and you can make yourself a decent gown. I'll find you some shoes, too. Van der Hest servants don't run unshod,'

'There's nothing wrong . . . '

'The first thing you'll need to learn is to speak when you're spoken to,' he said sharply. He turned once more to his wife. 'Have you anything more to say to her, my dear?'

Katherine lay back on her cushions. She was exhausted. She was always exhausted these days. 'No, I don't think so. I'm very tired, Jacob. Dionis, go and tell the wet-nurse to take the child to the kitchen when he is fed, for Jannekyn to mind.' She rolled her head on the cushion. 'Do you know about babies, Jannekyn?'

'Not much,' Jannekyn said truthfully. 'But I'm sure I'll learn.' She felt sorry for this poor woman who looked so ill. She looked much nicer than this dreadful man who was her uncle. Later, when he was out of the way, she would tell her the truth, that she was Jacob's niece, and after that all would be well, she was sure of it. She smiled at Katherine.

'Yes, you look intelligent, I'm sure you'll learn. And I'm sure you'll look after little Benjamin better than the woman who comes in to nurse him. She's little better than a slattern. But the child must be fed and I've no milk . . . ' Katherine closed her eyes wearily. 'He's a good baby. He rarely cries.' She waved her hand. 'Go to the kitchen now. Garerdine will find work for you.'

Jannekyn left the room. Jacob followed her and caught her by the shoulder before she was halfway across the hall.

'Just you remember, if anyone asks who you are or where you came from, you are no kin to me! I found you in the gutter, begging, and took you in out of the kindness of my heart. Is that clear?' His gaze swept her from head to foot. 'It shouldn't be difficult. God knows you look the part.'

Jannekyn lifted her chin and looked straight at him. 'Why should I say that, Oom Jacob? It isn't true.'

He grabbed her arm roughly. 'You'll say it because I've told you to. You'll say it because I have a name to uphold. I don't wish it to be known that I have relatives that are little more than peasants. Do I make myself clear?'

'Yes, Oom . . . Meester.'

'If you dare to say a word to the contrary to *anybody* I'll have you thrown out and you *will* be found begging in the gutter. And you know what would happen to you then, don't you? With no papers and nobody to speak for you?'

She shook her head, swallowing hard. 'I . . . '

'Then I'll tell you again. You would be flung into goal –locked in the dungeons at the castle yonder to rot among the rats; or thrown out of the town, where wolves and wild men roam. Because it is not legal for any member of the Congregation of Strangers, which is what our community is called here in this place, to come into the town without the special consent of the bailiffs. You have not got this consent! While you live under my roof this does not matter, I can speak for you and give you my protection. But if you were to leave my house, or if it were to become known that you had come to the town without authority . . . well, as I have said.'

He allowed his words to sink in. Then he added, 'Of course, your parents would be the ones to suffer most They should never have allowed you to come here in the first place without consent. It would go badly for them if it became known.' He stood back to see the effect of his words on her, the smile on his face more akin to a sneer. Then he put his face close to hers. 'Just remember that. And remember that I am not your uncle. You are no kin to me. Do I make myself quite plain?'

'Yes, Meester.' Jannekyn's shoulders sagged in defeat. She had no way of knowing whether his threats were real, whether she would be thrown into goal or out of the town – and worse, whether her poor parents would be made to suffer. But it was not a risk she could take. Life was difficult enough for them without adding to their troubles. Whatever happened, whatever hardships she had to bear, she would never risk adding to their burdens. For their sakes she must obey Jacob and never think of him as her uncle again. 'Yes, Meester,' she repeated quietly.

'Juist! Good!' With a nod he left her, satisfied that she would give him no further trouble.

But had he glanced round he might have felt less complacent. Because suddenly Jannekyn's shoulders lifted, and narrowing her eyes she stuck her tongue out as far as it would go at his retreating back. Then, having relieved her feelings in this childish gesture she looked round the great hall with its fine furniture and carvings, its expensive hangings and the glazed windows that were ostentatiously large so that no one should be in any doubt that a man of wealth lived there. Slowly, she walked over to the table and put her hand on the smooth, dark wood, rubbing it lovingly.

'He *is* my uncle,' she whispered so that only the house

could hear, 'and I hate him! I hate him for the way he has humiliated me this day. But he shall pay for it. I swear before God he shall pay for it. One day I shall humble him as he has humbled me.'

III

In the weeks that followed Jannekyn grew accustomed to the raw East Anglian winter: the biting east wind that penetrated even the most tightly fitting doors and casements; the damp mist that crawled up the river and curled itself insidiously round the town; and the rain that washed away the snow and flooded the streets with filth from the common gutter.

They were the longest and most miserable weeks of her whole life. Every morning she was up before the sun, raking the ashes into life so that the kitchen was warm when Garerdine came down to make the bread and barley cakes, and from then on she was kept hard at work. It was Jannekyn whose task it was to churn butter and press the cheese; Jannekyn who melted the tallow and made candles; Jannekyn who made soap from mutton fat and wood ash and perfumed it with lavender and other sweet-smelling herbs from the still-room. All day long she was run off her feet, with no time for anything but the task in hand. It was as well the baby was as good as his mother had promised; a fractious child would have made her life impossible because, apart from the time he spent with the wet-nurse, Benjamin was constantly in Jannekyn's care.

Fortunately, she was kept too busy even to be lonely, because Garerdine rarely talked to her, apart from giving her orders and shouting at her when she did not carry them out quickly enough.

It was quite obvious that although she was glad of someone to do the menial tasks the older woman resented Jannekyn. The reason for this was not hard to find. Garerdine could not reconcile herself to sharing the little room up under the eaves where she slept. Tiny as it was, the room was Garerdine's domain. Although it held little more man a truckle-bed and a straw-filled mattress this was luxury indeed to the woman whose only real possession was the tin box in the corner that held a few coins she had managed to save and a bible she could not read. To be forced to share her kingdom with a young serving girl dragged out of the gutter was an imposition she could not forgive and she vented her resentment on Jannekyn at every possible opportunity. The fact that the girl was so clearly well bred and fastidious in her habits only added fuel to the fire of her jealousy and animosity.

Night after night as the older woman lay snoring on her back Jannekyn would crawl into her hard little bed nearby and cry herself to sleep. She was desperately homesick. Even though her parents had been so poor that they had only a single room to live in she could remember every detail. It gave her a measure of comfort to picture it all: her father coughing in the bed in the corner, its threadbare curtains pulled back so that he could watch her and her mother busy with the fine sewing with which they made the few stuivers that kept them from starvation; the scrubbed table and benches, scrupulously clean like everything else in the room; the cooking pot hanging from its chain over the fire – she could almost smell the vegetables cooking as she saw it all in her mind's eye – and her little cat purring in front of the hearth. She hadn't realized until now just how happy she had been there, in spite of the poverty and the ever-present threat of war.

But there was no going back. It would kill her father if he were to find out how miserable she was. It would break his heart to discover how she had been treated by the brother into whose care he had so eagerly entrusted her, to know that she had been disowned because Jacob was ashamed to admit kinship with her. Because she was too shabby. He had admitted as much. At that thought the tears would begin to flow again as she remembered how carefully she and her mother had patched and darned her clothes so that she should not disgrace the family name.

And there was no danger that her parents would ever find out how badly she was being treated, Jacob had seen to that. Only a week after her arrival he had called her from the kitchen and taken her to his counting house.

'You can write?' he asked, handing her a quill.

'Yes, Meester.'

'Very well. Pen a letter to your father. I will see that he gets it.'

Jannekyn had looked up, her face shining. 'Oh, thank you . . . '

'I will dictate what you must say,' he had snapped.

So she had written, with Jacob cleverly making sure she told her father exactly what he would have wanted to hear – that Oom Jacob and Tante Katherine had made her more than welcome in their beautiful house and that she was very happy and contented in her new life and how thankful she was that he had sent her to Colchester. And when the tears had fallen and blotted the paper Jacob had torn it into shreds and forced her to start again, standing over her until the letter was completed in her neat, round hand to his satisfaction.

Then, triumphantly, he had sealed it. 'You will not need to write again,' he said.

Of all her tasks the one Jannekyn hated most was fetching the water from the stock well. The yoke with its two wooden buckets was no light weight when empty and when full it was cripplingly heavy. She learned to go to the well early, before the English gathered there to exchange news and banter idly with one another while their children played in the mud that surrounded the well even in the driest weather. Because she soon found out for herself that the Strangers, as her fellow countrymen were known, were not liked in the town. She could feel the open hostility as she approached the well in her neat grey dress with its plain white collar and she knew that her very neatness, plus the voluminous black apron and stiffly starched cap that she wore, marked her out as 'different'. For the people clustered round the well were at best shabby, and at worst downright ragged and all of them none too clean. When they saw her coming they would move aside, pulling their children with them, for all the world as if she were a leper, and watch in stony silence as she wound the heavy well bucket down into the water by its chain and hauled it laboriously back. No one ever offered her a helping hand, even when the winding gear stuck, despite the fact that she had to repeat the exercise three times in order to fill the buckets on her yoke. Her only defence was to get there before they arrived.

Even so, as she returned from the well so early one morning that she had had to crack the ice with the weight of the bucket before it could reach the water, she found she had still not escaped the inexplicable animosity of the townspeople. She was in sight of her uncle's imposing house in Frere Street when a man of about thirty, dressed in jerkin and breeches of well-worn leather, and carrying some shuttles in his hand, appeared from the direction of the castle. As they met he barred her way.

'Bin ta draw water, Stranger?' he asked, standing hands on hips astride her path.

'Yes,' she replied in her careful, slightly guttural English, 'I have been to the well.'

'Oh, my, that can speak English. Thass unusual for a Stranger.' He looked her up and down in cynical amusement, his little pig eyes glinting in a round, florid face.

She licked her lips. 'Ja, I speak a little English.'

''Thass a long way ta the stock well,' he went on, 'an' thass a heavy ole yoke you got there.'

'It is heavy. Ja. Please to let me pass. I wish to go back to the house where I can set it down.' She made to step round him.

'Hold on a minute, mawther. If thass too heavy . . . ' Quickly, before she could stop him he leaned forward and tipped the buckets, first one and then the other, spilling half the contents over the cobbles and over Jannekyn's feet. Ignoring her cry of protest he said, 'There, they ain't sa heavy now, are they?' and laughed. 'How much further hev you gotta go?'

'To Mynheer van der Hest's house.' Jannekyn pointed vaguely, trying to shake the water from her shoes as she spoke. 'Please let me pass. Garerdine will be waiting . . . '

'Van der Hest?' The man's amusement turned abruptly to anger. 'Thass th' ole bugger up at the Bay Hall. Him and his lot keep sendin' my cloth back 'ithout a seal. That ain't right that us English should hev our cloth examined at the Dutch Bay Hall, that ain't right at all, an' if that worn't for the likes of ole van der Hest we shouldn't hev to. I'll show you jest what I think of him an' his cronies!' He spat, substantially and accurately, into the nearest bucket and went on his way, shouting over his shoulder, 'An' you can tell 'im thass what Andrew Taylor think of *him!*'

Jannekyn gazed after him, tears of anger and frustration welling in her eyes. Then, with a sigh she tipped out what was left in both buckets and trudged all the way back to the stock well to refill them, trying to make as much haste as she could, knowing that Garerdine wouldn't even listen if she tried to explain why she had been so long. And it would be no use asking Garerdine why the English were so hostile towards the congregation of Strangers; shut up in the kitchen that was virtually her world, she probably didn't realize that they were.

In time Jannekyn learned, if not the reason for the hostility, at least how to cope with it. She learned never to mention that she came from Strangers' Hall on her trips to the market or the freshest vegetables and fruit would miraculously all have been sold, and only stinking offal would remain at the butcher's shambles. She discovered, too, that the English language was an invaluable asset. Used with discretion it commanded respect and gave her access to better meat and vegetables, which in turn mollified Garerdine and made her tongue a little less harsh. She realized that her poor father had been wise in wanting her to learn the English language, even though Minister Grenrice, just back from England, had dismissed it as unnecessary.

'No one uses it,' he had said, 'except for a few, like myself, who need to deal with the English officials.'

However, the offer of the family's most treasured possession, a carved oak coffer, had persuaded him that it would perhaps be a good thing for Jannekyn to learn English after all, and so he had agreed to teach her.

IV

Adam Mortlock whistled as he walked to work beside his master, Gabriel Birchwood. He carried the older man's tools and bag dinner over his shoulder as well as his own and he was careful to match his step to Gabriel's although in truth, on his long legs he would have been warmer striding through the icy streets at twice the speed.

Adam was twenty-two and had two more years before his apprenticeship to Gabriel would be finished and he would become a weaver in his own right. It was common knowledge that Gabriel was the finest weaver in Colchester – nay, in the whole of Essex and Suffolk – and he had taught Adam well. Soon the young man's skill would surpass even that of his master, a matter Gabriel viewed with great pride and satisfaction.

They were on their way to Strangers' Hall, which was the name local people had sarcastically given to Jacob van der Hest's great house. Jacob had heard of Gabriel's reputation and when he gathered together a select band of weavers to work in the special loom shed built on to his house he had invited Gabriel, although he was English, to be one of that number. Gabriel was reluctant, he did not want to work for any member of the Congregation of Strangers, but Jacob managed to convey that if Gabriel refused he would get no work elsewhere, because Jacob had 'influence'. Still Gabriel hesitated. There was his apprentice to consider. So Jacob offered to take Adam as well. Adam was furious, but he had no choice but to go with his master, and his nature was such that when his fury had subsided he made the best of the opportunity to work on the most up-to-date looms and with the most expensive materials that money could buy and to increase his knowledge as much as he could. The two other weavers in the loom shed were Strangers. They worked as far away from Gabriel and Adam as the looms allowed and had neither the desire nor the ability to have any communication with the two Englishmen.

'Here, howd on, boy, you're goin' too fast. You don't give

me time to ketch me breath.' Gabriel caught Adam's arm to slow him down. 'What you in sech a hurry about? We ain't late. Thass scarce light enough to see to work the loom, yet.'

'Sorry, master.' Adam slowed his step to Gabriel's, only then realizing he had begun to hurry in the hope of overtaking the girl ahead, struggling along with two heavy water buckets on a yoke. He felt sure it was the new servant at Strangers' Hall, a pretty, sad-looking girl of about eighteen. He had seen her once or twice in the garden, spreading the washed clothes on the bushes to dry. That was the advantage of working a loom, the room must have plenty of light, and that meant large windows all down the side. For most people that meant a lattice with shutters to close after dark, but there at Strangers' Hall the lattice was glazed so there were no cruel draughts to freeze a weaver's fingers till he could scarcely tell the warp from the weft. He had never had an opportunity to speak to the girl. Indeed, what was the use? The Dutch congregation were careful to speak no English and he could speak nothing else.

The girl turned under the archway that led to the courtyard of the rich clothier's house. The archway divided the house from the warehouse where the raw wool was sorted ready for spinning. Beyond it was the counting house. Opposite, and forming an extended wing to the house, beyond the dairy and the still room, was the specially built loom shed with its long glazed windows where Jacob's very finest cloth was woven. The rest was done by weavers in their own homes.

Adam and Gabriel followed the girl into the courtyard and they had almost drawn level with her when she stumbled in her effort to hurry. Adam quickly side-stepped and caught her or she would have fallen.

'That yoke is far too heavy for you,' he said, pointing to it and shaking his head in mime.

She braced herself and adjusted the yoke on her shoulders. 'No, I have much strength. I manage,' she replied in her careful English. 'But, thank you for your aid.'

Adam's face broke into a smile. 'You can understand! You speak my language!'

'Yes, I have some English.' She smiled, at the same time glancing nervously towards the kitchen. 'I should go. Garerdine waits. She will be angry that I have gone long.' She bowed her head and hurried off to the kitchen.

All day as Adam worked at his loom he watched for the girl to come into the garden to pick herbs or spread the washing, but there was no sign of her. He was unaccountably disappointed.

That night, lying in his warm bed under the eaves in the Birchwoods' cottage, Adam lay awake thinking about the girl at Strangers' Hall. This was unusual. Apart from the fact that he usually fell asleep the moment his head touched the pillow, thoughts of women didn't trouble him overmuch, although many of the local girls would have been glad of a glance from the tall, serious-looking man with the curly fair hair, neatly trimmed beard and deep-set brown eyes.

But Adam had been born to better things although he was now only a common weaver – albeit a very good one since he never did anything by halves. He had never been interested in frequenting the ale-house, nor indulged in the kind of horseplay that was an inevitable accompaniment to the three fairs that took place in the town every year: the Taylor's Fair held at St Anne's early in April, the Midsummer Fair on St John's Green at the end of June, and the big St Denis' Fair that was kept from the Exchange to the Market Cross in High Street for six days from the eve of St Denis'

Day, October the ninth. There was many a hastily arranged marriage in the town within three months of a fair.

This was not where Adam's inclinations lay. He had been a scholar once and his books were still precious to him. It was unfortunate that the very fact that he had been educated set him apart from the ordinary townspeople. They thought him snobbish. They didn't stop to think he might also be shy and a little lonely.

He knew that Bessie, Gabriel's wife, worried over him.

'Time you found yourself a wife, Adam, boy,' she would say, ladling out her thick stew in the forlorn hope of filling out his spare frame. 'Nice-lookin' lad like you. You could hev your pick. I seen the girls . . . '

'Leave the boy be, do, woman,' Gabriel would growl. 'He can't afford to marry time he's still a 'prentice, you know that, well as I do.'

'That don't stop him lookin' round.' Bessie would always have the last word.

Adam said nothing. He had never wanted to 'look round'. But now, lying in bed, his thoughts were full of how he could arrange to see the girl from Strangers' Hall again. He felt sorry for her. She looked so sad and forlorn. She intrigued him. Nothing more, he told himself.

His opportunity came the next day. He saw her taking a basket of washed clothes to spread on the bushes that separated the vegetable garden from the secret garden. He slipped away from his loom on the pretext of relieving himself at the vat placed behind the warehouse to collect the urine that would later be used to scour the wool. He hurried over to her.

'Did you hurt yourself when you stumbled yesterday?' he asked anxiously.

She shook her head. 'Oh, no, Mynheer. It was nothing,' she said.

'That yoke is far too heavy for you,' Adam insisted.

'You are kind.' She smiled shyly. 'But I am used to it. Every day I go for the water to the stock well.'

'Every day'. What time?'

'Very soon in the morning. I go before the English . . . ' She stopped, confused.

'I will come tomorrow and carry the water for you.' Adam smiled at her.

'Oh, no, Mynheer. It is not needful . . . '

Adam laughed aloud. 'It may not be "needful" but I shall come just the same. And my name is Adam.'

'A-dam.' She tried it carefully.

'That's right. And yours?'

'Jannekyn.'

'Yannikyn.' He copied her pronunciation. 'I like that. I'll see you tomorrow, Jannekyn. I must go now. Goodbye.'

'Goodbye, Adam.'

Jannekyn didn't expect to see Adam at the well the next day but he was there, waiting, when she arrived. He wound the heavy chain and filled the buckets for her and then shouldered the yoke and carried it back to the house.

'Don't worry, Jannekyn,' he smiled when she protested. 'I shall not be late at my loom. The sun is barely up. Weaving can't be done by candlelight, you know. Anyway, I work faster than all the others.' He said this without any air of boastfulness.

From then on she watched for the young weaver every morning and if he should be a few moments late her heart would sink with disappointment. She wondered if the feeling for Adam that was growing inside her was love or simply gratitude, because he was the only person other than Henrick de Groot who had shown her any kindness since she had come to England. She only knew that, far from dreading her daily visit to the well, she now regarded it as the one thing that made her life worth living.

And she could talk to him about the things that troubled her. One golden spring morning as they made their way back to the house Jannekyn said, 'Adam, why are my people called Strangers? Why have the English so much . . . ' she hesitated, searching for the right word, ' . . . haat . . . hate for us?'

Adam was silent for a while. To avoid being jostled by early risers preparing for market day they were slipping through narrow lanes and alleyways, where the houses were so closely crowded together that their upstairs windows nearly met and beneath them there was scarcely room for two people to walk side by side. Carrying the heavy yoke Adam had to adopt a kind of crab-like walk in order to stay beside Jannekyn.

'I think your people are called the Congregation of Strangers because that's exactly what they are,' he said at last. 'They've come to Colchester to live and work but they keep themselves quite apart from the townspeople.' He put down the yoke for a moment and began ticking off his fingers. 'They worship in All Saints' Church, but they have their own services, with their own ministers, in their own language. They have their own Bay Hall which they own and control. It's the only one in Colchester so the English have to take their cloth there to be examined. It's about the only place where Dutch and English meet' – he made a face – 'it must be like the Tower of Babel with neither side understanding what the other is saying.'

'Dutch we are not,' Jannekyn interrupted, shaking her head. 'For the most part Flanders is where we are from.'

'I know. But it's all the same to the English. Everyone coming from the Low Countries is labelled Dutch. And, another thing' – Adam shouldered the yoke again and they continued walking – 'hardly any of your community speak English even though some of them have lived here ten – perhaps even twenty years.'

'That I do not understand.'

Adam sighed. 'I suppose it's another way of preserving their identity, like the way they dress, always in dark, sombre clothes. The fact is, they don't *want* to be part of Colchester. They *want* to remain separate. Strangers.'

Jannekyn frowned. 'Yet it pleases Mynheer van der Hest that you and Master Birchwood should weave his special cloth.'

'That's only because Mynheer van der Hest is determined to have the very best weavers and my master has exceptional skills – skills he is passing on to me.' He gave a tittle laugh. 'I might tell you that it makes my master unpopular at the alehouse, being employed by a Stranger. Although of course it's partly jealousy because he always has a coin to jingle in his pocket while other poor weavers have empty bellies.' His brow creased. 'As I see it, it's all very well to come to England for refuge and to build up good businesses and become rich, but then to refuse to mix with the local people – whose livelihoods have often suffered as a result – and to refuse to even learn to communicate with them, well, it does seem rather high-handed, don't you agree?'

Jannekyn frowned. 'I cannot understand it makes any difference how high my people hold their hands,' she said seriously. 'It is their mouths from which they speak.'

'Oh, Jannekyn, you are funny.' Adam laughed aloud. 'I didn't mean ... oh, dear, how can I explain? It makes them appear arrogant – proud – superior. Is that better?'

'Ah, yes. I understand now what you are saying.'

'Well, then you can't wonder that the English are resentful and that they don't like the Dutch Community, can you?'

Jannekyn shook her head. 'No, that is true. I find it helps me greatly to speak English when I go to the market for Garerdine.' She fell silent, remembering her father's arguments with Minister Grenrice, who had declared that it was totally unnecessary for Jannekyn to learn English. Her father had won. The carved oak chest had been given to Minister Grenrice who had been the richer for it, and Jannekyn had gained something infinitely more valuable; a second language. She pulled her mind back to what Adam was saying.

'... and you must have found it useful to be able to speak English when you were begging in the gutter. How did you learn it? Did you just pick it up ... er, learn it, as you went along?'

She shrugged. 'Something like that.' One day she would tell him, tell everybody, the truth.

They had reached the castle bailey. Adam set the buckets down carefully and threw himself down on the grass, still damp with dew. Seeing Jannekyn hesitate he patted the ground beside him.

'It's early still. The house won't be astir for another hour. We've time to sit awhile.' He cupped his hands and took a drink from the nearest bucket.

It was true. By unspoken agreement they went earlier and earlier to the well, so that they would have time to loiter on the way back without fear of punishment.

Jannekyn sat down beside him and reluctantly accepted the piece of bread and cheese he offered. 'But this is your noon-piece, Adam.'

'Take it. I've plenty more. Mistress Birchwood is generous with food.' He smiled at her, his brown eyes warm with something she didn't quite understand. 'I like to share what I have with you, Jannekyn.'

'You are most kind, Adam,' she said, turning pink. 'But I do not want for food. There is always much to eat in the kitchen.'

'I'm glad. I should not like to think of you hungry.'

Jannekyn nibbled thoughtfully at her bread and cheese for several moments, gazing down the hill across the tenterfields, where the empty tenter-frames stood gaunt and skeletal in the early morning mist, waiting for the cloth to be hung on them to be dried or stretched. She was conscious that the young man beside her was watching her and she felt a surge of something inside her that she didn't quite understand, a warmth and contentment that she had never known before. Impulsively, she turned and put her hand on his arm. 'I am glad you are my friend, Adam, even though I am a Stranger and you are English. I hope nothing shall ever alter that.'

He put his hand over hers as it lay on his arm. 'If anything comes between us, Jannekyn, it won't be of my making,' he said seriously.

She was to remember his words.

V

Spring came. The weather grew warmer as the cruel east wind abated; the garden became bright with flowers and herbs, and daisies carpeted the castle bailey and the tenterfields beyond. In spite of the hardships she still had to endure Jannekyn went about her work singing.

She noticed as she passed the mirror hanging near the stairs that the pale, drawn look had left her face, her cheeks had filled out and her fair hair under its cap was thick and shining. She looked into the reflection of her clear blue eyes and was not dissatisfied. Whilst she was no beauty, her face, with its small, regular features and ready smile, was not unattractive. But she had scant time to spare on her appearance; Garerdine made sure that her hands were seldom idle.

Fortunately, the baby was good. Almost too good. At four months old it was not natural that he should sleep so much. Although it made Jannekyn's load lighter in that he was so little trouble, she worried about him. She mentioned him to the wet-nurse as she sat suckling him, but she was too dozy and stupid to see anything wrong.

'He thrives, don't he?' she said irritably. 'Look how he do grow.'

It was true. He was fat. Too fat. Jannekyn still worried.

She rarely saw the child's mother. Katherine spent her days in the solar languishing on her couch and her nights alone in the big bed to which her husband dutifully carried her and from which he was then dismissed, Katherine van der Hest was determined that someone should pay for a suffering pregnancy and a difficult birth and her husband was the obvious choice. The only time she altered her pattern of living was when he went on one of his infrequent trips to buy wool from the large fairs around the district. Then, if he was to be away for two or three days she would forsake her couch and walk in the garden if the weather allowed, or come to the kitchen and sit by the fire. Sometimes, she would summon enough energy to inspect the still-room and dairy – and even, if the mood took her, take a brief hand in the butter- and cheese-making.

On one of these visits Jannekyn spoke to her about the child.

'He sleeps too much, Mevrouw,' she said, careful never to call her Aunt.

‘Surely, you should be grateful he is so little trouble.’ Katherine peered into the cradle where her little son lay. ‘He thrives. I can see he thrives. Why, I swear he is bigger than when I saw him last.’

‘That was nearly a month ago, Mevrouw,’ Jannekyn said with a sigh.

‘That long? How time flies.’ Katherine turned away and picked up a barley cake cooling by the window and began nibbling it.

Jannekyn spoke to Garerdine.

‘Thank the good Lord he does sleep,’ Garerdine replied. ‘Think what the place would be like with a brat that squalled and yelled from morn till night. You should be grateful that the wet-nurse satisfies him with her milk. Why, I’ve known babies that none could satisfy save with a rag dipped in milk from a cow.’

Jannekyn picked the child up. Although she had been gone an hour he had the smell of the wet-nurse about him, a sickly-sweet smell that still seemed to cling however often Jannekyn washed him and changed his linen. He lay supine in her arms, taking no notice of her voice or his surroundings. Little though Jannekyn knew about babies she was convinced that his behaviour was not natural and that there was something very wrong with the child.

It surprised her that Jacob took so little interest in his baby son, although to be fair his business left him with little time to spare for anything else. And Sundays, whilst no work was done, were fully occupied with attending church, where he was an Elder and helped to minister to the spiritual welfare of those of the Congregation who were not, like him, one of the fortunate Chosen.

Often, Jannekyn would sit on the narrow bench, the child on her lap, while the homily of the Minister droned over her head, wondering why God chose those he did; like fat, slobbery old Minister Proost, who dropped food into his beard and whose voice went on endlessly in the same boring chant, all on one level, turning up slightly at the end of each phrase. Or like Jacob van der Hest. It was very evident from his prosperity that God had chosen him. And it was evident from Jacob's manner that he was fully aware of, and approved, God's choice. As an Elder Jacob was one of those responsible for presenting members of the Community who had committed misdemeanours, whether it be stealing half a loaf or loose and incontinent living, and he was quick to pronounce harsh judgement.

Jannekyn couldn't help feeling that the words of the psalm, 'God be merciful unto us and bless us', must have been left out of the bible Jacob van der Hest used, because mercy didn't seem to figure very largely in his judgements.

She was thinking along these lines as she sat with Garerdine behind Jacob and Dionis – Katherine was, of course, too delicate to attend and was excused the fine for non-attendance because she was visited privately and often by the new young Predikant who had recently moved to the town. Even in a dress made from her father's most expensive cloth, and with a cap set with pearls, Dionis was still plain and Jannekyn resolved to persuade her not to frizz her hair in such an unbecoming way as soon as the opportunity arose. Benjamin moved sluggishly in her arms and she offered up a silent prayer that she might find a way to discover what was wrong with him.

A prayer that was to be answered sooner than she expected.

At the end of the long, dull service people tended to gather in knots to discuss the sermon – or, out of earshot of Minister and Elders, more interesting things. This was frowned on in the case of servants, who were supposed to hurry back to their duties. But Jannekyn always used this as an opportunity to slip away from Garerdine in the hope – not often in vain – of seeing Adam. But today it was not Adam she saw as she skirted the crowd but Henrick de Groot, looking as raffish as ever, his cap cocked over one eye.

'Jannekyn, my child.' He beamed as he saw her. 'How are you?'

She smiled at him and shifted Benjamin to her other arm. 'I'm well, thank you.'

'And happy?' He looked searchingly at her.

'I have enough to eat and a warm bed.'

He gave a grunt at her evasive answer. 'Come home with me and meet Betkin, my wife. She's just been brought to bed with our eighth child. She'll be glad of some company.'

'I'd like to come, but Garerdine . . . ' She looked round and saw that the older woman was engrossed in conversation with two fat women. 'Yes, I'd like to come.'

The house in Grub Street was small beyond belief and overrun with healthy, happy children whose ages ranged from about ten years old down to a fat toddler of barely a year. Betkin lay on a straw pallet in the corner with the new baby at her breast Her round, motherly face was lined beyond its years but her eyes were full of serene happiness. She held out a welcoming hand to Jannekyn,

'I've been longing to meet you. Henrick has told me all about you,' she said. 'Come and sit here and talk to me. Henrick, give the children some broth and send them to play on the meadow. There'll be no peace while they're here.'

Jannekyn sat down and made Benjamin comfortable on her

lap while Henrick ladled out a watery broth and cut hunks of bread, using his maimed hands with surprising dexterity. The children fell on the food like ravening wolves, but not until grace had been said and the older ones had looked to the little ones.

'So that's the youngest van der Hest child,' Betkin said when the children were quiet with their food. 'He's very pale.'

Jannekyn raised the child higher on her arm so that Betkin could see him better.

'And fat. Far too fat.' Betkin ran an experienced eye over him; 'He's good?' she asked, looking up at Jannekyn.

Jannekyn nodded.

'Almost too good? Sleeps all the time?'

Jannekyn's eyes widened. 'How can you know that? But, yes, it worries me that he sleeps so much, although everyone says I should be grateful he's so little trouble.'

'How is he fed? A wet-nurse?'

'Yes. And I mustn't be away too long or she'll be waiting for him.'

'Give me the child.' Betkin eased herself up on the straw and took Benjamin to examine him more closely. 'This wet-nurse, does she make herself potions?'

Jannekyn frowned. 'I don't think so. Except once or twice I've noticed her make tea from poppy seeds because she slept badly the night before.'

'Ah, just as I thought,' Betkin nodded. 'I fancy she often sleeps badly and often seeks the relief of poppy-seed tea, although she'll be careful not to let you see. And the more she has the more she needs and the more she will pass on to the child through her milk.'

Jannekyn looked at her in surprise. 'Surely that can't be what makes Benjamin sleep so much!'

'Of course it can. I've seen it happen time and again. But doesn't the child's mother worry over him?'

'No. Everyone says I should be thankful he never cries.'

'Never mind being thankful he never cries, be thankful you brought him to me before it was too late.' Betkin pulled her gown aside and began to suckle Benjamin herself. 'I've milk and to spare, but, I warn you, he won't be so sleepy after he's had his fill from me.'

Jannekyn watched her in some alarm. 'But what about Maria, the wet-nurse? When she tries to feed him . . . '

'He won't take from her if he's not hungry, But you'll have to wean him from her gradually. Once a day at first, then twice, until he is no longer taking from her at all.'

'But what shall I give him instead?'

'Bring him to me when you can. When that's not possible soak some bread in warm cow's milk and feed him that. He'll cry at first, of course, but you'll have to put up with that. I'll give you something to quieten him for when he cries too much. In a week or two he'll be rid of her ill-humours and will turn from being, a fat, white slug into a healthy boy,' She reached inside the straw of the pallet and took out a packet. 'Pound this into a paste and put two drops in his milk. No more. And don't use it unless you have to.'

'I don't know how to thank you. I'm sure Mynheer van der Hest . . . '

'The best way to thank me is to keep quiet,' Betkin cut her short. 'My old grandmother handed down to me a knowledge of herbs and potions and because most folk don't know much about such things they whisper about me and say I'm peculiar. So, for the most part I keep my own counsel and only use what I know sparingly. I trust you to keep quiet and say nothing of what's gone on here today. Let them think it was your idea to wean the child. They'll think highly of you when he begins to thrive.' She handed a replete Benjamin back to Jannekyn. 'There, the wet-nurse will have a wasted journey this time.'

Henrick joined them. 'Noisy brats,' he shouted affectionately to his brood of children, as, their bellies filled, they ran off to play in the meadow.

'They're good children, Henrick,' Betkin said. 'And a great comfort to me when you're away. And, goodness knows, that's often enough.'

'They're still noisy.' Henrick took Betkin's hand in what was left of his own and sat down beside her on the pallet. Jannekyn couldn't help contrasting the obvious bond of affection here in this squalid little cottage with the cold formality of Jacob van der Hest's grand house in Frere Street.

'And how is your uncle?' Henrick said, as if he could read her thoughts.

She hesitated before replying, conscious that he was looking at her intently. 'Mynheer van der Hest is well, thank you,' she said at last, rather primly.

Henrick raised his eyebrows. 'Formal, aren't we?'

'De Meester prefers it that way.'

'Strange. And what about your aunt? You'll be telling me next you call her Mevrouw.'

Jannekyn glanced over her shoulder. 'Yes, that's right. I do. You see, nobody must know I'm Uncle Jacob's niece.'

'Whyever not?' Betkin asked. 'Surely, they treat you as one of me family?'

'Oh, indeed no. De Meester told me right from the start that I was to be his servant. He told his family that he found me begging in the gutter. He said I was never to say anything different.'

Betkin looked puzzled. 'But why, in the name of all that's holy?'

'Because I looked too shabby for him to admit I was his kin,' Jannekyn said sadly. 'I know I must have looked as if I'd just come from the gutter, but I couldn't help it – the weather was dreadful and I'd had a bad sea crossing . . . But there was another thing. I hadn't got any papers. I didn't know that no new Strangers were allowed to come into the town without the consent of the bailiffs. De Meester said that if I didn't do as he said he would turn me out and then I would be caught and thrown into prison with the rats until I could be sent back to Flanders.'

'Jacob told you that, did he?' Henrick scratched his beard thoughtfully.

'Yes.' Jannekyn lowered her voice. 'And he also said it would go badly for my family if it was known they had sent me here without authority.'

Henrick screwed up his face. 'You know, Jacob told me to forget I'd ever set eyes on you the day I fetched you up the river for him. I've often wondered why. It's true that no new Stranger can come into the town without someone to vouch for them, yes. But surely, as your uncle, Jacob wouldn't have had any trouble in doing that. He's a highly respected member of the Congregation. I can't understand why he should have disowned a pretty little thing like you . . . just because you were a bit travel-stained . . . I would have thought anyone would have been happy to . . . ' He shook his head. 'I can't understand it. I can't understand it at all. I've always found him a fair and just man in my dealings with him . . . in fact, he set me up with my boat when I first arrived here.' He shook his head again. 'It seems very strange to me.'

Betkin smiled at Jannekyn. 'Well, at least he's given you a roof over your head, that's something to be thankful for. And it's a beautiful house, too, so I've heard.' A wistful note crept into her voice as she looked round at her own humble surroundings. Then, suddenly, her face changed and her eyes narrowed. 'But there's no happiness there, is there? For all it's a great house with fine furnishings it's a house with no heart. No love.' She looked hard at Jannekyn. 'I'm right, am I not, Juffrouw?'

Jannekyn sighed. 'Yes, I fear you are.'

'A house needs love.' Betkin closed her eyes. 'Ah, I see it now. That's why you've come to it. You are the one that will bring love to Strangers' Hall.'

Jannekyn shook her head. 'I don't see how that can possibly be,' she said, with a sad little smile. 'I am only a servant, less than a servant, if that's possible.'

'It's true, all the same,' Betkin insisted. 'I'm sure of it. It will be through you that love will come to Strangers' Hall.'

Jannekyn left them, with Betkin's puzzling words in her ears. As she made her way past the ruined St Botolph's Priory and on up the hill towards the big house in Frere Street she talked to Benjamin about it. She often talked to him about her problems and usually he took not the slightest notice. But today, almost for the first time, his eyes followed her every movement, and now and again, as she bent her head towards him, he smiled.

After he had watched Jannekyn go, with the baby cradled in her arms, Henrick stood, rubbing his edging of wiry hair with the palms of his hands. Then he turned to his wife 'I don't understand it, Betkin. I don't understand it at all.'

'Don't understand what, my love?'

'I don't understand why Jacob should treat the girl like that.' He began to pace up and down the cramped little room.

'Dammit, she's his niece, and a pretty little thing at that. Why, in the name of Jesus, should he disown her?'

Betkin propped herself up on one elbow. 'I expect it's this business of no new Strangers coming into the town. They're very strict about it, and you said yourself, just now . . . '

Henrick waved her remark aside. 'I know. But there's more to it than that, if I don't miss my mark, although I didn't want to worry the girl by saying so.'

'What do you mean?'

He rubbed his beard thoughtfully. 'I don't know, exactly. But if ever I'm in Ypres . . . '

Betkin caught his sleeve. 'Now, Henrick, we've had all this out before. You promised me you wouldn't go back to the other side any more, it's far too dangerous. And now we've yet another mouth to feed . . . ' She looked down lovingly at the little dark head nestled in the crook of her arm.

He went and sat on the pallet. 'It's all right, lieverd, don't get yourself in a stew. I only said *if* I'm ever in Ypres. But I'm not likely to be, so we needn't talk about it any more. I'd still like to know, though . . . and that's where I think the answer might be.'

VI

There were times when Jannekyn almost regretted taking Betkin's advice over Benjamin. Days when she was busy in the bakehouse or dairy and he wouldn't stop crying; nights when he kept her awake; times when old Garerdine – not sweet-tempered at the best of times – railed at her for his fractiousness. But she persevered, weaning him gradually from his opium-sated wet-nurse, treasuring the times when she managed to steal him away to Betkin, who, while she suckled him, passed on some of her knowledge of herbs and hedgerow plants, secrets handed down to her by her grandmother. In time, she was rewarded by seeing the little boy become less and less bad-tempered and increasingly alert and lively, laughing and gurgling when she talked to him as he had never done before.

Even his mother noticed the difference and began to take an interest in him, sitting with him on her knee when she came to visit the kitchen in Jacob's absences from home, and even, on rare occasions, summoning Jannekyn to bring him to her as she lay on her couch in her solar, handing him back like a parcel at the first sign of a whimper. 'He is so heavy,' she would say, 'it exhausts me to hold him. It will be better when he is able to walk, then I will have him near me for longer.'

Dionis, too, began to take an interest in her baby brother, pushing him round the garden in the little wooden-wheeled cart that Tobias, the old man who looked after the garden, had made for the purpose.

Dionis was a strange girl, in some ways young for her years although she was already betrothed to Abraham de Baert, a middle-aged widower. How she felt about this Jannekyn could only guess, because Dionis maintained a haughty, superior air towards her, copied, no doubt, from her mother, and although Jannekyn would have liked to befriend her – sensing that at heart she was a lonely girl – Dionis never gave her the slightest opportunity.

Never gave her an opportunity, that is, until one afternoon in late July. Jannekyn was collecting in the dried washing from the garden when she heard the sound of crying. Not a child's crying but a long-drawn-out agonized weeping from the depths of despair. She put the linen down in a heap and looked for the source of the crying. It was some minutes before she saw Dionis, lying flat on her face on the grass behind a box hedge, sobbing as if her heart would break.

Jannekyn went over and knelt beside her and touched her arm gently. Dionis looked up, her face puffy and her eyes red-rimmed with tears.

'Oh, it's you,' she said rudely. 'Go away and leave me alone.'

Jannekyn sat back on her heels. 'You'll need to bathe your eyes before your father sees you,' she said in a matter-of-fact tone. They're all red and puffy. And your cap's all awry.'

Dionis sat up and jerked her cap straight 'Go away, Mistress Pry,' she repeated, nevertheless dabbing very carefully at her eyes. 'Haven't you anything better to do than spy on people? Why aren't you looking after my brother?'

'Your brother is asleep not twenty paces from where you're sitting. And if you will cry so loudly when I'm gathering in the linen I can't help but hear you.' She smiled at Dionis. 'If something's troubling you it sometimes helps to talk about it, you know.'

Dionis sniffed but said nothing.

'Very well, I'll do as you ask and leave you.' Jannekyn began to get to her feet.

'No.' Dionis put out her hand. 'Wait.' She shook her head. 'Not that you'll understand . . . '

'That's all the better, surely,' Jannekyn said cheerfully. 'Because you'll have got whatever it is off your chest without anyone being any the wiser if, as you say, I'm not going to understand what you tell me.'

'That's true.' Dionis blew her nose. Then, suddenly, her face crumpled and she began to cry again. 'I can't do it,' she wailed miserably. 'I can't do it.'

'Can't do what?'

'I can't marry Abraham de Baert. He's as old as my father and he's fat and ugly. I hate him.' She went off into another fit of crying.

Jannekyn was silent for a moment. 'But you won't be marrying him yet, will you? After all, you're only fifteen.'

'I'll be sixteen next month. And that's when we are to be married. As soon as my brother Pieter comes home.'

Jannekyn was silent again. She had heard of Pieter van der Hest, Jacob's nineteen-year-old son, away at sea with the Merchant Adventurers. He had travelled to the Baltic and was now somewhere in the Mediterranean in an effort to extend his father's already thriving business. 'So soon?' she said at last.

'Abraham is anxious for a son before he becomes too old to . . . ' The mere thought of sharing a bed with him sent her off into paroxysms of weeping again.

'Have you told your father how you feel?' Jannekyn asked.

'Oh, yes,' Dionis replied on a hiccup. Suddenly, her voice became flat and calm with despair. 'But my father says that I should be grateful that Abraham de Baert is willing to have me. Well, I mean, I'm not exactly pretty, am I? I'm fat, my face is too pale, my mouth is too small, my nose is too big . . .'

'Who told you all this?'

'I can see it for myself when I look in the mirror, can't I? But my father says so, too. He says his fine materials are wasted on me because my shoulders stoop and the sooner he can get me married off the better.'

Jannekyn drew in her breath sharply. She was surprised that even Jacob van der Hest could be that callous. But there was more to come.

'He says I should think myself lucky that Abraham offered

for me because nobody else was likely to. And at least I'll have a big house with plenty of land . . . ' she gulped, ' . . . he said.'

'Oh, Dionis, did he really say all that?'

Dionis nodded, sniffing. 'Well, he's right, isn't he? I should think myself lucky that someone's offered for me – even if it is fat, ugly old Abraham de Baert with his house full of servants that I don't like anyway.' She dissolved into floods of tears again.

Jannekyn put her arm round Dionis and this time the girl didn't rebuff her but put her head gratefulry on Jannekyn's shoulder.

'Have you told anyone else how you feel?' Jannekyn asked, stroking her hair. 'Your mother, perhaps?'

'My mother is too busy discussing wedding plans with Minister Verlender when he comes to see her. She doesn't really care about me. And who else is there to tell?'

'You've told me now. I care.'

Dionis lifted her head. 'Yes, but you can't *do* anything. You're only a servant, that my father rescued from the gutter.'

She didn't mean to sound rude and Jannekyn realized this. 'I once had a home, and parents who loved me,' she said, unable for a moment to keep the nostalgia from her voice.

'Did you? Tell me about them. Where are they? Why did you leave them?' For a moment Dionis forgot her own problems.

'One day I'll tell you,' Jannekyn promised. And she meant it. One day she would make sure that the truth was told. 'But for the moment . . . ' She put her heart on one side. 'Dionis, do you mink you could manage without some of the sweet cakes and peppermint drops you love so much? The gingerbread and spiced comfits?'

Dionis looked at her in bewilderment. 'Why do you ask?'

'Because I'm sure you are only fat because you eat too well

and walk too little. Also, all those comfits will turn your teeth black if you are not careful.'

'If I were not fat I would still be ugly,' Dionis pointed out miserably.

'Oh, Dionis, you aren't ugly,' Jannekyn laughed. 'It's just that you wear such a discontented look that your mouth looks all pinched up. If you were to smile sometimes . . . '

'I don't have much to smile about.'

'Rubbish. You live in a fine house and you have beautiful gowns and jewels to wear.'

'I've no friends.'

'I'm your friend. At least I would be if only you'd let me.'

'But you're only a servant.' A trace of the old haughty air reappeared.

'I'm still a person. And Dionis, I promise you this, a servant I may be now, but it will not always be that way. One day . . . ' Jannekyn looked up at the house, with its red bricks herring-boned between solid oak timbers, its richly carved bressummer supporting the upper storey, and the tiles on the roof that were bathed in a pink glow from the afternoon sun, and once again the feeling that had struck her on the day she arrived returned. Returned with such force that for a moment she was speechless – almost breathless – with the power of it, the sure knowledge that this was *her* house, waiting, in trust, for her to claim it. 'One day,' she repeated softly, 'I shall be mistress of my own house.'

She hadn't realized quite how intensely she had spoken until she heard Dionis give a nervous little giggle. 'Oh, Jannekyn, how can you be so sure? And you only my father's servant.'

Nevertheless, Dionis looked at her with a new respect Jannekyn noted.

Benjamin, lying in his cart in the shade, gave a whimper and pulled himself into a sitting position. This was a fairly new achievement and he gave a chuckle of delight when he caught sight of the two girls sitting on the grass nearby.

'Oh dear.' Jannekyn scrambled to her feet. 'I had hoped he might sleep a little longer. I still have work to finish in the dairy.'

'I'll look after him for you.' Dionis went over to her brother and picked him up. 'We'll make a daisy chain. You'll like that, won't you, Bennie?'

Jannekyn left them together and walked across the grass to the dairy. But before she had gone many paces she turned back. 'There is one more thing, Dionis,' she said hesitantly. 'I'm sure you'd sleep better if you didn't torture yourself with curl papers every night. And your hair would look so much nicer if it wasn't frizzed.'

'But it would be quite straight.' Dionis was quite shocked at the thought.

'What matter? It's a pretty colour. And well brushed it would shine.' Jannekyn lifted a lock of her own hair. 'See? Mine lacks curl, too.'

'Yes, I know. But you're . . . '

'Only a servant? I'm still a woman and anxious that my looks should please.'

As she said the words Jannekyn thought of Adam Mortlock, the young weaver, even now busy at his loom, as she could hear from the noisy clacking that came from the weaving shed nearby, and her face turned a delicate pink as she remembered the admiration she had seen, more than once, in his eyes.

'Anyway, it's too late,' Dionis called after her, the misery back in her voice. 'Why should I make myself pretty for old, fat Abraham de Baert?'

Jannekyn's thoughts were not with Dionis as she busied

herself churning the butter, they were with Adam. She recalled the conversations they had had on their way back from the well early in the morning, walking home from church sometimes, though not often, on Sundays, and walking through the woods on rare afternoons when they had both done their day's work early. Adam was ambitious. He admitted it. Not for him a life spent as one of Jacob van der Hest's band of weavers, however select they might be.

'What I want,' he had told Jannekyn more than once, 'is to weave van der Hest cloth on my own loom.'

'Many weavers work on their own looms,' she had teased him in her slow, halting English. 'But the finest quality cloth is made in Mynheer van der Hest's loom shed.'

'And that's the kind of cloth I intend to make. The special cloth, the mockados, stamells, oliotts and tametts,' he said earnestly.

'You cannot. You have no loom.'

'I shall have. Gabriel, my master, says I'm to have his. It stands unused in his cottage now that he works all his hours here at van der Hest's. He says he will never use it again. But *I* shall.' He'd smiled proudly at Jannekyn.

But Jannekyn had only frowned. 'I cannot understand why you should be so anxious to do that, Adam.'

'Can't you? Well, I'll tell you, then. Jacob van der Hest employs only the very best weavers at his house. Right?'

Jannekyn had nodded. 'Ja.'

'And he pays them sixpence a cloth more than he pays master weavers who work for him in their own homes on inferior cloth. Yes?'

'Ja.'

'Well, what I aim to do is to weave his best cloth on my own loom and charge him a shilling a cloth extra.'

'He will not pay. He will not trust that you will not steal the yarn. He has no trust for anyone.'

'He'll pay me. Because by the time I'm out of my time with Gabriel I shall be the best weaver in the district and he won't want me working for anyone else.' Adam had said the words as a simple statement of fact, without any hint of boastfulness. 'Even now my cloths are the most even, my selvedges the straightest and I can work my loom longer than any man there.' He'd laid his hand gently on her arm. 'I'm ambitious, Jannekyn. And one day I shall be successful. Then – well, we shall see.' And his smile had told her what his words had left unsaid.

She finished her daydreaming with the butter and setting it aside went back to the kitchen. Garerdine, in an uncharacteristic frenzy of activity, immediately rounded on her, calling her an idle, lazy scallywag, never there when she was wanted – look, she had let the fire die down – the pot boil over (Jannekyn wasn't sure how she could be guilty of both at the same time) – the dough hadn't been set to rise and the floor wasn't swept.

This tirade came all in a breath before Jannekyn could set her foot inside the door. When she did the reason for the outburst was plain to see. Over by the window, eating a plum selected from the bowl on the dresser, stood Jacob van der Hest himself. His presence had clearly reduced Garerdine to a quivering jelly.

'Which would you like me to do first?' Jannekyn asked coolly, refusing to be intimidated neither by Garerdine's outburst nor Jacob's presence. Since her arrival at the clothier's house she had seen little enough of him but what she had seen had given her no reason to change her first opinion of him – that he was a proud, arrogant and thoroughly hateful man.

'The dough . . . no . . . the . . . floor . . . no . . . take the basket and collect the eggs from the hens.'

'Very well, Garerdine.' Jannekyn picked up the wicker basket kept for the purpose and turned to go.

'Wacht even!' Jacob spat a plum stone out of the window. 'Wait. I wish to speak to you.'

Jannekyn waited. 'Yes, Meester?'

'What have you been doing with Benjamin, my son? The wet-nurse has come to me complaining that you dismissed her. Is this true?'

'Yes, Meester.' She brushed a wisp of hair away from her face as she spoke.

'Why? On what authority?'

'Because her services were no longer required by the child in my charge . . . ' a barely perceptible pause ' . . . Meester.'

'But the child is barely seven months old. I have known children suckled until they were three years old.'

'Benjamin would not have lived that long suckled by Maria de Haan, Meester. Have you not seen the difference in him of late?' She looked at him, her blue eyes clear and challenging, knowing that Jacob van der Hest would have no time to waste on children from whom no profit was to be made. 'Her milk was not good for him, it kept him weak and sleepy. I feed him gruel from a spoon. He is a fine boy now. Also, it saves you money, since you no longer have to pay the wet-nurse.'

Jacob's eyes glinted. 'This is true. Where is the child now??

'In the garden with his sister. I'll fetch him for you to see.'

Before he could protest Jannekyn ran and scooped Benjamin from his sister's lap and carried him, still draped with the daisy chain Dionis had put round his neck. He began to bawl loudly at being disturbed and by the time they reached the kitchen he was a red-faced, screaming bundle of fury.

'Ja, ja.' Jacob waved him away, scarcely looking at him. 'I can see he thrives. Take him back to his sister before he does himself a mischief.'

Suppressing a smile, Jannekyn did as she had been bidden and Benjamin's tears stopped as if by magic.

On her way back to the kitchen Jannekyn heard the hens that scratched round the back yard squawking and making a great commotion. As she neared the door she could see the reason why. An evil-smelling human heap of rags was standing at a short distance from it, his hands held out in supplication.

Jacob, with his hand to his nose, was waving the man away and Garerdine was advancing on him with a broom. 'We don't feed beggars,' she was screaming. 'Be off with you! Be off, you vagabond!'

'I have a message, lady. I have a message.' The man repeated the words over and over. But he spoke in English, and not understanding, Garerdine only shrieked the louder.

'Wacht even!' Jannekyn called to Garerdine. 'Wait! Listen to what the man has to say.'

'He's begging for food. Send him packing. He stinks to high heaven,' Jacob said, keeping his distance.

'He *isn't* begging for food,' Jannekyn said. 'He says he has a message for you. Can't you hear?'

Jacob shook his head contemptuously. 'I hear but I don't understand. He speaks English, a barbaric tongue. Send him away.'

'Who is your message from?' Jannekyn asked the man, ignoring her uncle and speaking in English.

'From Mynheer van der Hest. Mynheer Pieter van der Hest.'

Jacob recognized his son's name. 'Wat zegt 'ie? What's he saying? What does he know of my son?' he asked quickly.

'Tell me, what of Mynheer van der Hest?' Jannekyn asked gently.

The man held out hands covered in dirt and sores. 'Water first, and a crust, I beg you of your mercy, mistress. It is three days since a morsel passed my lips.'

Jannekyn went inside and took a wooden bowl from the shelf and ladled soup from the pot over the fire into it. 'He must eat before he speaks,' she said to the others, surprised at how easily she slipped from one tongue to the other. For once she was in command and even Jacob could not gainsay her if he wanted news of his elder son.

The three of them watched as the man consumed the broth, Garerdine with something akin to terror, Jacob with ill-concealed impatience and Jannekyn with compassion. She noticed that despite his disgusting appearance the beggar had an unexpected dignity. He was surprisingly well-spoken, his voice pleasantly modulated and polite and although he was starving he ate his broth in a slow and mannerly fashion. When he had finished he gave her back the bowl with a little bow. 'God bless you, mistress, you've saved my life this day, although to what purpose only he in his mercy can tell.'

'Wat zegt 'ie? What's he saying?' Jacob interrupted. 'Has he news of my son?'

'Aye, I have news of his son.' The beggarly Englishman was better at interpreting a foreign tongue than the rich Flemish clothier. 'I met him at Constantinople and he, discovering that my ship was bound for England, asked me to pass a message to you.' He waited while Jannekyn passed on the information. Then he continued, 'He is on the *Santa Maria*, yes?'

'Ja, ja, ja,' Jacob snapped eagerly, recognizing the name. 'Go on.'

'He said to tell you that new markets have opened for cloth that are likely to prove profitable.'

'He will be able to tell me that soon enough himself,' Jacob said, when Jannekyn had finished translating. 'He will be home within the month. Send this fellow packing.'

Jannekyn translated.

'No,' the beggar said. 'That is the reason I have come. Your son will not be home within the month, nor for many months, six at least. He is unlikely to be home until Christmas is well past. The captain of his ship has been paid a handsome figure to take men from Africa across the sea to the islands that are heavy with the scent of spices. It was an offer too good to refuse.' The man looked down at his rags. 'I only wish that I might have gone, too. It would have saved me from this.'

'Why? What happened to you?' Jannekyn asked.

'We were but a day and a night off Brightlingsea when there was a storm and my ship went aground on the Goodwin Sands and broke up in the heavy seas. Most of the crew were drowned, I fear, but I managed to cling to a beam. Even so, I was afloat for a full day before I was washed up on the Kent coast. From there I have walked . . . it has taken me three weeks to find my way here.'

'Oh, you poor man. Meester . . .' With her eyes full of tears Jannekyn related the man's story to Jacob, hoping that he would take pity on the man and give him employment.

But she was disappointed. All Jacob did was to take a coin from his purse and throw it into the dirt at the man's feet. 'Take that for your pains,' he said, and turned his back on him.

The beggar glanced at the coin at his feet, then with obvious reluctance bent and picked it up and concealed it among his rags. Then he smiled, almost apologetically, at Jannekyn. 'God be with you, mistress.' He raised his hand in salute and limped away.

Jannekyn watched him go, her heart full of sadness, wishing there was something she could have done for him, conscious as never before of how little she possessed, of her utter dependence on her hated uncle.

Then her spirits lifted. One person at least would be grateful for the news that the beggar had brought, and that was Dionis. Jannekyn hurried into the garden to tell her. But had she but known it, the beggar's visit was to have an effect more far-reaching than delaying Dionis's marriage. It was to change Jannekyn's life in a way she could never have imagined.

VII

August passed and September came, bringing with it gentle misty mornings that hinted at autumn's approach. Jannekyn loved these early mornings, the dew wet under her feet as she returned from the well. More often than not Adam was with her, bearing the burden of the water, although he no longer had any need to protect her from the taunts of the English. For since they had seen how Adam had befriended and protected her they had ceased to jibe at her for being a Stranger and, instead, wished her Good-day, and even gave her a helping hand when the well-handle got stuck, as it sometimes did. But Adam still continued to meet her and walk back with her across the castle bailey and she valued these all-too-brief meetings with the young English weaver.

Dionis, after her burst of confidence on that hot summer afternoon, had quickly returned to her former distant manner. Now that her marriage to Abraham de Baert had been put off she was not in such need of a shoulder to cry on and she once again treated Jannekyn with the lofty superiority she copied from her parents.

Jannekyn only smiled to herself. Despite the attitude Dionis displayed towards her it was obvious that she had taken her advice to heart. She noticed that the girl no longer stuffed herself with marchpane and gingerbread, with the result that her figure was already becoming quite trim and her face had lost its fat, puddingy look. Her hair, too, was no longer a frizzy halo and although it would never be very thick it fell in gentle waves from under her cap and framed her face softly. If only she would look a little less disagreeable she would be quite pretty, Jannekyn decided.

But at the same time, the prospect of marriage to Abraham de Baert was enough to make anyone disagreeable, Jannekyn had to admit.

She remembered particularly his visit to the house on Dionis's sixteenth birthday. He had brought with him a little jewelled casket as a birthday present, but even as he was giving it to Dionis Jannekyn was aware of him casting a lecherous eye in her direction and it wasn't long before she learned not to stand too close to him as she served at table.

It was strange that Jacob didn't object to the coarse, vulgar old man, he being so fastidious himself, but he welcomed him with every evidence of pleasure and appeared to pay no heed to his daughter's barely concealed distaste.

Her thoughts were running along these lines as she busied herself in the still-room. She loved working here among the fragrance, bunching sweet-smelling herbs to hang in all the rooms, pounding roots and crushing leaves to make remedies – some at Garerdine's instruction, some according to an old herbal she had found in a corner of the still-room. Today, she was making a syrup from rose-hips to drink through the winter and she was in a hurry because it was also baking day. Even now she could hear Garerdine shouting at her from the kitchen that the dough had risen and where was she, lazy good-for-nothing that she was, couldn't she see that there was work to be done. She tried not to listen, Garerdine always nagged and shouted. In fact, the woman was never quiet, she grumbled and nagged all day and snored all night. Jannekyn began to hum to herself to shut out the noise.

'You can put that down. I want you to come with me.'

Startled at the voice, Jannekyn swung round, nearly dropping the pan she was holding. Jacob van der Hest was standing in the doorway, a tall, black-clad figure, his cloak over his arm and a sheaf of papers in his hand. 'Yes, yes, you heard aright. I want you to come with me,' he repeated, tapping his foot impatiently, before she had a chance to speak.

She looked at her hands, sticky with juice and then at her plain grey gown, covered by a large black apron, but still spattered with syrup. 'But Meester . . . '

'Oh, put on a clean, apron and tidy yourself up. Hurry now.'

But Jannekyn, perplexed as she was, refused to be hurried. 'What about the baby, Meester? Who will feed him and tend him when he cries? And what about Garerdine? It's baking day . . . And my dress . . . '

'Bah!' He began to pace up and down. 'Dionis can look after the child. It will do her good to have something to occupy her. And Garerdine will have to manage as best she can for today. As for your dress . . . ' He paused and looked her up and down. It was true, the dress was beginning to bear witness to all her household tasks. 'No doubt my wife has an old cloak she will lend you to cover it. Now, are you ready? Come with me. I'm already late.'

Quickly changing her apron and pushing stray strands of hair back under her cap Jannekyn followed Jacob through the kitchen, where she was met with a cold glare from an unusually silent Garerdine.

'Wait for me in my carriage,' he called over his shoulder as they reached the hall.

Still perplexed, Jannekyn did as she was told. The carriage was standing outside the front of the house and as she climbed into it she recalled the last time it had carried her – not much more than six months ago – from the docks at New Hythe, full of hope and optimism at beginning a new life with her father's brother and his family. Little did she realize then what her life was to be.

Jacob hurried out to the carriage and flung a cloak at her. It was black velvet, trimmed with fur and lined with silk. 'Here, put this on. And mind and keep it close so that it covers your dress,' he said as he sat down opposite her.

The cloak rustled as she drew it round her and she could smell the lavender it had been stored in. She had never worn anything of such fine quality before and its feel gave her confidence.

'Where are you taking me, Meester?' she asked.

'To the Bay Hall,' he replied tersely.

'For what purpose?' She had heard of the Bay Hall and knew that it was the place where all the cloth made in the town must be taken to be examined before it could be sold. She couldn't imagine what it could possibly have to do with her. She looked at Jacob, waiting for his answer.

He didn't return her gaze. He was looking out of the carriage window as they passed the butcher's shambles and St Runwald's Church, staring as if he had never seen people milling round market stalls before.

'My clerk is ill,' he said briefly at last. 'I need someone to take his place.'

'But, Meester, how can I help? I know nothing . . . '

'You speak English. You translated for me when the English beggar brought news of my son.'

'But, Meester . . . '

'For the sake of all that's holy, stop saying "But, Meester". Can you not think of anything else to say?' He turned a hawk-like gaze on her, withering her into silence. 'Goed, dan. Very well.' He seemed to take her silence as acceptance of the situation. 'As I said, I know that you speak English with a certain fluency and that you understand when it is spoken. You will listen to what goes on at the Bay Hall and translate for me where necessary.' He nodded and permitted himself a ghost of a self-satisfied smile. 'There will be no need to divulge the fact that you speak the language. In that way, you – we may learn something of use.'

The carriage rumbled on past the market cross and finally stopped at the building known locally as the Red Row. It was an imposing building, heavily carved, with wooden columns supporting an overhanging upper storey that extended far enough to allow a carriage to be driven beneath it, allowing the occupants to alight and enter without being exposed to the weather. Big double doors gave easy access to those carrying in and out the bales of cloth.

Jannekyn had passed the Red Row many times and knew that the Dutch Bay Hall was situated in it. She also knew that it was a source of bitter contention between the English and the Dutch Congregation but she had never been able to understand why.

She followed Jacob inside, astonished at the amount of noise and activity.

'This way. And stay close,' Jacob said tersely over his shoulder. 'And remember to keep your eyes and ears open.'

In a daze Jannekyn followed him up the wide wooden staircase that led to the Dutch Bay Hall, jostled by weavers on their way down, most of them carrying heavy bales of cloth on their shoulders.

Despite the fact that everything was new to her Jannekyn found the morning passed slowly. She had little to do but wait while Jacob had long and involved conversations with officials with names like raw-hallers, white-hallers and provers of bays, and as time wore on the air became thick with the distinctive smell of cloth and the worse stink of unwashed bodies.

She noticed that there was a great deal of squabbling, mostly between Dutch and English, neither of whom could, for the main part, understand the other. A fight that broke out in one corner was swiftly stopped. Jacob took little notice of her, except to buy her a pie from the pie-seller who barged his way among the crowd; he gave most of his attention to a pallid young man, taller even than himself, with a stoop and an obsequious manner, called Wynkyn Eversham. She followed them, with feet and head aching, trying to make some sense out of a jargon she couldn't begin to understand, as they went from office to office, through the raw hall where the unfinished cloth was examined and sealed to the white hall where the finished cloth received similar treatment.

She was glad when at last Jacob called for his carriage and it was time to return home.

'Well?' he said, almost before she had seated herself. 'What was the fight about?'

'I . . . I don't know. It was over very quickly.'

'I know it was over quickly. I've got eyes in my head. I want to know what it was about. That's why I brought you here today, to keep your eyes and ears open.'

Jannekyn frowned. 'I think it was about a fault in a piece of cloth. The dyer, who was English, blamed the Dutch weaver and the weaver blamed the dyer.' She hesitated. 'I think that's what it was about but they were both talking so fast and shouting so loudly that it was difficult to make sense of what either of them was saying.'

'Hm.' Jacob nodded. 'That sounds about right. The English are always trying to shift the blame when there's a fault in their cloth so that someone else pays their fine.'

Jannekyn didn't altogether understand and at the moment she had no energy left to try. She was tired and her head ached; she had missed being out in the fresh air of the garden at home, the atmosphere in the Bay Hall had been stifling. She hoped she wouldn't have to go there again.

It was a forlorn hope.

Not only did she have to accompany Jacob to the Bay Hall every day, he also made her work in his counting house, keeping his accounts, sending out bills and making the ledgers balance. And it was useless trying to pretend she was illiterate because Jacob knew different. He had seen her clear, perfectly formed handwriting in the one letter he had allowed her to write to her parents. A letter to which she had neither expected nor received a reply.

It was Sunday, nearly a week since she had seen Adam. Now that she no longer fetched the water from the well she missed their early morning meetings more than she would have thought possible. For the first time she realized just how much she had come to depend on the young Englishman's friendship. No one else ever showed kindness or concern towards her the way he did and she was grateful to him. But was it simply gratitude that she felt? She didn't know. She had never had any experience with men to know what else it might be. But she sometimes wondered whether it was only mere gratitude that made her heart ache for the sight of his smile and the sound of his voice, or that filled her with such a warm glow when she was with him.

These thoughts were going round in her head as Minister Proost's voice droned endlessly on, extolling yet again God's providence to his chosen people – most of whom, it appeared, were sitting or standing in All Saints' Church at that moment. But at last he finished and the congregation spilled out into the weak sunshine. It was very hot and they all stood about in knots, ostensibly discussing Minister Proost's words before returning to their homes. Adam was right, she realized as she watched them, standing a little apart, these people were 'different'.

The men were all dressed soberly in black, the more well-to-do with white ruffs at neck and wrist, and wearing tall copotain hats. The less wealthy and the older men wore soft, flat caps with perhaps a feather or a jewel in the brim, and short, full-skirted coats with closely fitted and buttoned bodices. The younger men, however, sported galligaskins and doublets embroidered with silver or gold braid. The women, too, were dressed in dark colours although jewels and beads flashed on the bodices of wealthy matrons under their cartwheel ruffs. All the women wore long aprons over their skirts, black for servants and the poor, white for the rest. Of the white ones many were richly trimmed and decorated with lace as if to emphasize that they were purely decorative. All wore snowy caps with stiffly starched wings, and young matrons tended to wear their hair in two long thick braids that hung forward over their shoulders, sometimes reaching nearly to their waists.

But perhaps the greatest difference was in the hum of conversation. The guttural, almost clipped sound of Dutch conversation was utterly unlike the drawling vowels and slower speech of the local population. It was no wonder that the Dutch community were sometimes called Aliens. And it didn't help that no Stranger ever frequented an ale-house or played gleek or shovel-board. And as for attending a cockfight or bull-baiting . . .

Jannekyn scanned the crowd. Outside the churchyard the street was now thronged with local people taking their Sunday ease. In marked contrast to the Dutch congregation these people were gaily, even flashily dressed, the women in brightly coloured skirts and gowns, lavishly trimmed with ribbons and bows, the men in striking velvets and brocades. Even the poor among them managed a feather or a piece of brightly coloured glass to cheer a dowdy costume. She stood on tiptoe, looking for Adam. He was often waiting for her when she came out of church and she searched for him eagerly, her heart leaping as she saw the flash of his russet fustian. She caught his eye and began to walk out of the churchyard and down Queen Street, mingling with the crowd. Adam followed at a distance, not attempting to catch up with her until they were safely in the wood behind St John's Abbey.

In the cool, dappled shade of the trees he came up beside her and took her hand. 'I've been so worried about you, Jannekyn. Where have you been? I haven't seen you for several days. I thought you must be ill.' His eyes searched her face. 'Have you been ill, my love? You're very pale.'

'Pale?' She frowned at the word. 'I do not know what that means. I am not ill, Adam. Thank you, I am quite well. But I have helped Mynheer van der Hest in his counting house and I have been to the Bay Hall because Mynheer's clerk is ill.' She bit her lip. 'The Bay Hall I do not like. It is smelly and I do not understand what goes on there. And de Meester, he tells me nothing. Oh, I wish that he had asked that someone else might go there and not me.' She looked at Adam pleadingly. 'Why did he choose me?'

Adam led her over to a fallen tree trunk that was covered in soft moss and drew her down beside him. 'It's because you speak my language, of course,' he said. 'Mynheer van der Hest needs to be able to communicate with the English so that he can talk to the town officials. He needs you to act as his interpreter.'

Jannekyn gave an impatient sigh. 'That is not sensible at all,' she said in her slightly stilted English. 'Why does not *he* learn to speak the language? It would be very much more . . . what is the word?'

'Convenient?' Adam prompted, smiling gently at her irritation with Jacob.

'Ja, convenient for him.'

'You're right. Of course it would,' he agreed. 'But what you're forgetting is that you're dealing with a proud and arrogant man who would rather pretend that it is beneath him to attempt to speak English than to admit that he is unable to.'

'I think that is very silly,' Jannekyn said.

Adam frowned. 'I don't know, perhaps I'm being a little hard on de Meester,' he said thoughtfully. 'Not many of the Stranger Community are like you, Jannekyn, open, friendly and pleasant.' She flushed with pleasure at his words. 'For the most part they are proud and arrogant, all of them, not just Mynheer van der Hest And when you think about it I suppose you can't blame them. Persecuted, tortured even, some of them, for their faith, they had to escape to England with little more than the clothes they stood up in. Somehow, they have had to preserve their identity and restore their pride. And what better way to do it than by preserving their language? It's the one thing guaranteed to keep the Community together and to separate them from everyone else.'

Jannekyn looked at Adam, admiration in her eyes. 'You are very clever, Adam,' she said. 'Where did you learn . . . ? I would not have thought...' She stopped, realizing that what she had been going to say sounded rude.

But he only grinned. '. . . That an uneducated weaver's apprentice would be able to talk like that,' he finished for her.

She blushed. 'I am sorry, Adam. I should not even have thought such a thing. It was very wrong of me.'

'Don't be silly. You couldn't know.' He squeezed her hand. 'But, you see, I'm not entirely uneducated. I was at school until I was sixteen and I was expecting to go to university.'

'Then why . . . ? How is it that you are a weaver?'

Adam sighed. 'It's quite a long story.'

'Good. I like to hear stories.'

'All right, then. My father was a wealthy man. He owned trading ships and property and we lived in a big house with servants. We had our own carriages – not just one but two, maybe even three, I forget now. Anyway, there was no shortage of anything. But then, things started to go wrong. It was soon after my sixteenth birthday when two of his ships, carrying expensive cargoes of silk and precious spices, were lost in a storm. This was a terrible blow to him and in order to recover some of the money he had lost through this he began to gamble. Not in a very big way at first, but when he found he was winning he increased the stakes. Then, of course, he started to lose, and the more he gambled the more he lost, until in the end he'd gambled away everything he owned, including the house we lived in.

The shock of all this caused my mother's death and in the end it killed my father, too.'

'Oh, Adam, how dreadful for you. What did you do?'

'I was lucky, really, although of course I had to leave school. But my father had been a good and generous man in his prosperous days and he had once given Gabriel Birchwood a house when Gabriel had nowhere to live. Old Gabriel never forgot this and when he heard of my father's misfortunes he came to see him and offered to take me as his apprentice to repay my father's kindness.' He paused, then went on, 'He and his goodwife have been very kind to me. They treat me like the son they always wanted but were never blessed with.'

'But is that what you wanted? To become a weaver, I mean?'

He gave a little laugh. 'No, I have to say it wasn't a thing I would ever have chosen to do.' He frowned. 'I suppose, if I thought that far ahead at all, I had assumed that I would go into the Church.' His face cleared and he smiled at her, gently brushing a stray strand of hair away from her face, then, thoughtfully, he let his fingers trace the contours of her cheek till he tilted her chin so that he could look into the depths of her eyes. 'But then I wouldn't have met you, Jannekyn,' he said softly, 'so I'm glad things happened as they did.'

'I'm glad, too, Adam,' she said, a little breathless at his touch. As she gazed back into his deep-set brown eyes, the knowledge that he, like her, had had the course of his life altered in a way he could never have foreseen seemed to draw them even closer than before. For a long moment he held her gaze and she thought – hoped – he would kiss her. But the moment passed and he got to his feet. 'Come,' he said, 'we must go back. Garerdine will be searching for you.'

Jannekyn regarded her days spent at the Bay Hall and in

Jacob's counting house as nothing more than an interlude. An interlude to be endured along with Garerdine's scathing tongue, which every night in the little room under the eaves listed all the extra work that had fallen on Garerdine's shoulders whilst Jannekyn had been off enjoying life with de Meester. Jannekyn said nothing, knowing that when she did return to the kitchen she would again be labelled an idle slack-a-day who never lifted a finger to help. Garerdine apparently hadn't noticed her inconsistency and rather than point it out and be called insolent Jannekyn remained silent and allowed Garerdine to call her sullen. She was almost glad when the snoring began each night.

The interlude came to an end in an abrupt and, to Jannekyn, totally unexpected way. She had gone to the counting house early one morning to check some figures that refused to tally, hoping against hope that Mynheer Stowteheten, Jacob's clerk, would soon return and take the burden of books that refused to balance from her shoulders. She had not been there long when Jacob's black-clad figure loomed in the doorway.

'Juist,' he said, without even wishing her good morning. 'Good. I'm glad you take your duties responsibly because from now on they will be permanent.'

She looked up, her quill poised above the paper. 'Permanent, Meester? But what about Mynheer Stowteheten? Surely, he . . . '

'Mynheer Stowteheten died in the night,' Jacob said without emotion. 'I never expected that he would return to work when he became ill. I took you from the kitchen to see if you had enough intelligence to take his place. I'm sure that you have, although I detect a wilful disinclination to admit it. However, that we shall overcome.' He turned to go but came back before he had gone far. 'I shall arrange for a girl to help Garerdine in the kitchen . . . '

'A beggar girl, from the gutter?' Jannekyn asked, with a bitter twist to her lip.

There was an almost imperceptible lift of Jacob's eyebrows. 'There are many in our Congregation who would be glad of one less mouth to feed at their table,' he replied coldly. 'And as for you, I shall arrange for your possessions – such as they are – to be removed to a room more fitting to your new status. You will eat at my table and be paid whatever I think you are worth to me.' He pulled a gold watch from his pocket, looked at it and thrust it back. 'Be ready to come with me to the Bay Hall within the hour.' With that he strode off.

Jannekyn gritted her teeth and clenched her fists. She would *not* be treated like a parcel by that hateful man. She picked up her quill, almost beside herself with fury and frustration. She would . . . she would . . . she threw the quill down again, scarcely noticing that in her anger she had bitten it down to the stem, and put her head in her hands.

Oh, what was the use? What choice did she have but to do as he commanded? She had no money, no friends except Adam, and loving though he might be he could do little to help her. And where would she go if she ran away? If she didn't remain under Jacob's protection and she was caught she could be thrown out of the town, or sent back to Flanders. And what of her parents? There had been veiled hints that they could suffer and she couldn't tell whether these were simply idle threats or not.

She sat staring into space for a long time, feeling trapped and helpless. Then, slowly, but growing in intensity as the idea took hold, came the realization that here was not a trap but an opportunity. An opportunity to learn the ways of the wool trade. And when she had learned – well, who could tell? Maybe she would be able to free herself from Jacob's grasp . . . perhaps even gather together enough money to bring her parents to England . . . And Strangers' Hall. One thing was certain. Strangers' Hall would never be hers as long as she continued as nothing more than a kitchen slave. Perhaps, if she could but see it that way, this was the first step towards what she knew with such certainty was to be.

She began to apply herself with fresh vigour to the columns of figures before her.

'Of course, I am always the last to be told what is happening.' Katherine helped herself to one of the sweetmeats she kept beside her couch. Her head wasn't quite so bad today – at least it hadn't been until Jacob came rampaging in with his great booming voice. 'Who will care for Benjamin if you take the girl to work in your counting house? The wet-nurse no longer comes. No, Jacob, it is not to be borne, you cannot take her.' She closed her eyes against the great black figure standing by the window.

Jacob came over to her and knelt beside her couch, taking her white hand in his. 'I shall find another girl to mind the child, my love, never fear. And yet another for the kitchen; Garerdine, too, needs help. The house has been better swept and cleaned and the food tastier since she has had the help of the girl.'

Katherine allowed herself a little smile. Even the richest of her friends only had two servants. It would be well to be able to boast of three. She brushed a crumb from her bodice so that Jacob shouldn't see the look of satisfaction on her face.

'Does that make you happy, my love?' Jacob smiled at her and began to caress her neck.

'A house of this size needs three servants – at least three,' she replied briskly, brushing his hand away so that he knocked over a posset standing near. 'Oh, now look what you've done, you clumsy oaf. And all over my dress.' She shook the folds of crimson stamett irritably.

'It is no matter,' Jacob said smoothly, wiping away the few drops of liquid with his sleeve. 'It is time you had new dresses, my love. See, I have brought materials for you to choose . . . my new cloth, straight from the loom.'

Katherine's face lit up immediately. She loved new clothes although she hardly ever went out. 'Oh, Jacob, yes, let me see, let me see.'

He laid the swatches of cloth on the couch for her to examine.

'Oh,' she clapped her hands in delight. 'I'll have that one . . . No . . . ' she put her head on one side. 'I think I like that one better. Or shall it be . . . ? What do you think, Jacob?'

'Why not have one of each, my love?' He smiled indulgently at her.

'What *six* new dresses? All at once? Oh, Jacob, may I?'

'Of course, my love. I will call on Mistress Barlooe on my way to the Bay Hall and send her to you. She is a quick and neat sempstress, she will soon have the cloth made up to your liking.' Again he stroked her neck, and this time she suffered his caress.

After he had gone Katherine popped another sweetmeat into her mouth and got up from her couch, stretching her arms. In truth, she needed new dresses, all her clothes seemed to have got smaller of late, she couldn't think why. She went over to the window, drawing back into the shadows as Jacob passed on his way to the Bay Hall, the girl by his side. A turn in the garden might not come amiss before Mistress Barlooe arrived.

Chapter Two

I

By the time the New Year came in Jannekyn had learned a great deal about the cloth trade. She had discovered that the wool went through processes of being sorted, carded or combed and then spun before being handed over to the weaver for weaving. She found too that Jacob van der Hest had his own carders and combers and his own spinners, all working in their own homes. And when the yarn had been woven into cloth, again by van der Hest weavers working either in their own homes, or, in the case of the very best cloth – velvets, mockados and the like – in Jacob's special weaving shed, it was Jacob's men who took the cloth to the mill for fulling and thickening and then stretched it on the frames in his tenterhelds before more of Jacob's men dressed and finished it. He even had his own dyer, an elderly widower named Gyles de Troster. Few merchants were in such complete control from raw wool to finished cloth; most contented themselves on a much smaller scale, perhaps only buying and selling the finished product. It wasn't hard to see why Jacob was such a well-respected, if not particularly well-liked, member of the Dutch Congregation, Jannekyn decided. He was held in esteem at the Bay Hall, where his authority as one of the Governors went unchallenged; and at church as an Elder, holding strictly to the Calvinist principle that Christ died on the Cross not for all mankind, but only for the elect – of which he was unquestionably to be numbered.

Jannekyn hated him.

She hated him even more because he had elevated her to a sort of no-man's-land position between servant and family in his household. She had her own room, a tiny, panelled, cupboard of a room, with little space for anything more than her bed and a clothes press, but nevertheless, her own domain. And she had more skirts and bodices, gowns, ruffs, caps, shifts, stockings and shoes than ever before in her life. True, they had all belonged to Katherine and for the most part either needed mending or altering to fit, but everything was of the very best quality.

'If you are to accompany me as my clerk I refuse to have you looking like a serving wench,' Jacob said when he brought them to her.

Jannekyn, surprised and a little disconcerted to see him come to her room with the armful of his wife's cast-offs, watched as he laid them carefully on the bed. He picked up a dress of black mockado trimmed with gold. 'This will look well on you,' he said, holding it up against her, his head on one side.

She took an involuntary step backwards as his hand brushed her shoulder, but he appeared not to notice.

'This one; too,' He threw aside the black dress in favour of one of deep blue velvet trimmed with tiny silver flowers.

'Thank you, Meester.' She took the dress from him before he could hold it to her and held it against herself, looking down at the richly coloured folds. It was beautiful, she had never owned anything like it in her whole life.

'Wear one tonight.'

'Very well, Meester.' She wished he would leave her. He seemed to fill the tiny room like a great black bird of prey, with his hooded eyes and hooked nose.

'There are shifts here, too.' He began to rummage among the heap of clothes on the bed. 'And . . . '

'Thank you, Meester.' She laid the blue velvet over all the other things so that he couldn't search any further; she found it distasteful to see him handle things that she would wear. 'I'll sort them and put them away.'

'Yes. Yes. Very well.' He straightened up with obvious reluctance and looked about him. 'Perhaps I should have given you a bigger room,' he remarked thoughtfully. 'There's hardly room here to swing a cat.'

'As I've no wish to swing a cat that's of no importance, Meester,' she replied. 'There's quite enough room here for my needs. I manage very well, thank you.'

'Goed, dan. Good.' He turned to go. 'Remember, wear one of those dresses tonight. The blue velvet, I think . . . ' He came back into the room. 'Or perhaps the crimson . . . '

'I'll wear one, Meester.' She slid between him and the heap of clothes on the bed as she spoke.

'Yes, make sure you do.' He had no alternative but to leave her then and she heaved a sigh of relief. For some reason, in spite of his coldly impeccable behaviour towards her, she had not liked Jacob van der Hest entering her room – and even less had she liked him handling the clothes she was to wear. She had an uncomfortable feeling, too, that if she had looked up and met the eyes of the wealthy Dutchman she might have seen an expression there that would have made her even more uneasy.

Nevertheless, she did as she had been bidden and put on one of the dresses, the plainest and dullest one there. Then she went down to the hall where a great fire of sea coal burned.

'That's my dress she's wearing.' Katherine sat up, unusually alert, as Jannekyn entered.

'I know, my love, but you had cast it off, had you not?' Jacob smiled ingratiatingly at his wife. 'You removed them from your closet to make room for your new ones.'

Katherine frowned. 'I didn't think that was one of the ones I had discarded.' She stared at Jannekyn, galled to think that a dress that had grown too tight for her should hang on Jannekyn so loosely.

'But you never liked it. You always said the colour was too elderly for you,' Jacob lied.

'That is true. It's very plain and dull.' Mollified, Katherine allowed him to feed her with the choicest titbits.

From her place at the foot of the table Jannekyn watched Jacob fawning over his wife. She had plenty of opportunity to observe his behaviour because nobody spoke to her and Dionis in particular had studiously ignored her presence. It hadn't taken Jannekyn long to realize that mealtimes were always going to be difficult and she resented Jacob's insistence that she eat with the family. It came as a relief when Katherine demanded to be carried to her bed, because then she, Jannekyn, could escape, too.

She felt like an outcast, unwanted and unloved, not quite fitting anywhere. Even little Benjamin had grown attached to his new nursemaid and hardly recognized her. She thought of her poor, ailing father. This was not what he envisaged when he had planned so excitedly to send her to England. She often thought about him and her mother and she thanked God that they had no hint of her misery – for Jacob had never allowed her to write to them again and she had no means of getting a letter to them without his help. She didn't expect to hear from them. She knew the only way they would be able to send a letter to her would be through the chance visit of an itinerant hedge-preacher who might later be escaping to England. Any other way would be more than they could afford.

The only bright spot in her week now was her walk with Adam after church on Sunday. She looked forward to it eagerly and her heart would begin to beat a little faster the moment she spotted him in the crowd that milled in the streets. Their conversation never changed, from the days when the trees turned golden and orange and they walked through a rustling carpet of leaves, through the bleak November fogs when the air was raw and the trees in the wood beyond the great St John's Abbey where they walked were little more than ghostly shadows, to the crisp mornings when the frost made the undergrowth crackle under their feet.

'It'll be less man a year before I'm out of my time,' Adam said yet again, his breath cloudy on the icy January air and his face pinched with cold. 'Then I'll start as a master weaver and work from dawn till dusk . . . '

Jannekyn tucked her hand into the crook of his arm and huddled close to him, not entirely for warmth. 'You must be a journeyman first,' she reminded him.

'Why? I shall have my own loom to work.' He looked down at her, squeezing the hand in his arm. 'I told you, I'm to have Gabriel's loom.'

'Ah, yes, that is right. Very well, then I will buy yarn for you to weave. When de Meester pays me for the work I do . . . '

'Oh, Jannekyn, hasn't he given you any money yet?' Adam stopped in his tracks and turned to face her. 'You've been working in his counting house and at the Bay Hall for nigh four months now. It's time he paid you.'

'He gives me many dresses.' Jannekyn wouldn't look at him. 'This cloak . . . '

'They're his wife's cast-offs. They don't count. You must ask him, Jannekyn.'

Jannekyn was silent. In truth it was something that worried her, but her position at Strangers' Hall was such that she didn't dare to ask for money; indeed, she considered herself fortunate in being given so many clothes, although none of them were new. Her mood changed and she twisted from his grasp and scampered away from him into a clearing. 'Well,' she called, 'when he does pay me, I shall buy yarn for you to weave, and when you have woven it into cloth I will sell it for you and buy more yarn . . . '

He ran after her and caught her round the waist. 'And I'll weave such beautiful cloth as never seen before . . . ' Matching her mood he danced her round the clearing, laughing with her.

She threw back her head as they twirled faster and faster, ' . . . And everyone will want to buy it but only the very rich will have enough money . . . ' she said breathlessly.

' . . . And we'll grow rich and I'll build the biggest house in Colchester . . . '

Jannekyn stopped suddenly. Something was not quite right. Adam wanted to build his own house, but her destiny lay with Strangers' Hall, she knew this as surely as she knew that the sun would rise in the morning. Yet the thought of life without Adam was intolerable.

'What is it, my love?' Adam caught her to him anxiously. 'Is something wrong? Are you ill?'

She shook her head. 'Must you build a house, Adam?' she asked in a small voice, resting her head on his shoulder.

'But of course, sweeting. The richest merchant in Colchester must build a house fitting for his wife and family!'

They were standing under the spreading branches of a big oak tree. He leaned against it, and sliding his arms under her cloak he pulled her close. 'Oh, Jannekyn,' he murmured, burying his face in her hair, 'I want you so much for my wife.'

She twisted her head until her cheek lay against his. She could feel the lean hardness of his body as he held her, and every fibre in her cried out to match the need in him. 'And I want so much to be your wife, Adam,' she whispered, breathless from his nearness.

Gently, he kissed her eyes, then his lips travelled slowly over her face, until at last he reached her mouth, where her lips parted under his and they clung together, oblivious of everything but their desperate need for each other.

'No, it cannot be.' Suddenly, Jannekyn wrenched herself away from him.

He pulled her to him again. 'I want you, Jannekyn. We need each other . . . ' His mouth found hers again, hungry with love.

Again she twisted away from him, putting her hands on his chest to push him away. 'But there is so much to part us, Adam,' she cried desperately. 'You are English. I should be an outcast among my people . . . '

Her words had an immediate effect on him. 'You are right.' He held both her hands close to him, 'Oh, my love,' he said sadly, 'there is so much to keep us apart.' He took her in his arms again, but this time gently, his need for her held firmly in check. 'We must be patient. But one day, this I vow, we shall stand together as man and wife.' He bent his head to hers and held her close to his heart.

II

The second week in January Pieter van der Hest came home.

The house had been in a turmoil for a week since the news had arrived that the *Santa Maria*, the ship carrying Jacob's elder son, had been sighted off the Kent coast and was waiting for a fair wind to bring her into Brightlingsea. Katherine ordered a new gown to be made from tobine, the new striped material just on the market from Jacob's special looms, in honour of her son's homecoming, and even Jacob permitted himself a rare smile when his associates at the Bay Hall congratulated him on Pieter's safe return.

'Yes, yes,' he said, trying unsuccessfully to keep the pleasure out of his voice, 'it will be good to have him home. He's been gone two years and more. But I fear the boy that left will return a man and be unrecognizable to us.'

Dionis alone didn't share in the excitement. Pieter's return meant that her marriage to Abraham de Baert, already planned down to the last detail, could no longer be postponed. And so, Abraham's patience already wearing a little thin, the wedding was fixed for the fourteenth of February.

'The Feast of St Valentine. What could be more appropriate?' cooed her mother, ignoring the look, something akin to terror, that Dionis wore whenever her marriage was mentioned. 'And it will be a double celebration. We can celebrate Pieter's homecoming at the same time.'

It was noticeable that Katherine suddenly appeared to be less sickly, and that now she managed to walk about the house unaided, complaining that the servants – there were three now, apart from Garerdine, to do the work that Jannekyn formerly did – were lax in their duties, the tables were dull and lacked polish, floors were not swept and when fresh rushes were last put down she could scarce remember.

Jannekyn, who spent her time divided between the ledgers in the counting house and visits to the Bay Hall, the quay at New Hythe and anywhere else that Jacob commanded, felt detached from all the activity. She was mildly curious to see Jacob's elder son, but only mildly; their paths were unlikely to cross to any great extent. The son of one of the richest men in Colchester was unlikely to pay any attention to a pale, somewhat inkstained girl dressed up in his mother's old clothes.

In this assessment Jannekyn did herself an injustice. In spite of all her hardships she had blossomed into a very attractive girl, with a face that reflected her naturally sunny and optimistic nature. Although there was a determined, almost stubborn set to her jaw she had a ready smile that revealed teeth that were unusually white and even and her skin was as clear and soft as a ripe peach. But perhaps her greatest attraction – and one of which she was totally unaware – was her unexpectedly low and gentle voice.

Pieter van der Hest arrived home with an iron-bound chest full of treasures he had picked up on his travels. He had brought wines and sweetly scented oils, carpets from Turkey, strange musical instruments and grotesque masks. He had even brought a brightly coloured bird in a wicker cage that shrieked foreign obscenities to add to the general excitement and confusion of his homecoming.

Jannekyn was surprised to find that he was totally unlike his rather ascetic father. He was short and broad-shouldered, with a huge shaggy beard that completely covered the lower half of his face, contrasting strikingly with the neat, dark triangle that graced his father's chin. His voice was loud and boisterous and he went about the house like a tornado, causing his mother and sister to giggle admiringly and the servants to squeal when he discovered them in dark – and not-so-dark – corners. His stories were endless and, Jannekyn suspected, not always altogether truthful. He had brought nutmegs for his mother, silkworms for his father, a clasp made of mother-of-pearl for his sister and a set of carved wooden identical dolls that lived inside each other – down to the last, perfectly made replica, barely an inch high – for the brother whose existence he had learned of in Constantinople.

'I didn't bring anything for you, Jannekyn,' he said, down the length of the table, because she habitually sat slightly isolated from the rest of the family. 'I couldn't, could I? I didn't know you were here. But I've got a length of silk the colour of your eyes. I'll give you that.'

Jannekyn blushed, hardly knowing what to say.

'Oh, you don't have to give her anything, Pieter. She's only a servant,' his mother said, her manner off-hand. She laid a hand possessively on his arm. 'Dionis can have the silk for a bed-gown. You'll like that, won't you, Dionis?'

Dionis turned pale at this oblique reference to her forthcoming marriage but made no answer.

'I must say she doesn't look like a servant,' Pieter remarked, eyeing Jannekyn with open admiration. 'She's much too pretty and much too elegantly dressed? He winked at her. 'But never mind, Jannekyn, if you're not to have the blue silk I daresay I can find a coral necklace to grace that lovely white neck.'

Jannekyn flushed again and automatically put up her hand to cover the neck he was viewing with such obvious pleasure. She wished she hadn't chosen to wear quite such a low-cut gown.

'Jannekyn is not a servant,' Jacob rebuked his wife from his position at the head of die table. 'I have told you that before,

Katherine.' He turned to his son. 'Neither is she an object to be draped with your foreign baubles. She has been given the position of my clerk and general assistant . . . '

'But what about old what's-his-name? Wouter. That's it, Wouter Stowteheten. Where's he gone?' Pieter interrupted. 'I thought he was your clerk.'

'He was. But he died a few months ago. Jannekyn fills his place very well.'

'The devil she does,' Pieter said, half under his breath. 'God's blood, Father, you're a crafty old sod.'

'Please don't bring your shipboard language to my house, Pieter,' Katherine said plaintively, only half hearing what her son had said.

'Sorry, my lady.' Pieter inclined his head towards his mother, still with his eyes on Jannekyn.

But Jannekyn had heard every word and she stole a glance in Jacob's direction. She almost wished she hadn't. Jacob was staring at his son with an expression of venomous jealousy that could only mean one thing. Jacob regarded her as his exclusive possession.

The realization made her feel physically sick.

III

The house settled back into its normal routine after the excitement of Pieter's homecoming. Jannekyn saw little of him at first; she was kept more and more busy with Jacob's business, both keeping his books in the counting house and accompanying him on his visits to the Bay Hall. She learned very quickly and could soon recognize a good cloth from an inferior one and could pick out defects even before Jacob's practised eye had seen them. The officials at the Bay Hall respected her because she took the trouble to address them by name; she knew, too, each official title, of which there were a bewildering number, from prover of bays to searchers of the tenters, from raw-hallers to white-hallers to high searchers of bays. Moreover, she could speak to everyone in their own language, be it Dutch or English. This was an invaluable asset – so invaluable that she couldn't understand why Jacob allowed his stubborn pride to prevent him learning the language of his adopted country.

Almost wherever he went Jacob forced Jannekyn to accompany him. It seemed as if, although he talked little to her – and then invariably about his business – he couldn't bear her out of his sight Often when she looked up she would find him watching her, with an unfathomable expression in his eyes.

For her part, Jacob van der Hest filled her with loathing and disgust. She spent her days by his side because she had no choice, and so, to make life bearable, she threw all her thoughts and energies into learning about his business. And the more she learned, the more interested and eager to widen her knowledge she became. And the wider her knowledge, the more indispensable he found her. And so she bound herself to him with the very chains she had forged in a mental effort to escape from his continual presence.

'Jannekyn looks tired tonight,' Pieter remarked one night as she was sitting in her usual place, a little apart from the family, stitching.

Jacob frowned at his son. 'She has been at the Bay Hall with me for most of the day.' He turned to Jannekyn. 'Have you filled in those figures as I asked you, girl?'

'No, Meester. It was dark when we returned. I thought they

could wait until tomorrow when I shall be working in the counting house anyway.'

Pieter moved his chair and came and sat beside her. 'Well spoken, Jannekyn. I'm sure you've done enough for one day and deserve a rest.' He put his hand over hers. 'My word, you sew a very fine seam.'

Jacob shot him an ugly glance. 'Those figures should have been done,' he insisted. 'I shall be needing them early tomorrow.'

'Very well, Meester.' Obediently, Jannekyn put down her sewing. There was no point in arguing further with Jacob although she knew very well that she would have plenty of time to do the work before he needed it in the morning. She shivered a little as the wind shrieked round the house and the rain lashed at the windows and got up to fetch her cloak.

'I'll come with you to hold the lantern,' Pieter offered, getting to his feet.

'Surely, there's no need for that, my son,' Katherine interjected. 'It's a cruel night for you to be out.'

'It's a cruel night to send Jannekyn out,' Pieter said with a grin. 'I'm sure she'd appreciate a bit of company.'

'No, really, I'm quite able to manage on my own,' Jannekyn said uncomfortably.

'Rubbish. I insist on coming with you.' He followed her to the door.

'It's late. The figures will do in the morning,' Jacob snapped irritably.

Jannekyn turned in surprise. 'But, Meester . . . ?'

'I said they would do in the morning,' he repeated. 'Sit down.'

Jannekyn did as she was told and took up her sewing again. Pieter resumed his seat beside her, pulling his chair even closer.

'He's jealous,' he whispered. 'I do believe the old man's

jealous. He didn't want me to come with you to the counting house. Look at him watching us.'

'Nonsense.' Jannekyn tried to edge away a little. She found Pieter van der Hest a little frightening with his outspoken, blustering ways and she looked forward to the day when he would again set sail for foreign countries – and the further away the better, as far as she was concerned. Nevertheless, when she stole a glance in Jacob's direction he was indeed watching her every movement.

She told Adam little about this side of her life. She knew that it would worry and upset him and might even lead him to jeopardize his position in the loom sheds. Because Adam, too, was jealous, and could be fiery-tempered. She shuddered to imagine a confrontation between Adam and Jacob van der Hest. So she confined herself to telling him what she was learning about the cloth trade so that they could dream their extravagant dreams of prosperity together – dreams that neither really believed could ever come true but each pretended for the sake of the other. And Jannekyn repeated Pieter's tales of his travels in far-off lands.

'He was delayed in his return because of an errand of mercy,' Jannekyn told him one cold, bright Sunday morning. They were walking in the woods after church, an ill-assorted pair, with Jannekyn in an expensive fur-lined cloak that had belonged to Katherine until Jacob had replaced it with a better, and Adam in workman's leather jerkin and breeches and with an old sheepskin round his shoulders. But they didn't notice that they looked ill-matched, and if they had it wouldn't have worried them.

'An errand of mercy? What do you mean?' Adam asked, his breath cloudy on the frosty air.

'It seems his captain was asked to rescue some poor black people from Africa, where they lived little better than animals. Do you know, Adam, they actually *ate* each other? Even animals don't do that, do they? Anyway, Pieter's ship rescued them and took them to an island in the West Indies where they could start a new life.'

Adam stopped and turned to her, taking her hands in his. 'Is that what Pieter told you, Jannekyn?'

She nodded, surprised. 'Yes, why? It's true. And on the return journey they brought home new spices – cloves, mace and nutmegs. Pieter says they'll bring more next time.'

'So he's going again on this . . . errand of mercy . . . is he?'

'Yes. Adam, what's the matter? Why are you looking like that?'

'Oh, Jannekyn, don't you realize what he's doing? Have you never heard of the slave trade?'

Jannekyn looked mystified.'No. What's that?'

'It's a fairly new thing, trading slaves. But to put it briefly, those "poor black people" he rescued had been captured from where they were living perfectly peaceful lives in their villages, put in chains to wait for a ship to take them in indescribable filth and misery to islands where they didn't want to go, and where they would be sold into a life of slavery.'

'That can't be true. Surely, that can't be true.' Jannekyn's eyes widened. 'How do you know all this?'

'A few years ago Gabriel Birchwood's nephew was taken into the navy by the press. When he came home he told me tales that would make your hair stand on end. And he told me about these slave ships. He said you always sailed upwind of a slaver because of the stench. The slaves are battened down in the holds with no room to move, starved, lying in their own filth . . . '

'Oh, Adam, stop! You're making it up!'

'Making it up! If I hadn't heard it with my own ears I could never have imagined that human beings could treat each other so. No, Jannekyn, it's true, right enough. It's no errand of mercy that Pieter van der Hest's been on. It's a barbaric, gold-grubbing operation that only the most callous and unfeeling can stomach. He's not a man I admire overmuch, but I wouldn't have thought that even he would stoop to such a trade.'

They walked on in silence, Jannekyn thinking over Adam's words. The way he had described it Pieter van der Hest was indeed engaged in a despicable trade and knowing Adam as she did she was sure he had not exaggerated. She found it impossible to understand how human beings could treat each other so hideously; goodness knows she found it hard enough to bear the plight of the poor misshapen creatures she had seen on show at St Denis's Fair last October. She gave an involuntary shudder and moved closer to Adam.

He put his arm round her and drew her close. 'Are you cold, sweeting? Come, let's sit on this tree stump and I'll warm you.'

'No, Adam, I must go back. Abraham de Baert is coming to eat with us and discuss final preparations for the wedding.' She shook her head. 'Poor Dionis, she is still hoping it will not happen.'

'Just for a moment.' Despite her protest he drew her down beside him. 'I can't let you go back so soon.' He pulled her roughly to him. 'I wish we were preparing for our wedding, Jannekyn,' he said, his mouth coming down demandingly on hers.

'Oh, I wish it, too, Adam.' She clung to him with equal passion.

He lifted his head from hers and cupped her face with his hands. 'I swear that one day I shall marry you, Jannekyn,' he said, his eyes burning. 'Nothing can prevent that.'

But even as he spoke an icy finger seemed to trace the length of her spine, chilling her to the very marrow of her bone and making her shiver.

'What's the matter?' he asked, drawing away from her. 'Is the idea of marriage to me so distasteful to you?'

'Oh, Adam, you know there is nothing that I want more.' She clung to him as she said the words. 'It was your hands on my face. They're cold. They made me shiver, that's all.'

But it was not his cold hands that had made her shiver, it was the words he had spoken. She knew that and was afraid. Afraid and hopeless. Hopeless because Adam was English and she was Dutch – reason enough to make marriage between them impossible in the acrimonious climate that existed between the two communities; but the fear was something different – a nameless, intangible feeling of something inescapably dreadful in the future. And try as she would to shake it off it stayed with her long after she had left Adam and returned to Strangers' Hall.

The mood there was not exactly festive, although Abraham de Baert was in good spirits.

Dionis watched him shovelling food into his mouth. He disgusted her. And the thought that he would soon be her husband made her feel sick. She looked at the food on her own plate and closed her eyes against the nausea that rose every time she thought about him.

She looked round desperately for someone to help her. It was no use talking to her mother, she was too taken up with Pieter, always her favourite, and with the wedding preparations. Anyway, she wouldn't listen, and if she did she wouldn't understand.

Dionis sighed. She didn't mind the thought of being married, in fact she quite liked the idea of having a house of her own, if only it could be someone else she would share it with. In truth, she would be glad to get away from Strangers' Hall, where her father stalked about like some noisy black crow, finding fault at every turn and making sure everyone remembered what a great man he was, and her mother languished her days away in the solar. She was lazy, that was her trouble. She wasn't really ill now, she was only pretending; what she needed to do was to get up off that couch and chivvy the servants more. Garerdine had ruled the kitchen for too long, and since Jannekyn had been taken away from her the house no longer shone and sparkled the way it used to. Some corners were positively dirty. Dionis made up her mind that there would be no idle servants in *her* house.

That thought reminded her of her impending marriage and she crept away from the table and sat in the chimney corner, hoping no one would notice. But Abraham did.

'Come back here, my love, and take your place beside me, where you will so soon belong,' he leered, belching loudly.

She crept reluctantly back to him, shuddering as she felt his hand explore her leg.

Jacob stood up. 'Let us drink to the happy couple,' he said, smiling somewhat ingratiatingly towards Abraham.

Jannekyn had been watching Jacob out of the corner of her eye. He seemed in fairly good spirits although his joviality had seemed a trifle forced before he had a lengthy discussion with Abraham and he had only relaxed after she heard Abraham say, 'Then we need never speak of it again.' No doubt it had been Dionis's dowry under discussion, and Jannekyn couldn't help thinking it would do them more credit if they were to give even half as much heed to the poor girl's feelings.

IV

There was to be no last-minute reprieve for Dionis. The date set for heir marriage to Abraham de Baert drew closer and the preparations, so long planned down to the last detail, were all finished. Dionis crept about like a wraith and once again turned to Jannekyn, imploring her to intercede.

'My father will listen to you, I'm sure of it. Can't you tell him how I feel?' she begged, as they sat together on the window seat overlooking the garden.

'But surely you can tell him yourself. After all, you're his only daughter, he must have your welfare at heart.' Jannekyn was reluctant to approach Jacob on any subject that was not strictly business.

Dionis shook her head. 'I've tried, but he refuses to understand. He simply raises his eyebrows and reminds me that it is customary for a father to choose his daughter's husband.' She sighed, a sigh that turned into something like a sob. 'As if I didn't know that.' She pleated her skirt with nervous fingers for a few moments, then she looked up at Jannekyn. 'I'm sure he would listen to you. He always does. Can't you do something? Say something? Explain to him? It's not that I mind him choosing a husband for me, it's just that . . . I just wish he'd chosen somebody else. *Anybody* else.'

Jannekyn put her hand on Dionis's shoulder. 'I'll see what I can do,' she promised with a sigh, 'but don't expect too much.'

As she had expected, Jacob refused to discuss the matter at all other than to say that Dionis had known for long enough that she was to marry Abraham de Baert and that now was not the time to begin to object. The marriage was arranged, Abraham was a good friend and business colleague and there could be no going back on the … he nearly said bargain, but hastily corrected it to … arrangements.

'Mynheer de Baert has a new house in Lexden village,' he finished. 'It's finer, if anything, than this one. What more could a girl wish for?' As far as he was concerned that was the end of the matter and he turned and lifted a bolt of cloth from the shelf in the counting house and set it in front of Jannekyn where she was sitting with her ledgers. It was a fine-textured cloth, with the warm feel of wool yet with the sheen of silk, and its colours ranged from dark crimson to palest shot pink with a hint of lilac where it caught the light.

'Is this not a fine cloth?' he asked.

'Indeed, it is, Meester.' She smoothed the fabric, noticing the even texture and the skilfully blended colours. Only Adam could turn out work of such quality.

'Take it. Make yourself a gown from it.' He pushed it towards her.

'Oh, but, Meester, I have gowns,' she protested. 'More than I have ever had in my life before.'

'My wife's cast-offs, all of them.' Jacob dismissed them with a gesture.

'Nevertheless, they are good gowns and not to be wasted.'

'No, of course not. Wear them as you will.' He spoke impatiently. 'But have this one made up, too. It will look well on you.'

She glanced up. He was smiling at her. She couldn't ever remember seeing him smile before and she noticed that he had big teeth, like long, yellow fangs. At that moment he reminded her of nothing so much as a wolf.

She averted her eyes quickly.

He left her then and she picked up the bolt of material to replace it on the shelf. She would dearly have loved a gown made from material that Adam had woven, but not out of Jacob van der Hest's charity. She wanted nothing more than her due from that man. She smoothed the soft cloth; it felt warm and rich under her hand and somehow it gave her a feeling of closeness to Adam. She held it up to her cheek and buried her face in its folds. Why shouldn't she have a gown made from it? Although Jacob had promised to pay her twice a year she had received nothing so far for the work she did so this bolt of cloth would be no more man her due.

She replaced the cloth on the shelf. Tomorrow she would consult Mistress Barlooe, Katherine's sempstress. Satisfied with her decision she went back to her ledgers.

She worked on, entering the figures in her neat, round hand until the light was beginning to fade and the familiar clacking from the loom shed had long since finished. The weavers only worked during the hours of daylight; dusk or a flickering candle would not do for the high-quality cloth that they wove. She flexed her fingers and stretched her aching back. She hadn't realized that it was so late.

She yawned. She was very tired but there was still one thing that must be done before the light faded altogether, and that was to check the bales of wool in the warehouse before they were taken by the agents to the spinners the next day. Jacob insisted on a check being made every step of the way, from fleece to finished cloth, for he trusted no one, as Jannekyn had been quick to discover.

She put away the ledger and tidied the table at which she had been working and stepped out into the raw afternoon air. The day was damp and cold and mist lay like a blanket over the tenterfields beyond the garden, throwing out long grey tentacles that curled silently round the house and outbuildings.

She hurried across to the big warehouse that stood opposite the loom sheds. It had big double doors opening on to the road as access for the pack horses, so that the household should mot be disturbed by clattering hooves, but there was also a small door at the back so that it could be entered from the garden. It was to this door that Jannekyn had a key.

She hated the warehouse. She hated to see the children coughing as they sorted the raw wool into quality and length; she hated the stench of diluted urine which was used to scour out the dirt and grease; and she hated the reek of the oil mat the scoured wool had to be steeped in to make it supple enough to work. As she slipped through the door all these smells combined into a hideous stink that caught her throat and threatened to choke her.

The place was quiet and empty. Everyone had gone and the wool was all bundled into packs ready to be taken to the spinners the next day.

Each spinner would receive three packs, to be collected as spun yarn two weeks later. Jannekyn checked the bundles to make sure she knew how much yarn to expect back – Jacob insisted that the spinners were dishonest rogues, out to make a fortune at his expense. But Jannekyn suspected differently.

She was so engrossed in what she was doing that she didn't hear the door open and it was only when she felt the cold draught of air that she realized someone had come in. She turned to see who it was and was surprised to find it was Pieter van der Hest.

'I'm afraid your father isn't here,' she said. 'I think he's gone . . . '

'I wasn't looking for my father, Jannekyn.' Pieter smiled at her and in his smile she detected a shadow of Jacob's wolfish leer.

'Oh, then who . . . ?'

'Why, you, of course. Who else?' He leaned against the wall

and eyed her with cool amusement, his jaws moving rhythmically as he chewed a plug of tobacco.

'Me?'

'Yes. You. I've brought you a present. I promised you a coral necklace, don't you remember? Well, I've brought it.'

'There really wasn't any need . . . ' Automatically, she put her hand up to her throat.

'Of course there wasn't any need. It wouldn't be a present if there was any need to give it to you.' He didn't take his eyes off her as he spoke.

'There, I think I've finished here now.' Uneasy under his gaze she gathered up her papers and tried to make her voice sound businesslike. She didn't care for the way this man had sought her out; he could perfectly well have waited until she returned to the house. In fact, she was surprised that he hadn't; he always seemed to enjoy making his father jealous and the necklace would have provided a good opportunity for this. Not that she wanted the wretched thing, anyway.

'I'll just take these papers back to the counting house and then we can go back to the house,' she said briskly.

'Not so fast, Jannekyn. There's no hurry, is there?' He held up the necklace for her to see. 'There. Pretty, isn't it? Do you like it?'

'I – I can't really see it in this light. Perhaps if you waited till we're back at the house . . . the candles will be lit there. It's rather dark in here now . . . it would be a pity . . . ' She began to edge her way to the door as she spoke.

'What's the matter, Jannekyn? What's the hurry? You're not afraid of me, are you?' His tone was soft, intimate almost?

She gave a little laugh. 'No, no, of course not,' she lied. She licked her lips. 'But it was rather silly of you to come seeking me out in this cold, smelly old warehouse, wasn't it? I hate it in here.

Come on, let's go back to the house where it's light and warm and doesn't stink of fleece and worse.'

She'd nearly reached the door by this time, but suddenly he moved and in a flash was there before her, his back against it. 'No,' he said, 'I like it here.'

'Well, I don't.' She shuddered. 'It's too cold.'

'I could warm you.' He put out a hand and touched her cheek.

She took a step back, away from his reach and the tobacco-fouled smell of his breath, her uneasiness rapidly turning to terror.

'Oh, yes,' he went on, as if he hadn't noticed her movement, 'I like it here. It's quiet and nobody will be likely to disturb us. I've been waiting days for this opportunity. Did you know that, Jannekyn? Days, I've been waiting.' He was watching her as a cat watches a mouse. 'Come.' He held out the necklace again. 'Let me see how it looks on your fair skin.'

She instinctively put both hands up to her throat. 'No. I don't want it.'

'Don't want it? A pretty girl like you not want a coral necklace? Of course you want it.' His tone was soft and wheedling as he leaned forward and draped it round her neck, letting his rough hands caress the whiteness of her throat.

She stood stiffly as his hands slid idly from her neck to her shoulders and down the length of her arms.

'Please,' she said coldly, 'let me go or I shall scream.' There was no mistaking his intentions now and she was surprised how calm her voice sounded, considering that inside she was a quivering jelly of fear.

He began to play with the necklace at her throat. 'And what good do you think that would do? We're a long way from the house and the loom sheds are deserted so no one would hear you however loudly you screamed. Anyway, the mist outside would muffle any sound.' His tone was quiet and conversational, but with more than a hint of mockery in it. 'But why scream? What are you afraid of? I've done nothing but give you the present I promised you.' He paused. 'So far,' he added softly.

His face was now barely discernible in the darkness. Desperately, she tried to gather her wits, to think what to do, trying all the while not to give way to panic. She had tried unsuccessfully to bluff her way out. Now, she realized, her only chance was to make a run for it. In this, she had the advantage of knowing the warehouse better than he did. If only she could reach the big doors at the other end and lift the heavy wooden bar that secured them she could escape into the street beyond. The question was whether she could reach them and remove the bar before he caught up with her. It was her only chance. Already she could hear his breathing becoming heavier as his hands fumbled at her bodice.

Suddenly, the swiftness of her movement catching him off-balance, she twisted away from him and ran to the end of the warehouse, overturning bales of wool into his path as she went. She could hear him cursing as he tripped and went sprawling time and again.

But it gave her the time she needed and she reached the doors and with shaking hands heaved at the beam with all her strength. It wouldn't budge and with a sob of despair she realized that it was beyond her strength to move it.

In a moment he was behind her, catching at her skirt. 'You little –' she heard him curse as she ducked out of his reach and headed for the little door at the other end.

But she had forgotten the bales of wool she had strewn to impede his course and she tripped over first one and then another, sobbing with fear and frustration as she went, knowing that he was rapidly catching up with her.

'Ah, that's better,' she heard him mutter triumphantly as she failed to find her feet in time. Seconds later she felt the weight of his body on hers, pinning her into the soft, stinking wool. Hampered by her skirts as well as by his weight she tried to struggle free as her face was pressed into the wool, suffocating her.

'Good. I like a bit of spirit in my women,' he said thickly, and she felt his hot, wet mouth on her shoulder and his hands clawing at her bodice, as without seeming to shift his weight he turned her over.

He was very strong. He barely seemed to notice as she kicked and pummelled him, biting him and dragging his hair out by the roots. In fact, it only seemed to excite him further as he bruised her with loveless kisses, making her cry out with the pain and degradation of it all. A haze of fear and panic clogged her senses and turned her very bones to water. There was no escape. She could only pray for the blessed relief of oblivion.

But even this was denied her. As she clung desperately to her last remaining tatters of control black curtains of pain and degradation washed over her and she felt herself merging and becoming one with the horrible, stinking, stifling wool.

At last he finished with her and rolled away, laughing.

'You're a fiery little vixen,' he said admiringly. 'But next time perhaps you'll be a little more willing.' He caught hold of her hair and dragged her to him for another slobbering kiss.

As she tried to struggle free the warehouse door opened and a lantern appeared, flooding the place with light and revealing unmistakable evidence of what had taken place.

'There won't be a next time!' Jacob van der Hest thundered. He strode over to his son and struck him furiously again and again across the shoulders with a yard stick lying nearby. 'Get out, you lecherous young ram, and keep your farmyard habits for your dockside harlots!'

Pieter scrambled to his feet, fending off his father's blows. 'Hold, Father! Stand off! What ails you? I was only having a bit of sport with a servant girl – I gave her a necklace, and well, you know how these wenches lead a fellow on.' He moved away and began to straighten his clothing as he tried to bluster his way out of his embarrassment.

'Jannekyn is not a servant girl and not to be treated as one,' his father spat, breathless from his exertions. He held the lantern high, revealing Jannekyn's torn and rumpled figure in the pool of yellow light. 'And you lie! She was not willing! Look at her! Does she look like a trollop?'

Pieter shrugged. 'It was only sport, Father. That's what servants are for. Everyone does it!'

'Not everyone!' his father shouted, almost beside himself. 'Now, be gone. I want no more of your lechery in my house. If you cannot conduct yourself in a more seemly manner I will not have you under my roof!'

'Oh, come now, father, you're being too harsh. You didn't complain about the little jade you found me with in the dairy, did you, so why complain now? But as I've displeased you I give you my word it won't happen again.' He turned to Jannekyn with a leer. 'But. you'll agree Jannekyn's a comely wench.'

'That is no reason for you to defile her with your fornicating ways. If it were not for your sister's wedding feast I would turn you out of the house this very day. You have only your lady mother's feelings to thank that I allow you to stay.

'Come, my dear;' he said, turning to Jannekyn. 'I'll help you back to the house.'

He held out his hand to help her up but she ignored it and got to her feet unaided. She felt utterly degraded and defiled, and every part of her hurt, both mentally and physically. All she craved was to be left alone.

But she was not even to be allowed this. Jacob accompanied her back to the house and up to her room, his concern over her well-being unhealthy in its intensity. It was only with difficulty that she managed to prevent him from following her inside and she sensed in him a vicarious pleasure mingled with disgust at his son's behaviour.

He would have liked to have done it himself, she realized with a shock, and the thought made her retch into her washing basin. Then she flung herself on to her bed, shivering, too shocked even for tears.

A year had passed since she had first come to Strangers' Hall – a year almost to the day. She had tried to make the best of things for her poor sick father's sake, and she had become used to being treated as nothing more than a servant in her uncle's house, just as she had become used to being overworked and humiliated at every turn. But today had been the ultimate degradation. She knew that she could sink no lower. She wished that she could die.

Her wish was not granted. She did not die. She lay for a long time, shivering and exhausted, but then she became calmer and eventually summoned the strength to go and fetch water. She washed and scrubbed her flesh until it was almost raw in an effort to rid herself of Pteter van der Hest's touch, then she lay down on her bed again, to fall into an uneasy sleep.

'The girl is late,' Katherine said, helping herself to a fat, sticky sweetmeat and wiping her fingers on her dress. 'If she must eat with us at least she could do us the courtesy of arriving at the board on time. Pieter, go and summon . . . '

'Leave her be, she is doubtless tired, my love,' Jacob said smoothly, pouring his wife more ale. 'She has been with me to the Bay Hall. It was very crowded today. And then there was much to be done in the counting house.'

'It would seem you work her too hard, Jacob,' his wife said waspishry. 'She is with you at the Bay Hall or in the counting house from morn till night'

'But there is much to be done, my love. A man of my standing is never idle.'

'Oh, yes, there is much to be done.' Katherine gave an elaborate sigh. 'Indeed, this is a busy time for all of us. Myself, I am quite worn out, worrying over this wedding. Servants are so unreliable.' Her voice changed. 'And Dionis is little help, although it is all for her benefit. She cannot even be persuaded to leave her room to discuss matters.' She got up from the table and went to sit next to the huge fire of sea coal burning in me grate. 'Pieter, my son, come and sit beside me and tell me more of your travels. Your father tells me you will be rejoining your ship as soon as your sister is safely married so I am greedy for your company.'

Pieter got up from the table, shooting his father a venomous glance before joining his mother. But Jacob was giving all his attention to selecting an apple and didn't even look up.

When she woke Jannekyn felt a little better. She was very thirsty but what she needed most was something to soothe her nerves and heal her bruises. With a great effort she climbed stiffly from her bed and made her way to the still-room. She had always enjoyed working here; she had an interest in herbs and their healing properties and she found the aromatic atmosphere pleasant and calming. But since Jacob had taken her away from the kitchen she rarely had an opportunity to visit it and there was never the time to make up any of the decoctions or infusions from the old herbal she had found.

She lit a candle and held it high. The still-room was an untidy mess now, with jars and dishes of this and that strewn about with no indication of what they were, and bundles of herbs tied carelessly or simply thrown on the floor. She pursed her lips. Either Garerdine was less strict than she had been in Jannekyn's day or she had given up the struggle to make her kitchen slatterns take a pride in their work. She automatically began to tidy up before she searched for the right leaves to pound for a poultice to soothe her bruises.

She had been working quietly for some time when she heard footsteps approaching along the stone passage. Almost without thinking, she snuffed the candle and cowered back into the shadows, the memory of her ordeal of the afternoon too fresh to allow her to take any chances. She held her breath as the door was pushed open.

'Jannekyn? Jannekyn, are you there?' It was Dionis who spoke.

Jannekyn let out a sigh of relief. 'Yes,' she called softly. 'I'm here.'

'Why are you in darkness?' Dionis re-lit the candle from her own. 'And what are you doing here?'

'I came to get something for a bruise. I – I fell over a stool and bruised my leg,' Jannekyn lied. 'And the draught blew my candle out when you opened the door.'

'Oh.' Dionis seemed satisfied with Jannekyn's explanation. 'Something for a bruise, did you say?'

'Yes.' Jannekyn selected a sprig of catmint and began to pound it to a paste with some greenish liquid.

'That's strange. I was just looking for you to see if you had a cure for bruises. I know you have cures for most things.'

'Some things. Not most things. But where are you bruised? Let me see.'

Dionis unfastened her dress and let it fall to the floor and stood there in her shift. Slowly, she turned her back to Jannekyn.

An involuntary cry escaped the older girl. 'Oh, Dionis, who did that to you?' she whispered, staring at the great blue weals that swelled across the girl's back, trickling with blood here and there where the skin was broken. 'Who beat you like that?'

'Who do you think?' Dionis asked dully. 'My father, of course.'

'But why?'

'Because I told him I wouldn't marry Abraham de Baert.' Dionis turned back to face Jannekyn. 'I'd asked you to speak to him but I knew that wouldn't be any good, so tonight I went to him myself and told him I refused to marry that old man.' She shuddered. 'I've never seen him so angry. I think he would have killed me if I hadn't managed to crawl to the door and escape. At the end I don't think he even realized it was me he was hitting – he was beside himself with fury and I was just something to vent his anger on.' She covered her face with her hands. 'It was horrible, Jannekyn. He was like a madman.' After a moment she composed herself. 'But one thing is certain. I shall have to marry Abraham de Baert. I couldn't face another beating like that'

Jannekyn made some more of the green paste and spread it on a cloth and laid it carefully on Dionis's back. Poor girl. She had chosen the worst possible time to confront her father and had received the beating meant for Pieter. 'There, Dionis,' she said. 'Tomorrow the pain will be gone and in two days your back will be healed.'

'Just in time for my wedding,' Dionis said, with more than a trace of bitterness.

Jannekyn felt sorry for Dionis, especially in view of her own nightmare experience so short a time ago. She wished she could think of some way to help her. Suddenly she had an idea. She took down two jars from the topmost shelf and began mixing them. A sleeping draught, harmless enough, but at least it would afford Dionis peaceful nights.

She slipped the draught into her bodice, then she began to attend to her own bruises, although the effort of appearing normal to Dionis had left her almost too exhausted to bother. But she knew that if she didn't she would be too stiff and sore to move the next day. She pounded some more of the catmint into a paste and smeared it on her arms and shoulders where Pieter's rough hands had bruised her and on to her legs and thighs. She found herself trembling again at the dreadful memory of it all and as she blew out the candle and made her way painfully back to her room she was rent again with great racking sobs of hopelessness and despair.

V

No expense was spared at the marriage of Jacob van der Hest's daughter. He was a rich man and the event gave him the opportunity to parade his wealth before God and man. As God was called upon to bless the union of the ill-assorted pair, so Jacob made sure that he should be duly rewarded – with a new coat for the Predikant who ministered as his deputy and with a new bible from which his commands could be read.

As in Genesis, Jacob was determined that when God looked he should not only see that his own work was good, but also that of Jacob van der Hest. The Predikant in his turn had prepared an even longer thas usual wedding sermon, extolling the virtues of marriage for the mutual benefit and comfort of man and wife and for the procreation of children. Dionis, pale and half-fainting, dressed in the richest and most expensive materials her father could produce, listened with sickened horror to the Predikant's words before Abraham fumbled the heavy gold band on to her finger and made her his lawful wife.

Garerdine had prepared enough food to feed an army. Anne, Josine and Margarete, the three girls who between them did the work that Jannekyn had once done single-handed, were run off their feet and extra help had to be found in the end by calling in four poor weavers' wives, who were as grateful for the table scraps as for the few pence they earned.

The marriage feast lasted a week. The food was all laid out on long tables in the great hall. The centrepiece was a whole roast pig with a huge red apple in its mouth and stuck with cloves down the length of its back. Beside it were roasted chickens and capons, pigeons stuffed with gooseberries and huge venison and mutton pies, oysters stewed in wine – which Abraham was urged to indulge freely in – and dishes of tansy. On another table were bowls of syllabub and junket and all manner of sweetmeats, from plain gingerbread and decorated marchpane to little sprigs of rosemary dipped in egg-white and rolled in powdered sugar, and in the middle of it all an enormous bride-cake. On yet another table stood a great cheese that had taken three men to carry, whilst in the corner was enough bride-ale to ensure oblivion for everyone there if they wished.

Dionis ate little, but her bridegroom and the assembled guests ate their fill, slept and then began again. Abraham insisted on staying to the very end of the festivities, joining in the dancing and singing and listening to the long poem that had been composed in honour of him and his young bride. A poem that saluted them and wished them a long and fruitful marriage and carefully made no mention of Abraham's advanced years. Dionis was disgusted at the way her new husband gorged and glutted himself, even though it put off the evil hour when they must be alone together, because it had been deemed prudent to dispense with the public bedding in view of his age.

When everyone had sickened themselves of food the rotting remains were given to the grateful poor, who had never seen such fare in all their lives, and for the most part hailed Mynheer van der Hest as something akin to a saint. Those who knew better wisely held their peace.

At last it was all over. Just before Dionis left with her husband for their house in Lexden Jannekyn managed to slip the phial she had made up into her hand.

'Use it sparingly in your husband's cup before he retires,' she whispered. 'It will do him no harm other than to make him sleep. That is what you want, is it not?'

'Oh, yes.' Dionis took the phial gratefully. 'It isn't that I mind marrying him. He's got a nice house and a good many servants. And I shall like to be mistress in my own house. It's just the thought of . . . ' She shuddered. 'Ugh. Horrible old man.'

'Maybe you'll grow fond of him as time goes on,' Jannekyn said doubtfully. 'It has been known, you know.'

But this was something Dionis was never to discover for by the next morning Abraham de Baert was dead. She said she had woken to find him dead by her side.

The doctor shook his head. Clearly a new young wife had been too much for a man of his years. His heart must have given out under the strain.

The young widow was brought home to be comforted by

her mother. 'My poor child, to have suffered so,' Katherine wept. 'I knew no good would come of your being married to a man so old.'

'You should have spoken earlier, Mama. Then much suffering might have been spared,' Dionis, who seemed to have grown up overnight, said dryly.

'How could I? How could I gainsay your father? But it is over now.' Katherine held her daughter to her breast. 'You need never go back to that house, child, where your memories will be so sad. You shall stay here, with me . . . '

'Not go back, Mama?' Dionis pulled away from her mother's clasp. 'Of course I shall go back. It's my house now, and when my time of mourning is over I shall entertain. It's a fine house, Mama, better than this one. I shall enjoy living there.' Then she remembered her situation and wiped away a crocodile tear. 'It is just unfortunate that my poor Abraham can't be by my side to share my enjoyment.'

Jannekyn was less easy. Although the phial she had given Dionis was harmless enough taken in small doses, who could say what the consequences would be if it were to be taken all at once? Not that there was any suggestion that Abraham's death was not entirely natural – in fact there would be many digs in the ribs and ribald warnings to bridegrooms for many years to come reminding them of Abraham de Baert's fate. All the same, Jannekyn couldn't help wondering. But Dionis never ever mentioned the phial and Jannekyn never ever asked.

In any case, she soon had other things to worry about.

Life at Strangers' Hall returned to normal. All signs of the wedding festivities disappeared, Pieter rejoined his ship and Jannekyn was once again at Jacob's beck and call, working from early morning till late in the evening.

There was no doubt that Jacob was an important man in the community. As a Governor at the Bay Hall and an Elder at church he had influence in all aspects of life in the Dutch Community and as such he was feared and respected. Everyone deferred to his judgement in a way that gave him great satisfaction and added to his already not inconsiderable self-esteem. He was a great man; God had chosen him to be a great man and had rewarded him accordingly. Of that he was clearly in no doubt whatsoever.

Jannekyn was not so sure. She believed in God, but not in the discriminating God of Jacob van der Hest. Surely, she felt, a God who rewarded his chosen people here on earth would never have allowed his only Son to be nailed to a wooden cross, he would have made him the richest man in Galilee. So Jannekyn worshipped a caring God, to whom she poured out all her troubles on her knees each night and who she implored to deliver her from that which she most feared, with a fear that gripped her more and more as each day passed. A God who didn't always seem to listen.

Twice already she had fainted at the Bay Hall, overcome by its distinctive, oily, woolly, dusty, musty smell, and each day she looked for the sign that would tell her all was well and that what she dreaded most was not to be. But she looked in vain.

At night she tossed sleeplessly on her bed. Her knowledge of herbs did not include a remedy for what ailed her now for she had never thought to need one. In the end she went to see Henrick de Groot's wife, Betkin.

Betkin was in her kitchen, busily kneading dough and already bulging with her ninth child.

'It's for a friend,' Jannekyn lied, when she made her request.

Betkin ceased her kneading for a moment and tutted with impatience. 'One of the servant girls had a romp with the master's handsome son, home from the sea, and got herself with child by him, I suppose. And now wants to be rid of it?'

Jannekyn nodded. 'Something like that.'

Betkin sat down and shook her head. 'No, my dear, meddling with nature is not my way.' She patted her stomach. 'God knows we could have done without another, Henrick and me; eight we've had already and five of them still living, but as the Lord sends another mouth to feed so he'll send bread to feed it with. And each child brings its own love with it.'

'I fear she'll be turned out to beg from the gutter,' Jannekyn said, biting her lip. 'How will she provide for a child then?'

'Better that she should have to provide for a healthy child than one that is maimed, or blind, or, even worse, moonstruck,' Betkin said, wiping her floury hands on her apron. 'I have seen poor creatures that have lived after their mothers' attempts to miscarry them and I swore to have no truck with such devil-sent tricks. I'm sorry, Jannekyn, you've come to the wrong one for such remedies and my advice to you is to look no further, even though there are people who are willing to dabble in these things. Is she a pretty girl?'

Jannekyn blushed. 'Passably so, I think.'

Betkin looked hard at her and sighed heavily. 'In such circumstances I think she should tell her master what has happened,' she said slowly. 'A marriage with the master's son might even be arranged. Stranger things have happened.'

Jannekyn pushed a strand of hair back under her hood. 'The master's son has gone to rejoin his ship.'

'Then there's no time to be lost in calling him back. Get him to make an honest woman of . . . ' she hesitated ' . . . the girl . . . before he goes and gets himself killed by disease or pirates and the like. My Henrick . . . '

'Yes, how is Henrick? Is he here? I haven't seen him lately.' Jannekyn had never forgotten his kindness to her and had grown fond of him.

'No,' Betkin shrugged, 'fool that he is, he keeps going back and forth to Flanders. He said he'd only go the once, to fetch the son of an old friend who'd escaped from prison and needed a passage to England. But I knew what would happen. I knew once he'd started he'd go again. It's in his blood and there'll be no stopping him while there's breath in his body and wind in his sails.' She sniffed loudly, the only sign she allowed herself to show the distress his actions caused her. 'But, come now, no more of this talk. A barley cake fresh from the hearth, before you leave?'

Jannekyn ate the barley cake and then left. No good had come from visiting Betkin; even when she had guessed the truth the older woman had remained firm. And as for the idea of marrying Pieter van der Hest ... Even begging in the gutter would be preferable to that.

Deep in thought Jannekyn went on her way. When she reached the grounds of the ruined St Botolph's Priory she sat down on a stone. She chose a well-sheltered corner so that although there was a keen March wind the sun was warm on her face as she looked up at the towering columns and arches of the great, now almost derelict building.

But was that to be her destiny? Marriage to Pieter van der Hest? Her thoughts were in a turmoil of misery. One thing she had never doubted was that Strangers' Hall would one day be hers, but to come to it through Jacob's lecherous son ... surely that could never be. Surely that filthy thing that had happened to her in the warehouse couldn't be the beginning of some fateful plan. The very thought made her dizzy with disgust and she leaned her head back on the sun-warmed stone and closed her eyes against the tears that would not be held back.

'My child, are you in trouble?'

Jannekyn opened her eyes at the sound of the gentle voice and saw the black-clad tonsured figure of an old monk. He smiled at her and sat down on the stone beside her. 'I saw you as I was walking through the cloister. It's sad what this great place has come to, scarcely a corner fit for habitation now. But never mind that, can I help you, child? You seem deeply troubled.'

Jannekyn sighed. 'Oh, Vader, why is God so cruel?'

'God is not cruel, my child. It is man that is cruel. God is love.'

She shook her head. 'I wish I could believe that. If God is love why does he make us suffer so?'

The old monk put his hand on her shoulder. 'I don't believe God makes us suffer; we bring that on ourselves by not listening to him. I believe he suffers with us just as a human father suffers when his child hurts itself through not heeding his advice.' He smiled at her. 'You're a member of the Dutch Congregation, aren't you? I think they see things a little differently.'

'Yes, they believe that God chooses those he will favour. I just wish he had chosen me.'

The monk got stiffly to his feet. 'Trust in him, my child. Things may not go the way you want, nor indeed the way you expect them to, but remember that God can see the whole pattern, while you can only see the bit you are weaving.' He laid his hand briefly on her head and left her.

She watched him go. His habit was worn and threadbare, his sandals scarcely held to his feet and he looked thin to the point of emaciation, yet he radiated an inner calm and confidence quite unwarranted by his almost destitute situation. Jannekyn only wished she could feel even a little of his serenity.

She got up from the stone and made her way slowly back to the house, where she found Jacob roaring for her because he couldn't find the record of the last batch of cloth that had been shipped to London.

VI

In the end, when there was no possible room left for doubt about her condition, Jannekyn did what she had known all along that she would eventually have to do; she told Adam.

For several weeks on their precious Sunday walks after church Adam had expressed his concern for her, saying that she looked pale and drawn, but she had smiled at him as brightly as she could and blamed the long winter for the lack of roses in her cheeks, never telling him how violently she retched every morning, nor of the nausea that accompanied her through the day.

It was a bright, warm day in early April when she told him; a day when spring had settled a pale green haze on the frees in the wood, ready for the leaf buds to burst They were sitting on a fallen log and he held her close as she told him in dull, flat tones about that dreadful winter afternoon in the wool warehouse. 'And now I am to have his child,' she finished, in a voice of utter desolation.

Several times as she had been speaking she had felt Adam stiffen and his fists clench and now he swore, with a violence and fluency such as she would never have believed him capable.

'If I could get my hands on him, the . . .' He put Jannekyn away from him and began to pace up and down, white to the lips with rage and frustration. 'I'd kill him. With my bare hands I swear I'd kill him.'

'But what am I to do, Adam?' she wept. 'What am I to do?'

He stopped in his pacing and looked down at her, huddled tearfully on the log, crying now almost as much with relief at having unburdened herself as with anxiety at her situation.

'What do you mean, what are you to do?' he asked, surprised. 'You'll marry me, of course, and I'll claim the child as my own. It'll come a little early after our wedding, to be sure, but seven-month babies are not so uncommon.' He sat down and drew her to him. 'What else did you think, my darling? You surely didn't think I'd desert you when you need me most?'

She laid her head on his shoulder. 'Oh, Adam, I feel so safe with you.'

'And so you should, my love. I want nothing more than to care for you for the rest of our lives.' He stroked her hair and kissed her fingers, one by one.

'But, Adam, how can you keep a wife, and your apprenticeship not yet finished?' She lifted up her head and looked at him. Already she felt better, safer, in the knowledge that he would care for her, even though there were still difficulties to overcome.

'I'll explain everything to my master Gabriel and to Mistress Birchwood – oh, not quite *everything*.' He smiled at her tenderly. 'I'll tell them we were so in love we couldn't wait – they'll understand. I'm sure they'll make room for you under their roof with me. And I'll set up Gabriel's loom – you remember I told you he says it's to be mine – and do extra work to keep us.' He hugged her to him again. 'Oh, it's not how we planned to start, sweeting, but we'll be together. And we'll have other children, conceived in love, that will help you to forget this awful thing.'

She clung to him for a long time, dizzy with relief and love for him, caring and thoughtful as he was.

'I will not be a burden to you, Adam. I promise,' she

whispered, as he held her close to his heart. 'I have learned much about the cloth trade, I will help you with my learning. I will keep your accounts as I have learned from de Meester . . . ' Her voice trailed off.

Adam looked down at her. 'What ails you, sweeting? Why suddenly so quiet?'

'I am anxious what he will say.'

'Who?'

'De Meester. I must tell him.'

'Of course you must. I should think he'll give us a good wedding, too. After all, you're almost one of the family and I'm one of his special weavers.' He pulled her to him. 'Oh, Jannekyn, how happy we'll be. We'll dance and we'll feast and then we'll dance again to think that we'll be together for ever.' He became serious. 'Not many are lucky enough to marry for love, Jannekyn, as you and I will.'

But Jannekyn was still uneasy. 'De Meester may not allow it,' she said flatly.

'Why not?'

'Because you are English.'

'I hadn't thought of that.' Adam pinched his lip. 'You're right, Jannekyn, he could be difficult over that. No member of the Dutch Congregation has ever married an English person yet, have they?'

'No. They would fear to be turned away from the Congregation.'

'Would you risk that, Jannekyn?'

She nestled deeper into his arms. 'I would risk anything with you by my side, Adam.'

'Come then.' He stood up and pulled her to her feet. 'The first thing we have to face is Mynheer van der Hest. We'll go together, now, before your courage fails you.'

'What about your courage, Adam?'

'What do I need courage for? What can he do that could harm me? He needs my services too much to cross me.'

But in that Adam was being arrogant and only partly right.

When they reached Strangers' Hall Jacob was sitting in the small parlour trying the new fashion of smoking tobacco and not finding it very much to his liking.

Jannekyn went in and bobbed a curtsey. 'I have someone outside who wishes to speak to you, Meester,' she said.

Jacob drew on his pipe, choked and put it down beside him. He took his time in answering Jannekyn because she was looking very fetching in a nut-brown dress that fitted her far better than it had ever fitted Katherine. The bodice showed off the curve of her young breasts to perfection and he covertly savoured the sight.

'Who is it?' he asked at last.

'Adam Mortlock, the young English weaver who works in the loom shed yonder.' She inclined her head towards the garden.

Jacob frowned. 'What can he want? His work is there, ready. Surely, he's not wanting to break the Sabbath? What will these heathen English come to next?'

'It's not that, Meester.' Jannekyn kept her eyes lowered.

'Well, what then? Oh, very well, have him come in.' He shifted irritably in his chair. He'd had the first twinges of what he feared might be gout in his foot and the idea didn't appeal to him. Gout was an old man's complaint and he was not an old man. In fact sometimes, and particularly in Jannekyn's presence, he felt a stirring in his loins that made him feel positively youthful; a stirring that had to be swiftly suppressed.

Adam came in and stood beside Jannekyn. Jacob looked him up and down; he was a fine-built young man, his shoulders not yet bent from his long hours at the loom, fresh complexioned and with a clear, confident expression in his eyes. Jacob felt an unaccountable twinge of jealousy.

'Well?' he asked tetchily.

'Mynheer van der Hest. I ... wish ... to ... marry ... Jannekyn ... and ... I ... have ... come ... to ... ask ... your ... permission.' Adam spoke slowly and carefully, using Jacob's own tongue the way Jannekyn had taught him so that there could be no possible doubt of his intentions. As he spoke Jannekyn slipped her hand into his and gazed up at him.

Jacob paled visibly. 'No!' he thundered. 'It can never be. It's out of the question.'

Jannekyn had no need to translate his answer for Adam. There could be no possible doubt what he was saying.

'She ... is ... to ... have ... my ... child.' Again Adam spoke words that had been carefully rehearsed.

Jacob stood up. 'No!' he thundered again. 'You lie! You will *not* marry her.'

'Why not?' Quite forgetting himself, Adam shouted back in English.

Jacob raised his fist and for one dreadful moment Jannekyn thought that he was going to strike Adam. But he didn't. Instead, his lip curled and he sneered, 'You don't imagine that one of our Congregation would be allowed to marry an *Englishman*, do you?' He turned to Jannekyn. 'I'm surprised your native pride allowed you even to associate with this ... this ... upstart, let alone consider marriage to him.'

Jannekyn lifted her chin. 'I love Adam and he loves me.'

'Bah!' Jacob spat into the hearth, making a sizzling noise on the logs. 'What do you know of love? Where is your self-respect, girl?'

Jannekyn bowed her head. 'I lost my self-respect in your wool warehouse some two months ago,' she said sadly. 'True, I learned nothing of love there. But I know of Adam's love, a love that is strong enough even to accept your son's bastard as his own child, for my sake.' She looked up at Adam, with love and pride in her eyes. 'I should be glad to marry this Englishman, even though it means renouncing my own people.' She turned to Jacob and her lip twisted bitterly. 'I know I shall find more happiness and understanding with him than with my own narrow, bigoted countrymen, who have no charity and no compassion . . .'

'Be quiet, girl!' Jacob began to pace up and down the room. After a few minutes he stopped in front of Adam. 'You are a good weaver; one of my best. Lucky for you that you are exceptional or you would be out on the street tomorrow. As it is I shall continue to employ you. On condition that you have nothing more to do with this girl.'

Adam frowned, trying to follow what the Dutchman was saying. When Jannekyn translated his brow darkened. 'I will not . . . ' he began, but Jannekyn laid her hand on his arm. 'He would see to it that you got no work elsewhere,' she whispered.

'I don't care. I won't be . . . '

But Jacob, not understanding Adam's words, simply went on talking. 'However,' he said, 'I agree that it is time Jannekyn was married. I have thought so for some time and so I have arranged her marriage to Gyles de Troster. He is a widower, his wife died two years ago, childless, and he has agreed to take her.' He turned to Jannekyn. 'It is all arranged.'

Jannekyn's face turned ashen. 'Oh, Adam,' she cried, clinging to him. 'He says I am to marry a man called Gyles de Troster – a man I have never even met.'

Adam bent his head and said in her ear, 'We'll make a run for it. I won't let him do this to you. Stay close to me. We'll manage somehow, just as long as we're together.'

For a moment she nearly gave in. Adam was a first-class weaver and he would always find work – if Jacob van der Hest didn't prevent it. But Jacob's powerful fingers stretched into every corner of Colchester; Jacob could influence what was bought and what was sold. If he decided that Adam should starve through lack of work, then Adam would starve. And if Adam decided to leave the town to seek work elsewhere Jacob would know and would stop him. Jannekyn knew, as surely as she knew that the sun would rise tomorrow, that if she went with Adam now he was a ruined man.

'No,' she whispered. 'He will ruin you. That I cannot let happen. But always remember that I love you, Adam. Always I will love you. Never forget that.'

'I love you, too, Jannekyn. Far too much to let this happen to you. Come, we'll go. Now!' He made for the door, half-carrying Jannekyn with him. But Jacob, guessing what he planned, was there first.

'Get out!' he snarled at Adam, giving him a push and at the same time flinging Jannekyn out of the way. 'This girl is not for you, and if you make any attempt to take her she will be the one to suffer.' He slammed the door in Adam's face and locked it. Then he stood with his back to it, looking down at Jannekyn, who still lay where he had flung her, her shoulders heaving with great sobs as Adam hammered and banged on the door to be let back in. He put out his toe and gave her a push. '*I* decide who you will marry, not you, girl,' he said. 'And I have made my decision. You will meet your husband on the day of your marriage. And don't try to do anything foolish, like running away with Adam Mordock. If you do, he will be the one that suffers.' His voice dropped. 'I promise you, if you don't do my bidding Adam Mordock will never work again. A weaver cannot work without hands. Or without sight . . . '

Jannekyn heaved herself up on her hands and stared incredulously at him. 'You . . . you monster,' she cried. 'You couldn't . . . you wouldn't . . . '

He bent towards her so that she could smell his tobacco-reeking breath. 'Oh, yes, indeed I could. And if I see you as much as giving good day to that man you will find out whether or not I mean what I say.'

Defeated, she fell back in a crumpled heap on the floor.

Later, back in her own room, Jannekyn stood looking out of the window. She felt no curiosity about the man she was to marry, she didn't even feel sad to think that Adam had gone from her life. In fact, she felt nothing, nothing at all – just an empty numbness. As she stared unseeingly down into the sunlit garden Jacob came suddenly into view and the first spark of feeling began to return. It was a feeling of hatred, a hundred times stronger than she had ever felt for him before, and she clenched her fists, digging her nails into her palms until they bled. 'You will regret what you have done to me this day, Jacob van der Hest,' she said softly. 'I swear before God that you will pay for your acts and that I will humble you as you have humbled me.'

Chapter Three

I

Jacob had chosen Jannekyn's husband with great care. He had realized from the outset the possibility that she would need to be married and of course there was no question of allowing Pieter himself to marry her, he had been dispatched with great haste back to his ship and was now somewhere on the high seas. In any case he was already as good as betrothed to the daughter of an influential business acquaintance of Jacob, a betrothal that might or might not need to be honoured according to how things went at the Bay Hall. But in any event, Jannekyn was not a suitable wife for the eldest son of Jacob van der Hest. He had considered sending her back to her parents in Flanders but had decided against this for several reasons – the chief of which he didn't admit even to himself, being that he couldn't bear the thought of never seeing her again.

But Gyles de Troster was an eminently suitable husband for the girl. Not too young – his balding grey hair showed him to be well over fifty – he was unlikely to prove an ardent lover and so excite Jacob's jealousy. And, just as important, not too independent.

When de Troster's wife had died, some two years previously,

he had turned to the bottle to assuage his grief and it had very nearly proved his master. With frightening speed his business as a dyer had collapsed, leaving him penniless and almost destitute. Jacob had stood aside and watched it all happen and when the time was right and de Troster had come to his senses, Jacob had stepped in and put the man back on his feet, even providing him with a house to live in.

For this Gyles de Troster was profoundly grateful. So grateful that when Jacob asked if he would give a home to his serving girl and a name to her bastard child he had found it impossible to refuse. Anyway, had not a child been the one blessing the good Lord had denied him and Abigail in their life together?

And if Mynheer van der Hest required the girl's services in his counting house from time to time it would be churlish not to let her go, wouldn't it?

From the first moment Jannekyn saw him she felt sorry for him. He was an insignificant little man and it was plain that he looked upon Jacob as a wise and kind benefactor, which almost led her to despise him. At first.

They were married on an April day that held more showers than sunshine – a fact that Jannekyn regarded as an omen of their future together. There were few people at the church – the minister, Jacob van der Hest and another of the church Elders were the only ones to witness the ceremony. But Minister Verlender still found it necessary to preach a, wedding sermon – the same sermon he had preached to Dionis and Abraham de Baert such a short time ago. There was no feasting and merrymaking.

Jannekyn couldn't help contrasting her own quiet wedding with that of Dionis. Such a great junketing for a marriage that barely outlasted the festivities. She wondered how many years she was to be tied to this pale, elderly little man, and tried not to think of Adam.

After their wedding as there was nobody to celebrate with them, and indeed nothing to celebrate, Gyles took her to his home straight away.

He lived in an isolated cottage near the river, close to the water supply he needed for his dyeing sheds. Reached by little more than a rough footpath at the end of Maidenburgh Street, the cottage was on the edge of Jacob's big tenterfield. They walked in silence, with Gyles leading the way and occasionally looking anxiously back to make sure she was still following. Jannekyn gazed around her as she walked. The long rows of tenterframes were empty today, save for one forgotten piece of grey cloth, insecurely fastened, that flapped idly in the drizzling rain. Most days the tenterfields were gay with the brightly coloured lengths of fulled and dyed cloth, stretched to dry in the sunshine. But not today. Today their very drabness seemed to reflect the mood of her unhappy wedding day.

They reached the cottage and Gyles opened the door. It opened straight into the little living room, where there was a hearth and a rough chimney. In one corner stairs wound up to the bedroom and to the right a low doorway led through to the little kitchen and wash house that leaned crazily against the cottage wall.

It was a far cry from Strangers' Hall.

'I made a fire because I thought you might be cold,' Gyles said, watching her anxiously as she gazed round her new home. 'Let me take your cloak and you can sit by it.'

Obediently, she let her cloak fall into his hands and went and sat in one of the rough wooden chairs that stood either side of the fireplace.

'Here, this'll warm you, too.' Gyles dipped the ladle into a pot hanging over the fire and filled a bowl with rich brown broth. 'I made it specially.'

'You're very kind, Baas.' Jannekyn took the bowl and gratefully wrapped her hands round it. She was chilled to the very marrow although the day was not cold and there was such a feeling of despair inside her that it felt as if her heart dripped icicles.

He poured some broth for himself and sat down opposite her and they ate in silence. When he had finished he put down his bowl and cleared his throat.

'A servant brought your belongings from Strangers' Hall,' he said. 'I've put them all upstairs for you.' He cleared his throat nervously again. 'There is but one bedroom, I'm afraid. I have hung a cloth to divide it – you will see when you go up. Yours is the inner portion.' He turned a delicate shade of pink, even to the scalp from which his hair had receded. 'I shall not trouble you at night, my dear, never fear. You may lie easy in your bed, I shall be content to remain your husband in nothing more than name.' He smiled at her, a shy, almost diffident smile. 'There, now it's said and we need never speak of it again.' His tone changed and became brisker. 'Would you like some more broth?'

To her own surprise and his obvious delight she held out her bowl. 'Thank you, Baas, I don't know when I've tasted such delicious broth. I didn't think I'd be able to eat a morsel . . . ' She smiled at him, a sad, rather wistful smile.

He refilled her bowl and watched while she ate her fill, smiling at her encouragingly. When she had finished he took the two bowls out to the kitchen. While he was gone she looked round the room that was to be her home from now on. There was a table with joint stools set round it in the middle of the room and under the window stood a carved, oak chest. On the wall by the stairs a small hutch stood on a little table and opposite, on either side of the doorway to the kitchen, shelves held pewter mugs and plates and a few cherished pieces of blue and white delft. A brightly coloured rag rug took the chill off the stone floor. Everywhere was spotlessly clean and tidy.

Gyles came back into the room. 'I picked some gillyflowers for you,' he said, pointing to the jar of flowers that stood on the table. 'As a welcome, you understand.' He smiled at her and nodded encouragingly again.

'Oh, Baas, you are so kind – more kind than I deserve –' Suddenly, all her pent-up emotions overflowed and she, who thought she would never shed another tear, never feel any emotion again, began to cry.

She wept for a long time and he watched her helplessly, now and again patting her shoulder and saying, 'There, there,' but at last she stopped and dried her eyes. 'I'm sorry, Baas,' she gulped. 'It's the first time I've cried since . . . '

'That's all right, my dear. I expect the day has been a bit much for you, hasn't it?' He got up and fetched another log for the fire. 'Now, I suggest we spend a quiet evening getting to know each other a little. Did Mynheer van der Hest tell you that I was a dyer by trade?' He looked a little ruefully at his hands. 'Not that you would need telling when you looked at these. It doesn't seem to matter how much I scrub at them the dye never quite comes off.' He smiled up at her. 'I have all my vats and drying sheds at the back of the house. I'll show it all to you tomorrow.'

Jannekyn managed to return his smile. 'Yes, I knew you were a dyer. And a widower.'

A look of sadness crossed his face. 'Yes, for over two years now.' He shook his head. 'It was a bad time for me when my Abigail died. I thought I should never recover from it, for she was all the world to me.' He stared at the flames licking up round the log for a while, then he went on, 'I began to drink – somehow it didn't hurt so much when I'd got the fiery liquid inside me and I found that if I drank enough I could forget altogether, in fact I could forget everything.' He sighed. 'Of course, it was all right until I tried to stop, then I found I couldn't.' He paused for a while, then went on, 'I drank every penny I possessed. My house went so that I lived in my drying sheds, then they went, my vats, my dyes, everything. It wasn't until I reached the very bottom of the pit that I came to my senses and began to climb out, with the good Lord's help.'

'Oh, your poor man. I didn't know all that.'

'There's no reason why you should, my dear. Anyway, I never touch the stuff now. I know it would only take one drink to set me off again so I don't even keep it in the house.' He hung his head. 'My Abigail would have been so ashamed of me. It was when I realized how sad it would have made her to see me like that that I pulled myself together. By the goodness of the Lord I managed to get work with a dyer called Hendrix along by the Schere Gate and I'd only been there about two months when Mynheer van der Hest saw me and offered me a house if I would work for him. I must say that in the six months I've been doing his work I've no complaints.'

'Even if he has landed you with a wife you didn't want and the prospect of fathering somebody else's child,' Jannekyn said, with more than a trace of bitterness.

'I must confess I was not very happy at the idea when he first put it to me,' Gyles admitted honestly. 'I've no need of a wife – er – you understand what I mean, and I can manage my house and business quite well on my own. But then I thought, well, Mynheer van der Hest has been very good to me and this was something I could do to repay him for his kindness.' He leaned forward and turned the log over with his foot. 'You'll be company for me during the long winter evenings, my dear, and another thing, I've always loved children although we were never blessed with any of our own, Abigail and me. So it might not be a bad thing, it might not be a bad thing at all. The only thing is . . . ' he hesitated ' . . . I am prepared to take this child and bring it up as my own, but I should not like it if you were to prove . . . loose, if you take my meaning.'

She shook her head. 'There is no danger of that, Mynheer, I promise you. And I can assure you that the child I carry is no "love-child", whatever Mynheer van der Hest may have told you. It was forced on me against my will by his son, Pieter, when he was home from the sea.' Even now she couldn't recall that dreadful afternoon without a shudder of revulsion running through her.

Gyles nodded, partly with sympathy but more with satisfaction, relieved that here was no wanton creature ready to lift her skirts to the first hot-blooded youth that caught her eye. For a moment he even felt sorry for her.

She raised her eyes and went on bitterly, 'But when the man I love and who loves me would have married me and given the child his name, Mynheer van der Hest refused to allow it.'

'That surprises me. It's not at all what I would have expected of such a generous man. Who is this man who would have married you? Do I know him?' Gyles frowned.

'His name is Adam Mortlock. He is an English weaver.'

Gyles's face cleared immediately.

'An Englishman! Ah, I see. Then I don't blame de Meester, I don't blame him a bit. It would be quite wrong for a member of the Dutch Congregation to marry an Englishman, surely you must know that, my dear.' He turned a stern gaze on her. 'Mynheer van der Hest was quite right in forbidding such a marriage. An Englishman, indeed. Whoever heard of such a thing!'

He tutted to himself for several minutes and Jannekyn had the idea that he would hardly have been more horrified if she had contemplated marrying Satan himself. She thought of Adam; hard-working, thoughtful and kind, so different to some of the coarse and arrogant men of the Dutch Congregation that she knew. What did a man's race and nationality matter? Surely what a man was like was more important. She sighed. At this moment the gulf between her and the man she loved seemed wider than ever.

Gyles was still tutting and fidgeting about the room when there was a knock on the door and, without waiting for an invitation, Jacob van der Hest entered. He shook the rain off his cloak and stalked over to the fire and stood with his back to it, his hands behind him. Immediately, Gyles began fussing nervously round him, offering him food and the only beverage he kept in the house apart from water, herbal tea. But Jacob waved him aside.

'I wish to speak to your goodwife,' he said impatiently, turning to Jannekyn. 'There is a consignment of cloth to be dispatched to London tomorrow and you haven't yet entered it in the ledger,' he said.

Jannekyn looked up at him coolly. 'The ledgers were all up to date when I left them, Meester,' she said politely. 'In fact, it was late when I finished last night so that I should leave nothing outstanding. When did the cloth come in from the tenterfields to be sheared and folded?'

'This morning.'

'Then how could I have been expected to record it?'

Jacob shifted from one foot to the other irritably. 'I'm not suggesting that you should have recorded it. I'm suggesting that you should come and do it now.'

'On my *wedding* day, Meester?' Her lip twisted wryly as she spoke.

'Bah, what difference does that make? Your husband has agreed that you will still work for me.'

'Oh, I see.' Jannekyn nodded. 'Very well, I'll come and do it.' She paused, then added, 'Tomorrow.'

'Tomorrow! But the cloth will be shipped tomorrow!'

'Not before three in the afternoon if it's to go on the tide. I shall be there to see that the work is done in good time, Meester.'

'I really think . . . if de Meester wants you to go now . . . it's not late . . .' Gyles fussed, worried that already his new wife might be antagonizing his benefactor.

'It's nearly dark,' Jannekyn said. 'The work needs to be done in daylight if the cloths are not to be confused – a black with a blue, calimancos with chambletts, bustyans with baratos.' She took off her shoes and stretched her toes towards the fire. This was the first time she had ever defied Jacob and she was enjoying it: She lifted her chin and looked straight at him. 'I will come tomorrow.'

Jacob's brow darkened. Her argument was sound, the light was not good enough to distinguish one cloth from another and candlelight only confused colours. He had come to fetch her because he had wanted her in his counting house, where he could see her, so that he could watch the candlelight pick out the gold in her hair, and see the rise and fall of her breast as she bent over his ledgers . . . He flung himself to the door, furious both with himself and her for the sinful, carnal longings she excited in him.

'Very well,' he said, 'come as soon as it is daylight. There is much to be done.'

After he had gone and Gyles had finished admonishing her on her defiance – for above all Gyles was determined that nothing should happen that might put his new-found security at risk – Jannekyn sat staring into the fire.

Living under Jacob's roof, dependent on his charity, she had had no choice but to do his bidding. But now she had a husband whose home she shared, and although she knew she would have to be careful because Gyles owed everything to Jacob, at last she could begin to assert herself. Because Jacob van der Hest needed her, she knew that. She was becoming more and more indispensable to him in his business and at the Bay Hall. And, although she shied away from the thought, in other directions, too.

Slightly, almost imperceptibly, the balance of power was beginning to shift, as she had always known that in time it would. But who could tell where it would lead?

Katherine lay on her couch in the solar eating a sugared plum and waiting for Jacob's return. A small fire burned in the grate against the damp April day but she still felt the need to cover herself with a fur rug. As she heard his heavy step in the hall she rearranged the rug and lay back on her pillows.

'You've been a long time, Jacob. You know I get lonely now that our son has returned to his ship,' She sighed. 'I had hoped to keep him with us for a few months, we see so little of him. It was a great disappointment to me that he had to leave so soon.' She closed her eyes. 'Where have you been, Jacob?'

'To the counting house.' He went over to the window and stood looking out on to the knot garden, with its formal, symmetrical beds.

Her eyes flew open. 'But why, Jacob? I thought the girl – ah, the girl!' Katherine nodded sagely.

'The girl was not there,' he rapped. 'She was married earlier today.'

Katherine sat up. 'Married? Jannekyn? By whose permission?'

'Mine.'

'Yours, Jacob?' Forgetting herself Katherine threw off the rug and got to her feet. 'Who has she married?' she asked, going over to where he stood.

'Gyles de Troster.' Jacob didn't even look at her.

'But isn't he that old drunken dyer who lives by the river?'

'That's right. He doesn't drink now.'

Katherine leaned against the window, breathing heavily. There could be only one explanation for this. 'Is she with child?'she asked at last

'Yes.'

She caught his sleeve. 'Is it of your get, Jacob?'

He shook her free. 'No, it is not.' He still refused to look at her.

'I don't believe you, Jacob,' she said softly. 'I've seen the way you look at her, the lechery in your eyes.' She turned away. 'God knows, it's a look I've learned to recognize over the years.'

'It's not a look you've seen for many a long month, my wife though you may be,' he replied, his mouth twisting. 'I scarce remember when I was last allowed into your bed.'

'Nor shall you be when you tumble the servants and get them with child.' She almost screamed the words at him.

He caught her by the shoulders. 'Jannekyn is no servant,' he said, shaking her with each word. 'And I did not "tumble" her, as you so crudely put it. The child is none of mine.'

'You lie! Katherine said, throwing back her head so that she could look into his face. 'If it was not your child she carried you would never have bothered to see her decently married. You would have thrown her back into the gutter from whence she came. You . . . '

'If you will know, woman, it was your son, the boy by whom you set so much store, who got her with child.' Jacob looked at his wife with eyes that were cruelly cold.

Katherine staggered, 'I don't believe you, Jacob.' She put her hand to her head. 'You lie. You were jealous, jealous because Pieter spent all his time by my side. You wanted to be rid of him so you blamed him for your act.' She groped her way back to her couch.

Jacob watched her, making no move to help. 'I tell you, woman, it was your son,' he repeated. 'I found them in the warehouse, soon after his arrival home. No doubt the girl encouraged him,' he said with a shrug.

But Katherine was not even listening. 'Whatever your lecherous inclinations I have never found you out before,' she said, 'but I have seen the way you look at that girl and this time I am in no doubt. I will never again have you near me, Jacob, let alone in my bed. Please leave me.' He made no move to leave. 'Please leave me!' she screamed at him.

Without a word he turned and strode out of the room.

Katherine lay back on her pillows for a few moments, then, dismissing him from her thoughts, she leaned over and selected another sugared plum.

II

Jannekyn found life with Gyles de Troster less unpleasant than she had feared it might be. He was an honest and upright member of the Congregation, stern and strict in his beliefs and attitudes – the more so since his temporary lapse after the death of his wife – but as long as she adhered to his principles he was kind to her and as generous as he could afford to be. She came to regard him more as a father-figure than as a husband.

Each night when she returned from Jacob's counting house, taking a short cut across the tenterfields, Gyles would have a bowl of steaming broth ready for her or, as the summer became hot and her body heavier, a cold pie and fruit. For Jacob kept her continually at work and even when her ankles swelled with the extra weight of the child she carried he thought nothing of keeping her standing for hours on end at the Bay Hall, where she listened to the complaints of the English – who bitterly resented being forced to bring their cloth to a Bay Hall belonging to the Dutch to be searched and sealed, and lost no opportunity of saying so – and translated these grievances for Jacob's ear, only to have them swept aside with typical van der Hest arrogance. It was well that the English couldn't understand – it meant she was able to temper Jacob's rudeness and thus prevent many an ugly scene, of which there were quite enough, anyway.

She watched as the raw-hallers, all of them under oath to execute their work fairly and faithfully, with no discrimination, examined the cloth as it had come from the loom. They stood at long tables with the cloth laid out before them, working quickly but thoroughly, examining the quality, width and the number of threads in the warp. There were single bays, double bays and double-double, all of different lengths and weight, and

Jannekyn never ceased to be amazed at the speed and dexterity with which the cloth passed through the raw-hallers' hands. Now and again there was an ominous rending sound as a cloth was torn in half because it was not up to the high standard required, resulting in a fine of up to a third of its value from the man who had woven it. After the cloth had been passed to the dyers and fullers to be finished the whole process was repeated in the white hall. It was a complicated and thorough business and it was small wonder that Colchester bays had such a high reputation and that the Colchester seal was accepted without examination all over the trading world.

'What are you doing? I've been looking for you.' Jacob came up to her as she perched on an upturned bale of cloth in an effort to take the weight off her aching feet. 'Have you checked that the fines tally with the searchers' lists?'

'Yes, Meester, it all seems to be in order. But Matthew Bishop, a poor English weaver from Gutter Street, swears it was bad eyesight that made him tally too few threads in the warp for his single bay and not a desire to cheat. He says he has no money for the fine and his children are wont to starve.' She looked up at Jacob as she spoke, hoping she might have touched a chord of sympathy.

'He should have thought of that and checked his tallying more carefully,' Jacob snapped, closing his mouth in a thin, hard line. 'See to it that he is made to pay.'

Jannekyn turned away. She might have known there was not a shred of mercy in the make-up of Jacob van der Hest

It was late before they left the Bay Hall. Jannekyn was so tired that she was glad to sink back into the relative comfort of Jacob's coach. She closed her eyes wearily only to see figures dancing before them and her head rang with the quarrels and disputes between weaver and searcher, Englishman and Alien.

Suddenly, there was a shout and an egg sailed through the unglazed window into the coach. It splattered on the floor, sending forth unmistakable evidence of great age. It was immediately followed by more eggs, equally ancient, rotten tomatoes and cabbages picked out of the gutter by the market place and accompanied by the shouts and yells of ragged men who swarmed over the coach and poked their filthy heads in, shouting obscenities at its occupants.

'Drive faster, coachman!' Jacob shouted, lashing at the bearded faces with his cane, bloodying noses and splitting lips indiscriminately.

By the time the coach had reached St Runwald's the mob had fallen away, to vent their anger and frustration elsewhere.

Jacob wiped the slime of a rotten egg from his cheek. 'Barbaric heathens,' he muttered. 'English, all of them.'

'They're desperate. They have no work, their looms lie idle,' Jannekyn protested. 'They're starving.'

'They should be looked after by their own countrymen. We look after our poor, let the English look to theirs.' Jacob was still trying to clean himself, but the all-pervading stink remained. 'That's what the fines at the Bay Hall are used for,' he went on, 'and heaven knows, plenty are collected from the English for their shoddy work.'

Jannekyn was silent. It was true that the fines collected from the Bay Hall were used to help the poor, the Dutch fines helped the Dutch poor and the English fines the English poor. This was strictly carried out. But she couldn't help feeling that a system that collected money for the destitute by taking it from the very men who, in paying it, would themselves be in danger of starvation, left a lot to be desired.

'You look tired, my dear. And those men frightened you. Look there's filth on your gown.' Jacob leaned forward and brushed her skirt, letting his hand linger a shade longer than was necessary on her knee.

She shook her skirt, knocking his hand away. He often tried to touch her and she loathed him the more for it. 'I'm all right,' she said, 'a little tired, perhaps, nothing more.'

'Turn, down Maidenburgh Street,' he called to his coachman. He leaned back in his corner and smiled at her, his wolfish, unnatural smile. 'It will be less for you to walk.'

Jannekyn made no answer. She gazed out of the coach as it rumbled down the narrow hill that was Maidenburgh Street. Here, squalid little cottages huddled round clay-baked yards, leaning crazily against each other. And at the doors stood women, their distaffs ever busily employed, never wasting a moment that could be spent spinning, for they had to work long and hard to earn even a few pence to add to the family's meagre purse.

At the bottom of the hill, when the coach could go no further, she took the footpath along by the side of the river's green and flowery banks to the cottage.

A cool drink made from elderflowers and a cold mutton pie waited for her on the table.

Gyles was nowhere to be seen. This was unusual; however busy he was he always managed to be in the house to welcome her. She knew that he had become quite fond of her in the two months they had been married and almost unconsciously she had begun to put him in the place of her own father, whom she had not seen for such a long time.

She went through to the little lean-to kitchen and dipped herself a mug of fresh, cold water from the pitcher Gyles filled daily from the stock well. After drinking her fill she threw the dregs from the mug over her face and arms to cool herself and went to look for her husband.

His dyeing sheds were a little way from the back of the cottage and she could see steam coming from the open door as she crossed the yard, ducking between hanks of yarn that had been dyed in the wool and now were hanging in the hot sun to dry. Gyles was a master craftsman, the yarn was all a uniform colour, a delicate rose pink, and there were no streaks in the deeper pink of the woven cloth hanging on the tenter-frame nearby.

Peering through the steam in the dye-house she saw Gyles standing over his vats, gently stirring and lifting, stirring and lifting the cloth with a long, smooth stick. He looked up when he saw her.

'Hullo, my dear. You're home early,' he said with a smile, deftly lifting out the dyed cloth into a wooden tub and draining it carefully.

'Yes. De Meester brought me to the end of Maidenburgh Street in his carriage as it was so hot.' She followed him as he carried the tub outside, across the yard and out into the tenterfield and watched as he hung it on the frame to dry, fixing it carefully by means of iron keys in the wooden frame.

'There,' he said, lovingly smoothing the cloth and peering minutely at it to make sure that the colour had penetrated right through. 'It doesn't need stretching now, just holding firm until it dries.'

'Some cloth at the Bay Hall today had been over-stretched after it had been fulled,' Jannekyn said as she watched him. 'It was so badly done that you could almost see through it in places. I don't know how they ever thought it would get sealed.'

'Who did it belong to?' Gyles was still lovingly examining his work.

'Thomas Greenleaf.'

'Oh, him! I've heard of his bad dealings before. English, isn't he?' He looked round at Jannekyn.

She nodded.

Well, there you are, then. What more can you expect from such a nation of rogues and vagabonds?'

'That's not fair, Gyles. The English aren't all bad.'

'I'd like to see one that isn't.' Satisfied with his efforts, Gyles turned away and went back to the cottage. Jannekyn followed at a distance. For all his mildness, nothing that she could say would soften his attitude towards the English.

'I must change my dress before we eat,' she said when they reached the cottage. 'The carriage was pelted with rotten food as we came from the Red Row and some of it landed on my skirt.'

'You were not hurt?' Gyles turned to her, full of concern.

'No, a little frightened, at first, that's all. But, oh, Gyles, I know you hate the English, but I feel so sorry for them. So many of the weavers have no work – and I feel that we're somehow responsible – that we of the Dutch Congregation have taken away their livelihood.'

'Rubbish. In any case that's no reason for them to mob your carriage.'

'I'm not so sure. I think I can understand why they do it, poor things.' She turned to go up the steep staircase in the corner.

But Gyles came over and laid a dye-stained hand on her arm. 'Just a minute, meisje,' he said. 'Before you feel too sorry for the poor English, think of what happened at Halstead a few years ago.'

She paused, with a foot on the bottom step. 'Halstead? What happened there?'

Gyles turned back to the table and began slicing the mutton pie. 'Haven't you heard about that? Well, about thirty households moved to Halstead and set up their businesses. They had been asked to go to help provide work for the local people, which it did, both in the town and in the surrounding district However, the native bay-makers were so jealous of the way the Dutch Congregation prospered – you see they turned out cloth of much better quality than the English – that they made life unbearable. Why, they even counterfeited the Dutch Bay Seals; there was no end of trouble over that, as you can imagine. Anyway, the Congregation got fed up and came back to Colchester.'

'Oh, I didn't know about that'

'Ah!' Gyles pointed his knife in her direction. 'But that's not the end of it. Having rousted the Congregation out of Halstead the local people found they weren't so well off, after all. There was no work and people were beginning to starve again. So what did they do but ask the Congregation to go back again. Begged them, they did. Begged them to go back.'

'And did they?'

'No, of course they didn't. And not to blame them, either. Serve the English right if they starved, that's what I say.' Gyles sat down at the table. 'And now, make haste, child. Go and change your gown, I can smell it from here. And let's have no more talk of the poor English. Remember, those that work hard and well, prosper. Those that don't, starve.'

Jannekyn went slowly up the stairs to her room behind the curtain. Sometimes, she thought sadly, Gyles could be as heartless as Jacob.

III

Bessie peered short-sightedly at Adam as he pushed aside his half-eaten bowl of broth. 'Wass the matter with it, boy? Ain't it to your likin'?' she asked anxiously.

'It's delicious, Bessie. I'm not hungry, that's all. I think I'll go to bed.' Adam got up from the table.

Bessie caught his hand. 'There's somethin' wrong, boy, ain't there? Me an' Gabriel's bin watchin'. You ain't got no appetite an' you mope about. Now, why don't you tell ole Bessie about it while Gabriel's down at the ale-house?' She frowned. 'You ain't bin gambling' an' got yourself into debt, hev you? If thass the trouble we've got a bit put by, me and Gabriel . . . '

Adam put his arm round the old woman and kissed her. 'Oh, thank you, Bessie, you're so good to me. But it's nothing like that, I promise you.' He went over to the open door and stood looking out. 'I almost wish it was.'

'What is it then, boy? Can't you tell ole Bessie?'

He came back into the room and slumped down on his stool again. 'It's Jannekyn. She's a Dutch girl, a servant at Strangers' Hall.'

'Oh, Adam, you ain't bin an' got 'er into trouble, hev you?' Bessie said in a hushed voice.

'No, Bessie, I haven't. It's nothing like that. I love her and I want to marry her.'

'But she's Dutch,' Bessie said doubtfully. 'We don't marry the likes of foreigners, do we?'

'I couldn't, anyway. She's been married off to someone else,' Adam said flatly.

'Well, then.' Bessie dismissed it with a shrug.

Adam took her hand. 'You don't understand, Bessie. Look, I'll tell you . . . '

Bessie listened while Adam told her the whole story. When he'd finished she shook her head sadly. 'Thass the finish then, boy. There ain't nothin' you can do. She's married an' thass an end of it'

'But she won't even look at me now, let alone speak to me,' Adam said wretchedly. 'If only she'd smile once in a while ... I can see her working in the counting house from where I stand at my loom but she never as much as looks my way.' He put his head in his hands. 'I can't believe ... after all we meant to each other ... If we could just be friends I'd be content, but it looks as if she's allowed Jacob van der Hest to poison her mind against me.'

Bessie put her arm round Adam's shoulders. She loved the boy like a son and it grieved her to see him so unhappy. 'The best thing you can do, boy, is find yourself a nice little English girl. There's plenty about as 'ud be glad to call you husband.'

He turned on her, his eyes blazing. 'Never. There will never be anyone else. If I can't have Jannekyn I shall never marry.'

'Thass a rash thing to say,' Bessie said sadly. 'You're young, boy. You'll change your mind.'

He shook his head. 'No,' he said wearily. 'If I can't have Jannekyn I'll have nobody.'

Bessie pursed her lips. Time was a great healer, and with a little encouragement ...

Jannekyn found that the hardest thing to bear in her life with Gyles de Troster was being separated from Adam. Of course their precious walks after church on Sundays, when they had wandered in the woods and planned for a future together – sharing wild, impossible dreams that had made day-to-day living bearable – had had to cease. Each Sunday she accompanied

Gyles to church and sat beside him as a good wife should. But there was not even a chance to join the other matrons afterwards, to gossip and talk over the doings of the children, while the men discussed the finer points of the sermon – if, indeed, that was the topic of their often heated arguments. For Gyles, on his own admission, 'was not one to mix'. And so, after church Jannekyn was forced to accompany him straight home and to listen to his interpretation of the Predikant's words, which often amounted to another sermon.

She had no friends. Gyles's cottage, standing isolated as it did, made it difficult to be a part of the life of the community. But even more difficult was the attitude of the people themselves. They refused to accept Jannekyn, however friendly she tried to be with them. For didn't she wear finer clothes than most of the ordinary folk of me Congregation? (They weren't to know that Jacob insisted that she dress well, indeed, took a personal interest in her wardrobe, much to her annoyance. But he provided all she wore as payment for the work she did for him so she had no choice in the matter.)

And didn't she travel in the van der Hest coach, although she was only the wife of that drunken dyer? (They didn't know how she hated this and avoided it when she could.)

And, worst of all, didn't she work in Jacob van der Hest's counting house? Counting his money and looking after his interests?

Jannekyn found their resentment over this the most difficult to understand because didn't most of the people of Ball Alley and Angel Lane – known locally as the Dutch Quarter – also work for Jacob? The women at their distaffs, the men at their looms or teasels? And even the children were put to work sorting the raw wool, a stinking task that Jannekyn hated to see children put to but which she knew added a few necessary extra pence to the family purse. True, none of them were ever likely to become rich, but they all had a roof over their heads and food in their bellies. And at least they were paid in money and not in fine clothes, as she was.

'They are an ungrateful lot,' Gyles replied when she spoke to him about It. He would hear no word spoken against Jacob van der Hest. Jacob was good to him. Only last week he had provided him with the ground cinnabar needed to make the orange-red vermillion colour that was needed for a special order. This was expensive. Gyles could never have afforded to pay the Italian merchants who had brought it over from the Red Sea. And Jacob had imported madder and weld from France for him, too. Once again Gyles could hold up his head as a master dyer, thanks to Jacob van der Hest. Gyles was a snob, and his snobbery did nothing to narrow the gulf between Jannekyn and the rest of the Congregation, making her more lonely than ever.

She drew comfort and a kind of strength from the knowledge that when she was at work in the counting house Adam was not far away from her. Sometimes she could even feel his eyes on her as she worked at her ledgers, but remembering Jacob's threat she never dared to as much as glance in his direction, although at times the temptation to do so was almost more than she could resist. She often wondered, sick at heart, whether by this time Adam had found someone else to love, someone he could marry, with whom he could raise a family, with none of the problems and complications he had found with her. The thought made her shed bitter tears of misery and despair. She was thinking of this one afternoon near the end of July.

There had been no rain for nearly a month and the heat

shimmered over the tenterfields, baking the earth and drying the cloth in half the time it usually took. Jacob had gone to the Bay Hall alone for once. Even he had admitted that the stifling atmosphere there was no place for a woman in Jannekyn's condition. But today it was almost as bad in the counting house. She went to the door for a breath of air.

But the heat was like a blanket and as she leaned on the door post she hoped that she was not going to succumb to the sickness that was rife in the town. A sickness due, Gyles was convinced, to eating foul meat.

The poor were only too glad to buy the cheapest meat and in hot weather like this even the best meat was rancid almost before the breath had left the body of the slaughtered animals. The stench from the butcher's shambles testified to this as it mingled with the other everyday smells that came from the town gutter to be carried on the hot air. Gyles would not let Jannekyn buy meat while the weather was so hot. He went out at night and snared conies in the fields and made them into pies, which, if they were not eaten straight away, were covered to protect them from the flies and kept in the cellar under the living room, where it was cool. He swore that although he took a risk in catching the conies it was this that kept them both healthy while others suffered.

But Jannekyn didn't feel healthy today. With less than four months to go before her child should be born she felt heavy and lethargic; her hair was lank and lifeless and she felt tired through to her bones. And there was no air. If only she could get a little cool, fresh air into her lungs ... She fanned her face with her hand and took great gulping breaths to fight the faintness that was rising in her as the garden began to spin into blackness ...

'It's all right, my love. My dear love.' It sounded like Adam's, voice. It was such a long time since she'd heard him speak to her or felt his arms round her and she missed him so. But no doubt by this time he'd found someone else to put his arms round, someone else to love. Tears pricked her eyelids. She was dreaming. She wanted to go on dreaming, to hear his voice again and to feel him holding her close to his heart.

But they wouldn't let her go back to sleep. Someone was trying to force a cup between her lips. Cool water ran down her chin.

'That's right, darling. You'll feel better when you've drunk a little water.'

It still sounded like Adam. She opened her eyes. He was there, holding her in the crook of his arm and looking down at her with infinite tenderness.

'Adam?' She could believe neither her eyes nor her ears and she put out her hand to touch him.

'Yes, I'm real enough, my love,' he smiled. 'I was watching you from where I stood at my loom – I often watch you, Jannekyn – and I saw you were about to fall so I rushed out to you. You would have struck your head if I hadn't caught you,' He smiled at her again. 'Here, take another sip of water. It'll help you to feel better.'

'Dank U.' She handed him back the cup and rested her head on his shoulder, her eyes filling with tears. 'Oh, Adam, so much have I missed you. And never daring even to look over to where you work lest de Meester should see and make you to suffer . . . ' She drew away from him. 'Quickly, you must go. We must not be seen to talk together.'

Adam took no notice. 'It's not finished between us, Jannekyn. I don't know how or when, but one day we'll be together for always.'

She shook her head, the tears trickling down her face. 'Oh, Adam, if I only, could believe so. But how can it be? I have a husband . . . '

'Tell me, Jannekyn, is he good to you? Does he . . . ?' His voice faltered on the words he couldn't bring himself to say.

'He is good to me, Adam. He . . . he treats me as a daughter, nothing more.' Jannekyn looked over his shoulder anxiously. 'The loom master, he watches us . . . '

'Yes, yes, I'm going.' He held her close again under the pretext of giving her more water. 'You don't know how I've been torn apart with jealousy,' he admitted.

She touched his cheek, 'There is no need. I promise you there is no need.' Her face clouded. 'But Gyles hates the English. I told him about you but he had no sympathy. He is like de Meester, he would never agree to a member of the Congregation marrying an Englishman. He is very strict in all ways.' She shook her head sadly. 'Oh, I wish that I could believe you, Adam. I wish I could believe that we shall be together one day, but I cannot see that it can ever be. There are too many things that hold us apart.'

He bent his head. 'Your husband is an old man, Jannekyn. He won't live for ever, and when he dies . . . '

'No!' Jannekyn shook her head violently. 'You must not talk so, Adam. You must not even think . . . '

'How else do you think I exist from day to day?' he burst out wretchedly. 'Why else would I have begged Gabriel, my master, to let me have his loom now, instead of waiting until my apprenticeship is up? When I get some money to buy yarn I shall begin to weave my own cloth.'

'How can that be when you must spend all your daylight hours here at this loom?'

'I shall find a way.' He sighed ruefully. 'But first I have to find a way to buy yarn.' He squeezed her hands in his. 'But I *shall* do it, Jannekyn. And we *shall* be married. One day I promise you, Jannekyn, you will be my wife.'

She sighed, a sigh that seemed to come from the depths of her being. 'Oh, Adam, if it only could be so.' She gave him a push. 'But go now, please go. If de Meester should know we have talked he would do terrible things to you. He told me he would that terrible day when he threw you out of his house.' Her face was creased with worry.

He pulled her close to him and for a moment held her as if he could never bear to let her go, then, reluctantly, he got to his feet. 'Yes, I will go now. The loom master will be calling for me. Are you sure you're better now?'

She smiled up at him. 'Oh, so much better now that I have talked to you, Adam. I feared so much that you might have stopped loving . . . not that I have any right . . . '

'Never. I'll never stop loving you, Jannekyn, I shall always care for you. Remember that.'

'I love you, Adam.' Then in a loud voice in her own tongue for the benefit of the loom master, 'Dank U, Mynheer Mortlock. Your offer of water was timely. I was near to fainting.'

He left her then and went back to his loom to work frantically to make up the time he had lost.

Jannkeyn went back to her ledgers. Her heart was singing although she knew that nothing had really changed. She began to wrestle half-heartedly with the rough and ready accounts the agents gave her. These agents distributed the wool for spinning and the yarn for weaving to the spinners and weavers who worked in their homes. Some of these agents were not altogether trustworthy she felt sure, and she had voiced her suspicions to Jacob more than once. But with typical arrogance he had ridiculed the suggestion.that anyone might be managing to defraud him and she had not so far been able to pinpoint any particular discrepancies.

Today, she no longer felt in any mood to try. Adam still loved her. Jacob's business could go to the wall for all she cared.

IV

Jannekyn was not ill; she did not succumb to the sickness that ravaged the town. But Jacob did. On the last day of August he fell ill and for eight days leeches and purging and all the skills of his personal physician did nothing to improve his condition. Dionis came to see him when she thought it was likely that he would die. She had never forgiven him for forcing her to marry a man she loathed. And the fact that Abraham had died so soon – and conveniendy, some said – after the marriage, leaving her a young and healthy widow, did nothing to soften her feelings towards her father.

Jannekyn saw her walking in the garden with her mother – Katherine was always more active when Jacob was not there to see. Dionis had certainly bloomed in her widowhood. Clearly, she had remembered Jarmekyn's advice, given to her all those months ago in the secret garden. Her hair fell in two straight and shining plaits from under an elaborate, stiffly starched cap and careful attention to her diet had reduced her puddingy figure to an attractive shapeliness. Her apron, over a skirt of the most expensive blue and black striped tobine, was of finest lawn lavishly trimmed with lace, and a fan and a gold pomander hung from a girdle at her waist. Although her mouth would always be too small and pinched for her ever to be really beautiful, with a little artifkal colour added in the right place her face was quite pretty when she smiled. Jannekyn frowned as she sat in the counting house wrestling with her ledgers. Dionis, teetering along on the latest mode in high-heeled shoes, and her mother were laughing and chattering in a way that hardly befitted the wife and daughter of a man who was mortally ill. And the snatches of conversation that floated across to Jannekyn seemed to centre on the string of young men who paid court to the wealthy young widow.

'Silly boy,' Dionis said, speaking of the son of a rich merchant from the other side of Colchester. 'He's just like all the others. Seems to think I can't wait to be married again.' She fanned herself and tossed her head coquettishry. 'He's quite wrong, you know, and I told him so. I told him I should not even begin to think of re-marriage for at least another two years.'

'It may not be wise to wait too long, Dionis,' Jannekyn heard Katherine warn her daughter.

Dionis laughed, a false, tinkling laugh she had acquired since her widowhood. 'Never fear, Moeder. But next time I shall marry whom *I* choose, not a man chosen for me. At the moment, though, I am finding life very agreeable as it is.' She laughed her irritating little laugh again and whispered something to Katherine that sent them both off into paroxysms of laughter.

Right underneath Jacob's window, too.

Jannekyn went back to her work. She had more pressing problems to contend with than the way Jacob's wife and daughter behaved. Her accounting system was getting behind. Cornelis Provoest, one of Jacob's agents, had made no returns for almost a week. Each agent had his own spinners and weavers to keep supplied with raw materials, which were collected and paid for when they were spun or woven. The system worked well. The agent took the wool to his spinners to be spun into yarn, collected it from them a week later and took it to his weavers to be woven into cloth. He then took the cloth to the Bay Hall to be searched before it went on to the fulling mill to be washed and thickened and hung on the tenterframes to dry. In this way there was a constant turnover of materials and no time was wasted. Each agent kept his tally and handed over his somewhat rough and ready accounts to Jannekyn, who paid him a fixed wage plus the money he had handed over in payment to his spinners and weavers. But there had been no accounts from Cornelis Provoest since last Thursday and it was beginning to hold up everything else. It couldn't have happened at a worse time than when Jacob was too ill to advise her.

After some deliberation she decided to take the matter into her own hands and go and see the man. So she finished what she was doing in the counting house and made her way to Angel Lane, a lane to the west of the stock well. Cornelis Provoest's house was a neat, half-timbered house with the usual cantilevered upper storey. Jannekyn knocked at the door and a pale, thin-faced woman with her hair dragged back and screwed under her cap poked her head out of the upstairs lattice.

'Just a minute. I'm coming,' she said ungraciously, and closed the lattice.

A moment later she opened the door and Jannekyn stepped into the cool dimness of the house. As her eyes became accustomed to the light she could see that the room she was in was surprisingly comfortably appointed, with panelled walls and a heavy oak table and stools. The stone-flagged kitchen beyond had shelves stocked with pewter plates and mugs and there was a delicious smell of baking bread.

'You be from Strangers' Hall, old van der Hest's place, don't you?' Cornells Provoest's wife asked rudely.

'Yes, that's right. I've come . . . '

'I've heard about you. Married Gyles de Troster, the dyer, didn't you?'

'Yes, but . . . '

'Nearly drank himself to death, didn't he? I've seen him lyin' in the filth o' the gutter . . . '

'That's all in the past. He never drinks now.' Jannekyn bit her tongue on the words. 'Not that it's anything to do with you.'

'A good thing he've give it up, I should think, with a wife in your condition.' Margarete Provoest's eyes swept Jannekyn's figure insolently.

'I've come to ask about your husband,' Jannekyn said coldly.

'And well you might.' Margarete Provoest pursed her lips and glared accusingly at Jannekyn. 'He be down with the sickness that's all over the town. I'll wager he caught it from the hovels he hev to visit on his work – and much thanks he do get for his trouble.' She gave her head a disapproving toss. 'A pittance he do be paid. A pittance.'

Jannekyn was silent. It was true. Cornells Provoest was not well paid. Although both he and the other agents were provided with the distinctive van der Hest livery – which they were forced to wear until it fell, almost literally, off their backs – they were indeed poorly paid considering the work they did and the responsibility they took.

And yet, Cornelis Provoest's house was not the house of a man who lacked money. Whilst by no means ostentatious it was very comfortable by any standards. Paid for, no doubt, by the dowry of his rather bitter and discontented wife.

'I'm sorry your husband is ill,' Jannekyn said, ignoring the woman's barbs. 'Mynheer van der Hest has the sickness, too.'

'Hmph. I suppose I should say I be sorry to hear that,'

Margarete Provoest said with a sniff. 'But I daresay he do hev the best physician in the town at his bedside. Not like my man . . . '

'I think there is little the physician can do. The sickness runs its course. We should be thankful that it isn't plague. At least most people seem to recover from this, even though it leaves them weak.' Jannekyn smiled at the woman although she had been so rude and objectionable. But there was nothing to be gained by antagonizing her further. 'Now, may I see your husband? His spinners and weavers are . . . '

'No, you can't see my husband. He be far too ill to see anybody. But you can hev his tallyin's.' The woman turned away and rummaged in a drawer. 'Here, this be what you'll be wantin'.' She pushed a pile of papers at Jannekyn. 'Take them an' go. You must sort them out as best you can. And you can tell de Meester that we do hev no money to spare to pay any physician. My man must take his chance and trust in the good Lord's providence.' She almost pushed Jannekyn out of the door as she spoke.

Jannekyn was not sorry to leave. She had found Cornelis Provoest's wife a most unpleasant woman and could only feel sorry for the man who was married to her. She walked back to the counting house at Strangers' Hall through the market day crowds that jostled and haggled in the market place in the shadow of St Runwald's Church. Most people ignored her but now and again she was given a cheerful greeting from those who remembered her from the days when she used to be sent to shop by Garerdine. Days that seemed so long ago although it was in reality only the space of a few months.

Back in the comparative coolness of the counting house Jannekyn spread the papers that the agent's wife had given her across the table. Cornelis Provoest could read and write as well as tally and his accounts were written out clearly and fully – far more fully than was ever necessary for him to hand in to her. As long as money and materials tallied that was all that Jacob required that she record. She didn't have to know who did the actual spinning and weaving, all she needed to know was that nine spynning stons of wool had been given out, or that twelve pounds of yarn had been collected, or six pieces of cloth woven, and payment recorded accordingly.

She pored over the papers for some time before she could begin to make sense of the agent's system but gradually she began to understand and she could see that the accounts were faultless. One thing surprised her, however. Without exception, every name of Cornelis Provoest's list – both spinners and weavers – was English. Not a single member of the Dutch Congregation appeared to be employed in their own homes on work for Jacob van der Hest. Jannekyn checked the lists again. Mary Baker, spinner – Ann Carter, spinner – both of Trinity Lane; John Blackwell, weaver, of Queen Street. And so it went on, every name an English name.

She sat back and stared at the evidence in front of her. The last thing she would have expected was that Jacob van der Hest, with his hatred of the English and his contempt for their workmanship, would actually have employed them to work for him.

The whole thing was completely beyond her comprehension.

V

Jannekyn spent a sleepless night thinking about what she had discovered. It was totally uncharacteristic of Jacob to provide work for the English – unless, like Gabriel and Adam, their work was exceptional. But for the most part he maintained, quite unreasonably, that their work was never anything but shoddy. She listened to Gyles's gentle snoring from the other side of the curtain in the little room under the eaves. It was no good confiding in him, he saw everything in black and white. As far as he was concerned Jacob van der Hest was a good, honest and upright man, and if he chose to provide work for the heathen English then he was even more generous-hearted than his fellow men had given him credit for.

But Jannekyn knew better. She knew that it was not in Jacob's make-up to be generous to anyone, least of all the English, and the knowledge worried her. She wished desperately that she could talk to Adam.

She got up the next morning weary from lack of sleep, her body increasingly heavy and awkward from the child moving within her. Soon it would be born and would have to be fed and clothed. She couldn't imagine it. And even less could she imagine having any feeling for it. How could she love a child conceived as this one had been? She laid a hand over her swollen belly; oddly enough, she didn't hate it. She didn't feel anything for it except perhaps a weary irritation that it was making her so tired and ungainly.

She ate the oat cake that Gyles had left for her before he went to his dyeing sheds. Gyles always decided what they would eat and prepared it; Gyles cleaned the house and made the beds. It was very much Gyles's house and she felt rather like a guest – a very welcome guest, Gyles was unfailingly good to her – but nonetheless a guest. When she had finished her breakfast she began the walk over the tenterfields to Strangers' Hall. The frames were hung today with cloth that had been bleached in the fume house and the aroma of burning sulphur still hung like a pall over it. Jannekyn was glad to reach the counting house.

Hardly had she stepped inside when there was a tap at the window. She looked up and saw what looked like little more than a bundle of rags, but on closer inspection she could see that it was a scarecrow of a woman with a baby in her arms.

Jannekyn opened the window; 'What do you want?' she asked in her own tongue, then seeing the woman's perplexity she repeated the question in English.

'Work,' said the woman, when she understood Jannekyn's question. 'I ain't got no work. The agent shoudda bin a week ago wiv me wool ta spin but he never come. I went to 'is 'ouse but 'is wife said you'd got all 'is papers so I oughta come an' see you . . . ma'am,' she added as an afterthought.

'What is your name?' Jannekyn asked.

'Lizzie. Lizzie Fairley, ma'am.' The woman shifted the baby from one arm to the other.

'Wait a minute, Lizzie.' Jannekyn went over to the table and leafed through Cornelis Provoest's papers. After a minute she said, 'Lizzie Fairley – one spynning ston, twenty-third day of August. Is that you?'

'Thass roight, ma'am. Th' agent shoudda fetched it away a week ago yissday an' lef' me anuther lot. But 'e ain't never bin.' The woman looked anxiously at Jannekyn. 'I need the money, ma'am.'

Jannekyn was slightly nonplussed. She was not used to dealing directly with the spinners. Where is the yam that you have spurt from the wool left with you by Mynheer Cornelis?' she asked.

'Here, ma'am. Here it is.' The woman unwrapped several reels of yarn done up in a bundle carried over her shoulder. 'You'll find that tally with what the man left. I ain't kep' none back and I never damped it to make it weigh more. I only wetted it a little to stop it flyin' about like that alwuss do when there's thunder about but that soon dried orf.' She said all this in an anxious gabble, looking from Jannekyn to the reels and back again.

Jannekyn frowned. She found it difficult to follow the woman's broad dialect. The woman, misinterpreting her look, went on hurriedly, 'Thass all even – look. As even as ever that can be.'

'Yes, yes, that I can see.' Jannekyn pinched her lip. 'I think we should take these to the warehouse, Lizzie Fairley. You shall leave them there and take more wool. I will see that you are paid. Come, now. This way.'

With more assurance than she felt Jannekyn led the way to the warehouse. Even now she could not enter it without a shudder and a feeling of nausea but she fought it down and went inside, with Lizzie Fairley close behind, the child whimpering in her arms.

The place was full of wool and bodies; children scuffling about the floor half-naked sorting lengths from evil-smelling fleeces and several more women like Lizzie Fairley who had taken their courage in both hands and brought their yarn because the agent hadn't called for it. One of the other agents, Lucas Archer, was trying to gain some kind of order. Jannekyn went to him with Cornelis Provoest's records and together they dealt with the women – checking and weighing the reels and handing out more carefully weighed wool. Lucas Archer worked very quickly and it wasn't until the women had gone and also the string of weavers that had followed them, that Jannekyn began to get a glimmer of understanding as to what was going on.

Thoughtfully, she made her way back to the counting house. She couldn't believe that those poor wretches were as careless and dishonest as Lucas Archer had made out, but he had worked too swiftly for her to argue and for the most part they had gone away satisfied with their payment, little though it had seemed. There were still a few workers from Wyvenhoe and Boxted who hadn't brought their work in and Lucas Archer had agreed, to collect and deliver to them in addition to his own rounds. Jannekyn hoped it wouldn't be many days before Cornelis Provoest was back; it was as much as she could do now to cope with her own work without this extra burden.

But it still worried her. Lizzie Fairley's look of frightened apprehension as she watched her reels being weighed haunted her. She spoke of it to Gyles but he was totally without sympathy.

'Isn't that just like the English?' he said. 'Mynheer van der Hest gives them employment out of the goodness of his heart and what do they do? Cheat and lie and steal. No wonder the women looked frightened – they were afraid of being found out. The wonder is that de Meester wastes his time and money employing them. But he's a good man, one of the Lord's Chosen. He deserves to prosper.'

But Jannekyn was still not happy and on the pretext of a mistake in Cornelis Provoest's records she went along to Trinity Lane, where Lizzie Fairley and several of the others lived.

A cool September breeze tempered the sun's heat as she made her way from the market place through the narrow Pelham's Lane into Culver Lane and then on to Trinity Lane where the spinners lived in a block of hovels known as Trinity Poors Row. It was hardly a row; the one-roomed cottages stood in a kind of rough semicircle round a dust-baked yard where the children squabbled their days away until they were old enough to work – either in the fields or sorting wool.

Jannekyn picked her way between the grubby little urchins;

conscious of her elaborate gown. The people who lived in these hovels would not notice the tears in the lace and darns in the skirt, nor the sweat-marks under the armpits of Katherine's cast-off. They would only see the delicate ruched satin and the beaded bodice. She wished she had had the forethought to dress in something plainer.

'Lizzie Fairley. I am looking for Lizzie Fairley,' she said to the most intelligent-looking urchin.

The boy looked up and jerked a grimy thumb towards an open doorway. Jannekyn went over and knocked but as her eyes became accustomed to the gloom inside she could see Lizzie Fairley. She was cowering in a corner near the cold ashes of what had been a fire, with a blackened cooking pot hanging over it.

'Lizzie Fairley?' The woman didn't move. 'Lizzie Fairley? Can I come in? I mean you no harm.'

Still the woman didn't move.

'Wot d'yew want wiv comm' 'ere? Wot d'yew want wiv us?' A big, red-haired woman with no teeth came up behind Jannkeyn. 'Thass orl roight, Lizzie. We'll look arter yer,' she called to the woman in the corner.

Two more women had come to join the red-head and Jannekyn suddenly felt hemmed in and threatened. It was late in the afternoon and she'd told nobody where she was going. These women could kill her and nobody be any the wiser, she thought, in a moment of blind panic. She wished she'd never come.

She took a deep breath and turned to the three women behind her, barring her escape. 'Is one of you Mary Baker?' she asked.

'She is.' The red-head pointed to a straggly-haired blonde.

'Are you Ann Carter, then?' Jannekyn asked the red-head.

'No. She's Ann Carter.' The blonde pointed to the third woman.

'I ain't done nuffin',' Ann Carter said truculently. 'You come from Strangers' 'All, don't yer? Come to see we ain't kep' no yarn back, ain't yer?'

'No, indeed, that is not why I have come.' Jannekyn wasn't sure how to proceed. Her English was good but she was having difficulty in following the heavy dialect of these women and she had no idea how to overcome their understandable hostility. Again she realized the foolishness of her errand and wished she'd had the good sense to stay away from these people. If they were being treated badly that was their own look-out. Then she glimpsed Lizzie Fairley, still cowering in her corner. Poor woman. How could she ever hope to stand up for herself? Jannekyn passed a hand across her forehead. If only it wasn't so hot she might be able to think more clearry. But the cool breeze she had felt earlier didn't penetrate this dust-baked yard and the heat, coupled with the lingering smell of raw wool that came from the cottages, stifled her, making her feel faint and nauseous.

With as much dignity as she could muster under the circumstances she said, 'Do you mind if I sit down for a moment?' at the same time sliding gently to the ground as her legs buckled under her.

It was, in fact, the most fortunate thing that could have happened to her. Never quite losing consciousness, she could hear the women, at home with a situation they were all familiar with and which reduced them all to equals, fussing round her as they lifted her and laid her on the floor in the comparative coolness of the cottage. One of them put a battered cup to her lips and she tasted warm, brackish water that made her choke and brought her back to full consciousness.

'Poor mawther. Gettin' near yer time, ain't yer?' Mary Baker said, as the four women squatted round her.

'I think another month or so.' Jannekyn struggled to sit up as she spoke.

'Like me.' The red-head patted her belly. 'My fourth. 'Ow many yew got?'

'This will be my first'

'Thass allwuss the worst,' the women agreed. They settled Jannekyn on a rough stool and began to discuss their experiences and those of others they had known. Jannekyn listened to their tales, which were both colourful and lurid, yet told with the sympathetic compassion of women who shared a common painful lot, a sharing that included Jannekyn in a way nothing else could have done.

As they talked it became apparent that a woman called Susan, whom they must have summoned when Jannekyn fainted, was the midwife for the area. She was older than the rest, a small, witch-like creature with sparse grey hair and hands like claws, claws which could, as the others vouch-safed, be as strong as iron yet as gentle as silk. That they all loved and respected Susan there was no doubt.

'But, beggin' yer pardon, ma'am, yew won't hev no need of the loikes o' Susan at yor lyin'-in,' the red-haired woman said.

'Maybe not,' Susan said sagely. 'But jest because she's foreign and well-ta-do don't mean her labour'll be any easier or different from yours or moine.'

Impetuously, Jannekyn laid her hand on Susan's arm. 'I only wish you could come to me when my time comes. I think I should feel safe with you.'

'I doubt Master van der Hest . . . ' Susan said slowly, then, as if making up her mind, 'But if you called for me I'd come.'

'Not only Mynheer van der Hest,' Jannekyn said. 'My husband . . . '

''E's that ole dyer what live down by the river, ain't 'e?' Mary Baker asked.

'That is so. Gyles de Troster.' A shadow crossed Jannekyn's face. 'He does not like the English. He can be . . . ' she hesitated ' . . . sometimes he is a little awkward.'

All the women threw back their heads and laughed. 'Tell us a man that ain't,' they agreed.

'I'll tell yew who's the worst, too.' Suddenly, Lizzie Fairley joined in the conversation. She had hardly spoken up to now but Jannekyn had noticed that her hands had been busy with her distaff all the time.

'Yor ole man ain't no worse than anybody elses,' Redhead said with a laugh.

'I ain't talkin' about my ole man. I'm talkin' about th' agent.'

'Now, Liz, this ain't the toime . . . ' the other women warned uncomfortably, careful of this new, fragile friendship.

But Jannekyn leaned forward. 'Yes, it is,' she said. 'This is exactly the time. In fact, this is what I came to see you all about in the first place. Tell me, does Cornelis Provoest treat you all well?'

She looked round at the women. Susan, like herself, had been given a rough stool to sit on, the others squatted on their haunches or stood leaning against the wall. Each seemed reluctant to speak first. It was Lizzie, who had at the beginning been the most fearful, who again spoke up. She stepped forward.

'Here, ma'am, see: this?' She held out a length of the yarn she had just spun. Thass noice an' even, ain't it? No snags an' snarls, all the same thickness?'

Jannekyn ran her fingers along it. 'It feels perfect to me.'

'Well, yew should 'ear ole red-shanks – beggin' yer pardon, ma'am, but thass what we call th' agent 'cause of the red stockin's of 'is livery – he go through the reels an' complain somethin' terrible. An' if 'e find the least bit thass got through thicker or thinner 'e knock a penny orf a reel 'ere and tuppence orf there. Sometimes we don't git half wass due to us 'cause o' the fines he trump up. Thass roight, ain't it?' Lizzie turned to the others for support.

They all nodded in agreement. 'An' 'e complain we wet the yarn to make it weigh 'eavy so we can keep bite back for ourselves,' Mary Baker added, taking courage from Lizzie.

'You hev to wet it a bit when there's thunder about,' Ann Carter explained. 'Else that fly all over the place. But that soon dry.'

''E even say we put stones in to make it weigh 'eavier,' Lizzie went on. 'But that ain't true; 'E carry stones in 'is pocket and 'e slip 'em in when 'e think we can't see.'

'I don't remember the last toime I got paid my due,' Ann Carter said. ''E allwuss manage to dock our money for somethin'. 'E's a rogue, ma'am, an out an' out rogue. There ain't no other word for it. But what can we do?'

'Ye see, at least we git *somethin'*, which is more'n some poor folks do,' Lizzie said. 'So we dursen't complain too loud or 'e'll give the work to other people an' we shan't hev none at all. There ain't that much about'

'No, mere ain't,' Ann Carter agreed. 'An' thass how 'e manage to git away with it. Moind yew, th' agents are all the same. They're all as bad as each other. My man's a common weaver.' She jerked her thumb through the open door towards one of the other cottages and Jannekyn realised that the dull click of a loom had been constantly in the background throughout her visit. 'Ole red-shanks treat 'im somethin' cruel. Allwuss complainin' and finin' 'im so 'e scarce make enough to buy bread for the children. But there's so many poor 'earts wivont work that 'e dursen't argue.' She sighed. 'At least we do git a few coppers. Thass better'n hevin' to go on the parish.'

Jannekyn listened, growing more and more concerned at what she was hearing. There was little she could do at present to improve their lot but she offered them sympathy and promised to do whatever she could.

'I don't see there's much you can do, ma'am, beggin' yer pardon, but thass noice to know somebody care about us,' Mary Baker said.

Jannekyn left them then and made her way home. What Mary Baker had said may have been true, maybe there was little she could do to improve their lot, but Jannekyn understood what was going on now in Jacob van der Hest's empire of corruption.

It was always easier to fight a battle when you knew what the enemy was up to.

VI

Jacob's illness left him weak and listless. He went to the Bay Hall each day and to church on Sundays but such was his reliance on Jannekyn that he was content to leave a good deal of the day-to-day management of his business in her capable hands.

Of course he visited the counting house. He brought more of Katherine's cast-off gowns and insisted that Jannekyn have yet another one made up from a bolt of the new blue chamblett.

'But I have gowns,' she protested as he dumped the heap of clothes on the table in front of her. 'More than enough. I have no room ... '

'Give them away. They are misshapen from the child you

carry. Have this blue made up for after your lying-in.' He had missed her; he couldn't take his eyes off her; he wanted to give her things, to burden her with gratitude towards him. It incensed him that she should regard him so coolly, with as little feeling as if he had been a beetle under her foot. He hated her and himself for this mad, adulterous longing she roused in him, a longing that had to be stifled at all costs and only allowed to break out in little, unimportant things like showering dresses on her.

When he had gone, Jannekyn fingered the expensive materials. Some of the gowns Katherine had hardly worn before casting them off. She gave a wry smile; it was typical of Jacob that his generosity confined itself to making use of his wife's extravagance, he could never bear to part with hard cash if there was any possible alternative. Even the blue chamblett had come from stock so it wouldn't be missed. She held it against her cheek. It was nice, and Adam had made it, she was sure. She would have it made up in the same style as the crimson Jacob had given her at the beginning of the year. That was still her best gown. She had worn it on her wedding day to help her not to feel quite so far from Adam. Tears pricked her eyes. Dear Adam, how she longed for him.

Stifling these thoughts she turned back to her work. She was going through each agent's accounting system, finding some easier to decipher than others, and she had discovered that although every agent had at least one or two English people on their books, for the most part all the spinners and weavers were of their own Congregation. Only Cornelis Provoest and Lucas Archer had extensive dealings with the English. But she suspected that they all augmented their meagre wages by fines and exploitation in some way or other. No wonder Jacob had been reluctant to investigate when she had told him of her suspicions regarding his agents. He was content to let them exploit the poor – indeed, he encouraged it. It meant he could keep their wages to a minimum.

Quietly, Jannekyn had begun to alter this: She had doubled the wages of the agents in return for their promise of fair treatment of the spinners and weavers. Several of the agents, chosen in the first place for their lack of scruples, thought they could have it both ways and continued to exploit their workers. When she found this out Jannekyn dismissed them and shared their work among the others.

'She do be a hard one, that,' one complained, fresh from tasting her displeasure that his accounts were not in order. 'She do be as hard as old van der Hest himself, in her way. The way she do carry on she might almost be his kin.'

'You're right, there,' said another. 'And her so pretty and gentle-lookin'. You wouldn't think she had it in her.'

'Must be near to 'er time, too. She'll do the child a mischief, carryin' on the way she do.'

Jannekyn sometimes felt that way herself. There was so much she wanted to do, so much that needed to be looked into without Jacob's beady eye watching her, that she worked longer and longer, ignoring her body's aches of protestation and the way her feet swelled so that she could hardly walk and her fingers so that she could scarcely hold a quill. But she was slowly, painfully slowly, improving the lot of the poor creatures who had for so long been exploited.

It was inevitable that Jacob should discover what she was doing. She knew he would but she had hoped that by the time he found out everything would be working so smoothly and efficiently that he would regard it as an improvement.

She might have known differently.

The day started badly. She got up feeling sick and ill. Even early in the morning she had difficulty in getting her shoes on because her feet were so swollen,

'You ought to stay at home and rest,' Gyles said anxiously. 'The child will soon be born. You must tell de Meester that you will not go to the counting house any more until after you are brought to bed. He is a good man. He will bring the work here to you.'

Jannekyn smiled to herself. Gyles knew how to look after himself. He hadn't for a moment suggested that she should no longer do Jacob's work, only that it should be brought here to her. She flexed her fingers. They weren't too stiff and swollen today. If only she could get through the next week everything would be sorted out. Then it wouldn't matter.

She walked slowly up through the tenterfields. The gentle upward slope of the land seemed like the side of a steep mountain and she had to stop and rest several times on the way, but at last she reached the counting house.

Jacob was already there.

He was sitting at the table with her ledgers spread in front of him, his thick black eyebrows drawn into a straight line above his beak-like nose and his mouth set in a thin, downward curve.

He looked up as she came through the door.

'What is all this?' he snapped, without so much as a good morning to greet her, tapping the ledger with a long finger. 'Who gave you leave to pay the agents more money, idle rapscallions that they are? They do little enough to earn their bread, without paying them more man their due.'

Jannekyn supported herself against the door frame for a moment to recover from the walk up the hill. 'It's not costing you a penny more than before,' she said with a trace of sarcasm in her voice. 'As you'll see if you look more carefully.'

'I can see perfectly well what has happened,' he said tetchily. 'And that's another thing. Who gave you leave to sack half my agents?'

'They were greedy and dishonest, so I dismissed them.'

'You take a great deal on yourself, madam! How dare you dismiss men who have been in my employment for years? Men who have worked for me faithfully and well?'

'Because they were rogues.' She moved wearily from the door into the room. 'No,' she said, correcting herself, 'they were not rogues. They were so badly paid that they had no choice but to make what extra they could from the poor wretches they supplied with work. If they were rogues it was *you* that made them rogues because you paid them scarcely enough to live on.' She shook her head sadly. 'I should have known. I should have realized long ago what was happening.'

'It is none of your business!' He stood up, towering over her like a great, black crow. 'You are here to do *my* bidding, not to do as you please. You will see the agents today – *all* of them, and you will reinstate those you had the audacity to dismiss.'

'Very well, Meester. But it will cost you twice as much.' She watched him cynically. She knew the struggle that was going on inside him.

'Do the agents that are left get through the work?'

She nodded. 'I've re-organized their routes to make it easier.'

'Good.' He pulled thoughtfully at his beard. 'But they're being paid too much, far too much. I can't afford . . . '

'Their wage bill is no bigger than it was before.' She sat down. There was a nagging pain in her back which every now and then shot a sharp stab through her. She rubbed her side to ease it.

'It was always too much.' He consulted the ledgers again. 'A system of fines will soon take care of that, I think.' He picked up a quill.

'If you fine the agents they'll only make up their money from the spinners and weavers.'

He looked up at her with a ghost of his wolfish smile. 'Of course they will, my dear. Didn't you realize, that's how the system works.'

'But it's not *fair*. Those poor wretches . . .'

'. . . Are luckier than those who have no work at all and depend upon poor relief.' As he spoke he was busy calculating on a scrap of paper.

'That's not the point.' She got up and leaned across the table. 'They deserve just payment for the work they do.'

He spared her little more than a glance. 'Rubbish, madam. They should be grateful to be given work at all. Now, listen to this. You can dock sixpence from the agents every time they . . .'

'I will *not*!' She banged her hand down on the table. 'I will not have anything more to do with a business that makes its money from starving the poor. You are a hard man, Jacob van der Hest. I have worked hard to give a fairer share to those people. It would cost you no more and gain you respect from them. But you will have none of it. Very well, I will have no more of your ways, either.'

'That is an idle threat and you know it.' He waved it aside and said more gently, 'You are young, Jannekyn. You don't understand the dog-eat-dog ways of business! To prosper a man needs to be hard. It's a hard, cruel world we live in. Now, come along, I'll show you what I have in mind. Plainly, we can't reduce the agents' wages when you have only just put them up but there are other ways of cutting them . . .'

'No,' she said quietly, but her voice was icy with fury, 'I meant what I said. I will have no more of your scheming, miserly ways. I uncovered this corruption – and if there'd been the time I've no doubt I would have found the same story right through, from the broggers who sell you the raw wool down to the cloth you export. Jacob van der Hest, you have built your business on the rotten roots of corruption. How can you hold your head up as a pillar of the Church and a respected member of the Bay Hall? You make me sick!'

He paled. 'Enough, madam! I will hear no more of this talk. Remember your position!'

'I am remembering my position.' She drew herself up to her full height. 'For the past eighteen months and more I've had little chance to forget it. I came here from Flanders as your niece, your own brother's daughter, but you disowned me and allowed me to be treated as less than a servant. Why you should have done this I have never yet discovered.' She lifted her chin. 'But now I don't care. In fact, I'm glad. If you hadn't disowned me, *Uncle Jacob*, by all that is holy, I would disown you, for the callous hypocrite that you are.' She turned and went to the door.

'You'll regret those words, madam.' His voice was like a whiplash. 'You are in no position to do as you please. Remember, you are dependent on me.'

She came back and stood looking at him. 'For what? For a roof over my head?' She tossed her head. 'Not any longer. *You* married me off to Gyles de Troster. Don't you realize that in doing that you pushed me the first step along the road to freedom? I am no longer dependent on you, Jacob van der Hest. I am the wife of Gyles de Troster.'

'De Troster is in my pay. I'll see he starves.'

'Will you, Mynheer? Will you deprive yourself of the services of the best dyer in Colchester? Will you turn us out of our cottage so that we are forced to go and live in the cottage Mynheer Lewys de Hase holds ready for us?' She smiled, a mirthless smile. 'Ah, yes. You may turn pale to think that your nearest rival cannot wait to get his hands on my husband's services.'

'You lie.' His voice was barely more than a whisper.

'Turn us from our cottage and you'll see.' She leaned forward and picked up the ledger lying in front of Jacob and snapped it shut. 'I have finished with you, Jacob van der Hest. No longer will I allow you to treat me like dirt under your foot, no longer will I be a party – albeit an innocent, ignorant party – to your wickedness and corruption. You may look for some other poor innocent fool to do your bidding.'

Before he could reply she turned from him and walked out of the door, her head held high and her back straight, leaving him staring after her with an expression of pure venom mixed with an incredulous disbelief that she could have so deliberately defied him. Nobody had ever done that to Jacob van der Hest before.

Jannekyn made her way slowly and painfully home, stopping every now and then to hold her side against the searing pain that knifed through her. She was halfway across the tenterfields before she realized that in her fury she had forgotten that Jacob still held the trump card. A trump card he would not hesitate to use. Adam, the man she loved.

She sank to her knees in pain and despair. 'Oh, God,' she cried, 'what have I done?'

Chapter Four

I

After she had gone Jacob began to pace up and down, his hands behind his back, repeatedly thrusting the ball of his fist into his cupped hand in a gesture of rage and frustration.

Nobody had ever dared to speak to him like this before; not even Katherine, his frigid, hypochondriac wife; not even Dionis, in her desperate defiance before her short-lived marriage to Abraham de Baert.

'She's near her time. Women are not themselves at such times,' a little voice inside him said. 'Speak reasonably to her and she'll come back.'

Grovel to her? Never! It was not in Jacob van der Hest's nature to grovel. Let her go. Let her find out just what she had brought on herself today. A little pressure on Gyles de Troster and he would turn her out of his house.

'To starve?' the persistent inner voice said. 'To lose the shapely curves of that lovely body, which even pregnancy can't spoil? That lovely body that you will no longer be able to feast your eyes on?'

Yes, let her starve. Why shouldn't she suffer? It would be a fit punishment for the torment she had caused him. He sat down to try to think more rationally. It was no use, Gyles de Troster wouldn't turn her out. She was his wife so he would do his right and proper duty by her. And he couldn't afford to antagonize de Troster because to do so would lose him the best dyer in Colchester. He thumped his fist on the table. He thought he had been so clever in marrying the girl off to the old dyer, but now, here he was, thwarted by his own initial cunning.

He began to walk about again, blind hatred in his heart for this girl who could rouse in him such feelings as he'd never experienced before, yet who looked on him with such cold disdain. She had never given him more attention than absolutely necessary, regarding him most of the time with a passive obedience which infuriated him and performing her duties with efficient disinterest. Never once had she given him so much as a warm smile. No, her smiles and warm looks were reserved for that young upstart of an English weaver . . .

Jacob ceased his pacing and looked over towards the loom shed. Adam Mortlock would soon be out of his time and want paying a man's wage. Jacob had already made provision in his mind for that. Gabriel Birchwood, Adam's master, was an old man and becoming slow with the shuttle, and his eyesight was failing. Jacob had planned to get rid of him when the time came and keep Adam on in his place. He stroked his beard. Young Mortlock was a fine weaver, the best in the district. It would be a pity to lose him, but to throw him out now was the one sure way to bring the girl to her senses. True, it might be a week or two before the news filtered through to her, but as soon as she realized that her beloved Adam had joined the ranks of the hungry unemployed weavers who rioted all over the town she would come crawling back. And there would be no more nonsense about raising wages; when he'd finished with her she'd know once and for all who was master. The thought gave him a thrill of satisfaction.

He picked up his cane and walked briskly across to the loom shed.

As soon as he reached the door the clacking of the looms speeded up. Everyone feared the grim-visaged Dutchman and heads bent a little closer and shuttles flew a little faster in his presence.

He walked over and stood behind Gabriel. The old man was threading up his loom and when he became conscious of Jacob's presence he became nervous and began to fumble, breaking threads and mixing the wrong colours.

Jacob pushed him to one side impatiently and leaned forward to examine the work. Then he turned to the loom master. 'Pay him and send him away. He's too old; his eyesight is failing. His work is slow and full of faults.' He gave Gabriel another push that caught him off balance and the old man fell to the floor.

Adam had been watching and he left his loom and hurried over to his old master's assistance. Over the years he had picked up enough of the language of the Dutch Congregation to know exactly what Jacob was saying, and he was furious at this unjustified attack on Gabriel.

'Get back to work!' Jacob barked, raising his cane to him.

Adam put up his arm to fend off the cane just as Jacob took a step forward and he caught the rich clothier a blow to the side of the jaw that sent him reeling.

It was purely accidental but it played straight into Jacob's hands. When he recovered his balance his face was a mask of fury.

'You, too!' he shouted, pointing to the door. 'Take your belongings and go!' He was beside himself with rage.

After a first involuntary gasp the other weavers buried their heads industriously in their work, watching nervously out of the corner of an eye so that they didn't miss what was going on, but anxious not to suffer the same fate as the two unfortunate Englishmen.

Adam knew it was useless to argue. He hadn't meant to strike Jacob but it had happened and in this strange, wild mood the rich clothier would never listen to excuses or apologies. Not that Adam wanted to apologize. After the way Gabriel had been treated Adam only wished he'd hit Jacob harder. He helped the old man to gather up his few belongings and together they left the loom shed.

'Whatever ails the man?' Gabriel said anxiously. 'D'you think he've taken leave of his senses? I never seen a man in sech a way afore.' He caught Adam's arm. 'Here, boy, let me ketch holda your arm. I'm all a-tremble. Oh, Lor, I dunno what'll become on us. We shall hetta go on the parish, I doubt. My ole woman 'on't think mucha that. Why'd 'e do it, boy? Why'd 'e chuck us out? I ain't never seen anything like the way 'e carried on. That look like a put-up job to me. Here, stop a minute, let me ketch me breath.'

Adam stopped. He was only half listening to Gabriel's gabbling, he knew it was fear and shock making the usually taciturn old man so garrulous. While the old man stood, panting, he looked about him, his eyes going first, as they always did, to the counting house, to catch a glimpse of Jannekyn. But today she wasn't there.

'No!' Jacob's voice roared from the door of the loom shed. 'It's no use looking for her there. She's gone!' He waved his arm in the direction of the tenterfields.

Adam turned his head and followed Jacob's gesture. Far

across the tenterfields he could see a slow-moving figure that could only be Jannekyn. Surely, Jacob wouldn't have sent her to walk home in labour. No, there was more to it than that, he was sure of it. If only he could see her, talk to her . . . He looked down at Gabriel, clinging to his arm. He couldn't leave him and follow her. Gently, he tried to hurry the old man along.

'Wass ter become of us? Wass ter become of us?' was all he could say, over and over again.

'Don't worry, master, we'll find a way,' Adam soothed automatically as he led the trembling old weaver home.

Gabriel's wife was putting lavender between the linen in the clothes press when they arrived home. Adam explained to her what had happened while they put Gabriel to bed with a posset.

'But, why?' she asked. 'Why should 'e do this to yer, boy?'

'I can only think it must have something to do with Jannekyn,' Adam said, his brow furrowed with worry.

Bessie sat down heavily by the hearth. So it was that young Dutch girl again. She sighed. Oh, why couldn't the boy take up with some decent English girl instead of courting trouble with a foreigner? He knew very well the Dutch and English didn't mix. She wished Gabriel had never gone to work at Strangers' Hall in the first place, she'd always known no good would come of it.

Weren't no call for 'im to treat Gabriel so, as I see it,' Bessie said sadly. 'Pore ole man, that ain't nothin' to do with 'im.'

'No. It was Master van der Hest's way of getting at me. I'm sure of it. And that's what makes me think Jannekyn must be at the bottom of it all.'

'I dunno what you mean.' Bessie shook her head.

Adam squatted down beside her. 'One. Master van der Hest was in a foul temper.' He began ticking off his fingers. 'Two.

Jannekyn wasn't in the counting house, she was making her way home.'

'P'raps 'er time 'ad come. It must be pretty near.'

'I'd thought of that. But I can't see why that should put Master van der Hest in such a filthy temper, and he'd surely never make her walk home like that.'

'No, thass right enough, boy.' Bessie nodded, her gnarled fingers, always busy, absently pleating the folds of her skirt, 'So what d'you reckon?'

'I reckon she's walked out on him. And the only way he could think of to get back at her was to get rid of me. He knows that what'll hurt her most is to know that I'm suffering through her actions. Same as he knew he'd only got to treat the master badly to get at me.' He smiled sadly at Bessie. 'It's always harder to watch the suffering of someone you love than to bear it yourself.'

'Thass right enough, boy,' Bessie said again. 'And Master van der Hest is wiry enough to know that.'

'Oh, he's shrewd, all right,' Adam agreed. He frowned. 'I just wish I knew about Jannekyn . . . If only I could see her . . . speak to her . . . '

Bessie laid a hand on his arm. 'Why don't you go along then, boy? It'd set your mind at rest.' And perhaps that'll put an end to it, she thought privately.

Adam shook his head. 'No, that would play right into his hands. But if she doesn't know he's put us out . . . ' He was silent for a moment, then he went on, 'Oh, Mistress Bessie, it'll break my heart never to see her, never to know what's caused all this, but whatever it is, it would only make it harder for her to bear if she knew I was suffering for it.' His voice broke and he put his head in his hands. 'There's only one thing for it. Whatever happens, I must make sure she never sees me again.'

II

Jannekyn struggled on. The pain in her back and side was becoming worse and she had to keep stopping to let it wash over her before going on again. Eventually, she reached the cottage.

'Gyles,' she called weakly as she clung to the door post. 'Gyles, help me.'

Gyles came hurrying across from the dyeing shed, up to his elbows in blue dye. He took one look at her. 'Oh, my dear child,' he said. 'Here, give me your arm. Let's get you up to your bed.'

He helped her up the stairs and undressed her down to her shift. Then he went downstairs and scrubbed the dye off his hands and arms. When he had done this he went back to her. She lay, bathed in sweat despite the chill day, screwing her face in pain as each spasm overtook her.

'Is de Meester sending the midwife?' he asked anxiously.

'De Meester will send nobody ... ' She paused for another pain. ' ... And I wouldn't have her if he did. I've done with him for good.'

Gyles looked at her in alarm. Had she taken leave of her senses? 'Done with him?' he said. 'What do you mean? You can't have done with him.'

'I've done with him,' she insisted, breathless from the pain. 'I'll have no more of his evil, corrupt ways.'

Gyles frowned. The child was clearly not herself to speak of de Meester in such terms. Everyone knew what a high-principled man he was, a pillar of Church and Bay Hall alike. However, now was not the time for argument; there were more pressing matters to attend to. He had seen birth before, although it was the one blessing his Abigail had been denied. But he knew what was required. He went downstairs again and put a large pot of water to heat over the fire.

By evening it was plain that all was not well. Jannkeyn was exhausted by the pains that racked her but the child still seemed reluctant to make its appearance. Helplessly, Gyles mopped her sweat-drenched face and let her drag at his arms as she screamed with pain.

'Fetch Susan,' she muttered, during a brief respite. 'For God's sake fetch Susan. She'll know what to do.' Another pain tore at her. When it had subsided she went on, 'Trinity Poors Row. Ask at Tripity Poors Row.'

'But de Englesen live there,' he muttered. He wanted no English under his roof. But another scream from Jannekyn sent him rushing from the house.

He never remembered how he got up the hill that was Maidenburgh Street and across the market place and through the lanes to Trinity Poors Row.

'Susan.' He managed to say with what little breath he had left in his body. 'Susan. For Mevrouw de Troster.'

The people gathered round him and gabbled sympathetically in their strange English tongue. But they didn't seem to understand him. 'Susan,' he kept repeating. 'For Mevrouw de Troster.'

Eventually, a wizened stick of a woman appeared and pointed to herself. 'Susan,' she said, nodding. Then, indicating a big belly and screwing her face in imitation pain, 'Mevrouw de Troster?'

'Ja! Ja!' Gyles nodded eagerly and caught her hand to pull her away with him.

She held up her free hand. 'Wait' She hurried to her cottage and came back a moment later with a bundle. Then she allowed him to hurry her back with him to where Jannekyn still writhed, exhausted, in the agony that would not let her be.

Susan took one look at her. 'The child or the mother?' she asked Gyles. 'I doubt I can save both.' Gyles nodded uncomprehending. He didn't understand a word of what the old woman had said and Jannekyn was too far gone to translate.

Dawn was breaking over the tenterfields when the child was at last born. It was only due to Susan's strength and skill that it was born alive and for three days and nights Jannekyn hovered between life and death, unknowing and uncaring of what was going on around her.

On the fourth day, when her son was placed at her breast, she opened her eyes and saw the little downy head and was filled with an overwhelming, possessive love.

Susan, watching, saw this and looked across at Gyles, who had scarcely left his wife's side. 'She'll live,' she said with a nod.

Gyles understood and with a sigh of profound relief went back to his dyeing shed. Twice already Jacob had sent his servant to see if the green stamett was ready, in spite of Gyles's message that his wife was sick and likely to die so he couldn't leave her side. He glanced across the tenterfields as he tended his vats. 'Bless my soul,' he said to himself as he saw the red-liveried servant coming yet again. 'Has de Meester no heart?'

But in a way hie couldn't help feeling relieved. Although he hadn't taken too much notice of Jannekyn's wild ramblings in the delirium of pain, it would have been awkward if she *had* fallen out with de Meester as she'd claimed. True, Lewys de Hase had offered work but the pokey little cottage that went with it was in Angel Lane and every drop of water would have to be lugged from the stock well, no mean distance when you used as much water as a dyer did. No, Gyles was very happy with things as they were, and if Mynheer van der Hest was impatient for his cloth, well, at least that was better than having his home and living taken away because of some stupid argument between de Meester and de meisje, as he always thought of Jannekyn.

As for Jannekyn, as far as she was concerned that episode in her life was finished. The moment she set eyes on her little son his beginnings were forgotten and to her great surprise her heart swelled with fierce, protective love. He was perfect and he was hers. He belonged to her as nothing had since her little cat in the village outside Ypres where she had been brought up. It was a long time since she had even thought about her home across the sea. She wondered if her poor, sick father was still alive. Her eyes filled with tears at the memory of their last farewells and a tear fell on the baby's face, making him give a little whimper of surprise.

'I shall call you Jan, after my father,' she whispered to him softly. 'My little Jan.'

Jannekyn's return to strength was slow. After Susan had left her she crept about the house unable to do much more than attend to the baby's needs, the cold November fogs doing nothing to assist her return to health.

Gyles had tolerated the old Englishwoman with a grudging acceptance that had turned to respect as he recognized her extraordinary skills; not only with the ergot of rye that had eased Jannekyn's pain but for her manipulative skill that had delivered the almost-doomed child alive, using fearsome-looking articles that were swiftly tied back in the bundle she had brought with her. And after the birth she had tended Jannekyn with a gentle competence, encouraging her back to life and feeding her back to strength. Maybe, he decided as he went about his work, just maybe, he had misjudged the English and they were not as bad as he'd thought. But this was not an admission he voiced aloud.

As the weeks wore on Gyles became surprised that Jannekyn

had no work brought to her from Strangers' Hall – he knew very well how much Jacob depended on her – but there had been nothing, not even an inquiry after her health. He began to wonder if perhaps there had been something in her strange outburst, after all. However, Jacob's servant still delivered and collected yarn and cloth regularly so there could be nothing very wrong.

After a great deal of thought, and in a round-about way, he broached the subject one evening as they were sitting by the fire, the baby asleep in the wooden cradle Gyles had made.

'He is a good child,' Gyles said, nodding towards little Jan. 'And thriving. I can see him grow daily.'

Jannekyn bent over her little son, smiling. 'Yes, he's very little trouble.' She moved the blanket away from his face.

'He can stay with me when you go back to the counting house,' Gyles offered. 'He will be warm in the drying shed and I will watch him carefully.'

She sat up straight, her eyes flashing. 'I'm never going back to that place. I told you that, Gyles, don't you remember?'

'I thought you were speaking in delirium,' he said, puzzled. 'I didn't pay much heed. Of course you'll have to go back. What will de Meester do without you, meisje?'

'I care nothing for Jacob van der Hest. He can manage as best he may. I will not go back to him. He's an evil man and corrupt in his dealings.' She spoke fiercely.

'Hush, meisje, someone will hear.' Gyles shifted the log on the fire with his foot, sending up a shower of sparks, at the same time looking over his shoulder as if he expected someone to be listening at the window. A worried frown creased his brow. 'It won't do to upset de Meester,' he said. 'We depend on him for everything.'

'I wish we didn't,' she said vehemently. 'I wish we could be done with him. He is evil. Wicked.'

'How can you say such things?' Gyles said, shocked. 'De Meester is a good man. He is a pillar of the Church and the Bay Hall . . . '

'He makes himself rich at the expense of poor creatures who have no defence against him.'

'He is no worse than the others. Lewys de Hase . . . '

'He is worse because he holds himself up to be better,' Jannekyn insisted. 'I will *not* go back to him.'

'What if he turns us out of our cottage?'

'He won't. Has your work for him fallen off?'

Gyles shook his head. 'No, I do as much for him as ever.'

'As I thought. You are the best dyer in Colchester. Nobody else blends colours as cleverly as you do. He knows very well that if he turns you out Lewys de Hase will be only too glad to have you as his dyer. He will not turn us out, never fear.'

Gyles chewed his beard. He didn't know how to cope with this new, rebellious mood in his wife. He was a peaceable man and wanted no trouble from any quarter. He decided to leave the matter for the present. Doubtless, before long, Jacob would come to fetch her and the matter would sort itself out. Until then, there was no point in discussing it further.

St Nicholas Eve and Twelfth Night came and went with little celebration in the de Troster cottage.

Jannekyn was still pale and listless. She tended the baby with a fierce love but deep in her heart there was an ache that gnawed at the very depth of her being. She realized now that just seeing Adam from time to time and knowing that he was working nearby in the loom shed had sustained her more than she had known, and she longed for the sight of him. It was for this reason and no other that she missed her work in Jacob's counting house. She worried, too, that Jacob might have made Adam suffer for her actions and she prayed nightly that this might not be so. Almost the worst thing was not knowing, but there was nobody she could ask. And so she fretted her time away, hiding her misery as best she could from Gyles, who worried that her return to health was so slow.

So, although he was still anxious for her, it pleased him when one bright morning in January, she announced that she felt strong enough to go to the market.

'Leave the child with me, then. He is too heavy for you to carry up the hill. See, I've made a corner for him in the drying shed on some bales of yarn.' Gyles was growing to love his little stepson and often looked after him while Jannekyn rested. 'Mind and put your thickest cloak on, meisje. The sun may be bright but the wind is chill and you are not yet strong.'

'Very well, Gyles.' Jannekyn smiled at her husband. He had been very patient with her listlessness of the past months and she owed it to him to pretend a brightness even if she didn't feel it.

She took a cloak lined with fur from her press. She had far too many clothes for a woman in her position, all showered on her by Jacob. Even to think of him sent a shudder of disgust through her. One day, she was sure, he would be shown up for the evil man that he was. She had not seen him since that fateful day she had walked out on him. Who now did the work that she had done she neither knew nor cared. She did know, though, that he would not have found it easy to find someone to take her place.

Slowly she walked along the river bank and up Maidenburgh Street. The market place was noisy with stall-holders shouting their wares and thronged with bystanders, most of them little able to do more than cast a longing eye on the goods displayed. Jannekyn bought fruit and vegetables, looking all the time for someone who might give her news of Adam. But she saw no one. All the news she gleaned was of starvation and unemployment among spinners and weavers. Too little work to spread among too many people had inevitably led wages to fall below living standards, and consequently to riots, bloody in places. She offered up a prayer of thankfulness that at least Adam had work – for Jacob would never risk losing his most skilled weaver, of that she was sure. But she feared he might have suffered in other ways. If only she knew . . . If only she could find out. She sighed and searched the crowd for a familiar face. But she searched in vain and at last, disappointed, she made her way home.

Gyles was talking to Nicholas Vrost, Jacob's servant, when she reached the cottage. He had brought yarn to be dyed in the new pale green colour that Gyles had recently developed by experimenting with his vegetable dyes.

'This is a special order. De Meester would like it within the week,' Nicholas Vrost was saying. He was a nasty little man, who tried to make up for his lack of stature by an imperious manner. Jannekyn had never liked him. Why, Mevrouw de Troster. I hope your health is improving and that we shall see you back at the counting house soon,' he said ingratiatingly.

Jannekyn looked at him warily. Could it be that Jacob had told nobody of their quarrel? It would be easy enough to explain her absence; it had been nothing short of fortuitous as far as he was concerned that it had coincided with the baby's birth. In that case, was Jacob simply waiting for her to go grovelling back to him?

She smiled. 'Not yet, I think, Mynheer Vrost. My time is fully taken up with my child at present.' She picked up little Jan from the bales of yarn where he lay cooing and looking at his fingers, newly discovered.

Nicholas Vrost turned back to Gyles. Within the week, then. Shall we say Friday?'

Gyles looked anxious. 'I don't think I can manage Friday, Baas,' he said. 'The yarn must be kept for two or three days after it has been boiled in the mordant before it can be dyed. And then it has to dry.' He shook his head. 'I doubt it will be ready before next Wednesday. Tuesday at the earliest'

'Can't you dispense with the mordant?' Nicholas Vrost said impatiently.

'Not if you want the dye to set, Baas. This is a new colour. I'm unwilling to experiment with a different mordant because I fear it may alter the shade.'

'Oh, very well, next Tuesday it will have to be, then. I dare-say it will be time enough now that there are fewer weavers in the loom shed and this is a special order.' Nicholas Vrost turned to go.

'Fewer weavers?' Jannekyn caught his arm. Then, lest he should think her over-anxious she let go and half-turned from him. 'Yes, I hear there is becoming less and less work about. Soon the whole town will fall into decay, I fear.'

Nicholas Vrost drew himself up to his full height. 'Mynheer van der Hest has no shortage of work for his weavers,' he said haughtily. 'It was insubordination that led him to dismiss the Englishman, not shortage of work.'

Jannekyn's mouth went dry. 'Insubordination?' she said weakly.

'Yes.' The little man swelled with his own importance. 'I'm told – it's only hearsay, mind, because the weaving sheds are not my province – but I'm told that the young English weaver knocked de Meester down and walked out. Nearly broke de Meester's jaw, I believe.' He turned to Jannekyn. 'Do you know the one I mean? Mortlock, I think the name is. Naturally enough, de Meester refused to have him back.'

'Yes, I think I know who you're talking about.' Jannekyn knew she had turned pale and she laid little Jan back in his nest and looked round for something to hold on to. 'But why should he have done such a thing?'

'Search me. It strikes me these weavers don't know when they're well off.'

'I thought you said there were two of them,' Gyles reminded him.

'That's right. The other one was the old Englishman; young Mortlock was his apprentice. De Meester had allowed young Mortlock to come too when he took the old man on because the youngster was in the middle of his apprenticeship, and this is how he got repaid. So he got rid of the pair of them, and not to blame him, either. Bah, I wouldn't trust these English any further than I could throw them.'

And that wouldn't be far, Jannekyn couldn't help thinking, you nasty, weedy little man. But aloud, she said, 'Ad ... the young man must surely have had a reason, if what you say is true. People don't just go around knocking their employers down ...'

Nicholas Vrost shrugged his shoulders. 'I couldn't say. I know it was all round the town at the time but I've forgotten the details now. Heaven's sake, it must be nearly three months since it all happened.' He turned to Gyles. 'I must be off. I'll see you next Tuesday, Mynheer de Troster. Make sure the yarn is ready by then, won't you?'

'I'll do my best, Mynheer Vrost.'

Jannekyn picked up little Jan and went into the cottage.

Nearly three months ago. That would take it back to All Saints' Tide. And little Jan had been born on the Eve of All Saints', the last day in October.

III

For several days Jannekyn worried and fretted over Adam. Her one fear had been that Jacob would make him suffer for her actions on that fateful day when she had walked out on him. But although something had obviously taken place it didn't sound as if it had been of Jacob's designing. She was completely baffled by what Nicholas Vrost had said and questions kept going round and round in her brain. Whatever had come over Adam to do such a dreadful thing? And, even more important – where was he now?

The following Sunday she accompanined Gyles to church for the first time since little Jan's birth. Gyles took his step-fatherhood very seriously and insisted on carrying the child up the hill to save Jannekyn's strength. He was as proud of little Jan as if he had fathered him himself and treated him with a firm gentleness that Jannekyn found quite touching. She had grown very fond of Gyles in the months they had been married. There had never been so much as a cross word between them and Gyles clearly cherished her as the daughter he had always wanted but been denied. If it were not for the persistent, gnawing longing for Adam she would not have been at all unhappy as Gyles de Troster's wife.

Which was not what Jacob van der Hest had intended at all.

He saw de Troster enter the church and take his seat with Jannekyn by his side, the child in her arms. Illness had given her face an almost transparent loveliness, showing up her delicate bone structure and the long, white line of her neck. Her figure, too, was slim again and softly curved. She gazed down at the child sleeping in her arms; motherhood had made her even more beautiful. He dragged his eyes away from her as he felt the old familiar stirring in his loins that only she could arouse.

He hated her. He hated her for the feelings she aroused in him. He hated her for making herself indispensable to him; the stupid fool who did her work now was an incompetent nincompoop. And he hated her for forcing him to get rid of the best weaver in Colchester. It wasn't even as if the ruse had worked. She *hadn't* come begging to come back to the counting house in order that he would reinstate young Mordock, as he'd expected her to. He couldn't imagine that she hadn't heard what had happened so perhaps her feelings for the young puppy weren't as strong as he'd thought.

Irritably, he shifted in his seat. Business wasn't going so well, either. She'd made the agents dissatisfied; they were being difficult about their increase in wages being eroded away again by fines, and he hadn't been able to find anybody skilled enough to replace the two English weavers. But at least he'd seen to it that young Mortlock wouldn't get work within thirty miles of Colchester. He allowed himself a grim smile of satisfaction on that score.

Jannekyn glanced across at him as he sat on the great padded seat reserved for the mighty. He sat alone, the household servants below and behind him. Katherine, of course, never came. Her health wouldn't allow it

He was dressed in his habitual black, his face set in deep, disagreeble lines and his mouth turned down at the corners in a thin, disapproving curve. She studied him. What pleasure had his wealth and position brought him? What comfort was it to him to know that he had been chosen by God if he found no comfort in his fellow men? For a moment she felt almost sorry for him, sitting in lonely isolation in his exalted place; but then she thought of Adam and her pity turned sour.

The Predikant droned on, mumbling into his beard words that brought no joy to the poverty-stricken families who huddled obediently below him, their minds more on their empty bellies than on the smug clichés that fell from his lips.

'Many are called but few are chosen,' he droned. 'And how fortunate those that are of the chosen few.' He cast a sycophantic glance in Jacob's direction.

'And what about the God of Love?' Jannekyn wanted to shout. 'What about the commandment that says "Thou shalt love thy neighbour as thyself"? How can you say that God chooses people who ignore mat commandment and become rich by grinding their neighbours into the dirt?'

But she didn't. She kept her thoughts to herself as she nursed her little Jan and worried over Adam. By the time she left the church she knew exactly what she must do.

She even risked talking it over with Gyles. Since having had cause to be grateful to Susan for her competence and common sense at the birth of little Jan, and afterwards for saving Jannekyn's life, he had not been quite so ready to condemn the English at every turn and she felt he might lend a more sympathetic ear than in the past.

'I've been thinking, Gyles,' she said that evening as they sat together in the firelight as was their habit in the long winter evenings. Little Jan was asleep in his cradle between them.

'Tell me, meisje. I know something's been troubling you for a long time.' He smiled his fatherly smile at her.

'It's about what Nicholas Vrost told us the other day. About Adam and his master, Gabriel.'

Gyles gave a deep sigh. He had hoped, indeed he had convinced himself, that the baby had taken the place of the young Englishman in Jannekyn's affections. It would seem he had been wrong. 'What about them, meisje?' he said.

'I can't understand it.' She puckered her brow. 'Adam isn't a man to use his fists without the greatest provocation and I fear' – she shook her head – 'I fear it may all have something to do with my quarrel with Mynheer van der Hest. Oh, Gyles, I'm so worried that Adam may be suffering on my account.'

Gyles stared into the fire. After a while he looked up. 'You are my wife, Jannekyn, and I will stand for no . . . ' He searched for a word, then began again, 'There must be no other man . . . '

She laid her hand on his arm before he could say any more. 'You're a good man, Gyles, but when I married you you knew that I loved Adam. I never made any secret of the fact. I still love him; nothing can alter that. But I give you my word that there will never be anything more than friendship between us while I'm your wife.'

He nodded, satisfied.'I believe you, meisje.'

'But I feel I must know what has happened to him, Gyles. If only I knew he was all right I would be content. Will you give me leave to visit the house where he lives with Master Birchwood?'

Gyles didn't answer for a long time. Perhaps this was what ailed Jannekyn, he thought. Perhaps fretting over the young Englishman was what was keeping the roses from her cheeks. He experienced a sharp stab of envy for his own long-lost youth. At last he said, 'I'm not happy about it, meisje, but you've given me your word and I know you'll keep it. Very well, go and see the young man, if it will put your mind at rest.'

Impulsively, she got up and put her arms round her husband's neck and kissed him. 'Oh, thank you, Gyles, thank you. I would so much rather go with your blessing than without it.' She sat down at his feet. 'Because, you see, I know that I must go. It came to me in church on Sunday – sometimes I have these feelings, Gyles, I can't explain them – but I knew I had to go to Adam; that he needed me.'

'You'll come back,' Gyles said sharply.

'Oh, yes, I'll come back, Gyles. I'm your wife.' She watched the flames licking round the log for a while, then she looked up at him. 'You'll look after little Jan while I go, won't you?'

He nodded.

Early the next day Jannekyn made her way to the cottage in Wimbles Lane where Adam lived with his master and his master's wife. Bessie Birchwood opened the door to her knock, stepping back in surprise to see the fine lady in her fur-lined cloak standing there.

'May I enter your house, Mevrouw Birchwood?' Jannekyn asked. 'I have come to see Adam.'

Bessie shook her head, her eyes dull with despair. 'He've gone, my lady. You won't find 'im 'ere. 'E've bin gone these past four weeks and the Lord in 'is mercy knows when 'e'll be back. But you can come in, all the same, whoever you be.'

Jannekyn stepped into the cottage. It was bare except for a table and a stool and a bed in the corner on which an old man lay. Everywhere was spotlessly clean. She undid her cloak and let it fall to the ground.

'I am Jannekyn, Mevrouw Birchwood. Jannekyn de Troster. Please tell me about Adam. You tell me he is not here? Where, then, is he? I have worried so much about him.'

Bessie looked at the pale slip of a girl. So this was the cause of all Adam's troubles and heartache. She wanted to hate her and yet her heart went out to this girl who looked so pale and ill, and with such anxiety in blue eyes that were too big for her thin, white face. 'An' well you might worry about 'im.' Bessie's eyes filled with tears. 'Oh, Lor, I dunno wass to become of us, I surely don't.' Then she bit her lip and pulled herself together. 'I'm sorry, my'lady, but it comes over me at times. I can't help it. Please to sit down, I'm afeard I can't offer you much – we don't keep a lot in the house now.' She looked round at the bare board.

Jannekyn took Bessie's hand in both her own. 'Mevrouw Birchwood, please do not call me m'lady, call me Jannekyn, for I know Adam has told you all about me.' She kicked the cloak as it lay on the floor. 'These fine clothes mean nothing. I must wear what Mynheer van der Hest provides because I have nothing else. Please tell me about Adam. I have worried so much about him. I would have come before but I have been ill since my child was born. I did not know until the other day that Adam and Mynheer Birchwood no longer worked in the loom shed at Strangers' Hall.'

Bessie sat down on the bed and took Gabriel's hand in hers while Jannekyn sat on the stool by the bed. 'My Gabriel ain't left this bed since the Eve of All Saints', or was it the day before? Yes, thass it, the day before. Thass when it all 'appened.'

Jannekyn leaned forward. 'When what happened, Mevrouw Birchwood?'

'When Master van der Hest turned on my Gabriel, sayin' 'e was too old, an' 'is work was full o' flaws. A pack o' lies, it was, all a pack o' lies. My Gabriel was still the best weaver this side of Ipswich. I dunno why the Master shoudda said what 'e did, I can't make it out at all.'

'So what happened?' Jannekyn's eyes never left the old woman's face.

'As far as I can make out, Adam went over to see what all the fuss was about and the Master went to strike out at 'im. Adam put 'is arm up to ward off the blow – jest like anybody would if they thought they was gonna be hit – and caught 'im on the jaw.' Bessie shrugged. ''Course, that was the finish. They was both put out on the street afore you could turn round. An' that was that. Adam brought Gabriel home an' we put 'im to bed an' there he've bin ever since, struck powerless all down one side.' Bessie wiped her eyes with the corner of her apron. 'I dunno why it all 'appened, but the worst of it is, young Adam, good boy that 'e is, can't get work nowhere now. 'E's out of 'is time now, and a finer weaver there never was, but nobodyll give 'im work. There's the loom idle upstairs an' 'im with the skill at 'is fingertips, an' 'ere we are with empty bellies. Tain't right.' Bessie shook her head from side to side, the picture of desolation.

Where is Adam, then?' Jannekyn asked. Things were even worse than she had imagined.

'Gone to Sudbury to see if 'e can get work there. 'E's bin gone near on four weeks. Y'see, 'e thought 'e might fare better further afield. I do miss 'im, though.' Bessie bit her lip again.

Jannekyn sat silent. She had never dreamed that her actions would have such far-reaching effects. It was wicked. Cruel. But it was typical of Jacob van der Hest.

'I'll tell Adam you called,' Bessie said politely, remembering her manners, 'when 'e get back. If 'e ever do come back,' she added sadly.

Jannekyn stood up. There was nothing more she could do. 'I shall come and see you again, Mevrouw Birchwood,' she promised.

*

'Now will you believe me when I tell you what an evil man Jacob van der Hest can be?' Jannekyn said, when she had finished telling Gyles Bessie Birchwood's story. She hung her head. 'And I'm to blame. Oh, Gyles, I'm to blame.'

'You mustn't say that, child,' Gyles admonished.

'But it's true, Gyles, it's true.' She began to cry bitterly. 'Don't you see? All this happened after I quarrelled with de Meester. He wanted to make Adam suffer to punish me and so he made Gabriel suffer to punish Adam. Oh, he's wicked, wicked! So it's all my fault those poor people are starving.' She rocked back and forth, sobbing.

Gyles watched her for a long time. Seeing her like this he could not doubt her love for the young English weaver; but he could never condone it. However, there could surely be no harm in her doing something for the old people. 'You must take them some broth,' he said at last.

She nodded. 'Yes, that's the least I can do.' She sniffed and wiped her eyes. 'I can look after Gabriel and his wife until Adam gets back.' She gave Gyles a watery smile.

Gyles picked up his pipe and began to ram the tobacco home. 'That's right, child.'

But the same thought was uppermost in both their minds, and the words hung between them, unsaid: 'If he ever does.'

IV

Jannekyn visited the Birchwoods' cottage daily, taking them broth and doing what she could for them. On her fourth visit she took little Jan with her, much to Bessie's delight.

'My word, 'e's a fine boy an' no mistake,' Bessie said, holding him on her knee, and even Gabriel held out his good hand to tickle the little boy and gave him a lopsided smile. Little Jan loved the attention and gurgled and laughed contentedly, while Jannekyn looked on. She noticed that the old couple were looking better now; Bessie had lost her drawn look and was even putting on a little weight now that she was having more to eat and Gabriel was looking a little less grey. She was glad that she had been able to help them, it seemed somehow to bring her closer to Adam, wherever he was.

'I must go, Bessie,' she said, taking little Jan from her. 'Did the boy bring you logs for the fire? Gyles said he had ordered some for you.'

'Yes, dearie, 'e did, thank ye kindly. We're warm now an' our bellies are satisfied, thanks to you an' your good man. All we could ask for now is that our lad should walk through that door.' She wiped her eye with her finger. 'I do worry about 'im so.'

Jannekyn laid her hand on Bessie's arm. 'Oh, Bessie, so do I.'

'I often think I hear 'is step comin' along the lane,' Bessie said, 'but 'e never come. They do say there's wolves in the woods this side o' Sudbury . . . '

'Hush, Bessie, you must not think such things,' Jannekyn said. But her heart was sad as she carried little Jan home.

When Jannekyn had been visiting the little cottage in Wimbles Lane for nearly three weeks Adam came home. They didn't hear his step in the lane because he had no shoes. The door simply opened and he fell inside.

Jannekyn wondered afterwards if she would have recognized him if she'd seen him in the street, he looked so gaunt and ill. His beard was thick and matted, his clothes, what there was left of them, hung in tatters and his feet were raw with broken blisters.

She helped Bessie to get him into the other end of the bed

where Gabriel lay – he was too weak to reach his own bed up in the loft beside the loom – and fed him broth, and then she left him to sleep the sleep of utter exhaustion. He was home, he was alive, at the moment nothing else mattered. Not even the wince of pain that fleeted across Gyles's face when she told him the joyous news.

After a good night's sleep Adam woke, weak but refreshed. Bessie brought him water and bathed his sore-covered feet and as she rubbed them with her own soothing ointment he told her a little of his experiences. But only a little, he was far more concerned with her and Gabriel.

'How have you and my master fared without me, Bessie?' he asked. 'I worried about you so much.'

'It was bad, boy, there's no denyin' that. We was near to starvation when your little maid came to our aid,' Bessie said truthfully.

Adam frowned. 'My little maid?'

'Why, yes, Jannekyn. She've bin bringin' us broth and her husband sent logs for the fire. A fine little babby she've got too, Adam.'

'Jannekyn came here?' A look of pain crossed Adam's face. 'Is she happy, Bessie?'

Bessie finished binding his feet, considering her answer. 'Happy, boy? That I can't say. But she've got a good, kind man for a husband, that I will vouch for. He've bin generous to a fault in lettin' her look after me an' Gabriel. An' there's no doubt she dote on 'er little Jan.'

Adam signed deeply. 'Then it would be very wrong of me to come between them, wouldn't it?'

'Yes, boy, it would,' Bessie said sadly. She put her hand on his arm. 'You know, Adam, there's nothin' I want more'n to see you happy an' settled. But I couldn't feel it right that you should be so at the expense of such a good man, Dutch though he be. An' you know there could never be marriage between you, even if the little maid was free. She's Dutch and you're English. Thass like fire an' water, boy, the two don't mix. You know that as well as I do.' She shook her head. 'I've thought an' thought about this, boy, you bein' as dear to me as a son an' seein' as I've taken to Jannekyn like she was a daughter, but I can't see no good comin' of it, no matter how I try. You still love 'er, don't you, Adam?'

'More than life itself.'

'Then you've got a hard furrow to plough, boy, for I reckon the kindest thing 'ud be to let 'er think you don't care no more. I know thass hard, Adam, but thass the way I see it.' Sadly, Bessie did what she had never done before, she took Adam's face between her hands and kissed his forehead.

Adam was silent for a very long time. Then he said, 'Tell me, Bessie. Do you think Jannekyn still loves me?'

Bessie thought for a while. It was not in her nature to tell a lie. 'I think she's very fond of her husband and little boy,' she answered at last, evading the question not very skilfully.

Adam bowed his head. 'Then I vow I'll never come between husband and wife.'

When Jannekyn went back to the little cottage in Wimbles Lane the next day Adam looked a different man. Dressed in breeches and a jerkin that had belonged to Gabriel, he had bathed and trimmed his beard and although still pale and thin to the point of emaciation and unable to walk much on his poor feet, he looked a little more like the Adam she knew and loved.

But with a difference. There was a coolness in his manner

towards her that had never been there before. The hand she offered him so eagerly when she saw him was barely touched – a slight that made her thankful she *had* only offered him her hand and had restrained herself from flinging herself into his arms as she so dearly wanted to – and, in fact, only her promise to Gyles had prevented her from doing this.

'I must thank you, Jannekyn, for caring for my master and mistress,' he said politely. 'Bessie has told me of your kindness.'

'I could do no less,' she replied, equally politely.

In vain she searched his face for some glimmer of warmth and affection, knowing all the time that it was something she no longer had any right to seek. Yet hadn't he vowed, 'I will always love you, Jannekyn. Nothing can alter that'? But something clearly had made him alter his mind. It wasn't difficult to see what it was. Who could blame him for turning against her when it was her actions that had brought this suffering not only on to him but on the old couple who were like parents to him?

''E says 'e's goin' off again as soon as 'is feet's healed,' Bessie said to Jannekyn, her face lined with anxiety. 'I say 'e shouldn't go. If 'is name's bin blackened as far as Sudbury wass the use o' goin' south to Brentwood? The same thing'll have 'appened that way.'

'Bessie's right, Adam.' Jannekyn went over to him. 'I am sorry. I am truly sorry. I am to blame for this dreadful thing that has, happened to you all. I know that and I can understand how it has made you feel about me, Adam.' Her eyes were downcast so she didn't see the look of naked anguish that crossed his face at her words. But he said nothing and she went on, 'If I had only left things as they were none of this would have happened. But I thought I could improve the lot of those poor wretched spinners . . . ' She shook her head. 'I should have known it would only cause more trouble. Oh, Adam, if only I had realized sooner . . . but I was ill . . .'

'Is your child well? I hear you have a boy.'

She nodded. 'Little Jan. Yes, he is well. I have left him with my . . . with Gyles.'

'Tell 'im not to go to Brentwood, dearie.' Bessie nudged Jannekyn, desperate to prevent Adam from leaving again. She turned to Adam. 'Tell Jannekyn 'ow all the people turned agin you when you asked for work, Sudbury way. How word 'ud gone ahead that you was an idle slack-a-day an' stole from your master.'

'But who could believe such lies?' Jannekyn said, shocked.

Wearily, Adam waved it aside. 'It's no matter. I'll find work somewhere, sooner or later.' He turned to Jannekyn. 'I'm truly grateful to you for caring for my master and mistress, Jannekyn, and I would be much indebted to you if you would continue, then I can go further afield to look for work with an easy mind. Indeed, it won't matter' – he dropped his voice – 'if I never return.'

'Indeed, it *will* matter, my boy.' It was Gabriel's voice, weak and difficult to understand, that came from the bed.

Bessie hurried over to the bed and took her husband's hand in her own. 'Praise be to God, I never thought to 'ear you speak again, 'usband,' she said, wiping away a tear. She turned, still holding Gabriel's hand. ''E's right, Adam. We won't stand for you goin' off again. The Lord knows we worried enough about you when you went off to Sudbury, but knowin' what 'appened there – an' you livin' on berries and sleepin' in the hedge – no, we'll find a way but what you don't go off again, even if we all starve in our beds.'

'We'll see,' Adam said, to placate the old couple. 'I'll stay for a day or two anyway.'

'You'll hev to. Them feet won't carry you out o' the door the way they are at the minute,' Bessie said, ever practical. 'An' *then* we'll see, when they're better.' She pursed her lips, a force to be reckoned with.

Jannekyn had remained silent while the argument was on, busy with her own thoughts. Now she said, 'Adam, if you wove your own cloth, would it sell?'

Adam gave a mirthless laugh. 'Oh, yes. If I wove cloth there's not a merchant in Colchester or Brentwood or Sudbury would refuse to buy it I know,' and he spoke without conceit, 'that I am without doubt the best weaver in the district, and any clothier worth his salt can recognize a good cloth when he sees it. But how can I prove my worth when nobody will try me? With no yarn to weave how can I prove I am a fine weaver? Oh, Jacob van der Hest was thorough,' he said bitterly. 'He left no corner of the district out when he spread his lying rumours about me.'

Jannekyn winced at these words, sick at the suffering she had unwittingly caused Adam. But now was not the time to dwell on that. She went on, 'Adam, will you weave for me? You have a loom here, your master's loom, if I bring you yarn . . . '

'Beggin' your pardon, dearie, but where'll you get yarn from? Your husband is but a dyer . . . ' Bessie reminded her gently.

'I wouldn't ask my husband for money for this. I have another plan.'

Adam's head shot up. 'Are you back with Jacob van der Hest? I'll have none . . . '

'No. Nor ever likely to be.' She waved the question aside. 'But, answer me, if I bring you yarn will you weave it?'

For a moment Adam struggled with himself. Then he answered, 'Yes. I have no choice. I must, for the sake of my master and mistress.'

'Very well. By the time your feet are healed enough to treadle and you have regained the strength to throw the shuttle I shall be back with yarn.' She put on her cloak and left, first making sure that there was nothing further they needed.

Gyles was not altogether happy about her idea but he could see that he could not reasonably forbid her to sell her own clothes. Clothes that were the only payment she had ever received from her avaricious Dutch master, clothes that were so numerous that they took up much wanted space in the little cottage.

She kept only two gowns back, the crimson that she had worn for her marriage to Gyles and the blue stammett, both made from cloth that Adam had woven. It was no use, she couldn't help loving him still, even though the treatment he had received through her actions had plainly killed the love he had had for her.

She took the clothes – bodices, skirts, gowns, ruffs, underproppers, stomachers, stockings, everything she could lay her hands on to a smelly little shop in Pelham's Lane. She had to make several journeys and each time she found it so dark that she had to blink several times before she could see Old Mother Hickstead. The old woman was so fat she could scarcely move, and with yellowish white hair wisping from under a filthy cap, she sat in the dim, windowless room, surrounded by mountains of clothes, a good many of which had seen better days.

She drove a hard bargain, clawing at the clothes with grimy hands and handing over coins dragged reluctantly from a bag she wore round her neck.

'Where d'ya git all these from?' she demanded, when Jannekyn had made two visits. 'They ain't bad; Got some more?'

Jannekyn looked at the coins Old Mother Hickstead had

passed over. 'Not if you cannot pay me better than this,' she replied.

The old woman looked up, her fat chins wobbling as she chewed her toothless gums. She had heard the faint foreign inflection in Jannekyn's voice. 'Yer can't expect much fer stolen goods. I gotta pass 'em on, remember.'

'These things are not stolen. They belong to me,' Jannekyn met her gaze coolly.

'Ha! Need the money, do yer? Got yerself in trouble so you gotta sell the clothes orf yer back?'

'I do not need it so badly that I have to haggle with you,' Jannekyn bluffed, turning away. 'It will not be difficult to find someone who will pay me more than this pittance.'

'Orl right.' There was a further chink of coins. 'Ain't no need to git wroughty, mawther. Bring me some more termorrer.'

'I might.' Jannekyn could see the avaricious gleam in the old woman's china blue eyes. 'I will see what I can find.'

She made her way home and, put the money in a tin with the rest. Soon she would have enough to go to the market and buy raw wool. She allowed herself a wry smile at the irony of a situation in which Jacob van der Hest, albeit unknowingly, was financing Adam to set up his own business, when he had been so thorough in preventing him ever finding work with a master.

When she had sold enough of the clothes Jacob van der Hest had given her she got up early one morning and went to the market to buy raw wool. On previous visits to the market she had noticed a stall, tucked away in the shadow of St Runwald's Church, where raw wool was cheap. She knew that this was because the brogger selling it had no licence and therefore paid no licensing fee and not because the wool was inferior, so she had no hesitation in buying from him, even though she knew he was trading illegally. She bought as much as she could afford, her last sixpence going on having it carried back to her house. It was sixpence she begrudged having to pay, but there was nothing else for it, because she knew she couldn't carry it herself.

But she managed the sorting, in a little lean-to attached to the dye-house, teasing apart the filthy, stinking fleeces and sorting the wool according to its length and texture, just as she had watched Jacob's sorters do, a great many of them choking children. When this was done she fetched water from the river and washed the wool and scoured it with urine. Then she spread the wool in layers, soaking each layer in oil before placing the next layer on top. After that she had to leave it until all the oil was absorbed and the wool supple enough to work. It was all a hard, dirty process and the stench reminded her of the warehouse at Strangers' Hall, where she had watched and pitied the workers, little thinking that one day she would need to remember what she had seen in order to carry out the work herself.

It also reminded her of the day she had lost her virginity to Pieter van der Hest in that nightmare of stinking darkness. That memory still made her feel sick in her stomach.

Now and again Gyles came to see what she was doing. 'This is no work for you, meisje,' he would say, holding his nose against the sour, suffocating smell, 'Come away. Find someone else to do it.'

'I can't afford to find someone else to do it, Gyles,' she would tell him, wiping oily hands on her apron and pushing strands of hair back under her cap. 'I shall have to pay for it to be spun, but this much I can do myself. It's the least I can do after all the suffering I've caused.'

It was as if she needed to do the filthy work as a scourge for her guilt. Gyles pursed his lips in disapproval. He felt it unnecessary. But he left her alone.

When the wool was ready she carded it. This was a laborious, arm-aching task, using cards, two boards spiked with metal. The wool fibres had to be rubbed together between these until they formed a tight mass. Then they were ready to be spun. Jannekyn gave herself respite from this by taking what she had prepared in batches to Trinity Poors Row.

The women there greeted her as a friend. They hadn't forgotten how she had improved their lot, short-lived though the improvement had been, and they were only too willing to spin for her. They would have done it for less than the meagre pittance they were once more receiving from Jacob if she had allowed it.

'Oh, no,' Jannekyn said firmly. 'I will not pay you less. And as soon as I can afford to I will pay you more. Much more.'

When the wool was spun she took it to Adam. He was more like the old Adam now. The gaunt, haggard look had gone, and although he was still very thin, his face held more colour. His eyes lit up as he fingered the yarn, but they were wary as he questioned her.

'Where does this yarn come from?' he asked. 'I won't work it until I know. If it comes from Jacob van der Hest' – he pushed it away – 'I'll have none of it.'

Jannekyn shook her head impatiendy. 'Do you think that *I* would have dealings with that man?' she said sharply. 'No, I will tell you where the yarn came from.' She paused and gave a mirthless little laugh. 'I suppose you could say, indirectly, that it came from de Meester, but only indirectly, and by God, I earned it. Because Jacob van der Hest never paid me a penny for all the work I did for him. All he gave me was clothes; clothes his wife had tired of, for the most part. Only this blue stammett' – she fingered the dress she was wearing – 'and one other were made for me from material he provided. These two I have kept. The rest were sold to buy wool for my friends in Trinity Poors Row to spin for me – oh, yes, I paid them for their work, never fear. And now I have brought it to you. Gyles has agreed to dye it – for a price – when you are ready.' She held her head high. 'You may regard it purely as a business arrangement, if that is what you wish.'

He fingered the yarn again. 'It's very kind of your husband to agree to dye it,' he said stiffly. 'I'll weave the cloth and then it can be dyed.' In spite of himself he became enthusiastic. 'The pattern will be in the weave – perhaps later we'll introduce colours into the pattern, but for the moment . . . '

'It'll be a start, boy. It'll be a start,' Bessie said excitedly. 'Oh, it'll be a treat to hear the old loom workin' again.'

Adam smiled at the old woman, a wealth of affection in his eyes.

'I will have more yarn to bring you when the spinners have finished it,' Jannekyn said, catching Bessie's mood.

'Thank you. You're very kind, Jannekyn.' But the gaze Adam turned on her was bleak and held none of the warmth he had shown Bessie.

V

When Adam had woven the cloth. Gyles dyed it for him as he had promised. Then Adam took it to a friend in Boxted who had agreed both to finish the cloth and also to take it to the Bay Hall for the all-important seal of quality.

'Where will you sell it, now that it's ready, Adam?' Jannekyn asked, fingering the soft, even-textured cloth. She had come to the cottage in Wimbles Lane to bring more yarn spun by her friends in Trinity Poors Row. 'I have no more money left to buy wool.'

Adam darted a swift glance at her. 'Did you pay the spinners for this?' He pointed to the yarn.

'Oh, yes. Everything is paid for. But I can't buy any more until this cloth is sold.'

He stroked his beard. 'Mm. That's the next thing, isn't it? Of course, we'd get the best price if we could get it to London . . . '

'Lor, boy, it'd cost a fortune to send it there,' Bessie said.

Jannekyn's eyes lit up. 'No, it wouldn't. Henrick would take it for us. Henrick de Groot. I know him well. He often takes cargoes to London. Shall I go and ask him?'

Adam looked doubtful. 'Do you really think he would?'

'Oh, yes, I'm sure of it. I'll go and ask him right now.' Jannekyn made a sling for little Jan in her shawl and went to the door. Adam followed her. 'It's very good of you, Jannekyn,' he said, putting out a finger for little Jan to grasp and watching as the little fingers curled round his own. Jannekyn had noticed that he avoided meeting her eyes whenever he could, and it saddened her. She still loved him, his nearness still sent the blood pounding through her veins – nothing, it seemed, could alter that, not even his new coldness towards her. And, in truth, after what he had suffered through her actions, who could blame him if his love had died? But she had at least hoped that they could be good friends and not merely business partners, unwilling ones at that.

Henrick was at home, much to the delight of Betkin, his wife, and their brood of children. There was an atmosphere of love and warmth in the tiny cottage such as Jannekyn had not seen since the day she had left her own home in Flanders. It made her realize with a new understanding just what a sacrifice her parents had made to send her to England and a better life. A better life. Her mouth twisted wryly at the thought.

When Betkin and the children had finished fussing over little Jan, Jannekyn told Henrick the reason for her visit.

'You do still carry goods to London?' she finished anxiously.

'He does when he's not risking his neck to bring refugees over from the other side,' Betkin said, her voice bitter with disapproval.

'Hush, woman, hold your tongue.' Jannekyn had never heard Henrick speak so sharply to his wife before.

'I will not hold my tongue. It's me and the children that'll suffer if you don't get back one of these times.' She raised her eyes to heaven. 'God forbid that such a thing should happen.'

'You'd be well looked after, I've seen to that. There are some in high places who have cause to be grateful to me for a safe passage to England. They'll see you come to no harm,' Henrick said, with a trace of impatience.

'Are things still bad over there?' Jannekyn asked in a low voice.

He gave a shrug. 'Things have quietened, but it's an uneasy quiet. I fear the bloodshed is not yet finished, even after all this time.'

'I often wonder about my poor father and mother and how they are faring,' Jannekyn said with a deep sigh.

'You never hear about them?'

She shook her head. 'Letters are too expensive for them to send and messages are not always delivered. In any case, it's not always easy to find someone going in the right direction.'

'That's true. But, tell me, where does your father live? I could try to get a letter to him when I'm over there.'

'Oh, I would be grateful for that.' Suddenly, at the thought of her father and mother Jannekyn's eyes filled with tears. Brushing them away she gave Henrick directions to the tiny cottage near Ypres that was once her home. 'I should so much like them to know that I am well and that I am married and that my son is called Jan, after his grandfather.'

Henrick nodded. 'I make no promises,' he warned. Then his sombre mood changed and he grinned. 'But as for taking your cloth to London to sell: the law is strict over the shipment of goods by Aliens, but if I can smuggle men across the sea I reckon I can smuggle a bit of cloth down the coast, don't you?' He smacked what was left of his hands down on to his knees. 'After all,' he roared, 'what are laws like that made for, if not to be broken?'

Thanking him, Jannekyn started for home, stopping on the way to tell Adam that if he took his cloth to Henrick's house in Grub Street Henrick would see to it that it was sold in the London market. She had a long walk ahead of her and the baby was heavy on her arm, but her step was light. They had made a beginning; it was only a small beginning, but it was a beginning all the same. There was little doubt that Adam's cloth would fetch a good price in the London market and she felt proud to think that she had played no little part in the venture. Letting her mind rove over future possibilities and successes, she made her way down Maidenburgh Street and along the river bank to the cottage where she lived with her husband the dyer. As she pushed open the door her face was pink from the cold winter breeze.

But the colour drained from her face and the smile on her lips died when she saw who was sitting in Gyles's chair by the fire.

It was Jacob van der Hest.

She closed the door and stood with her back to it, the baby clutched to her breast, her eyes wide with alarm. Surely, he couldn't have heard about Adam already?

Jacob, for his part, saw that motherhood had made Jannekyn quite lovely, rounding her figure to make her even more desirable, and putting a glow on her features that bordered on beauty. Either that or he had forgotten just how lovely she was, which was unlikely, since she haunted his dreams and his waking hours until he hated both himself and her for his enslavement.

He smiled at her. 'Jannekyn.' His voice was silky. 'You are well? You look blooming.'

She licked her lips, suppressing a shudder of revulsion at the sight of him. 'Thank you, I am well enough.'

'Good.' He nodded. 'How long is it since the child was born?' An unnecessary question. He knew to the hour how many weeks and months he had been without her.

'Four months, Meester. Four months and a few days.'

Gyles came over and took her cloak and then laid little Jan in his cradle. 'Come, meisje, come to the fire. You're cold.'

It was true. She was cold to the marrow. But it was Jacob van der Hest's presence, not the freezing March wind, that had chilled her. She allowed Gyles to draw her to her chair by the fire.

'De Meester has come to see if you are ready to return to his counting house,' Gyles said, gently chafing her hands in an effort to warm them. 'I've told him I think you have recovered sufficiently from the child's birth to consider it.'

Jannekyn looked at Gyles and then at Jacob. She could hardly believe her ears. 'You are asking me to come back and work for you?' she repeated slowly.

'Why not?' Jacob smiled the wolfish smile again. 'It was always assumed that you would return to me when your health allowed.'

She stared at him in astonishment. Had he forgotten how she had left his counting house? The things she had said? The accusations she had made? Or had he simply chosen to ignore them and pretend that the events of that last day had never taken place? If that was the case, what was his motive? Why should he want to do it?

As if in answer to her question Jacob continued, 'As a Governor of the Bay Hall I need to associate with the English Bailiffs and aldermen to some extent. They for their part are too stupid to learn Dutch and I refuse to converse in such a barbaric tongue as theirs, so I need an interpreter. An interpreter I can trust. I shall not, of course, expect you to spend your time poring over ledgers, my dear.'

She shook her head. 'No,' she mumbled, feeling for all the world as if she were fighting off the effects of a bad dream, 'I won't come . . . '

'You are not yet ready?' Jacob looked at her closely. 'A few more days, then?'

'No.' She cast her eyes round until they lit on the cradle. 'The child. I couldn't leave the child.'

'Of course you couldn't,' he said smoothly. 'I've arranged for that. Benjamin's nurse will look after him for you. Benjamin is over two years old now, his nurse will like a young baby to care for.'

She gazed at him open-mouthed. He was speaking as if there had never been any doubt that she would return to him. 'I . . . ' she began.

'My wife is tired and needs to rest, Meester,' Gyles intervened. 'She needs to have time to get used to the idea of allowing her child to be in someone else's care. Perhaps we can talk about it again in a day or two.' He went over to the door and held it open.

'Yes. Very well.' Jacob hesitated a moment longer, but seeing that Gyles was very obviously waiting for him to go he had no option but to leave. 'I shall come and see you again in a few days,' he said over his shoulder to Jannekyn as he went through the door.

When he had gone Jannekyn rounded on Gyles. 'Talk again in a day or two? Come and see me again in a few days? What are you talking about? I'm not going back to that man, ever! I told you that when I left him, Gyles. I don't know how you could have listened to him, let alone allow him to think I would go back to him. Why did you let him into the house? Why didn't you send him packing?'

Gyles gave a deep sigh. 'Because, meisje, I live in his cottage and I depend on him for money to feed and warm you and the child.'

Jannekyn tossed her head. 'Lewys de Hase would provide for us just as well. You know there is work and a cottage to be had there for the asking.'

'Jannekyn, have you seen the cottage? A miserable hovel in the middle of the town. All the water would have to be drawn from the well and carried to it. Here, I live beside it, and have a plentiful supply at hand. I'm an old man, child, I have to think of these things.' He spoke with asperity.

'I will not go back to that man.'

'You must, meisje.'

'I will not.'

Little Jan whimpered and she picked him up and put him to her breast. She looked down at him, and a tear dropped on to his curly head. She hated defying Gyles. He was good to her and she had become very fond of him, but surely he must see the impossibility of what he was asking her to do. She brushed her hand across her eyes and looked over to where he sat in the chair Jacob had so recently occupied, smoking his pipe and gazing into the fire. He was getting old, it was true; his hair – what there was of it – was quite white. But he was dressed neatly and well, his linen fine and white, his jerkin and breeches of good-quality material, not the everlasting leather that the poor people wore. And she knew that his dye-house was well stocked with dyes and mordants that Jacob had imported at his own expense. No wonder Gyles was unwilling to sacrifice all this for her sake. After all, hadn't he already sacrified enough in marrying her and sharing his home with her? And that out of gratitude to his master.

All the same, she was determined not to weaken. She would not go back to Jacob van der Hest. If only she could hold out until Adam had established himself, Gyles would be able to cut himself free from Jacob . . .

But that was a long way ahead.

They didn't speak of the matter again, but it hung between them like a heavy, invisible curtain, and as the days wore on Jannekyn knew that it was not done with.

In due course Adam came to the cottage with the cloth he had woven from the new lot of yarn she had provided. He came, at Gyles's request, under cover of darkness because the old dyer was not happy to be seen to associate with the English, and they discussed colours and shades. This took some time, because although Adam had picked up a smattering of Dutch over the years, Gyles had never felt the need or inclination to learn the English language and so everything had to be done through Jannekyn, sitting between them and interpreting.

Gyles couldn't help liking the young Englishman in spite of himself and he tried to stifle the fierce jealousy that rose in him – jealousy not only because Adam had Jannekyn's love, but also because of his youth and vitality, his lean, straight body and the sinewy strength in his arms.

Adam, for his part, valued the wisdom and knowledge of the older man and, in the way of one craftsman recognizing the skill of another, expressed his gratitude with dignity and respect.

'When Mynheer de Groot returns from London with the money for the cloth he is selling for us we shall be able to buy more wool,' Adam said, and Jannekyn noticed with pleasure his use of the words 'us' and 'we'. 'And I think next time it would be better to be dyed in the wool instead of in the woven state, that way I can make colour patterns in the weave. I have ideas . . . ' He broke off with a slight, almost apologetic smile. 'But one thing at a time.' He turned to Jannekyn. 'You are keeping a very careful tally of what is spent, Jannekyn, aren't you?'

'Yes, of course.' Jannekyn went upstairs and fetched the little leather bag in which she kept the money from the clothes she had sold. There was not much left. She spilled the coins on to the table. 'There is just enough here to pay your friend at Boxted for the finishing, but we shall have to wait until Henrick brings us money from London before we have enough to pay Gyles for the dyeing.'

'Money will have come from London by the time this piece is dyed,' Gyles said quietly.

Jannekyn turned to him in surprise. 'How can you be so sure, Gyles? Henrick has been gone barely a week. These things take time, you know.'

Gyles returned her gaze steadily. 'Indeed they do, my dear. I, too, am very busy. The young man's cloth will have to wait.'

'Oh, come, Gyles, you're not that busy,' she laughed. 'I know . . . ' Then her voice died away as she realized what her husband was telling her. It was his way of forcing her to go back to Jacob van der Hest. It was simple: until she returned to Jacob, Adam's cloth would not be dyed. She hung her head, defeated. 'Very well, Gyles,' she said, her voice barely above a whisper.

Gyles went over to the hearth and picked up his pipe. 'A bluish pink rather than an orange pink, you said, young man?' He gave the log on the fire a prod with his foot, sending a shower of sparks flying before it broke into a blaze. 'Look, that colour, in the middle of the flame, there. Is that the shade you're thinking of?'

Adam came forward. 'Yes, that's exactly right. But I thought you said . . .'

'Good.' Gyles nodded. 'Come and see me in ten days.' He sat down in his chair, his eyes closed, drawing on his pipe, putting an end to the conversation.

Adam frowned and looked to Jannekyn for an explanation of Gyles's sudden change of mind, but Jannekyn kept her eyes down and merely shrugged. 'You must have misunderstood. Your Dutch is not that good,' she said. 'Anyway, Henrick should be back in another ten days, so we shall be able to buy more wool.'

But after Adam had gone she put her head in her hands and wept.

Gyles said nothing for a long time. He had put Jannekyn's love for the young man to the test and was almost disappointed that it had stood up to it. But it would make life very much smoother all round if she went back to Mynheer van der Hest, and above all Gyles valued a smooth and peaceful life. Oh, he realized that de Meester was not all that he might be, he'd listened to Jannekyn's tirades on the subject many times; but she was young and full of ideals, she'd yet to learn that the world was a hard place and everyone, however high-principled, ultimately had their price. He glanced at her, still weeping in the corner. Even Jannekyn.

Chapter Five

I

Jannekyn spent several sleepless nights trying to see a way out of the trap she was in, but there was no way round it. Adam's cloth must be dyed and Gyles was the person to do it. Not only was he the most skilled dyer in the town – that in itself a vitally important factor – but, and at present almost equally important, he would not overcharge and was prepared to wait for payment until the cloth was sold. She lay listening to the regular snoring coming from the other side of the say curtain that divided the little bedroom under the eaves. She almost hated Gyles. A mild and gentle man he might be, but he could be quite ruthless in his determination to get his own way.

And he would get his own way. There was no escape for her. She would have to go back to Jacob van der Hest. But – and she became calmer as the idea formed in her mind – she would go back on her own terms. Jacob need not know that she was returning under pressure from Gyles.

Jacob was oily in his pleasure to have her back with him and she despised him for it.

'I have a man in the counting house so you will have no need to concern yourself with that side of things,' he said, leading the way into the house. 'Besides, it is cold there. Come and take a glass of wine in my smoking room whilst I summon the nurse to take the child from you.'

Jannekyn followed him, wondering wryly why the temperature in the counting house should suddenly have gained so much importance. She could remember the time, not so long ago, when he couldn't have cared if her fingers had dropped off with cold as long as the work was done.

The nurse was a young girl who appeared to have little control over Benjamin. He had grown into a wayward two-year-old, full of energy, bearing no resemblance to the sluglike baby Jannekyn had rescued from his opium-sated wet-nurse. The girl took little Jan from his mother with an obvious affection for small children and this allayed at least some of the misgivings Jannekyn felt at being parted from her little son.

She drank her wine and listened with inward amusement to Jacob's explanation of her duties.

'You know that Minister Verlender has been called to London?' he began.

She nodded.

'No doubt you know, too, that he used to mediate between members of the Dutch Congregation and the English bailiffs and aldermen.'

She nodded again. 'Because he could speak both languages.'

'Partly,' Jacob admitted grudgingly. 'Anyway, as an Elder of the Church and a Governor of the Bay Hall, I have been appointed to take his place.' There was more than a hint of his old arrogance in his tone.

'But you don't speak English. How can you mediate?'

'Hardly anybody in our Congregation has any knowledge of the barbaric tongue the English speak. As long as I have an interpreter – which is where you come in, my dear' – he inclined his head in her direction – 'I am by far the best person to sort out their grievances.'

'*You*, sort out *their* grievances?' Jannekyn raised her eyebrows. 'Surely, you mean it the other way round?'

'What do you mean?'

'Surely, it's for us to go to them to sort out *our* grievances. After all, Colchester is their town. *We* are the aliens here.'

'That may be, but we have the protection of their Queen. We have letters from the Privy Council. We are to be allowed to carry on our trade unmolested. Don't forget we have brought prosperity to the town. Look at the houses we have built and repaired. Look at the work we provide for spinners and weavers and the like. We have shown them better methods in all sorts of industries, not only in the manufacture of bays and says . . . '

'One moment.' Jannekyn surprised herself at her readiness to argue with him. '*Shown* them better methods? How can you show them better methods when you do not even communicate with them?'

'They copy us.'

'If they can discover what you are doing – which for the most part you're careful to make sure they can't. Oh, yes, you're right, the English do have grievances. And it's no wonder.'

'You don't understand what you're talking about.' Jacob got up to pour her more wine and then stood looking down at her. 'You need new dresses.' He bent to finger the stuff of the dress she was wearing. It was the dress of blue stammett, one of the only two she had left since selling the rest to buy wool for Adam, and both of which were becoming a little shabby.

She brushed his hand away and stepped back out of his reach in a very obvious gesture of repulsion. 'When I receive payment from you for the work I do I will buy myself new dresses. Until then, what I have will do. They are clean and there is no disgrace in darns.'

'I'm sure I can find you dresses that are better . . . '

'I've told you, I will choose my own dresses,' she repeated firmly. She lifted her head. 'And I shall have clothes of the best quality, because doubtless you will pay me well. After all, my skills are invaluable to you.'

He sighed, a little nonplussed by this new, hard Jannekyn. 'My intention was never any different,' he said, garnering up papers from his desk.

She watched him for several moments. Then she said, 'There is another thing. Adam Mortlock is back in Colchester.'

'I wasn't aware that he had ever left the town,' he replied smoothly, without looking up.

'I'm surprised at that,' she said. 'For there's precious little that goes on in Colchester that you don't know about.'

'Well, I didn't know that.'

'Then perhaps you didn't know that Gabriel Birchwood has never left his bed since the day you turned him out of your loom shed.'

'He was an old man, past useful work.'

'He was one of your best weavers. And Adam was the other. Yet Adam could find no work this side of Sudbury. He found his name had been blackened wherever he went. I suppose you didn't know that, either?' She waited a moment and then went on, 'You knew very well that Adam had left Colchester, because you'd seen to it that he would find no work here. And you made sure he would find no work anywhere else, either. Well, in case you didn't know this, he's back in Colchester and he's weaving his own cloth on his own loom.'

'His *own* cloth? Where would he buy yarn to weave his own cloth? You mean he's working for a master. Who is he working for?' Jacob's face was ugly with contempt as he said the words.

'He is his own master. I told you he is weaving his own cloth.'

'He will never get it sealed at the Bay Hall and he will never sell it without a seal. I have given orders . . . ' He stopped, realizing that in his temper he had already said too much.

She smiled to herself, remembering the bale of cloth already on its way to London.

'I think it's time those orders were changed, then.' She sat down and continued quietly, 'Before I leave this room I want your assurance that Adam's cloth can go to the Bay Hall *in his own name*, and be sealed *with his own seal*.'

'It's out of the question. You don't know what you're asking.'

'I know perfectly well what I'm asking. Adam is a master weaver. He has every right to his own seal.'

Jacob took a gold watch from his pocket. 'We are already late. We'll talk of this another time,' he said impatiently.

'We'll talk of it now or you can go to the Mote Hall alone,' she said, without raising her voice. She pushed a piece of paper over to him, then picked up a quill and examined the point. 'There,' she said, 'a note from you is all that's needed.'

'I will not give it.'

'Then I will not come with you to the Mote Hall. And it won't be much use your going alone, will it?'

He rounded on her. 'You little fool. Do you think you can force me into this?'

'I am simply making a not unreasonable request.' She sat in her chair with her hands folded in her lap. 'You treated Adam badly. Now you can make amends. That's all there is to it.' She looked up at him. 'Well, Uncle?'

He paled, and his lips were a thin, straight line. 'Don't call me that. I told you never to call me that'

She gazed at him dispassionately. 'I wonder why? But no matter. I'd be loathe to let it be known I was your kin so it's not something I'm likely to let slip . . . accidentally.'

He took a step towards her, his arm raised. His face was dark with fury. 'Why, you little . . . '

She didn't flinch. 'If you strike me I shall walk out of this house and never return. I have received enough ill-treatment in this house, I'll take no more,' she said. She handed him the quill. 'Now, we've wasted enough time. Are you going to write this note?'

He slumped in his chair, his shoulders sagging, and snatched the quill from her. She watched him as he wrote. The tide had finally turned. Jacob van der Hest could no longer hurt and humiliate her; his power had gone. Now it was she who had the upper hand. Strangely, the thought gave her no pleasure; it simply made her despise him more than ever.

When he had finished writing he almost flung the paper at her. She read it carefully, then folded it and tucked it in her bodice. 'Thank you,' she said. 'Now, shall we go?'

He gathered together the documents he needed and called his carriage. Jacob travelled everywhere by carriage, even the short distance to the Mote Hall in the market place, because he liked to show off his wealth. Besides, it was safer, with all the riots and discontent that there was in the town.

The Mote Hall, seat of the local government, was a singularly unimpressive place and they were shown into a small room facing the street, where a rather tired-looking man with grey hair was waiting for them at a desk littered with papers. He looked up as they entered.

'Mynheer van der Hest?' he said, scrambling to his feet in some surprise. 'To what do I owe this honour? Usually, your Minister, Mynheer Verlender . . . '

Jacob gave Jannekyn a prod. 'Tell him Mynheer Verlender has been transferred to London,' he interrupted, as he recognized the name. 'Tell him it was unfortunate that Mynheer Verlender had to go, being the only member of the Congregation who spoke English, but it was unavoidable. Tell him I've come in Mynheer Verlender's place and I daresay we shall manage very well with you translating.'

Obediently, Jannekyn repeated the message to Robert Lamb, the English bailiff. He frowned at her words.

'This language barrier makes things very difficult,' he said sadly. 'It's no wonder that there's trouble in the town. However, we'll do the best we can. What are the complaints this time?'

Almost majestically, Jacob unrolled a parchment and began to read in measured tones. Then Jannekyn repeated what he had said to Robert Lamb, who then discussed each matter with her whilst Jacob looked on uncomprehendingly, waiting for her to report to him, so that he could argue, through her, with the Englishman. Jannekyn had never been in such a ridiculous situation in the whole of her life, and halfway through the morning she had an irrational desire to laugh out loud as Jacob, trying to remain pompous and arrogant, had to keep asking 'Wat zegt ie? What is he saying?'

At the same time, she could see the gravity of the situation. Starving English weavers had tried to set fire to the house of a wealthy Dutch clothier, claiming that the Dutch were stealing their livelihood. Jacob pointed out, not without justification, that the Dutch clothiers would employ the English if only they would work harder and more conscientiously. At this, Robert

Lamb reminded him that the Dutch had taken over the use of the fulling mills which made it difficult for the English to get near them, thus making their work suffer.

'The Dutch Congregation has brought money into the town,' Jacob snapped. 'Look at all the houses we have repaired that would otherwise have fallen into ruin. And our poor are no drain on your resources – we look after them ourselves. Not only do fines from the Bay Hall support them, we have a weekly house-to-house collection for them. Of course, you English would have no need of a house-to-house collection, the fines you have to pay at the Bay Hall for bad workmanship would keep the poor of all Christendom in luxury!'

Jannekyn modified that before she repeated it to Robert Lamb. She liked the elderly Englishman. He was clearly trying to do a difficult job in trying circumstances to the best of his ability, and she felt irritated that the Dutch Congregation should be so persistently clannish and unbending. After all, they'd been glad enough to seek refuge in the little town.

The argument raged back and forth and at the end of it nothing was solved. Jannekyn was glad to collect little Jan and go home to Gyles.

'It made my head ache,' she said, as Gyles fussed round her, drawing her chair nearer to the fire and cutting her a slice of mutton pie. 'All the arguments and disagreements and neither of them understanding what the other was saying.' She giggled. 'It was quite funny, really, Gyles, to see Jacob trying to look haughty and arrogant when he didn't understand a bit of what was going on.' She took a bite of pie and chewed it, staring into the fire. 'If only he could see how much simpler all round it would be if he and some of the other Elders learned to speak English,' she said after a bit.

'Oh, no, that would never do,' Gyles said hastily.

'I don't see why not. I don't feel any less Dutch because I speak the language of the country I'm living in. And it makes life so much easier.'

'That's not the point. If we're going to stay as a community we need to show that we're different.'

'I think it's a mistake.'

'You don't understand, meisje. One day we shall go back to our homeland and it's important for our children's sake if nothing else that we should keep our own ways, so that they won't feel strangers in their own country.'

Jannekyn was silent. She doubted the truth of what Gyles was saying. Too many members of the Dutch Congregation had prospered for them to want to give up their fine houses and thriving businesses and go back to begin again in the ruins of their strife-torn native land. Sooner or later they would have to accept the fact that they were here to stay.

For her part, she was beginning to feel that she straddled a kind of no-man's-land between the Dutch Congregation and the English townspeople; her allegiance to one weakened by her sympathies towards the other.

Dionis paced back and forth across the solar, her skirt swishing expensively at each turn. 'No, Mama, I've told you before, you cannot come to live with me. Your place is here, with Papa.'

Katherine watched her daughter's impatient movements from her couch. Dionis had changed. She was as thin as a stick and her face was painted like a doll's, covered with that thick white paste she used and relieved only by a round red patch of rouge on each cheek and the bright red lip paint that pointed up her narrow, pinched mouth. And she could scarcely turn her head because of the size of her ruff: Katherine leaned over and selected a piece of marchpane and popped it in her mouth. 'I am not well, Dionis,' she said, with her mouth full.

Dionis stopped her pacing and stared at her mother. She had grown very fat, but it was hardly to be wondered at since she spent all her lime simply lying on her couch picking at food. 'You have *never* been well, Mama,' she said unsympathetically. 'Ever since before Benjamin was born you have spent your days on that couch – except, of course, when it suited you to do otherwise.'

Katherine's face crumpled. 'You don't understand, daughter. You don't know what I've suffered from your father's excesses.'

'What *are* you talking about, Mama!'

Katherine turned her head away. 'Of course, you wouldn't know. Your husband died before he could subject you to his animal cravings.'

Dionis went over to the window and stood looking out so that her mother shouldn't see the smile that played around her mouth. Dionis did not spend many nights alone in her bed these days. She had enjoyed the company and favours of many suitors since Abraham did her the good service of dying and leaving her all his wealth. Life was good and she was enjoying it to the full. One day, perhaps, she would remarry, but not yet. Not while the little sponge that she used nightly was still effective and kept her childless.

'And now he's brought that girl back to work for him.' Katherine's words cut across her thoughts.

'What girl? Do you mean Jannekyn?'

'Yes.' Katherine spat the word out.

'And not before time, I should think. The whole house looks as if it needs a good clean.' Dionis ran her finger over, the window ledge and left a line in the dust. Her own house was spotless and sweet-smelling, which was more than could be said of Strangers' Hall.

'Oh, she hasn't come to look after the house, Garerdine has to do that. She's come to work for *him*. He takes her to the Mote Hall now, if you ever heard such a thing. He can't bear her out of his sight.' Katherine's eyes narrowed. 'That child of hers – you know how quickly he married her off. Didn't turn her out into the gutter, mind you, married her off. Well' – she nodded sagely – 'surely that speaks for itself. And now to bring her back. It's more than I should be asked to bear.' She put her hand up to her brow. 'Why won't you take me to your house, daughter?'

'Because your place is here. If you were ill, really ill, it would be another matter.' Dionis allowed herself a tiny piece of marchpane. 'And as for Jannekyn, you're being, stupid and jealous, Mama.' Dionis had her own thoughts about that. She had seen Pieter sneak into the warehouse after Jannekyn and months later – after her own widowhood and Jannekyn's hastily arranged marriage – she had pieced together the events: Jannekyn in the still-room after salve for bruises and her own beating at the hands of her father. And had come to her own conclusions. 'Jannekyn had a tumble in the wool with Pieter. That's why he was sent back to his ship so soon, surely you realized that, Mama. Now get up from that couch and take a turn in the garden with me before I return to my own house. I don't wish to be out after dark and get my carriage mobbed by hungry weavers.'

Realizing that she would get no sympathy from her daughter Katherine did as she was told and got clumsily to her feet, reaching for the stick without which she didn't feel safe to take a step. Dionis came over to her and brushed the crumbs of food from her mother's crumpled ruff. 'There,' she said, more kindly. 'You would feel so much better if you walked about more, Mama. Heaven knows, there is plenty you could do. What are the servants about? The whole place needs a broom taking to it.'

'There is only Garerdine. The rest have gone. Your father is mean. He swore we could not afford to pay them,' Katherine began to complain again. 'But he can afford to pay *her*. Oh, it is not to be borne, the way he treats me.'

'Well at least we can hang fresh bunches of herbs on the walls,' Dionis said cheerfully, ignoring her mother's complaints. 'Come with me and we'll gather them and tie them in bundles. Then I must return to Lexden. I am entertaining friends tonight and I want things to be just so. The servants scamp their duties if I am not there to watch.'

'I wish you would take me with you, Dionis.'

'No, Mama, your place is here, with my father.' Dionis took her mother's arm and led her into the garden.

II

Jacob didn't demand her services every day and for this Jannekyn was thankful. For one thing she hated to be parted from little Jan and for another she was anxious to help Gyles in the dye-house. Apart from the fact that the dyeing processes interested her, both she and Gyles recognized that he was no longer a young man and he was as anxious to pass his skills and secrets on to her before it was too late as she was to learn them. In the evenings as they sat by the fire with little Jan in his cradle between them he would pass on to her the tricks of his trade and she would write them down. But when it was daylight he liked to see her in the dye-house, experimenting with different vegetable dyes, discovering for herself the advantages of soaking or boiling, learning which dyes needed a mordant and which would set without.

Jannekyn also managed to persuade Gyles to take on an apprentice. Thirteen-year-old Johan de Groot, or Joey as he was known, was the oldest son of Henrick and Betkin, a lively, intelligent boy who was both willing and able. Gyles soon came to rely on him for the heavier tasks, admitting freely that he sometimes wondered how he'd ever managed without him. Jannekyn smiled at this; it had taken all her powers of persuasion to get Gyles to take him on.

She was in the dye-house, preparing a brown dye from lichen, her hair escaping from her cap in the steamy atmosphere and an old piece of sack tied round her middle to protect her dress, when Adam came to fetch his cloth.

He stood for a moment, savouring the sight of her humming quietly to herself as she worked, and it took all his will power not to stride over to her and take her in his arms. He sighed. Bessie had foreseen that it would be hard but even she could never have realized the constant struggle he would have to keep his feelings under control.

Gyles came over to him. Adam knew the old man didn't care for him visiting the cottage, but Adam had a reason for forestalling him today.

'Your cloth is ready,' Gyles said in his own tongue. 'The colour has taken very well.' He fingered it with practised hands. 'It's a fine cloth you weave, young man.'

Adam frowned in his effort to follow what Gyles had said although he could understand Dutch better than he could articulate it. He smoothed the material. 'Yes, it has come up well and is exactly the colour I had in mind,' he said in his halting Dutch. 'Now, what price is it, Meester?'

Jannekyn dried her hands on her sacking apron and hurried over to them. She caught his sleeve. 'But, Adam, I told you. The money is all gone. We shall have no more until Henrick returns from London.'

Adam turned and smiled at her, a privilege he rarely allowed himself these days. 'Henrick is back from London, didn't Joey tell you? He came to see me – and look what he brought!' His eyes were bright with excitement as he putted a soft leather pouch from inside his shirt and spilled silver coins from it over the bench. 'There, Jannekyn, count that! Enough there to pay for the dyeing and finishing, as well as to pay my friend at Boxted his price for putting the cloth through the Bay Hall in his name. And there'll still be a profit, even after we've bought more wool.'

Jannekyn counted the coins carefully. When she had finished she looked up, her eyes shining. 'It's far more than the cloth would have fetched if it had been sold in Colchester' she said.

'And the merchant he sold it to is anxious for more.' Adam's voice held a note of triumph. 'I'll take this piece to Boxted now, for Samuel Fox to finish . . .'

Now it was Jannekyn's turn to sound triumphant. 'You no longer need to pay Samuel Fox to put your cloth through the Bay Hall.' She fished inside her bodice and brought out Jacob's reluctantly written note of authority. 'You are to have your own seal, Adam.'

Adam looked at the foreign scrawl. It meant nothing to him. Then he recognized his own name and, at the bottom of the paper, that of Jacob van der Hest. 'What is this?' he asked suspiciously.

Jannekyn nodded encouragingly. 'It gives you authority to have your cloth searched at the Bay Hall and sealed in your own name. You no longer have to pay Samuel Fox to put it through in his name.' She looked at him, eagerly waiting for his response.

'Where did you get it?' He was still suspicious.

'Why, from de Meester, of course. He was the only person with power to give it to me.'

Adam felt sick with disappointment. How could she go crawling to that man after all he had done in the past? Did the suffering he had caused mean nothing to her? Bessie near to starving and Gabriel who would never walk, let alone work again, and his own suffering – was it all of so little importance to her? He flung the note down on the bench. 'I want no favours from that man.'

He turned to pick up his bale of cloth but Jannekyn got between it and him. 'It was no favour he did,' she said hotly. 'It is nothing more than your right as a master weaver. And you are in no position to refuse it, Adam Mortlock. Your friend Samuel Fox has said he will have your cloth sealed in his name *for a price* and, you mark my words, it will be an ever increasing price. He will bleed you dry in time. Nobody takes risks like that for nothing, surely you must realize that'

'His price is high, that I will own,' Adam conceded.

'And it will become higher.' She pushed the note over to him. 'Take it. Regard it as a favour if you must, but for God's sake, take it. Heaven knows, you need it.'

He stared down at it, still not able to bring himself to pick it up.

She leaned over the bench towards him. 'I'm doing the best I can to help you, Adam. Do you have to make things even more difficult? Am I going to have to fight you every inch of the way?' She picked up the note and looked at it, then she flung it down.

'Oh, take it. Use it or not as you please,' she said wearily, pushing a strand of hair back under her cap. She turned back to the vat of liquid bubbling in the corner. 'But leave me enough money to buy wool at the wool market tomorrow,' she said over her shoulder. 'The broggers will be there and their prices are best if you know what you're looking for.'

Adam stared at the note. She was right, of course, he desperately needed his own seal. Samuel Fox was already asking a higher and higher price for putting the cloth through as his own, because it was a highly illegal procedure. But how did she come by it? What price had she been forced to pay Jacob van der Hest? It must have been high because Adam Mordock was the last person on earth that man would lift a finger to help. Oh, God, he thought, why can't I stop loving the woman and be done with it all? Why do I care what she does for Jacob van der Hest? It's plain enough where her loyalties lie – she is only helping me in order to pay off what she considers to be a debt. The best thing to do would surely be to help her to discharge that debt and be done with her. Reluctantly, as if it would burn his fingers, he picked up the note and put it inside his shirt.

When Adam had gone Jannekyn went over to the bench and stood looking down at the heap of coins tying on the bench. Then, slowly, she let them trickle through her fingers, suddenly weary to the marrow. At least he had taken the note, but what a struggle it had been. She was so tired. Tired of fighting. It seemed as if her life now was one long fight; a fight against Jacob van der Hest; a fight against Gyles for Adam's sake; and now, it seemed, she was having to fight Adam himself. She sighed. Perhaps she should simply give up and let life take whatever course it would. It would be so much easier just to let things drift. After all, why was she fighting to help Adam, stubborn, independent fool that he was? Was she simply doing it to make amends for all the suffering she had unwittingly caused him? She owed him a great debt and she had no other way of repaying it.

But deep down inside herself she had to acknowledge that this was only the half of it. She would willingly work her fingers to the bone for the chance to see him and be near him. And the fact that he treated her with nothing more than a cold formality made no difference to her feelings for him at all.

The next day she got up early and went to the wool market, leaving little Jan with Gyles. The jostling crowds, with not infrequent rioting among the hungry weavers, often made her nervous although she tried not to show it, and the added encumbrance of a child would only make matters worse. But she knew exactly what she wanted and she haggled fiercely with the broggers to get the best deal. She enjoyed the cut and thrust of bargaining and at the end of the morning had amazed even herself at what she had managed to achieve.

She looked round for a boy to carry the load home for her – a strong boy, for it would take him several journeys.

'Can I carry the wool for you, Mevrouw de Troster?' A small, pinched-looking man in shabby breeches touched her elbow. He had a rough wooden hand-cart with him.

She turned. 'Lucas Crowbroke!' she said in surprise. 'Why aren't you at work? Surely, you're one of Mynheer van der Hest's combers? I've seen you at work in the warehouse there, haven't I?'

'That's right, Mevrouw. And my children sort the wool. But odd days there's no work for us so I come and wait by the broggers' stall to earn a penny where I can.' He hefted the fleeces on to his hand-cart. 'Where do you want them taken, Mevrouw? Who does your sorting and combing?'

She looked at the daunting heap of stinking fleeces and

made a mental check of what money she had left. Her heart sank. Once again she would have to do it herself. She couldn't afford ... Then she remembered. Jacob had paid her, expecting her to buy herself a new gown. But that could wait. There were more important uses for the money. 'Will you do it for me, Lucas Crowbroke? Will you bring your children to sort the wool? And then will you comb it for me? I can't employ you on a regular basis but when I have work and you have not will you do it?'

Lucas Crowbroke nodded eagerly. 'Aye, Mevrouw, that I will, and right willingly. And my woman will spin for you, too.'

'Good. Then take these fleeces to Gyles de Troster's house. There's a lean-to shed beside the dye-house. It's not very big but I'm sure we'll manage.'

'I'll fetch the children on the way and they can make a start – I'll help them till there's enough done to start the scouring. Wouter, my eldest, he's sick in his lungs from the fleeces, but when he has a good day he'll come, too.' The man was pathetic in his eagerness.

Jannekyn walked home, leaving him to follow with the cartload of fleeces and his family. As she walked her brow furrowed. It was strange that Jacob should have no work for his people; the business had been thriving six months ago when she had left and since she had been back nothing appeared to have changed. 'Odd days,' Lucas Crowbroke had said. There were always off days when the fleeces hadn't arrived, or the sorters hadn't finished or the wool wasn't sufficiently steeped. Probably it meant nothing.

All the same, she had noticed that Jacob was at pains to keep her out of his counting house these days. Could it be that there was something he was anxious to hide?

III

The summer came and went. Jannekyn worked herself so hard that she scarcely noticed. If it hadn't been for snatching enough herbs from the fields to stock her tiny still-room against winter ailments she wouldn't even have noticed that the flowers in the hedgerows had bloomed and died.

Jacob continued to demand her services and she answered his requirements dutifully and mechanically. She discovered that she had a gift for smoothing ruffled tempers and managed to turn many a potentially ugly situation into an amicable agreement. She liked Robert Lamb, the English bailiff with whom they often had to deal, although it was plain that Jacob despised him – quite unreasonably, and that Robert Lamb had difficulty in concealing his dislike for Jacob.

This was hardly surprising. Jacob had begun to develop a kind of desperate truculence; throwing his weight around to an extent that was making him unpopular with his own countrymen as well as with the English population. In Church matters Jacob was the first to condemn transgressors and his judgements were never tempered by any degree of mercy. He was hated and feared by those who worked for him and Jannekyn had even heard Katherine, his wife, threaten more than once to leave him and go to live with Dionis. But this threat was soon appeased, Jannekyn noticed, by a new and expensive gown.

She spoke to Lucas Crowbroke about him. Lucas was spending more and more of his time in the little lean-to by the side of the dye-house. He had built himself a clay fireplace in the corner where he could heat the combs he used for combing the wool. Jannekyn often wondered how such a thin, weedy-looking little man found the strength and stamina to wield the heavy combs for such long periods. But he did, although the sweat ran in rivulets down his face and back as he worked. He stopped at her words and mopped his face with a tangle of discarded wool.

'Aye, he do be a hard master,' he said in reply to her remark that Jacob seemed to be making himself more and more unpopular. 'But then, he always has been, so there's nothing new in that. But I'll tell you this, Mevrouw' – he picked a comb out of the fire and spat on it to test the temperature – 'he's a worried man. There's not the work about for us combers in his warehouse these days. And the spinners are often idle, too. His business ain't what it was. Not by any means it ain't.' Rhythmically, he began to swing the comb through the long strands of wool that were fixed by one end to a stake in the wall. 'I might tell you I'm glad enough to come here and work for you, Mevrouw. My children's bellies 'ud scrape their backbone oft times if it worn't for that.'

Jannekyn was silent. It was no more than she had suspected. Jacob had never allowed her in his counting house but he couldn't prevent her noticing that the loom shed was often silent and the warehouse deserted. Neither could he conceal the tremor in his hands which she suspected went with an unhealthily flushed complexion and the smell of spirits on his breath. But she was less worried about this than about the way he tried to cling to her, depending on her so entirely as a kind of moral prop so that he could still present a successful and authoritative face to the world. And from this there was no escape, with Gyles behind her, subtly reminding her where her duty lay. He had only to be 'too tired' to attend to Adam's cloth so that it remained too long in the vat for her to realize that any idea she might have of rebellion was out of the question.

She grew thin. But it was hard work not unhappiness that caused her to shed weight. She had no time to consider whether she was happy or not happy and the dull ache of longing for Adam's love was so much a part of her that she accepted it as she accepted the ice and snow of the long, hard winter. She did nothing but work when she had tended little Jan. When she was not doing Jacob's bidding she spent her time either in the dye-house with Gyles and Joey or working to keep Adam supplied with yarn, driving herself out of bed before sunrise to buy the best fleeces at the market for the best prices, making sure they were cleaned and combed in readiness for the spinners to keep pace with the insatiable appetite of his loom. Marketing the cloth was no problem. Word had spread of the special, fine-textured cloth that he wove and there was soon no need for it to be taken to London in Henrick de Groot's hoy. Merchants came knocking at the door of the humble little cottage in Wimbles Lane, demanding as much, and more, than he could supply them with.

The money they made grew too much for the leather purse and Jannekyn had to find a bigger one, then a bigger one still, that she kept under a loose board near the leg of Adam's loom.

She was counting it one day, while Bessie looked after little Jan downstairs. 'There's quite a lot of money here, Adam. Don't you think you should consider moving to a bigger house?'

'Half that money belongs to you.' Adam spoke over the clack of his loom, without taking his eyes from his work. 'You can take it if you wish.'

'I don't want it. I've nothing to spend it on. I'd rather keep it in the business.'

'Well, it wouldn't be right for me to use it to buy a bigger house for myself.'

'Why not? It would be better for business. It can't be good, conducting it from this tiny little cottage. What must people think?'

'I don't care what people think. I get as much business as I can handle.'

'Mr Gurney's house at Scheregate stands empty. You could have a workroom that was completely shut away from the rest of the house. And you could have a proper bedroom. I hate you having to sleep beside your loom the way you do.'

He shrugged. 'It doesn't bother me where I sleep.' All this time he had never so much as glanced in her direction. This was nothing new. He rarely looked at her these days and only spoke to her when he was forced to discuss business matters. And things had been even worse since she returned to Jacob's service. She didn't blame Adam for this but neither could she explain to him that this was the only way she could persuade Gyles to continue dyeing their cloth. She tried to accept the situation but as she looked at him, intent on his shuttle, her heart was heavy. She knew that however Adam treated her she would never, ever stop loving him.

'I'm sure Bessie would like Mr Gurney's house. And Gabriel could lie and look out of the window at the passers-by.'

Adam ceased weaving to examine his work. 'Oh, yes, Bessie would like it, I'm sure,' he said. 'But I'm not so sure about Gabriel. I think he'd rather die where he is. He's very feeble now and he loves this little cottage so I wouldn't want to hasten his death by uprooting him. I doubt he'll last much longer, anyway.'

'You're very good to the old couple.' Jannekyn put the money back in the leather bag and bent down to replace it under the loose board.

'How could I be otherwise? They've been good to me. Gabriel taught me all I know and Bessie couldn't have treated me better if I'd been her own flesh and blood. Anyway, they're all I have in the world. I shall never leave them.'

Jannekyn looked up but his face was hidden by the fine threads of the warp stretched over the length of the loom. 'You may marry,' she said in a low voice, although the mere thought cut her to the heart.

'Marry? I shall never marry.' His voice was harsh. 'What would I want with a wife?' And the bitter way he spoke cut her still deeper. There was no plainer way he could have told her that his love for her had died. Not that she blamed him. She had caused him nothing but suffering in the past and could offer him little in the way of hope for the future. But it didn't stop her loving him; nothing, it seemed, could do that, and tears of despair ran down her cheeks on to the board as she replaced it over the bag of money. She thought of the plans they had made together such a short time ago; plans to work together and become rich. The irony of it all was that they *were* working together, just as they'd planned. And they *were* becoming prosperous, just as they'd hoped. Only instead of bringing them happiness there was nothing but misery. Sadly, she got to her feet.

'I'm going home now,' she said.

'Goodbye.' He didn't even look up. But after she had gone he left his work and got up to stare for a long time out of the window, his expression full of bleak hopelessness.

IV

Jannekyn walked home with little Jan wrapped in a sling made from the corner of her shawl. He was growing fast now and when they were at home he often had to be tethered to the door post by a strip of cloth tied round his middle to prevent him crawling away and falling in the river. But on the whole he was a good child; in fact Jannekyn often thought her little son was the only thing in her life that made it worth living. Little Jan and the business she was building with Adam.

She paused as she passed Mr Gurney's house at Scheregate. It was a small house compared with Strangers' Hall but it was solid and well built and there would be plenty of room there for the merchants who travelled from London to examine and choose their cloth.

But Adam was right. It wouldn't be kind to uproot old Gabriel.

As it happened there was no question of uprooting him. He died in his sleep less than a week later, stealing away as quietly as the yellow fog that crept up from the river and shrouded the cottage where he lay.

'Now there is really no excuse,' Jannekyn said to Adam, when Gabriel had been decently laid to rest and a reasonable time had elapsed. 'You need a bigger house, you can't deny that, and Mr Gurney's house still stands empty.' She turned to Bessie. 'You'd like to live in Mr Gurney's house, wouldn't you, Bessie?'

'Thass a rare fine house,' Bessie agreed. She had made several journeys there, all by herself, and had stood on tiptoe, peering in at the large rooms through the lattice – lattice with glass in, at that.

'I'll think about it,' was all Adam would say.

When Jannekyn had gone. Bessie got meat and bread and put it on the table. 'If you don't want Mr Gurney's house then we won't go there,' she said. 'But that'd be a sight better for you if we went there. You could hev a proper room for the loom, and wouldn't need to sleep in a truckle bed beside it . . . '

'I know all that. Jannekyn has already pointed it out to me,' Adam said irritably, stretching his feet towards the fire in a moment of unaccustomed idleness.

'Then what's stoppin' you?' Bessie cut a hunk of meat and handed it to him on a trencher of bread.

He ate in silence for a while, staring into the fire. Then he said, 'The money isn't mine, it's half Jannekyn's. If it was all mine I'd say yes, right away.' He continued to stare into the fire.

'Do Jannekyn want her money out, then?' Bessie asked.

'No. But I want her to have it.'

'But why? I thought you was workin' together?' Bessie frowned, her slow mind trying to understand. 'I know she'm Dutch, but . . . '

'She's back with Jacob van der Hest,' Adam broke in. 'She can't serve two masters – not that I'm her master, but you know what I mean, Bessie. As you say, she's Dutch, and her loyalty clearly lies with her people, Jacob van der Hest in particular. Surely you realize, Bessie, that she only helped me to build this business out of a sense of conscience? Because she felt she was to blame for what happened to Gabriel and me and the fact that I couldn't find work. Well, she's paid her debt, or what she considers to be her debt, and there's an end to it. The sooner I can pay her what's due to her and be done with it the better. You were right, Dutch and English don't mix,' he added bitterly.

Bessie gazed at him sadly. 'I ain't sure as you're right, boy. An' I ain't so sure as I was, either. Jannekyn's a rare nice little maid, an' although I know I'm speakin' contrariwise to what I said afore, nuthin' 'ud please me more than to see you two wed.'

Adam got up from his chair with such violence that he knocked it over. He didn't stop to pick it up. 'I'm going back upstairs. I've work on the loom that must be finished tonight,' he threw over his shoulder as he climbed the stairs to the loft

Nevertheless, within a month he had trundled his own and Bessie's possessions from the cottage in Wimbles Lane to the house at Scheregate on a hand-cart, making more than one journey to fetch the precious loom, insisting all the while that he was only doing it for Bessie's sake.

There were plenty of rooms in the new house, enough for him to rebuild his loom on the top floor where there was plenty of light. This became his workroom. No longer did he have to sleep on the truckle bed beside the loom, he had a proper bedroom with a mattress of feathers to lie on. Not that he paid much attention to where he slept; he worked such long hours that he often fell asleep over his shuttle, waking again hours later, cramped and cold, to crawl into his bed and sleep again until it was light enough to begin work once more.

Bessie loved her new house with its oak-panelled walls and glazed windows. After the cottage where she had lived for so long it was little short of a palace to her and she hummed to herself as she polished the dark oak table and benches or made bread and oat cakes in the faggot oven, the like of which she had never seen before.

'Mind yew, Gabriel wouldn't ha' liked it,' she told Jannekyn as she proudly showed her over her new home. 'It 'ud bin too big for his likin'.'

Jannekyn smiled. She knew what Bessie meant, although compared with Strangers' Hall this house was still very small. But it was more than adequate for Adam's and Bessie's needs and it was far superior to the Dyer's House where she lived with Gyles.

'But you like it, Bessie, don't you?' she asked.

'Lor, yes, I should think I do.'

'And Adam?'

Bessie's face grew serious. 'To tell the truth I don't believe he notice much difference. All 'e do is eat, sleep an' work. An' often times I hev to take 'is food up to 'im and clear a space for it near the loom or 'e wouldn't eat at all. You can hear the loom goin' upstairs now, an' it's like that from morn till night. He've even got a young boy now to do the fetchin' and carryin' so 'e don't hev to stop and fetch the yarn an' go to the finishers hisself. Thass all work, work, work. He'll kill hisself afore he's much older, if 'e don't watch out.' She looked anxiously at Jannekyn. 'Why don't yew go and speak to 'im, dearie? 'E won't take no heed o' me, but p'raps 'e'll listen to yew.'

'I'll try, Bessie.' Jannekyn put little Jan on the floor – only to see him scooped up into Bessie's ample lap – and threw her cloak over the settle that stood in the corner by the fire. 'But I doubt he'll listen to me.'

She made her way up the oak staircase. It was built round a large square pillar, with wide steps and a cupboard built into the pillar at each turn. The cupboard at the top of the stairs was smaller than the rest and had a lock. It was here that their now depleted store of money was kept.

Adam didn't stop working as she entered his workroom; she doubted if he had even heard her come in, he was so intent on his work. She stood for a moment watching him. He was thin, almost gaunt, and his face had the pallor of a man who rarely saw the sun. It was true what Bessie had said. He was working himself to death.

He looked up as her shadow fell across his work but he didn't stop the rhythmic clack of the shuttle for one moment.

'I'm running out of purple,' he said, over the noise. 'Has Gyles got that other batch nearly ready?'

'Yes. Joey will be bringing it later on today.' She no longer expected a smile or word of greeting from him. She stood looking out of the window over the higgledy-piggledy of roofs.

Will you move along. You're standing in my light,' he called.

She moved. 'Oh, I wouldn't want to get in your way,' she said, with more than a trace of sarcasm.

'What did you say?'

'I said I'm sorry I'm in your way,' she shouted.

'Oh, you're not in my way. You're all right if you stand there.' He carried on working without a second glance at her.

She bit her lip and stood silent for a while. 'Do you like the house?' she said, after a bit.

'What did you say?' It was almost impossible to hold a conversation.

'I said . . . ' Suddenly she put her hands over her ears. 'Oh, for God's sake, can't you stop that thing for a minute!' she screamed.

It was surprise more than anything that made him stop and look up. For a moment the silence hung between them like a thick blanket. Then he said quietly, 'It's only while I work at my loom that I earn any money.'

'But surely you're making enough money without working *all* the time? You've been able to buy this nice house . . . '

'Only by paying for it with money that was half yours. Money that I intend to repay as soon as possible.' He spoke stiffly.

'Oh, Adam, you know I'm not worried about that.'

'Maybe not. But I am. I don't want to be in your debt any longer than I have to.'

She frowned. She'd never seen him like this before. 'Adam, what's the matter? We're business partners. You can't talk about being "in debt" to me. I told you a year ago, when we began, that if I chose to leave my share in to help things along I would. Well, I have left it in and I shall continue to leave it in if I choose. So I see no point in your working yourself to death in order to repay money to me that I've no intention of taking.'

'I'd prefer that you did.' He didn't look at her.

She was silent for a long time. 'You mean you don't want me to work with you any longer,' she said at last, her voice flat.

'That's right.'

'May I know why? I thought we worked well together.' She found herself automatically counting the threads in the warp as she spoke. Anything rather than look at him.

'I just think it's best. For one thing you're Dutch and I'm English . . . '

'That's never mattered to you before.'

He ignored that and went on, 'It's quite plain that your husband doesn't care for our association and now that you're back with Mynheer van der Hest – well, it's obvious where your allegiance lies. And who can blame you? After all, he's done a lot for you. If he hadn't been kind enough to pick you up out of the gutter goodness knows where you'd be.'

'He didn't . . . '

'Oh, I'm not blaming you, Jannekyn, don't think that. Mynheer van der Hest is good to you so it's only natural that you should serve him. But you must surely see that you can't go on serving him and working with me. And it's not even a question of asking you to choose because you've already made your choice. As I see it there's no more to be said.'

She went to the window and stood looking out. 'Very well, Adam, if you no longer want me I'll leave you in peace. I'll make sure you have a list of all the people I deal with and all the people who do work for us. We'll have to come to some arrangement over the dyeing, that is, unless you've found someone else to do it.' She smiled, a bitter little smile. 'It's ironic, isn't it? It was only by agreeing to go back to Jacob van der Hest that I could persuade Gyles to continue dyeing your cloth, yet it's precisely because I'm working for Jacob that you now want to be rid of me.' She shrugged. 'Well, at least Gyles won't have a lever to force me to serve that man any more if you take your dyeing elsewhere.'

Adam left his loom and came and stood behind her. 'I didn't know that,' he said quietly. 'I thought you'd gone back to him of your own free will. Out of gratitude . . . '

At this, Jannekyn laughed out loud, but it was a hollow, mirthless sound. 'Oh, yes, I've a lot to be thankful to Jacob van der Hest for.' She turned and looked at him. 'Do you know who he is? He's my *uncle*, but he disowned me the moment I set foot on English soil. He told everybody he'd picked me up out of the gutter and he treated me as if it was true. He treated me as if it was true to such an extent that I almost began to believe it myself. He humiliated me in front of his family, yet he couldn't bear me out of his sight.' She turned away again. 'Worst of all, he parted me from the only man I've ever loved and forced me to marry a man nearly old enough to be my grandfather. And now he's come between us again, Adam, to ruin the only thing I have left to make my life bearable – the business I'm building with you.' Tears were running down her cheeks but she didn't bother to check them. 'Oh, yes,' she said bitterly, 'I've a lot to be grateful to Jacob van der Hest for.' Blindly, she turned to stumble from the room.

'Oh, Jannekyn, Jannekyn, my own dear love. I didn't know.' Suddenly, she was in his arms and he was holding her as if he would never let her go. 'Forgive me. I didn't know. I thought you were happy with your lot. I thought you'd forgotten all we'd been to each other.' He smoothed her hair back from her face. 'I've been so eaten up with misery and jealousy because you appeared so happy and contented that I could hardly bear to look at you.'

'Happy!' She clung to him. 'Oh, if only you knew the torture

I've been through. I thought you hated me for all the suffering I'd caused you.'

'Never,' he groaned, his lips against her hair. 'I think I love you more each day that goes by, if that's possible. I only live for the moments when you're here, with me.'

She looked up at him in surprise. 'Yet you barely speak to me.'

'Lest I should humiliate myself by letting you see how I long for you.' His lips came down on hers and he kissed her with such passion that she was shaken to the very depths of her being and she found herself responding with equal ardour. It was as if floodgates had been released and she felt herself drowning ... drowning in his love.

Then, with a supreme effort she pulled herself away. 'No, Adam. It can't be. You know it can't be,' she said breathlessly.

He gazed at her hungrily, seeing the quick rise and fall of her breasts, and took a step towards her, pulling her to him again. 'We've waited so long, Jannekyn,' he said thickly.

'But we must wait longer.' With a superhuman effort she pushed him from her. 'Oh, Adam, it's as hard for me as it is for you. But I promised Gyles we would never be more than friends while he lived ... He's an old man,' she added weakly.

'And healthy. And wiry. And good for at least another ten years,' he said savagely, trying to take her in his arms again.

She twisted away and instead took his hand and cradled it against her cheek. 'Isn't it enough for the moment to know that I love you, Adam? That I've always loved you and that I'll go on loving you till the day I die?'

'No, it isn't,' he said roughly. 'I want you. *All* of you. Why do you think I never stop working? Well, I'll tell you. I never stop working so that when I fall into bed at night I'm too tired to be tortured by dreams of having that lovely body of yours lying beside me.' Once again he took her in his arms and this time she had no resistance to offer, returning his kisses with a passion that equalled his own. He was right. They had waited too long. Suddenly, an agonized scream rose from the room below.

They sprang apart. 'Little Jan. Oh, my God, it's little Jan.' Jannekyn rushed down the stairs, tying her bodice strings as she went, with Adam close on her heels.

Bessie was sitting by the fire, rocking back and forth, the screaming child in her arms and a pan of scalding water overturned on the hearth. 'I musta fell asleep and he musta clawed holda the pan,' she moaned. 'Hush, my pretty. Let Bessie see what yore done.'

'Let me see.' Jannekyn took little Jan from her. 'There, there, come to Mammie, little one.' She comforted him until his screams had subsided enough to let Adam examine him to see where he was hurt.

'It's his hand. I don't think he's hurt anywhere else,' Adam said after a minute.

'Thank the good Lord for that.' Bessie hurried to the door. 'I'll get some balm for it. Is it bad?'

'No, there's no blister. It's just red. It's all right, liefje. Bessie's gone to get some stuff to take the hurt away.' Jannekyn rocked the little boy in her arms. 'It's my fault, I shouldn't have left him for so long,' she said to Adam, over the child's whimper.

'It was my fault, too.' Adam was still kneeling beside her and he stroked little Jan's silky hair. 'But perhaps it happened for the best,' he went on in a low voice. 'If he hadn't screamed as he did . . . I'm sorry, Jannekyn, I got carried away. But you were right, of course you were right. I promise it won't happen again.'

She put out her hand and touched his cheek. 'It didn't even

happen this time, Adam, did it?' she said, with a sad little smile. 'I almost wish it had.'

'We can wait, my love. It won't be for ever.' In full command of himself now he kissed the palm of her hand and then got to his feet as Bessie came back into the room.

'There, there, my pretty, this'll take the fire outa yore pore little hand.' She wrapped a rag soaked in green liquid round little Jan's hand and put a gingerbread man into the other one. 'An' thass for bein' a good, brave boy. Adam, fetch a clout, now, and clear up the floor. Thass only water, so that won't do no harm.'

Little Jan, quiet now, sat on his mother's knee, munching the gingerbread man and watching what was going on with enormous blue eyes.

''E's gettin' to be a big boy, aren't you, my lovely?' Bessie was still fussing, trying to make amends for her negligence.

'And heavy, too, I'm sure,' Adam said. 'I'll carry him home for you, Jannekyn. It'll do me good to get a breath of fresh air and I can bring back the yarn Gyles has dyed for me.'

'Thass a good idea,' Bessie agreed. 'An' thass a pity yew don't go out a bit more often. Stuck upstairs at that loom all the time . . . '

They left Bessie still wittering and set off for the Dyer's House by the river, taking a short cut through the castle bailey and across the tenterfields, barely half hung with cloth from Jacob's looms. Jannekyn stopped and looked back up the hill at Strangers' Hall. It stood in the shadow of the wintry afternoon sun and suddenly the old familiar feeling struck her, more forcibly than ever before, that it was *her* house, and that it was waiting for her to make it live.

'What's the matter, my love?' Adam was sensitive to her every mood.

'It's the house – Strangers' Hall. I know I've had nothing but unhappiness there, and yet – somehow it calls me. I can't explain.' She shook her head. 'It's as if it's there waiting for me, waiting for me to bring love and laughter to it. Oh,' she gave a little laugh. 'You must think I'm stupid. I daresay you're right, too.'

'Is it the first time you've felt like that?' he asked seriously.

'No. It happened the first time I set foot inside it and it's happened several times since. It's funny; I ought to hate it, I've suffered so much misery there. But I don't I love every stick and stone of it.'

'I'm afraid I can't see Jacob ever giving it up,' Adam said.

'No, neither can I. And I'd never live in the same house as him again, ever.' She shrugged. 'Oh, it's just a silly feeling that comes over me. I suppose it's because it's such a beautiful house. I'd never known such a place before I came to England.'

She turned and continued to walk down the hill with Adam at her side, with little Jan on his arm, utterly content in his company.

Suddenly, he said, 'So much has happened this afternoon that I'm not sure I heard aright, but didn't you say earlier that Jacob van der Hest was your *uncle*, Jannekyn? Or was I dreaming?'

'No, you weren't dreaming. It's perfectly true. But he said I was never to tell anyone.'

'Why, for goodness' sake?'

'I never really knew,' she confessed. 'I used to think it was because I looked so awful when I arrived in England. You see, my parents had no money so my clothes were full of darns. And they were very dirty from the dreadful crossing over the German Sea' – she shuddered – 'I can still remember it.' She gave a little laugh. 'Hardly a fit creature to be welcomed as the niece of the great Jacob van der Hest.'

'Didn't you ask your aunt?'

'No. I dared not talk to anyone. You see, I had no papers, no authority to be in Colchester. He told me that it was only while I was under his roof and he spoke for me that I would be safe. He said my parents would suffer . . . Oh, he really terrified me into silence, I can tell you.'

Adam frowned. 'But he must have had a reason for disowning you.'

'Yes. I used to think about mat a lot. But, you see, if he had accepted me as his niece he would have had to treat me as one of the family. It was much cheaper to treat me as a servant I'm sure that would be reason enough as far as he was concerned. You know how mean he can be.'

'Do your parents know all this?'

'Heavens, no. And I wouldn't have wanted them to. He allowed me to write to them once, to let them know I had arrived safely, but he made sure I only put down what he told me to. I don't even know if they ever received it.'

'Where are they?'

'When I left they were living in a little village to the north of Ypres. I don't know whether they're still there. My father was too ill to make the journey to England and of course my mother wouldn't leave him. But he desperately wanted me to come because he thought I'd have a better life here.' She gave a mirthless laugh. 'Little did he know what he was sending me to!'

'So you don't even know if they're still alive?'

'No. But Henrick goes over sometimes.' She lowered her voice. 'He doesn't talk about it but I think he still helps people to escape. Did you know he lost his fingers to the Spanish? He was in prison for five years, just like my father.'

'No, I didn't know that'

'Well, it's true. I've told him where my parents live – or rather lived – and he's going to try and get a message to them.' She looked at little Jan, asleep now against Adam's shoulder. 'I should like mem to know they have a little grandson.'

Adam looked at her, a wealth of love in his eyes. 'And I should like them to know that there's someone who loves you and would give anything to be able to take you and care for you for the rest of our days.'

For a moment she clung to his arm. 'Oh, Adam, if only it could be so.'

Gyles was waiting for her when they arrived at the cottage. He was paternally possessive towards her, chiding her because she was late for the lample pie he had cooked. And he fussed round little Jan, insisting that the perfectly adequate dressing should be changed for ointment that he had made. He dismissed Adam with hardly more than a nod.

'Never mind,' Adam whispered to Jannekyn as he picked up the bundle of yarn that Gyles had almost thrown at him. 'At least he dyes it well and at least he doesn't stop you from working with me.'

She glanced over her shoulder to where Gyles was still tending little Jan. 'I fear he would if he guessed.'

'Then we mustn't let him guess.' He grinned and in a louder voice said, 'I give you Good-day, Mevrouw de Troster.'

'And to you, Master Mortlock.'

She closed the door behind him. Nothing had changed. The cottage was the same; Gyles, although he was increasingly fussy and possessive, was the same; Jacob, rude and demanding, was the same; yet she was happy. Suddenly, her heart sang and everything looked brighter.

And all because she was secure in Adam's love.

Chapter Six

I

Jacob van der Hest was not unaware of Adam Mortlock's growing success and, coupled with a decline in his own business, it was a double blow. He had, on occasion, managed to bribe searchers at the Bay Hall to reject the young Englishman's cloth, but this was an expensive business and searchers were naturally reluctant to tear in half perfect cloth, as was the custom with cloth that was not up to standard. So there was little he could do but watch Adam's increasing success.

Knowing that Jannekyn was a part of it didn't help. He tried threatening her with Gyles's eviction from his cottage, but it was a threat he knew he would never carry out because there was nowhere else that he could get cloth dyed so cheaply – indeed, if things were difficult he could even 'forget' to pay altogether.

'You may evict us if you wish,' she replied coolly, facing him across the table in his smoking room. 'There's a cottage not far from East Mill that will suit us very well. In fact, I had already been to look at it. But, of course, that would mean you would lose my services as interpreter – not that you need me now. Surely, you have learned enough of the English language to manage for yourself.'

He was silent. True, he had picked up a smattering of English, but it was a difficult language and he found he often got it quite wrong and would have given in to what he considered to be quite outrageous English demands simply because he had forgotten to put in a simple word like 'not'.

'We will let things remain as they are for the present,' he said stiffly.

Jannekyn left then, leaving behind her a faint smell of lavender to remind him of her presence, of the tilt of her head, of the whiteness of her neck that he so longed to touch ... to run his fingers down its length and to feel the soft smoothness of her shoulders ... Savagely, he got up from his chair, sending it crashing to the floor in the process, and went over to the hutch in the corner. He threw the door open and took out a bottle, splashing the amber liquid into the glass that stood ready by its side, his hands shaking so much that it spilled on to the floor as he raised it to his lips. This was his only comfort now, the only thing that afforded him oblivion from a business that was sinking further and further into debt, a frigid wife and an obsession with a girl who despised him but who, God help him, he would take in spite of everything but for the dreadful charge he would have to answer at the Day of Judgement.

II

Jannekyn walked home from Strangers' Hall deep in thought. There was no doubt Jacob van der Hest's business was not what it had been. The spinners in Trinity Poors Row now worked exclusively for Adam – and it was not simply because he paid them more than Jacob and didn't accuse them unjustly of dishonesty and fine them unfairly – the agents – or agent, there was now only one – simply had no work to bring them. Likewise, Lucas Crowbroke spent most of his time in the lean-to beside the dye-house, working for Jannekyn, and his family with him. And it was not that there was any shortage of weavers to produce the cloth once the yarn was spun; they still rioted through the town begging for work, just as they'd always done. It was very odd.

At the same time, she had been bluffing when she had said the cottage at East Mill would suit. Gyles would never agree to moving there, his allegiance remained faithful to Jacob in spite of everything. In truth, she had to play her cards skilfully in order to persuade him to continue dyeing Adam's cloth. Sometimes she even did it herself, helped by Joey, when Gyles was out of the way, and she was increasingly pleased with the results she achieved.

Joey was waiting for her when she arrived home and he dashed out into the yard from the dye-house, his ginger head tousled and with streaks of green and red dye running down his face.

'My goodness, Joey, you quite frightened me! You look for all the world like the evil spirit in a mummer's play,' she laughed. 'What have you been doing?'

He looked down at the old shirt belonging to Gyles that he wore to protect his own clothes. 'Oh, not the evil spirit,' he said with a grin, 'I'd be better as Joseph, with my coat of many colours, wouldn't I?'

'Yes, perhaps you would.' Jannekyn turned to go into the house.

'Wait, Mevrouw. I have a message for you.' Joey caught her sleeve. 'It's from my father. He's been away for several weeks, I don't know where, my mother wouldn't say, but I know she's been worried about him. He says will you go and see him.'

The message could only mean one thing. News of her father. Jannekyn smiled at Joey. 'I'll go right away. Is little Jan still asleep in the dye-house?'

'He was a minute ago.'

Jannekyn went into the dye-house and looked at her little son asleep in the nest of cloth that Gyles had made. 'He'll be all right there till I get back. I shan't be long,' she said to Gyles, adding in a low voice, 'I think Henrick may have news of my father.'

It didn't take her long to reach the little house in Grub Street and Henrick was there with Betkin, pregnant yet again. They were both delighted to see her.

'You have news of my father?' Jannekyn said eagerly when she had been seated on a stool by the fire and given oat cakes and ale.

'Indeed I have.' Henrick scratched the rim of wiry hair round his bald head with what remained of his hands. 'And how to tell you about it . . . ' He sighed, gazed into the fire and shook his head. Then he sighed again. 'I really don't know where to begin . . . '

'He's dead. You're trying to tell me he's dead,' Jannekyn said flatly.

'No, no, he's not dead, my dear. He's ill, that no one could deny, with a cough that would rattle the bells in the church tower; but, no, he's not dead.'

'My mother?'

'She's well'

'Then what? What have you got to tell me?'

'Start at the beginning, Henrick,' Betkin said, putting another log on the fire. 'That's always the best place.'

'Yes, that's always the best place,' Henrick nodded. He continued to stare into the fire.

Jannekyn watched him expectantly. She had never seen him so at a loss for words. Finally, he took a deep breath and began. 'Your father belonged to a wealthy family. Clothiers they were,' he said, looking up at her.

Jannekyn raised her eyebrows. 'Did he? I didn't know

that. In fact, I don't ever remember a time when we weren't very hard up.'

'Well, the van der Hests were a rich and notable family in Ypres. There was the father, your grandfather, my dear, and two sons. Jan, your father, was the eldest and he had a younger brother, Jacob. At the time of the reign of terror in 68 they were, as I say, wealthy and of some standing in the town. When Alva decreed that even more taxes should be squeezed out and that estates should be seized they decided that they had had enough and they would do what thousands were already doing, and emigrate to England. However, before they could arrange a passage your grandfather was taken before the Blood Council and charged – I don't know what with, some trumped up charge like they all were, I expect. I understand he died a pretty horrific death. When they heard about this the two brothers realized that they'd better get out quickly before the same thing happened to them.'

Jannekyn licked her lips, her eyes never leaving Henrick's face. 'Go on,' she said.

He took another deep breath. 'Jan and Jacob, together with their wives, left their home in Ypres secretly, taking as much of the family silver and valuables as they could carry and made their way to Antwerp. It was not an easy journey, they had to hide by day and travel by night. But at last they reached Antwerp and went to an address they'd been given. There, they met up with another man who was bound for England, a Predikant, Minister Weller, a man with a price on his head for preaching openly against Catholicism.' Henrick paused. 'Leven Weller was a brave man, one of the bravest I ever knew,' he said soberly. Then he went on, 'Friends of Leven Weller had arranged for me to pick him up from a little cove a few miles below Antwerp. What I used to do was deliver my cargo at the port and then collect my "passengers" further down the river with whatever fresh cargo I'd picked up and deliver them to England.' He waved his hand. 'It was no problem, I'd done it before, scores of times. In fact, it was the recognized escape route for anyone with a price on his head.'

'But my father hadn't got a price on his head, had he?'

'No, not exactly. But the Spanish didn't particularly want him to leave the country and he knew it, so this route seemed the safest. *Seemed*, I say.'

'Why? What happened?'

'Well, they all hid in the cellar of this house for four days. The Spanish had apparently got wind that something was afoot and they were pretty watchful. But at last it became imperative that they should move because I couldn't stay in Antwerp any longer without arousing suspicion. So, they went, escaping over the rooftops with nothing but what they stood up in, while the Spanish walked the streets below.'

'So they had to leave all the silver and valuables behind?'

'Yes. Everything.' Henrick paused to light his pipe, which consisted of a thick straw poked into half a walnut shell. Jannekyn watched him, amazed at the dexterity with which he used what was left of his fingers. When he had got the pipe to draw he went on, 'What happened next had always been a mystery to me. I'd been told to expect two men, Hans and Jacques – I was never given proper names, it was safer all round if I didn't know the real identity of my passengers – and their wives, plus another man, who I knew simply as the Predikant, although it didn't take much to work out who *he* was. But when I arrived to pick them up there was only one man and his wife and the Predikant. Hans, as I knew him, insisted that we wait for his young brother. Apparently, he'd been taken ill on the way and would be along with his wife, who'd stayed with him, a little later.' Henrick shook his head. 'I should have smelled a rat then. I blame myself to some extent; I'd been doing the job for long enough to know that it's not safe to hang about for *anything* at times like that. But the man was clearly concerned about his brother and didn't want to leave him behind, so we waited. We waited an hour. The brother never showed up, but the Spanish butchers did. They crept up on us. and took us before we had any chance to escape. And all Hans could say was, "Thank God my brother hadn't arrived, or he'd have been taken, too. At least he'll have a chance to get away."'

'Hans was my father?'

'Yes, but I didn't discover that until I searched him out for you. And all those years I'd had no idea that Jacob van der Hest was the missing younger brother, Jacques.'

'My father must have found out, though, or he couldn't have written to him.'

'Yes, he learned from a Predikant who'd returned from England.'

'Minister Grenrice, who taught me English?'

'I don't know. It may have been. Anyway, it was years later. Of course, when the poor man found out he was overjoyed to think his young brother had managed to escape and he decided to send you over to him.'

Jannekyn frowned. 'It's strange that my uncle didn't welcome me a bit more warmly, then. I've always thought it very peculiar . . . '

'Ah, but my dear, you haven't heard the whole story yet'

'What do you mean?'

Henrick took his pipe out of his mouth and laid it carefully on the shelf. 'Well, doesn't it strike you as even more odd that the Spanish should have discovered that escape route on that particular night, when Minister Weller, the most wanted man in the district, was there? And that the younger brother and his wife, who should have been there too, were not? And even more odd still that the younger brother should later arrive in England and very quickly become one of the richest men in Colchester?'

'What are you saying?'

'I'm saying that the younger brother, Jacob, tipped off the Spaniards that this escape was going to take place and then faked illness so that he wouldn't be there. Remember, if the brothers had both reached England they would have had nothing but the clothes they stood up in. Nothing. And neither of them was used to poverty. The temptation to betray the Predikant, even though it meant sacrificing his own brother, was too much for Jacob, seeing that in return he was guaranteed a safe passage to England for himself and his wife, plus all his family's wealth, or, more strictly, *some* of his family's wealth. The fact that he smuggled the rest of it out under the Spaniards' noses is another story.'

'What happened to my father, then?'

'Like me, he spent an uncomfortable five years,' Henrick said, in a masterpiece of understatement. 'Although' – he looked at his hands – 'he did manage to get out without actually losing anything. In fact, I believe the rack can add an inch or two to a man's height. And we both fared better than the Predikant, poor brave soul, he died a most horrible death.' He paused and sat gazing into the fire for a long time. Then he pulled himself together. 'However, that's all water under the bridge, as they say. And speaking of water under the bridge, did your, father ever tell you how he escaped?'

'Yes. He said that when the Prince of Orange's men rose against the Spanish the prison guards panicked and executed most of the prisoners. Those they didn't execute they tied back to back and threw into the Scheldt to drown. My father was tied like that but by the time they got to him the guards were in such a frenzy that they didn't tie him properly to his partner and my father managed to get the bonds off. He said it was difficult because the man who was with him, who had been his friend ever since they were captured together, couldn't help . . . ' Jannekyn's eyes widened. ' . . . He'd been tortured and had had all his . . . fingers . . . cut . . . off . . . All these years and I didn't think . . . I didn't realize . . . '

Henrick nodded. 'Yes, all these years and we neither of us knew that you were the daughter of the man I'd been through hell with.'

'And it was all Jacob's fault'

'Yes.' Henrick gave a bitter smile. 'Of course I can understand now why Jacob was good to me when I came to England. He realized that he'd sacrificed me as well as his brother to save his own skin and feather his own nest.'

'I can't see why he should have disowned Jannekyn and treated her as a servant, though.' It was the first time Betkin had spoken.

'Oh, I think it was simply cheaper to keep me as a servant than as a member of the family,' Jannekyn said, dismissing it. 'Jacob's a mean man, we all know that.' She turned to Henrick again. 'But where did you learn all this? Did my father tell you?'

'Yes, but it's only lately that he's managed to piece it all together. I might tell you he was very relieved to hear that you were safe, he'd never have sent you to Jacob if he'd known what the man was capable of.'

Jannekyn sat silently looking into the fire, digesting all that Henrick had told her. 'My mother?' she said at last. 'What about my mother?'

'She didn't suffer too badly compared with some. She was released from prison after a couple of years and managed to live by her distaff. It wasn't what she'd been used to but she managed to find a hovel and make some kind of a home, praying for the day when your father would be released.'

'Oh, they should never have been made to suffer so much at that man's hands,' she said through clenched teeth. 'I could *kill* him. With my own bare hands I could *kill* him.'

'Hush, child.' Betkin glanced furtively towards the door. 'Be careful what you're saying. Haven't you heard?'

'Heard what?'

'That the witch-hunters are about. They've been to St Osyth and ten women were denounced as witches for less than what you've just uttered.' She spoke in a low voice as if afraid she might be overheard.

'I'm no witch,' Jannekyn said. 'If I were, I'd . . . '

'Hush. Don't even say it,' Betkin warned, putting her finger to her lips.

'I shall go and see him.' Jannekyn stood up, tossing her head. 'I shall go and see him and tell him what I know. I shall demand that he pays to have my parents carried to England in comfort.'

'I fear it's too late for that, my dear,' Henrick said sadly.

'It may not be. We'll arrange a litter for my father. The summer is coming . . . '

'You can try. But I doubt he'll live that long.'

'Nevertheless, I shall go and see him!' Then she hesitated. We've no proof, though. And my father can't help because he's still in Flanders. It's just my word against Jacob's.'

'Your word and Henrick's,' Betkin reminded her.

Henrick got to his feet. 'There's also Wynkyn Eversham. He's an official at the Bay Hall. In fact, I believe he's now one of the Governors, which may, in itself, be significant. Jacob and his wife stayed with him when they first arrived in Colchester and I'm sure he knows all about it, although when I went to see him he wouldn't talk. However, I gathered, more from what he didn't say than what he did, that he knows what went on. I'd be reluctant to draw him in, but I would if I had to.'

'It may not be necessary,' Jannekyn said. 'Maybe the threat will be enough, After all, the only thing I'm asking is that my father's last days shall be spent in comfort, here in England if possible, where he so desperately wanted to come, and that my mother shall be looked after, too. Surely, even he wouldn't deny that to his own flesh and blood.'

'He already has,' Henrick reminded her cryptically.

'Well, he couldn't be callous enough to do it a second time.'

III

Jacob was pacing up and down the solar, with Katherine's complaining voice whining in his ear. New clothes. She needed new clothes. Didn't he realize she hadn't a stitch to wear that could be called respectable? Dionis was always having new . . .

'Yes, my dear. Very well. I'll have patterns sent and you can choose what you will,' he placated her. She could choose, that would keep her quiet, but it didn't mean he would ever afford to let her have it made up. Debts were piling up on every side; he could only afford to hire inferior workmen now and inferior cloth fetched inferior prices. It was a downward spiral that was gathering momentum at a frightening speed.

Garerdine pushed open the door without knocking. She was the only indoor servant left now and she was old, shuffling along on bad feet, leaving a sour, unpleasant smell of unwashed body behind her. 'Mevrouw de Troster to see yer,' she muttered and banged the door shut, leaving Jannekyn on the inside.

'Jannekyn, my dear.' He went forward to greet her with a smile. She looked young and fresh and more comely than ever in a new blue gown that exactly matched the colour of her eyes. And she was clearly quite unconscious of the provocative picture she presented, with tendrils of hair escaping from under her cap to frame her face.

For her part, Jannekyn remained just inside the door, stepping aside as he advanced on her with his wolfish leer. She could see Katherine, fatter than ever, lying on her couch by the window, petulantly plucking at the covers, dressed quite unsuitably for a woman of her size, all frills and ribbons, with food stains down the front,

'Come and sit down.' Jacob drew up a chair for her. It was unheard of that she should visit without a summons delivered by his servant. 'To what do we owe the honour of this visit?'

'Oh, for goodness' sake, Jacob,' Katherine interrupted irritably. 'Anyone would think it was the Queen herself visiting us.'

Jacob turned an ugly glance on his wife and then smiled ingratiatingly again at Jannekyn, holding the chair invitingly.

'No, thank you. What I have come for is better said standing up,' Jannekyn said, her voice icy with fury.

'Oh!' Jacob raised his eyebrows in surprise. 'Is something wrong?'

'Yes. Something is *very* wrong, Uncle Jacob.'

Jacob shot a warning glance at her and then at his wife.

Katherine sat bolt upright. '*Uncle* Jacob? What does she mean, *Uncle* Jacob?*

'Nothing, my dear. A slip of the tongue.' He fussed round his wife, saying over his shoulder, 'My wife is unwell. She must not be disturbed. We will go to my smoking room.'

'I am perfectly well.' Katherine brushed him aside and put her feet to the floor. 'Now, what is all this about''

'I am your niece, Aunt Katherine.' Jannekyn went forward to Katherine, ignoring Jacob, who was still trying to come between them. 'I am the daughter of Jan van der Hest and his wife Bettris.'

Katherine frowned. 'No, you lie. That can't possibly be. Jan and Bettris were killed when we tried to escape to England in 68. And that must have been years before you were even born.'

'No, Aunt Katherine, they were not killed. They were imprisoned, but they did not die. They are still alive . . . '

Katherine tried to marshall her muddled thoughts. She rarely put her mind to much thinking these days and she found the task difficult. 'But Jacob,' she said, 'you always told me . . . surely they must have died. You told me they were dead when we were on the boat coming to England. You did tell me that Jan and Bettris were dead, didn't you?'

'I told you I thought they were dead. I didn't know . . . I wasn't sure . . . ' Jacob blustered.

'No, no, you told me they were dead, I'm quite sure of it.' Katherine shook her head from side to side, trying to remember all those years back.

'I thought they were dead. You remember, I was taken ill, so I didn't really know what happened to them.'

'That's right.' Katherine's fat face cleared. 'You were taken ill on the journey to be picked up by that boat. I remember how relieved I was that you made such a quick recovery when the others, Jan, my dear friend Bettris and the Predikant, Leven Weller, were only just out of sight. It would have been such an easy matter to catch them up but you wouldn't. You insisted on turning back. I never could understand that.' She sniffed. 'I hated being separated from Bettris and I wanted desperately to go on with them but you wouldn't. You refused and dragged me back to that dreadful cellar. I was terrified.' She frowned. 'I could never understand why there was all that secrecy because in the end we came over quite openly on a boat from Antwerp and brought a lot of the family valuables with us. So it was all for nothing that Jan and Bettris died.'

'They didn't die, Aunt,' Jannekyn insisted. 'They are still alive.'

Slowly, so that Katherine could take it in, Jannekyn recounted Henrick's story, and all the time Jacob continued to bluster and deny everything she said.

'Lies,' he said, over and over again. 'Take no notice. It's all lies.'

'Wynkyn Eversham didn't say that it was all lies when Henrick spoke to him,' Jannekyn said when she had finished her story.

Jacob paled. Wynkyn Eversham. For twenty-five years he had paid for that night at Wynkyn Eversham's house when he had foolishly and drunkenly let slip more than he'd intended. On the strength of what he'd guessed from a few indiscreet phrases Wynkyn Eversham had begun to demand money; money that Jacob had been foolish enough to hand over. And once the first payment was made he had demanded more and more as the years went by and Jacob's position in the town became more and more important. Even now he was demanding money that Jacob had not got and could see no prospect of obtaining, in order to hold his peace. He sighed. Oh, what was the use?

He turned to Katherine. 'I did it all for you, my dear. Don't you realize that it took a great deal of money to begin a new life in a new country if we weren't to start at the bottom? There simply wasn't enough to share between the two families. It was the only way I could make sure you wouldn't have to suffer the hardships of other immigrants. It was the only way. I did it all for you.'

Katherine threw back the dornicle that covered her and stood up. 'Did it all for me!' she said scornfully. 'Of course you didn't do it all for me. You did it out of your own greed and avarice. You knew that I would a thousand times rather have had my Bettris here in England, safe beside me, than all the riches in Christendom.' She pushed her face close to his. 'I don't care about you, Jacob van der Hest I don't care about your fine house and your fine clothes. I'm sick and tired of your avaricious greed.' She turned to Jannekyn. 'It seems I've wronged you, child. I'm sorry for that. You would never have been treated as a servant in my house had I known who you were.' Tears, genuine tears, were running down her face. 'Can you ever forgive me?'

'You weren't to know, Aunt. It was not your fault. And I was too frightened to tell you,' Jannekyn soothed.

'No, child. God forgive me, I didn't know.' Katherine lifted her head and shot a glance of pure venom at her husband. 'And you wouldn't tell me, would you? After twenty-five years of lying to me that Jan and Bettris were dead it would have been difficult to explain the appearance of their eighteen-year-old daughter, wouldn't it? Much easier to say you'd picked her up from the gutter and to treat her as a servant. Easier – and cheaper, too.' She drew herself up to her full height and clenched her fists above her head. 'Jacob van der Hest, before God I curse you. May your soul rot in hell,' she cried, the final words coming in a strangled gurgle as she fell backwards on to her couch.

'She's dead,' Jacob said, giving her scarcely more than a glance as he stepped towards Jannekyn. 'We can forget all that's been said this morning, my dear. I'll see that your parents . . . '

Jannekyn brushed him aside. 'She is not dead. Her heart is still beating, I can see it from here. Help me to get her back on to the couch,' she commanded, hardly listening to him. 'I'll burn feathers under her nose while you send a man to fetch the physician and Dionis.'

The feathers did no good. One side of Katherine's face was dragged down into an ugly grimace and her arm and both legs were useless. 'She's had a seizure,' Jannekyn said when Jacob came back into the room. 'I've seen it happen before. Gabriel Birchwood suffered much the same.'

'It was your fault,' Jacob said softly.

Jannekyn turned sharply to look at him. He was smiling. A secret, crafty smile.

'What do you mean, my fault?' she asked.

'It was you. You put the evil eye on her.'

'Oh, don't talk such nonsense,' Jannekyn said impatiently. She took no further notice of him but made Katherine as comfortable as she could and then waited with him until the physician came. It seemed a very long time, for neither of them spoke again.

IV

Gyles stirred the yarn in the vat gently. It was being dyed in the wool, before weaving, and he was anxious that the colour should be even. He lifted it with his long stick. Yes, the colour was just right, it was ready to come out.

'Joey,' he called. 'Joey, bring the tub over here. I want to drain this batch.'

Joey came running in with the big wooden tub, its base

slotted to let the water drain, and placed it on top of a barrel to catch the excess dye.

'Hold it steady, now,' Gyles commanded and began to lift the heavy skeins out of the dye and into the tub. Just then, little Jan woke and began to crawl out of the little nest where he'd been lying when his mother left, an hour ago.

'Drat it, he would wake just now. Joey, go and tie him to the door post so he can't crawl over here and get himself scalded. But be quick, boy, I need you to hold this tub steady.' A few years ago – months, even – Gyles would have happily managed the whole operation single-handed. It was a sign of his advancing years that he no longer felt confident to do it without the help of a good strong lad.

The length of cloth that was used to secure little Jan was left permanently nailed to the door post so it didn't take Joey a minute to tie it round the little boy's middle, giving him a good long circumference to crawl round and explore. This, together with a bunch of bobbins tied together so that they rattled and a rag doll that Bessie had made him, kept him contented for long periods at a time.

Gyles and Joey finished draining the yarn and hung it up to dry in the drying shed. Then Gyles sent the boy to deliver a piece of finished fabric to Adam, telling him he could go home when he had delivered it.

Gyles prevented Adam visiting the cottage as much as he could. He realized he could not refuse to dye the young Englishman's cloth or Jannekyn would stop helping Mynheer van der Hest. And that would never do. But Adam Mortlock was becoming prosperous, he'd even moved to a bigger house and this was due in no small measure to Jannekyn's efforts. Gyles didn't like it. He didn't like the fact that Lucas Crowbroke and his family sorted and combed wool for Adam's business in the lean-to behind the dye-house, either, and he lived in fear that de Meester would discover this.

But most of all, he didn't like the change in attitude between Jannekyn and Adam. Oh, it was nothing you could put your finger on, but he was not blind, he could see that the coldness, the almost hostile attitude that had existed between them was no longer there. It had been replaced by – he didn't know what exactly it had been replaced by, but he knew mat Jannekyn sang to herself as she went about her work, which she had never done before.

Little Jan began to whimper.

'All right, little one, I'll go and fetch you a cup of milk from the house.' Gyles bent and ruffled the child's curly head as he spoke. 'I won't be a minute.'

He was a little more than a minute because he decided to warm the milk as there was a cold March wind blowing. When he came back little Jan had gone. It was obvious what had happened. The child had strained at his makeshift leash and the cloth had torn from the nail that secured it. The old man put down the milk and ran inside the dye-house, fearful of the boiling vats there, but little Jan was not there. Neither was he anywhere in the house or yard, nor the lean-to, closed up today because Lucas Crowbroke was not there. Shading his eyes Gyles looked across to the tenterfields. One piece of cloth, insecurely pegged, flapped in the wind, but nothing else moved. Frantically, he ran to the riverside, just in time to hear a splash and see a little blond head disappear.

He rushed over and tried to grab the long leash of cloth that was still tied round little Jan's middle but it slipped away before he could grasp it. Without a second thought he waded in after it. The river was narrow at this point, it ran swiftly and was icy cold. Gyles took no heed of this and flailed along, up to his neck until at last he could grab the end of the leash. Then he pulled.

It took all his strength to drag little Jan to safety against the pull of the tide but at last he managed to haul him in and scramble with him up the bank.

'It's all right, little one,' he said, with what little breath he had left. 'You're all right now. Pappa's got you. Now, let's get indoors and take those wet clothes off you.'

He didn't have time to think of his own condition as he peeled little Jan's wet clothes off and placed the frightened, shivering little boy in a warm bath in front of the fire. Then he dried him and put clean clothes on and put him in his cradle – a bigger one now that he had grown – warmed first with a hot brick wrapped in a piece of bay.

'I'll make us both a hot drink when I've changed my clothes, little one,' he said through chattering teeth, conscious for the first time of his own wet clothes clinging to him and chilling him to the bone.

But even a change of clothes and a hot posset in front of a roaring fire did nothing to take the chill from the very marrow of his bones. Little Jan, warm and snug in his cradle and with a full belly, slept, none the worse for his ordeal. But when Jannekyn returned from her confrontation with Jacob, Gyles was in no fit state to listen to her story. He felt he would never be warm again.

Jannekyn put him to bed with two hot bricks and piled her fur cloak on top of his bedcovers in an effort to warm him. She made him hot herb tea and would have mulled him wine but she knew he would never touch it, gleaning the story of what had happened in snatches as she ministered to him. And all the while little Jan, the cause of it all, lay in his cradle, pink-cheeked and rosy, asleep with his thumb firmly in his mouth.

For a week Jannekyn nursed Gyles, hardly leaving his side except to tend little Jan, who was none the worse for his dip in the icy waters of the Colne.

Adam came to bring cloth to be dyed but took it home again when he saw how things were. 'I'll bring it again when Gyles is better,' he said. 'There's no hurry for it.' He smiled at her and there was a wealth of warmth and affection in his gaze. 'I only brought it along today so that I could see you for a few minutes.' He dropped his tone. 'I love you, Jannekyn.' He made no attempt to touch her.

'I love you, too, Adam,' she said in a low voice. 'But . . . '

'Hush, I know.' He laid a finger on her lips and smiled into her eyes. Then he raised his voice a little. 'Has the physician seen Gyles?'

She shook her head. 'The worst is over now. As long as he remains warm in bed and doesn't overtax himself he'll take no harm. He's very weak now, that's all. There's no need to call the physician.'

'I'm glad he's on the mend,' Adam said and she knew he meant it.

By the time Gyles was allowed downstairs to sit in his chair by the fire Jannekyn had heard, through Lucas Crowbroke, that, although she could not speak, Katharine had recovered sufficiently to make signs indicating that she would have nothing more to do with her husband and that Dionis had arranged to have her mother removed to live with her in her fine house at Lexden, leaving Jacob to the slovenly ministrations of Garerdine.

'I think you must go to church tomorrow,' Gyles said as she made him comfortable by the fire. 'You will be fined if you don't go.'

'I've had good reason not to go these past weeks,' she reminded him. 'You've been too ill to be left.'

'Well, I'm not too ill to be left now. You must go. Leave little Jan with me, he'll be company for me. He'll come to no harm, I'll see to that.'

'Very well, Gyles.' She was happy to leave the child with him, partly because he often became fractious during the long service, but also because she didn't want Gyles to think she no longer trusted little Jan in his charge.

It was a crisp, frosty morning as she walked along the river bank and up Maidenburgh Street to the church. As usual it was full. As she slipped into her usual seat she saw Jacob, as chief Elder, sitting a little apart from the rest, his hooked nose dominating a face that was set in deep, disagreeable lines. For a moment she felt almost sorry for him: his way of life had brought him nothing but misery and isolation. But he had chosen his path; he had chosen to rise at the expense of others. And by them he deserved to fall.

The Predikant spoke for an hour. Minister Lamote was not quite such a sycophant as old Minister Proost had been but his theme was the same. God chose those that he would favour and 'By their deeds shall ye know them'. These deeds appeared, according to Minister Lamote, to be largely their efforts to prosper – part of their duty to God was to make themselves rich and it didn't seem to matter if the poor were ground down in the process. It all seemed very strange to Jannekyn, especially when she remembered the words 'Consider the lilies of the field, they toil not, neither do they spin . . . ' but she tried to listen and make sense of it all because Gyles would expect her to repeat it almost word for word on her return.

At the end of the service the Congregation rose to leave, as they usually did, and were surprised when Minister Lamote asked them to sit down again.

'One of the Elders wishes to speak to us on an important matter,' he announced.

Everyone looked round. There was no sign of any transgressor, which an announcement like that usually heralded, such as an adulterous woman, dressed all in white and carrying a white wand as a mark of her shame. They waited expectantly.

Jacob van der Hest stood up. It was always he who introduced these solemn proceedings. But today there was no introduction.

'I wish to denounce a witch,' he announced in a voice of doom.

A shocked murmur went through the congregation and everyone looked apprehensively at his neighbour.

'I wish to denounce *that* woman.' He raised his hand and pointed dramatically. 'Mevrouw Jannekyn de Troster.'

A gasp went up and all eyes were turned to Jannekyn.

She closed her eyes, feeling the colour drain from her face. For a moment she feared she would faint. It had never crossed her mind that Jacob would stoop to this. But in spite of a thumping heart and sweating palms she managed to maintain an outward semblance of calm. 'It is not true. The accusation is false. I am no witch,' she said quietly.

Minister Lamote stood up. 'On what evidence do you denounce this woman?' he asked. But it was a half-hearted question. Jacob van der Hest's word was never seriously in doubt.

'On my own evidence. On what I have seen with my own eyes.'

'Tell us.'

'First, I must deny this cock and bull story she has been

putting about to the effect that there is some family relationship between her and myself. Some of you may have heard it.' He waved his hand. 'Utter rubbish, of course. Utter rubbish. However, my wife was very distressed when she came to hear these lies and summoned the person in question' – he pointed vaguely at Jannekyn – 'and demanded that she retract her statement that she was a blood relative. Whereupon the creature turned her evil eye upon my dearly beloved wife.' There was a hushed silence. Jacob bowed his head for a moment, then went on in a low voice, 'My wife was immediately struck dumb and fell into a trance from which I doubt she will ever recover.'

Immediately, hubbub broke out. Everyone knew that Mevrouw van der Hest was sick and being nursed by her daughter at Lexden.

'Do you know of any other people who can corroborate your word?' Minister Lamote asked, unnecessarily because nobody was likely to doubt the word of the great Jacob van der Hest.

Jacob bowed his head gravely. 'Indeed, I do. My servant, Garerdine Fromiteel will give evidence.'

'Is she here? Stand forward, Garerdine Fromiteel.'

Garerdine came forward, the sound of her shuffling feet loud in the silence.

With something akin to alarm Jannekyn noticed that suddenly – nobody was sitting near her, despite the fact that the church was full and all the other benches crowded, just as the one where she was sitting had been only minutes ago.

'What have you to say, Garerdine Fromiteel?' Minister Lamote asked.

'I have to say that it be true that my mistress be took bad while *she* was with her.' Garerdine jerked her head towards Jannekyn as she spoke.

'Is that all?'

'She did make up a potion for the pains in my joints, onceover. But they got worse instead of better, till I couldn't hardly walk at all.' She looked down at her flat feet, misshapen from the weight of a too-heavy body. 'I still have trouble and my poor hands do swell so much I can't hold so much as a broom,' She held them up.

A gasp went round at the sight of her fat, pudgy fingers.

'Silence!' the Minister said. 'Go on, Garerdine Fromiteel.'

Garerdine lifted up her head. 'She did wean my master's youngest son from the wet-nurse. She did say that the nurse's milk did make him unhealthy. I did see her give him potions to stop the crying . . .'

'Did the child die?' Minister Lamote asked.

'No, Minister.'

'Is he a healthy child now?'

'Well, yes. He don't ail much, that I will own.' Garerdine was grudging.

Minister Lamote shook his head. 'Then I – cannot accept that as evidence of withchcraft. All children have to be weaned. And if the child is healthy . . .'

'He may grow up with the devil in him,' someone suggested.

'That is true.' Minister Lamote admitted. He turned back to Garerdine. 'Have you anything else to say, woman?'

'Yes. I have.' Garerdine took a deep breath. 'On the day my master's daughter was married to Mynheer Abraham de Baert I did see *that person*' – another jerk in Jannekyn's direction – 'give her a phial. "Use it sparingly in your husband's cup before he retires," was what she said. Them were her exact words. I know, because I did hear her speak them.' She looked around. She was beginning to enjoy herself now that every eye was on her. She had never been the centre of attention before and was determined to make the most of it. 'The next day . . .' she paused dramatically. 'The next day Mynheer de Baert was dead.'

'It was only a sleeping draught that I gave her for him,' Jannekyn said involuntarily. This was all a bad dream. It couldn't be happening. In a moment little Jan would cry and wake her up. Then she looked up and saw Jacob's face, glaring at her, ugly with gloating triumph, and she knew it was no dream.

A general hubbub broke out. Mevrouw de Troster was always pleasant but she did live in an isolated spot with that old husband of hers. And who had ever heard of such an old man fathering a child before? Didn't she have dealings with the English, too? Especially with that young weaver from Scheregate, who seemed to be doing very well for himself all of a sudden. And she could speak the language like a native, which wasn't natural, it wasn't natural at all. Oh, no, there was no smoke without fire. And another thing, hadn't she been seen gathering her own herbs from the hedgerows when any self-respecting body would have paid a ha'penny and bought them from the apothecary?

But the crowning argument, and one nobody in their right mind would ever dispute, was that her condemnation had come from the lips of Church Elder and Governor of the Bay Hall, Mynheer van der Hest himself.

'Witch!' somebody called from the back of the church. 'Witch!' the cry was taken up. 'Witch!' 'Witch!' Witch!'

Jannekyn put her hands over her ears. It was all horrible, too horrible to bear. She got up to run out and everyone stood aside to let her pass, the women even holding back their skirts, afraid that they might become contaminated if they so much as allowed her to brush past them.

But the Predikant was at the door before her, his cross in his hand as a safeguard.

'There is no escape,' he said sternly. 'You cannot be allowed to walk free to continue your evil works. I have a warrant for your arrest, I shall take you myself to the castle, where you will be locked up out of harm's way until your fate is decided.'

V

The witchfinders had done well in Colchester. There were ten others lying in the squalor of the castle prison, all accused of witchcraft and all protesting their innocence. Jannekyn, thrown roughly in among them, got to her feet and found herself a space against a wall dripping with damp, and leaned there, fighting the nausea that overcame her as the evil stench met her nostrils.

'Stick yer 'ead down atween yer knees, ducky,' a toothless old woman beside her advised. 'Yor'll soon git used, ter the smell.'

Jannekyn did as she'd been bidden, although blessed oblivion would have been preferable to this hell. It couldn't be true. This couldn't be happening to her. It was all part of the dreadful dream and she would wake up and find Gyles and little Jan . . . What would happen to Gyles and little Jan? Would someone tell them where she had been taken? Would someone look after them? Gyles wasn't strong enough to look after himself yet, let alone the child as well. What would they eat? How would they keep warm with nobody to tend the fire?

She went to the door and hammered on it in desperation.

'Ain't no good yew doin' that. They 'on't take a mite o' notice. Yew moight as well save yer strength,' somebody called in a tired, flat voice.

She went back to her place by the wall and sank down on to the straw, too miserable even to weep.

The next day Betkin was thrown in to join them. The two

women clung together, weeping, for a long time. 'Oh, Betkin, not you, too,' Jannekyn sobbed.

Betkin sat down wearily on the floor. 'There's such a fever against witches that it's become dangerous even to keep a herb in a still-room, let alone have a cat as a pet. I've never known anything like it. Everybody testifying against everybody else while the witchfinders stalk the streets. They're all mad, the whole lot of them. Mad.'

'What's to become of us?' Jannekyn whispered, clinging to the older woman.

Betkin looked round at the other women, huddled in the gloom. One old crone had died in the night and her body had not yet been removed. She shook her head. 'God in his mercy knows,' she said. 'But surely hanging would be better man rotting in this stinking hole.'

'But I'm innocent,' Jannekyn protested. 'Why should I die?'

'Aye. Why should any of us?' a weary voice from the gloom agreed.

A week went by. Half the women were taken away, Betkin among them and some more brought in. Jannekyn worried about Henrick and his six – or was it seven? – motherless children; but soon she ceased to worry about anything, even Gyles and little Jan, in her fight to stay alive, to keep a corner for herself that was reasonably free from the filth that surrounded her and to snatch her share of the watery gruel that was all they were given to eat. Soon she lost track of time altogether, sustained only by the brief periods of sleep when she dreamed of Adam.

She didn't know how many weeks she had been there when the gaoler came for her. She didn't even know whether it was part of the fantasies by which she kept herself alive as she stumbled into the daylight and blinked owlishly at Minister Lamote.

'If it goes badly I'll bring her back to wait for trial at the Assizes,' Minister Lamote told the gaoler, speaking in passably good English. 'But this is really a matter for our own Congregation to deal with.'

'That don't make no difference to me who deal wiv 'em,' the gaolkeeper said Sullenly. 'I on'y look after 'em time they're 'ere.' He let them out and the door banged shut behind them.

Jannekyn took great gulps of the fresh, cold air, trying to clean her lungs of the stinking atmosphere she had existed in for the past – she didn't know how long;

'Where are you taking me?' she asked at last, trying to keep up with the Predikant's stride.

'To the church. Evidence has come np. It must be put before the Congregation.' Gerard Lamote was not happy. He tried not to look at the sorry creature hurrying along beside him. She was dirty, she smelled vile, her dress was stained and torn and her hair hung in limp rats' tails from beneath her filthy cap.

'Is it Sunday, then?'

'It is.'

She looked down at herself as she stumbled along. 'I'm dirty. I can't go into church like this.'

'You must. They are waiting for you.' He smiled at her briefly. 'It may not be as bad as you fear.' He felt sorry for her but he could not let pity overrule duty. He only wished he could. He wanted no part in the scene he knew was to come.

Once again the crowd in church parted to let Jannekyn through, but this time they added the further insult of holding their noses as well. The Predikant led her to the front where she was forced to stand up before the sea of hostile faces. Jacob van der Hest, seated higher and to one side of the rest, like a great, black vulture, turned on her a look of utter contempt mingled with surprise.

Minister Lamote climbed to his place. 'New evidence regarding this woman has come to light and must be publicly heard,' he said, with an apologetic glance in Jacob's direction.

A general murmur of speculation went round the congregation.

'Captain Henrick de Groot. You have something to say. Will you come forward, please.'

Henrick came forward. Jannekyn felt a surge of pity for the bluff seaman, dressed today as neatly as he knew how and with his unruly fringe of hair plastered down as well as it would go. She knew how fond he had been of Betkin, his wife; he must be finding life very hard without her. She dragged her mind back to what he was saying.

'... and took my own wife for a witch. However, as is the custom, they let her go free without trial because she was with child ...'

At this, relief flooded through Jannekyn. Of course, she had forgotten. A woman with an unborn child could not be convicted. And Betkin was with child, and the child not due for several months yet. By the time it was born perhaps this wave of persecution would be over. Once again Jannekyn had to drag her attention back to Henrick.

'... was allowed home she told me that Mevrouw de Troster was still imprisoned. At this I began to make inquiries for myself. I'd been at sea when the matter was first brought up so I didn't know what it was all about.' He drew himself up to his full height, which was not great, and threw his cap on the floor. 'I have never heard so much rubbish in all my life,' he shouted. 'On my oath on the Holy Bible' – a ripple of consternation ran through the congregation at these words – 'I swear that Mevrouw Jannekyn de Troster is no witch! I also swear that Mynheer Jacob van der Hest is lying when he suggests such a thing and, further, that Mevrouw de Troster is, in truth, the daughter of Jan van der Hest, the elder brother of Mynheer Jacob van der Hest.'

A great noise broke out at this and the Predikant had difficulty in restoring order. That the great Jacob van der Hest should be accused of lying was tantamount to denying the existence of Adam and Eve.

'On what grounds do you make these accusations?' The Predikant, secretly relieved at the uproar, at last managed to make himself heard.

Henrick told his story, leaving out no detail and ending with his visit to Jannekyn's parents, just outside Ypres.

'You have brought them with you today?' the Predikant asked.

'No. Jan van der Hest is too ill to travel and his wife will not leave his side.'

The Predikant pulled his beard and glanced anxiously at Jacob van der Hest to see how he was taking all this. He was not reassured by the thunderous expression on the face of the chief Elder but neither was he surprised. It was unheard of that the word of a man in his position should be challenged. But Gerard Lamote was in a difficult position. He had had it in mind to refuse Henrick de Groot – who was, after all, only a common seaman – a hearing when he had come to him with his story yesterday. But there was a ring of truth about what the man said that could not be denied; because Gerard remembered, and it would have been about the right time, twenty years or so ago, the whispers that went round hinting that Leven Weller was being smuggled to England to escape the Spanish. He remembered, too, that the great preacher had never arrived. Yet it was unthinkable that Jacob van der Hest, that pillar of the Church, should have betrayed him. After Henrick had gone Gerard had spent the night on his knees, praying for guidance and that God would continue to look after his Chosen, though largely with an eye to his own salvation here on earth.

He pulled at his beard again. 'This is much too serious a matter to deal with on the word of one man alone. Without further proof . . .'

'But I have further proof. Mevrouw de Troster will testify,' Henrick said.

'The testimony of a witch is not valid,' Minister Lamote said with something akin to relief.

'She *is* no witch. But no matter.' Henrick shaded his eyes with his hideous hands and scanned the congregation. 'Mynheer Wynkyn Eversham. Is he here? He has agreed to testify.'

Minister Lamote sighed. Another Elder and a deputy Governor at the Bay Hall. Who could doubt his word? It would be well to get the matter cleared up once and for all. 'Very well. Let him come forward.'

Wynkyn Eversham stood up, his shoulders stooping, and told his story to the hushed congregation. He told how Jacob and his wife had stayed with him twenty-five years ago when they first arrived in England, and how impressed he had been by the fact that they had managed to escape so openly, bringing so much wealth with them; and how Jacob, in his cups one night, had boasted of what he had done, and how a word in the right ear had ensured his and his wife's safety. Wynkyn Eversham looked round the assembled Congregation. 'News was just coming through that Minister Leven Weller, whom everyone had heard about for his bravery, had been betrayed and captured. It didn't take me long, by a little devious questioning, to piece together the rest of the story, including the fact that Jacob had betrayed his own brother at the same time.' He paused and then went on in a low voice, 'When Jacob van der Hest made me a present of a silver flagon I thought little about it, other than that it was given in gratitude for my hospitality. But as the presents continued to come, particularly each time after I had asked if there was any news of his brother, I realized that he was paying me for my silence.' He bowed his head. 'I swear before God it was *years* before I fully understood what was happening, but, may God forgive me, when I did begin to understand, to my eternal shame I have to admit that I traded on it.' He lifted his head. 'There, I've told what I know; I swear it is the truth. May God forgive me for my part in it.'

The Predikant turned to Jacob. 'Is this true, Jacob van der Hest?'

Jacob sniffed haughtily. 'It is true that my brother was with Leven Weller. But what happened to them I never found out until much later. I worried about them, of course, but I had been taken ill on the journey and this had proved fortunate for me and my wife. For that I thank the good Lord.'

'And you may thank the good Lord that you weren't found out before!' It was Dionis who stood up now. Jannekyn hadn't noticed her before. She was dressed in the highest fashion and her face was already beginning to show the ravages of the heavy cosmetics she used.

'Everything Captain de Groot has said is true,' she cried, 'It is exactly as I heard it from my mother's lips.'

'Your mother is sick. She has no speech,' Jacob shouted.

'My mother is recovering. She is still very ill but her speech has returned and she has told me everything, *everything*.' She turned a contemptuous glance on her father. 'She says she will never go back to live with *that man* ever again! And I don't blame her. It was only after he had forced me to marry Abraham de Baert – a man old enough to be my grandfather – that I discovered that *I* was the price of *his* silence.' She looked at Wynkyn Eversham. 'He couldn't give me to you, you were already married, so he had to think of other ways to silence you.' She turned to Jannekyn. 'And as for the accusation that this woman caused my husband's death with her potion' – she rummaged in a leather bag she carried – 'I can prove that to be a lie because I have it here.' She held the phial high. 'I never gave him any, I never needed to. He never needed a sleeping draught, he was an old man and near to death when I married him.'

There had never been a day like this. Even the day the dancing bear had run amok at St Denis's Fair hadn't provided so much entertainment as this.

Lucas Crowbroke stood up, twisting his cap in his hands. 'Mevrouw de Troster hev always bin very good to me and my family. She hev always treated me right and paid me my dues for the work I hev done.' He nodded towards Jacob. 'Which is more'n I'd say of *him*, cheatin' old, scoundrel.'

There was a murmur of agreement.

Another man stood up. 'I've never told anybody this. I hev bin too ashamed. But, I'm a searcher of bays and he did bribe me to find fault with the cloth of the Englishman, Adam Mortlock.' He bowed his head. 'I only did it twice, I wouldn't do it again, for a finer bay I never had pass through my hands and it did grieve me to see it rent.'

After the first expression of horror at this other people began to raise their voices against Jacob; little grievances that had rankled for years, bigger ones that had never been uttered before because they feared the consequences of complaining. At the end, Jacob stood, head bowed, revealed to everyone for exactly what he was.

The revelation had eclipsed the purpose of the meeting, until Minister Lamote reminded them.

'Mevrouw de Troster, you are a free woman. May God go with you.'

Chapter Seven

I

Jacob listened to the words being hurled round the church. How dare they accuse him of all these things? Didn't they understand? He was an Elder; he was a Governor of the Bay Hall; and as such he was beyond reproach. He gazed disdainfully at the rabble milling about the church. They were like a lot of silly sheep, where one led the rest would follow. None of them had enough sense to think for themselves. He watched the girl, dignified even in her filth, make her way down the church and out of the door, the people now stretching out their hands to her, where before they had cringed away. Disgusted, he slid quietly from his seat and slipped out by the back way. It said much for the stupidity of the crowd that no one had even noticed him leave.

He walked home and let himself into the house. Strangers' Hall. A good name. It was a big house, the best in Colchester, just right for a man of his standing. But he would never have been able to build it if he hadn't had a good start in England. He'd been right to do what he did; what kind of life could two penniless brothers have made for themselves in a new country? Money was absolutely essential. And he'd always intended to find out if Jan was still alive and to send for him. He'd just never got round to it.

Going across the hall to the solar he ran his fingers over the long table, leaving four distinct lines in the dust He needed a drink. More than anything he needed a drink. He took the bottle out of the hutch and poured himself a generous measure, gulping it down and pouring another before he slumped into his chair, the bottle still in his hand.

He sat there, staring at the couch, empty now, where Katherine had spent the past years. She'd never appreciated what he'd done for her, how he'd schemed to make a good position for himself in the town to please her. And had it pleased her? Had it, hell. She'd played the invalid for years, keeping him from her bed, denying him *everything*, even a civil word. He poured another drink. Even his children had turned against him. Dionis, what was she now but little more than a trollop? And Pieter. He'd never been home since he'd sent him back to his ship in disgrace. For all he knew the randy young pup had died of yellow fever, or worse, long since. Even Benjamin, the fruit of the one night in years he'd claimed his rights as a husband, had gone. Dionis had taken him when she took Katherine. So they'd all gone, leaving him alone in the house he'd built for them.

He poured another drink, emptying the bottle. He threw it into the fireplace among the cold ashes, then he went to the hutch and took out another one, slopping the brandy into the glass with shaking hands.

It was all through that bitch. If he'd never agreed to her coming to Colchester this would never have happened. It was his one mistake. He'd even paid for her to come over from Flanders, fool that he'd been. An attack of conscience, something that didn't usually trouble him overmuch, was what it had been, and he'd paid dearly for it. If she'd never come to Colchester to torment and finally to expose him none of this would ever have happened. He would still have been the most feared and respected man in the town, instead of this humiliation.

But he'd show them. He'd show all of them that he was still a force to be reckoned with. He dragged himself out of his chair and lurched to the door.

'Grarerdine!' he bawled. 'Garerdine! Bring candles. And food. Garerdine!'

'I'm comin'.' A disgruntled voice yelled back from the other side of the hall.

She took her time but appeared at last with a taper and a platter with a piece of stale bread and a lump of mouldy cheese on it. She put the platter on the table beside him and lit candles, placing one at his elbow.

'Is that the best you can do?' he barked.

'There do be no more food in the house. If you do want more you must give me money to buy it.' She picked up his glass and sniffed it, then took a gulp. 'So that's where all your money do go,' she said insolently. 'No wonder there do be none left for food.'

'How dare you drink from my cup, woman.' He dashed the glass from her hand. 'Get out!'

Garerdine shuffled to the door. 'I'll be glad to. There do be more comfort in my kitchen than in this freezing hole. At least I do have the warmth of a fire.'

'Light me a fire then.'

'Light it yourself.' She went out and banged the door behind her.

In a fury he lurched after her, knocking the candle off the table beside him as he staggered from his chair. The candle flickered and would have gone out, but, formed by the draught as he opened the door to shout after the old woman, it flared and caught the corner of the dornicle that covered Katherine's couch.

'Garerdine!' he shouted, unaware of what was going on behind him. 'Garerdine, you filthy, lazy slut, bring coals for the fire.'

He banged the door shut as the flames reached the painted cloths that hung round the walls. 'Garerdine!' he screamed, frantically tearing the painted cloths from the walls and trying to stamp out the flames, too far gone in his drunken state to realize the futility of his efforts. As the flames began to lick round his legs his screams grew louder . . .

. . . But Garerdine couldn't hear. She shut herself in the warm kitchen and ladled herself a good helping of chicken broth from the pot that hung over the roaring foe. The fire that did seem to roar a bit louder than usual tonight and seemed a trifle smokey, too. She finished her broth and helped herself to another ladleful.

II

Jannekyn stumbled from the church, barely conscious of the kind and encouraging words that followed her, and made her way home in a daze. She neither knew nor cared what would become of Jacob, all she wanted was to go home to Gyles and little Jan and to see Adam again. But not until she had washed the stink of prison from herself.

She slipped through the castle bailey and across the tenter-fields, shuddering as she passed the great bulk of the castle and thought of all the poor creatures still incarcerated there. But it was better to go home that way, even if it meant passing that awful place, than to have to walk through the streets with the filth of her shameful imprisonment on her clothes for all to see.

She hurried down the hill towards the cottage, slightly alarmed that she could see no sign of life, not even a curl of smoke from the chimney. She hoped it didn't mean that Gyles was ill again. And what about little Jan?

She reached the cottage and cold fingers of fear curled round her heart. It was deserted. The ashes on the hearth were cold and a bit of cheese that stood on the table was covered in a blue mould, except for a corner that was eaten away, leaving tiny, rodent teeth marks.

Little Jan's cradle had gone.

Jannekyn sank down in front of the blackened ashes. What could have happened? Where was Gyles? Surely, if he had been in church he would have called to her. Unless, when he discovered that she'd been imprisoned as a witch, he'd gone away and taken little Jan with him. Away from the taint of a mother who was a witch.

Suddenly, it was all too much. The strain of the false accusation, the imprisonment and then today's ordeal, finally coming home to this, a cheerless, empty place, was all too much and she began to cry with great racking sobs that shook her body from head to foot. She cried for a long time but when all her tears were spent she found that her mind had cleared and that she could begin to think more rationally.

The first thing she must do was to clean herself up. But before she could do that she would have to light a fire and heat water. She gathered sticks and made a fire and sat before it, waiting for the water to heat. She realized as she stretched her hands out to the welcoming warmth that she was cold through to the marrow.

When the water was hot she dragged the big wooden tub in from the yard and set it before the fire. Then she dropped her prison-stained clothes outside the door and scrubbed her flesh until it was red, in an effort to rid herself of the taint of the place she'd been in. After that she washed her hair and brushed it until her scalp tingled. Then she wrapped herself in a cloth and went upstairs to find clean clothes to put on.

She paused in Gyles's half of the little bedroom. His bed was rumpled as if he'd just got out of it and his best clothes were gone. She was right, then. He'd gone away and taken little Jan with him, doubtless because he couldn't face the stigma of her shame.

Calm now, she dressed herself in a plain grey gown and put a clean cap and apron on. Very well, if that was what he wished she wouldn't try to find him. A tear dropped on her hand at the thought of never seeing her little son again, but if that was what was best for him she could bear it. She had borne much in the past. Better that she live her life out here, in isolation, than that she should bring shame and unhappiness to those she loved most. Adam. Never seeing him would be the most difficult thing of all. Slowly, she went down the stairs.

Adam was there. He was sitting in Gyles's chair by the fire. At first she didn't believe her eyes, she had imagined so much during the past weeks that she didn't trust what she saw.

'Adam?' she whispered, half afraid that the sound of her own voice would break the spell.

He turned his head and smiled at her. 'I came as soon as I knew you were home. Come and sit down, my love, we've much to talk about?'

She did as he had bidden and sat down beside him. Everything she did had a dreamlike quality; nothing seemed quite real, in fact she almost questioned her own reality. 'Gyles has gone,' she said flatly. 'He's taken little Jan with him.'

Adam leaned over and took both her hands in his. 'Little Jan is with Bessie, Jannekyn. He's waiting for you at the house at Scheregate.'

'He is? Gyles hasn't taken him away? I can see him again?'

'Of course you can see him, my love. I've told you, he's waiting for you.'

'Oh, thank God for that' It was almost a sob. 'But what about Gyles? Where is Gyles, Adam? Where has he gone? Couldn't he bear the shame of a wife taken for a witch?'

Still keeping hold of her hands Adam left his chair and knelt beside her, 'Gyles is dead, Jannekyn,' he said.

She frowned. 'Dead? How can he be dead? He was getting better.'

'Oh, Jannekyn, my dear love, do you know how long you've been away?'

She shook her head. 'A week? A month? I don't know. Time didn't mean much in that place. You know where I've been, Adam?'

'Yes, I know where you've been. And that you were there for exactly twenty-one days. We tried to get you out sooner . . . '

'We?'

'Henrick and me. I went with him to Wynkyn Eversham to persuade him to speak out against Jacob van der Hest. He didn't want to, he was so ashamed of what he'd been doing. But he agreed in the end.'

She shuddered at the memory of those hours in church. 'But what about poor Gyles? Was it the shock of having a wife taken for a witch?'

'No, it was nothing to do with that, my love. It was simply

that when you were taken off to prison so suddenly there was no one to look after him and little Jan.'

'But the others . . . Joey and Lucas . . . '

'It couldn't have come at a worse time. Unfortunately Joey wasn't well, so he didn't appear for several days and Lucas Crowbroke had work to do for Jacob so it was nearly a week before anyone realized the plight they were in.'

'Oh, Adam, how awful.'

'They'd managed. At least, Gyles had managed. But after being so ill he was in no fit state to chop logs out in the cold winter wind, but he had to do it to keep the fire going. What with that and tending to a lively child it was all just too much for him.'

'When did he die?'

'Let me see. Joey came along on the Friday and saw how things were and fetched me. I came straight away and persuaded Gyles that he and the child must come with me to Scheregate. He didn't want to, he wanted to wait here for you but in the end he agreed. I took little Jan with me and went to fetch a cart to carry Gyles – he was too weak to walk far, but when I came back for him he was dead. He'd just sat in his chair and died. I think he'd have died sooner but he made himself stay alive because there was no one else to look after little Jan.'

Jannekyn looked over at Gyles's empty chair. 'Poor Gyles.'

'Minister Lamote saw to his burial,' Adam said. He was silent for a while, then he drew her head on to his shoulder. 'You know what it means, Jannekyn, don't you?'

She nodded against the rough stuff of his coat. 'Yes. And I will marry you, Adam, but not yet. It mustn't be too soon.'

'I've waited this long, my love. I can wait a little longer.' He bent his head and kissed her, very gently, holding her close in the warmth and comfort of his arms, bringing her at last to the realization that what was happening was indeed real and no dream.

'Bessie is making one of her special pies,' he said, after a while. 'Come with me now. I came to take you back with me.'

She smiled. 'I think it's a long time since I ate a proper meal. And I want so much to see my little Jan.'

'Fetch your cloak, then.'

They left the cottage and with Adam's arm firmly holding her for all the world to see they began to walk up through the tenterfields.

'It's very light,' Jannekyn remarked. 'Have the days drawn out so much since I last saw proper daylight?'

'No, it's not that. It's not that at all. Look!' Adam pointed as a tongue of flame shot into the sky, followed by a shower of sparks. 'My God, it's Strangers' Hall. Surely, that madman hasn't set the place to burn!' He began to run up the hill, leaving Jannekyn to follow as fast as her weak, half-starved condition would allow.

Crowds had gathered to watch the spectacle. Some were frenziedly pouring buckets of water on to the outer fringes of the fire to prevent it spreading further, but for the most part they stood and gaped, jostling each other to get the best view, their faces yellow in the light of the roaring flames.

'They got the old woman out,' Jannekyn heard someone say. 'She was half asleep. Hadn't realized anything was wrong.'

'What about him? Old van der Hest?' another asked.

'Didn't you hear?' A third person joined in the conversation. 'They found him half hanging out of a window. At least, they think it was him. There was precious little to recognize him by.'

Jannekyn felt sick. She wished she hadn't heard that last remark. Much as she had grown to loathe Jacob van der Hest, much though she and those she loved had suffered at his hands, she would never have wished such a horrific death on the man. She remembered his humiliation – was it only hours ago? – in the church, brought about through her in a way she could never have foreseen when she swore, the day she arrived in England, to humble him as he had humbled her. The victory brought her no sense of triumph or satisfaction, only sadness and a great feeling of pity. Jacob was her father's brother. Things should have been so very, very different.

She turned away, looking for Adam, as a great roof timber crashed down, sending showers of sparks and tongues of flame reaching up into the night sky.

'Take me away from this, Adam,' she begged as she buried her head in his shoulder. 'Please take me home.'

Yet even as she spoke the words, the old feeling came over her, stronger than ever, that here, even in this blazing inferno, was her home. She lifted her head and stared into the flames as the feeling grew, stronger and stronger.

Epilogue

They said that the spot where Strangers' Hall had stood was haunted and that nobody would ever build there again, but it was not true. In due time another house rose there, not quite so grand, but a good solid house, nevertheless. It was called Mortlock's and it was to this house that Adam took his bride and her little son.

Adam Mortlock and Jannekyn de Troster were married in the English Church in Colchester. They were married in the English Church because the Dutch Congregation still regarded the English with hostility. But it was the beginning of the breaking down of barriers. Within fifty years marriages between the two communities were commonplace and in a hundred years the Dutch were totally integrated with the English. Today, only a few surnames are left as a reminder that a separate community ever existed in Colchester.